PLAUSIBLE DENIAL

PLAUSIBLE DENIAL

BY

F.W. RUSTMANN, JR.

REGNERY
FICTION

Cataloging-in-Publication Data on file with the Library of Congress

ISBN 978-1-62157-750-8
eISBN 978-1-62157-740-9

Published in the United States by
Regnery Fiction
An Imprint of Regnery Publishing
A Division of Salem Media Group
300 New Jersey Ave NW
Washington, DC 20001
www.Regnery.com

Manufactured in the United States of America

10 9 8 7 6 5 4 3 2 1

Books are available in quantity for promotional or premium use. For information on discounts and terms, please visit our website: www.Regnery.com.

It is ten thousand times cheaper to pay the best spies lavishly, than to pay even a tiny army poorly

Sun Tzu
The Art of War

DEDICATION

For Carolyn

PLAUSIBLE DENIAL

F.W. RUSTMANN, JR.

PROLOGUE

MACAU

MacMurphy watched the speck on the horizon grow into a full-sized hydrofoil. The sleek craft arched around the breakwater and throttled back, splashing down from its pontoons onto its hull as it entered Macau harbor.

He walked slowly toward the ferry terminal and watched the boat maneuver into its docking position. He felt run down and tired, and couldn't shake the butterflies from his stomach—that horrible feeling of trepidation. He did not like the feeling at all.

His condition was worsened by the physical injuries he had received in the fight with Lim. His left arm was held in a loose sling. Broken ribs scraped across his lungs with each breath. The sunglasses he wore did not completely hide the ugly bruise on the left side of his face. He wore tennis shoes, jeans, and a short-sleeved denim shirt. He looked a mess and felt like shit.

He was also quite certain that the news the courier was bringing from the DDO was not going to make him feel any better.

He saw him first as he passed through the double doors of the customs area and entered the main terminal. He wore baggy blue jeans, a rumpled white shirt with an open collar and an unbuttoned blue blazer. His graying hair was tosseled and he walked with a familiar limp. He looked like he hadn't slept in days. Mac's eyes widened and his heart quickened. He realized the news couldn't be as bad as he had expected—not if Edwin Rothmann was the courier delivering it.

The DDO flashed a weary smile when their eyes met. He hefted the backpack slung loosely over one shoulder and quickened his pace. When they met, the big man enveloped Mac gingerly in a loose bearhug, frowning at his condition. "You look terrible," he growled.

"You should see the other guy," Mac replied sheepishly. "But you know all about that by now. I guess you're here to tell me what happened after I left, and what's going to happen next."

They entered the first cab in the queue and Mac directed the driver to take them to the *Pousada de Macau*. They made small talk during the short drive to the inn, not wanting the driver to overhear anything he shouldn't.

When Rothmann saw that the driver was concentrating on weaving his rattletrap through the traffic around the gaudy Lisboa Hotel and surrounding casinos, he decided it was safe to break the silence and assuage Mac's greatest concern. Mac was gazing thoughtfully out the window. The DDO leaned close and spoke to him in a low, gravelly voice. "Lim's alive; he made it—what's left of him."

The taxi dropped them in front of the old *Pousada de Macau*. Mac paid the driver and led the big man up the old wooden steps of the inn, through the small entrance hall and directly out to the veranda overlooking the bay. The sun hovered a few feet above the horizon, casting a crimson spell over the sparkling blue-green waters.

They chose a table a discreet distance from the other people. A stately old waiter in starched whites arrived instantly. Rothmann ordered a scotch and Mac a vodka-tonic. When the waiter returned with their drinks, Mac lifted his in a toast. "*Kam-bei*, boss, thanks for coming." The rim of his glass touched the DDO's slightly below its rim, honoring him in an ancient Chinese way, like a deeper bow from a Japanese.

Mac leaned forward and touched Rothmann's arm. "Okay, let's have it . . . all of it . . . from the beginning. How about starting with why you came yourself."

The DDO looked up at him wearily. "I came because I like you, Mac. I wanted you to hear this from someone close to you, someone who respects you, not from one of the assholes who are taking over this fucking outfit."

The DDO sipped his scotch and gazed out over the water. The red sun was slipping slowly into the cool and soothing sea. "Anyway, I decided the best thing was for me to come personally. The fact that no one else could figure out where the hell you had gone when you bugged out also helped a lot. You really had them doing back flips.

"I got the back channel cable you sent via Rodney and didn't tell another soul about it. I just called in sick and beat my way out here A-S-A-P to see you.

"And let me tell you, we're both damn lucky Lim didn't check out, because if he had, the Director would have had an excuse to crucify me and push me out. Not to mention what he would have done to you."

MacMurphy adjusted his position, grunting as one of his cracked ribs stabbed him. "What about Lim? When I left him, I thought he was dead. I thought I had killed him."

"Well, from what I hear, it wasn't from lack of trying. When the police found him, he was indeed at death's door. But he survived. The Chinese have already returned him to Beijing. Only problem is he suffered extensive brain damage from the loss of blood and oxygen and the pounding you gave him. So not only will he be the ugliest guy in his neighborhood—I guess you really did do a job on his face—he will also be the village idiot."

MacMurphy grimaced. "You must think he got what he deserved."

"You better believe I think he got what he deserved. I've got no sympathy for that murdering SOB whatsoever. I'm just glad you're not facing a murder rap."

"What about the police?"

"It was reported as an attempted robbery." His large finger spun the ice in his drink absentmindedly. "They think Lim caught someone trying to rip him off and decided to take the law into his own hands. Only problem was he obviously bit off more than he could chew." He grinned.

"And he's in no shape to tell them any differently . . . even if he wanted to . . . and from what I heard, he never will be. Actually, that's the way it is with your entire theft operation at the Chinese embassy. The French know nothing, the Chinese won't say anything, and the Agency will deny everything.

"So the Chinese would prefer to let the whole matter drop. They don't want the news to get out that they smuggled fifty million euros into France through the diplomatic pouch—especially if people were to find out the money was to be used to fund illegal covert operations in Europe to support Iran's terrorist activities and efforts to replace the U.S. in Iraq.

"Furthermore, they are thoroughly embarrassed by the defection of one of their senior MSS officers and want that kept quiet too. For our part, we agreed to keep mum about the defection—no publicity—and to give Huang a new identity so he can live out his years in the U.S. in anonymity.

"And you can be sure the Company won't be jumping to advertise the fact that one of theirs pulled a heist right under the noses of the French and then pulverized a friendly third country diplomat."

"So Huang did defect," said MacMurphy.

"You knew he would. He had no choice. Losing fifty million euros of the people's money and allowing Lim to run amok the way he did would not win him any medals in Beijing. He would have spent the rest of his days in whatever the Chinese equivalent of Siberia is."

He thought a moment before continuing. "But I'm getting a bit ahead of myself, that's only part of it. The induced defection of Huang was so important, the Director's putting you in for the Intelligence Star. He doesn't want to, but he has to. Huang is the highest-level MSS officer ever to defect to the west."

Mac was not surprised, but he expressed obvious pleasure.

"I'm glad everyone is so pleased," his voice was laden with sarcasm. "But it all didn't come without cost. The lives of François and Le Belge and Wei-wei . . ."

"Well, yes, but don't be too proud of yourself. The medal is just half of it—the good news. The bad news is you're . . . fired. The Director wants you out of there." He looked at Mac levelly, watching for his reaction, but Mac didn't return the gaze.

MacMurphy stared into his drink pensively. "Can't say as I didn't expect it. So . . . I guess it's really over. . . ." His voice verged on cracking.

"Yes Mac, it's over. At least this part of it . . ." He reached over and patted his arm gently. "People like you and I are dinosaurs. The cold war is over. They castrated the Agency through budget cuts and all the rest, and now they want to reorganize it out of existence. It's just not the same organization anymore. You said it yourself. It's time to leave anyway, don't you think?"

"Yeah, I suppose . . ." Mac looked out over the calm, moonlit bay. Shards of silver moonlight glinted on the nearly still waters, broken only by an occasional small wave or the wake of a boat. "Let's take a little stroll along the quay before dinner."

MacMurphy paid the check and led the DDO down to the quay. The bright full moon, competing with the flashy neon lights of the distant Lisboa Casino, danced on the bay. A gentle breeze came off the water. Mac took a deep, painful breath, and inhaled the fresh salt air. They walked silently along the path on the water's edge.

Mac broke the silence. "What about the money?"

"Oh yeah, I almost forgot about the money. No one wants to hear about it. As far as the Agency is concerned, there is no money."

"No money? There's fifty million euros sitting in that Swiss bank!"

"Yes. The money's a problem. A big problem for all concerned. The Agency can't return it unless the Chinese government asks for it, and they won't even admit to ever having it. And we can't give it to the Treasury without having to explain how we got it. So, there simply is no money . . ."

"You're joking!" exclaimed Mac, grunting from the pain in his ribs. "Just what the hell do they expect me to do with the fifty million euros?"

The DDO stopped and turned to face him. He spoke very softly. "This is serious, Mac. We're not done. Not by a long shot. Listen, I want you to set up some sort of a cover business and wait for me to contact you. Keep the money safe because we're going to need it to fund operations this politically correct outfit can't do anymore. We're going back into business."

CHAPTER ONE

Khun Ut directed the operation from the balcony of an apartment building directly across the muddy Mai Ping River from the sprawling U.S. Consulate General in Chiang Mai, Thailand.

As the protégé and successor of the notorious drug warlord Khun Sa, who ruled the Golden Triangle for three decades with his twenty-thousand-man Shan United Army, he was no stranger to meticulous military operations. And like his predecessor, he was a hands-on leader.

Observing the gate of the consulate through powerful binoculars, he spoke into his lapel microphone. "One, what is his location?"

The voice in his earpiece responded. "I am behind him, just passing the Muangmai market on Wichatanon Road. You should be seeing us shortly."

Khun Ut scanned his binoculars to the right. "I see you. Two, pull out when I tell you. Five, four, three, two, one, go-go-go-go . . ."

The ten-wheel dump truck pulled out of Witchayanon Road at the corner of the consulate compound and headed south toward the entrance, falling in behind a grey Toyota Corolla driven by young, first-tour CIA case officer, Jimmy Steinhauser. The surveillance vehicle dropped back to follow the truck. "Two, drop back a bit more. Make space. You are too close."

The truck slowed, leaving three car-lengths of separation between the two vehicles. It was past mid-day and traffic was light along Wichatanon Road, the north south thoroughfare running along the bank of the peaceful Mai Ping River.

It was hot in Chiang Mai in the summer; people tended to stay indoors during the siesta time. Except for the Americans at the consulate. They were on American time—always.

The Consulate General and the ConGen's residence were located on a ten-acre, manicured compound that once belonged to the last Prince of the Lanna Kingdom. Stately palm trees and lush banyans shaded its historic sand colored buildings, covered with red barrel-tile roofs. The compound was surrounded by a beige, twelve-foot concrete wall topped with identical red tiles.

Coils of razor wire to deter would-be wall jumpers were strung on top of the wall. Security was tight among drug lords and terrorists.

The sliding gate at the main entrance was strong enough to stop a small bulldozer, and if a vehicle made it past the gate, a pop-up two-foot high pneumatic barrier was raised by the ever-present Marine Security Guard installed in the bullet proof gate house next to the entrance. The only chink in the security armor occurred when the gate had to be opened and the barrier lowered to let a consulate vehicle through.

Khun Ut had learned this from weeks of observation, and he was counting on it today.

CHAPTER TWO

At that moment a Country Team meeting was being held in the Consul General's office on the second floor of the main Chancery building at the far end of the compound. The office was in an L-shaped, two-story building that once housed the prince's stables and servants' quarters. Present were the ConGen and his deputy, the head of the DEA, the CIA base chief and his deputy, the Army and Air Attachés, the AID chief and several other ranking consulate officials.

The group sat around a large conference table. The CIA base chief, Marvin Sadosky, was giving an intelligence briefing on the latest overhead photography of the poppy fields taken by the CIA's Porter STOL aircraft. Map-like photos covered the conference table and PowerPoint images were flashed on the screen to his side. The country team was discussing Khun Ut's increasing boldness.

"Next slide, Charly," Sadosky said to his deputy.

An aerial view of Khun Ut's heavily guarded palatial villa in the highlands north of Chiang Rai, in the area of the famed Golden Triangle, was displayed on the screen. "This is where the bastard lives," he said, circling the villa with a laser pointer. "Not bad for a half Akha, half Chinese peasant from Ban Hin Taek, eh? The sonofabitch has more than doubled the acreage of poppy fields under cultivation since the last estimate was done two years ago."

The CIA base chief was a tall, athletic man with a shock of longish blond hair hanging over one eye. "It's not back at the level it was when his step-father, Khun Sa, was running the operation back in the seventies and eighties, but it's getting there."

He paused until the next chart appeared on the screen. "As you can see, the opium production from the region amounts to ten percent of the worldwide supply, with the rest—or most of it—coming from Afghanistan. At last count it was over 2,500 tons, but that ten percent accounts for almost half of the U.S. heroin supply. He sends most of his shit straight to us."

A frustrated Sadosky tossed his notes on the table. "And the worst part is that he's becoming more and more aggressive, attacking Thai and Burmese police forces, eliminating his rivals, openly bribing officials— you name it. Chiang Rai is becoming Dodge City."

The DEA chief, a brash, balding former New York cop named Peter Wollner, was sitting at the foot of the long conference table. He raised his hand, got a nod from Sadosky, and said, "He rules his empire like Gengis Khan—far worse than Khun Sa ever did—taking out his enemies with a brutality never before seen in this part of the world.

"And that's accelerated ever since his new Cambodian security chief joined him a couple of years ago. Guy by the name of Ung Chea. He's a vicious snake. You never see him around town because you would recognize him on sight. Story is he took some shrapnel from an RPG round when he was fighting the Vietnamese with that Khmer Rouge bastard Ta Mok in northern Cambodia. Took off one of his ears and left a gash in his face to the corner of his mouth. He's an ugly sucker alright. Can't smile—face just screws up in a menacing scowl when he tries." Wollner screwed up his face in a mimicking snarl that drew snickers from the rest of the group.

He continued with the briefing. "Okay, okay, I'm a bad actor, but no kidding, Ta Mok, the most brutal Khmer Rouge leader of them all, was his mentor—like a father to him. Story is Ung Chea's mother was a nurse who saved Ta Mok's life when a land mine blew off his leg at the knee. He's known in these parts simply as 'The Cambodian.'"

"That's right," said Sadosky. "We're going to have to deal with that bastard along with Khun Ut. We've got a pretty good dossier on him. Couple of good surveillance photos as well."

He turned to his deputy, an attractive thirty-ish Eurasian woman sitting at the back of the room, operating the projector. "Charly, would you do me a favor and go grab Ung Chea's file off my desk? I want to show the group what a pretty bastard he is."

They exchanged smiles as she rose and he winked at her.

"You bet." Charly Blackburn pushed her shiny black hair back away from her face, and hurried across the room to the exit. Sadosky watched admiringly as her hips bounced under her light summer dress.

The entire Country Team had the same thought as they turned their attention back to Sadosky. *You are one lucky bastard, Marvin.*

She walked to the end of a long corridor, turned left to the CIA wing of the building, and punched in the three digit code on the cipher lock on the entrance door. She entered the office suite, turned into the COB's office, located the file on his desk, and went back into the hall. Then, full of the morning's coffee and anticipating another hour in the meeting, she made a lifesaving decision to make a brief bathroom break before returning.

She was there when she heard the first sounds of gunfire and screams coming from the direction of the compound entrance. Almost immediately, she heard a deafening explosion and the building erupted, tossing her hard against the wall and showering her with plaster from the ceiling.

CHAPTER THREE

The Cambodian slowed the ten-wheeler to allow more distance between him and Jimmy Steinhauser's vehicle. "We are about one hundred meters from the entrance. He has right turn signal on," he said into his lapel mic. "I will let another car pass. Do not want to get too close."

"Okay, Unit two," said Khun Ut, "I see you. Wait until the rabbit is almost through the gate before you hit him."

"Yes, okay . . . Hold on, hold on, gate is opening. Turning in now. Hold on . . . there he goes . . ."

The Cambodian hauled the wheel to the right, hitting the gas and horn at the same time. The case officer's Toyota was mid-way through the gate when the dump truck slammed into his rear bumper and accelerated, pushing him through the entrance, the blaring horn adding to the shock and confusion of the moment.

The Marine in the gate house stood, stunned, for a moment too long before he uttered, "Oh, fuck!" and hit the switch to raise the internal barrier. He screamed into his microphone: "May Day, May Day, May Day, intrusion alert, intrusion . . ."

The pneumatic barrier began to rise and caught the back wheels of the truck, raising them off the ground. The truck slammed over it, hit the ground hard and screamed into the compound, engine revving, pushing the Toyota in front of it.

Steinhauser spun the wheel of the Toyota in an attempt to pull away from the charging dump truck, but the truck's bumper caught the left rear fender and flipped the car on its roof. The truck ran over the rear end of the up-righted vehicle, its rear wheels crushing the Toyota and rupturing its gas tank. The car burst into flames, leaving the young case officer trapped and screaming inside.

The Cambodian yelled, "We're in, we're in. Bail out now. Go-go-go." He pushed a heavy cement brick against the accelerator, set the wheel to continue the truck on its journey toward the main building, opened the door and rolled to the ground. He came up firing back towards the gatehouse with his AK-47 rifle, taking out two local guards before they could raise their pistols.

There were better automatic weapons, but the AK-47 was the one he had used since joining Ta Mok's Khmer Rouge army as a teenager. It was like an extension of his arm. What he aimed at, he hit.

The passenger hit the door, rolled on the ground, and came up shooting with his automatic weapon. Several more men leaped out of both sides of the bed of the truck, hitting the ground and firing their weapons at whatever moved inside the compound.

The Cambodian screamed, "The guards, get the guards," concentrating his fire on the area around the front gate. Two of the local guards returned fire with side-arms but were quickly cut down by the intense automatic weapons fire.

The ten-wheeler reached the end of the driveway, crashed through the front entrance of the chancery building and exploded, bringing the second floor of the building and all that it contained, including the entire Country Team, down upon it.

The Cambodian's men directed their fire up at the windows of the office buildings that cirled the courtyard. People inside, foolishly drawn to the windows by the firing and explosion, were hit with bullets and flying glass.

The Marine on duty returned fire with his M-16 from behind the bullet proof guard shack. He stepped out into the open to optimize his shooting and hit one of the Cambodian's men before several rounds stitched across his chest, sending him flying backwards, killing him.

Several of the insurgents directed their fire toward the fleeing visa applicants, who moments earlier were standing patiently in a line that wound like a snake in front of the consular section. People were screaming and crawling through bloody trails in their attempts to get away from the chaos.

Three more Marines came out of their barracks firing M-16 automatic weapons. They took out another one of the Cambodian's men in a fusillade of automatic weapons fire. Chaos reigned, and then the Cambodian screamed over the din and into his mic, "Out, out, out, out . . ."

Khun Ut watched intently with great satisfaction through his binoculars. He heard the Cambodian's signal to retreat and spoke into his microphone: "Vans up now. Move, move, move . . ."

Two white vans were waiting about a half-block down the road from the entrance of the consulate. Upon receiving Khun Ut's command, the drivers screeched away from the curb, rushed toward the consulate, and skidded to a halt in front of the consulate gate.

The gate was wide open with no guards in sight. Smoke, fire, and screams accompanied the withdrawal of Khun Ut's men as they backed out of the gate, firing their weapons at anything that moved within the compound.

The men turned, ran, dove into the van's open doors and were gone, tires screeching, down Wichatanon Road.

Police sirens wailed in the distance, the sounds getting stronger and stronger, but Khun Ut's men were gone.

Khun Ut stood at the window of his observation post and watched the escape with the smile of a man proud of his work. He glanced down at his watch. The whole operation, from the time the truck crashed through the front entrance to the time his men jumped into the waiting mini-vans, had taken less than three and one-half minutes.

CHAPTER FOUR

Rising from the floor, a dazed Charly Blackburn pulled a pistol out of her handbag. She was bleeding from a scalp wound and had a splitting headache. Shaking cobwebs from her brain and trying to stop the ringing in her ears, she hurried downstairs and out into the courtyard in time to see the Cambodian's men backing out of the front entrance, firing at anything that moved in front of them.

She dropped to one knee, took careful aim holding the pistol with two hands, and emptied the .380 Walther PPK at the retreating terrorists. She slapped in a fresh magazine and prepared to fire off a few more shots, but they were gone, speeding off in identical white mini-vans.

One of the CIA communicators, a lanky Texan, came out of the building behind her and laid a hand on her arm. "You won't be doin' any good with that little pea shooter, Charly. They're all gone anyway," he drawled.

She spat back, "The hell I won't. I hit what I aim at and I just hit one of those monkeys in the back as he was running for the van. I saw the sonofabitch hop."

Heart racing, she sat down heavily on the steps of the building and surveyed the courtyard around her. Blood matted her hair and stained her dress, and her shoulder ached. The terrorists were gone and all that remained was carnage. The communicator sat down beside her.

They watched as the chancery building burned, timbers creaking and crashing to the floor. Dozens of dead and injured were strewn about the courtyard. Cries and moans from the injured replaced the cacophony of shooting and screaming.

Police and militia forces began arriving, sirens blaring, pouring through the main gate. Charly thought about her colleagues and realized that no one could have survived. There was only a huge burning hole where the chancery building once stood. No human sounds came from the wreakage.

She stood up slowly, glanced around the courtyard one more time and walked purposefully back to the CIA's suite of offices on the second floor. "Come on, Gene," she said to the communicator, choking back the emotion, "We've got to report this to Headquarters right away."

They hurried up the stairs, taking them two at a time. The communicator worked the dial of the combination lock on the vault door. He heaved the heavy door open and they entered the commo room lined with whirring communications gear.

"Send a flash precedence cable back to Headquarters. Make it 'eyes only' to the DDO with an info copy to the COS in Bangkok."

The CIA communicator sat down at a console, typing the message as she dictated. "Say the following: 'Consulate attacked by unknown terrorists at approximately 1100 hours. Truck bomb exploded under ConGen's office during Country Team meeting. All presumed dead including ConGen and COB. Small arms fire in courtyard inflicted additional casualties among staff and locals. Details follow shortly." She choked up again and paused briefly before regaining her composure, such as it was, and continued, "Sign it: 'DCOB Blackburn Acting.'"

"Got it," he said.

The message would be automatically encrypted and arrive in the CIA operations center within seconds. It was approximately 2330 hours–eleven thirty in the evening—in Langley. The Ops Center would call the DDO, Edwin Rothmann, at home on a secure STU phone, and he would head into the office. It would be a long night for him and several key case officers and analysts in the CIA's East Asia Division.

Charly Blackburn headed back down to the courtyard to help with the wounded and to assess the damage. Two of Khun Ut's men lay dead. One had been shot in the face by the Cambodian as he lay wounded, crying for help—the Cambodian wanted no potential prisoners left behind for questioning.

Directly in front of the entrance to the consular section, just north of the front gate, was the worst carnage. A dozen or more bleeding bodies of innocent Thai visa seekers were strewn about. Whole families mowed down as they waited in line for permission to visit America.

A third severely wounded terrorist sat near the guard shack beside the gate. The dazed and dying man was being interrogated by one of the Marines who stood over him with an M-16 jammed in his face.

The Marine screamed, "Who do you work for you fucking little maggot? Who sent you here?"

Charly Blackburn got there in time to hear the terrorist wheeze; hands held out in front of his face, "Please, please, no, no shoot" he begged, "Khun Ut is boss. Please not shoot . . ."

Charly put a hand on the Marine's arm. "Don't kill him Corporal. He's more valuable to us alive."

The Marine lowered his rifle. "I understand what you're saying Ms. Blackburn, but I'd really rather kill the dirty little sonofabitch right here and now. Anyway, probably don't matter none anyway, the way the little shit's wheezing and oozing blood like he is. He won't last long from that chest wound anyway. Fuck the little maggot. Let him die, real slow and painful like."

Nothing in Charly Blackburn's background had prepared her for this moment. She was now the thirty-five-year-old Acting Chief of a decimated CIA base amidst a ruined consulate general. It would be her job to pick up the pieces and bury the dead, including her lover, Marvin Sadosky.

She would have to get on with the business of collecting intelligence on the narcotics business in the region and bringing down Khun Ut. She steeled herself; she could do it. She would get that sonofabitch.

CHAPTER FIVE

The Cambodian's white mini-vans sped out of the area. One turned right on Thywang Road and headed west toward the outskirts of town. The other continued down Wichatanon Road before crossing the Mai Ping River heading east. When their drivers were certain they weren't being followed, they slowed to the posted speed limit and took circuitous routes out of town before heading north toward Khun Ut's main warehouse, in a forested area north of Chiang Rai.

There were nine of them left, including the Cambodian. Two received minor gunshot injuries. One took a .380 round in the right buttocks as he was running toward the mini-van. Three were left behind in the courtyard and presumed dead. One had been shot by the Cambodian during their retreat because he didn't have time to drag out the wounded man. The Cambodian was not aware that a third man was left alive in the courtyard.

They joined up at Khun Ut's heavily guarded warehouse. After driving their vans inside, they stood in the middle, surrounded by bales of marijuana and pallets of heroin and raw opium.

Khun Ut, dressed handsomely in his signature uniform—a grey, short sleeved safari suit, starched and tailored to perfection—surveyed the remaining nine fighters, two of whom were on cots receiving medical first aid.

The one who had been shot in the buttocks moaned loudly on a cot as a medic probed the wound and retrieved the .380 round from his right butt cheek. A dozen members of the security staff and warehouse workers surrounded the group, listening intently to Khun Ut's words.

"I am very proud of what you men accomplished today." His voice echoed through the vast room and he liked the sound of it. "We have taught the Americans a well-deserved lesson. They will think twice before meddling in our affairs again.

"You have struck a huge blow against the DEA and the CIA who have tried to disrupt our business. And they have no way to retaliate against us. They are impotent. The United States is tied down fighting wars in Afghanistan and Iraq, and their erstwhile allies, the Burmese and Laotians no longer fear them or support them.

"And as for the Thais," he paused for emphasis, "the Thais have been bought and paid for by us. We own them. There is nothing they can do, or will do, to stop us. They will ring their hands and cry foul. But they will stop meddling in our business."

He paced among his troops, chin up and limping on a stiff right leg, drawing strength from their presence. "Before my dear father died in that stinking Burmese prison, he had built an empire in these hills. Twenty years ago Khun Sa was responsible for seventy percent of the heroin consumed in the U.S. But pushed from behind by the stinking Americans, the Thai government went after my father with a vengeance and all but destroyed his empire."

His troops nodded and muttered in agreement. Many had heard this speech before but none of them dared let on.

Khun Ut turned to face them and raised his voice. "In their assault on Ban Hin Taek they killed his natural son, my closest friend in the world, my brother, and destroyed my leg." He reached down and rubbed his right knee with both hands for emphasis.

"With your help we have regained much of that lost ground and are now well on our way to once again cornering the U.S. heroin market. Leave the cocaine to the Colombians. We are once again the kings of the heroin trade. Khun Sa would be proud of what we have accomplished in such a short time. He would be gratified, just as I am."

By now Khun Ut was sweating profusely. The air was still in the warehouse, despite dozens of whirling ceiling fans. "We left three fine men on the battlefield today and they will be remembered. Their families will be well taken care of. I will see to that personally. And the rest of you will be generously rewarded as well. We have struck a hard blow at the Americans. This has been a glorious day for which you should all be very proud."

He turned to the Cambodian. "Ung Chea, I have a special note of thanks to you. Your father would have been extremely proud of you today. Your operation was executed perfectly, absolutely precisely. Your keen attention to detail during the planning stages was clearly well worth the effort, and your men performed with precision. You left nothing to chance. I am honored to have you with me and I am grateful that you traveled all the way from Anlong Veng in Cambodia to join me here in the hills of Northern Thailand. I recall vividly how sad you were at the passing of Ta Mok in that filthy Phnom Penh prison. We shared the grief of losing both our fathers that same year. You have become my right hand, and I thank Buddha every day for bringing you to me."

The Cambodian did his best to look stern, but his scarred face glowed red from the praise that was being heaped upon him by Khun

Ut. He had indeed found a new home here in the Golden Triangle, and a new mentor in Khun Ut. The crowd erupted in applause as Khun Ut limped victoriously past them and out the main door.

Khun Ut may have been right about the impotence of the U.S., but what he did not count on was the wrath of the CIA's deputy director of operations, Edwin Rothmann, the DDO.

CHAPTER SIX

SUZE-LA-ROUSSE, SOUTHERN FRANCE

MacMurphy paced nervously at the edge of the ancient town, his eyes flicking to the old Roman stone bridge that separated the village from the highway. It was six minutes past noon. He was late, which was unusual for a case officer coming to an operational meeting.

Then he saw a taxi pull to the side of the road and discharge a big man.

The man headed directly for the bridge, his feet crunching on the gravel at the side of the road. He walked with a John Wayne swagger, one shoulder dipped lower than the other, and with a slight limp.

He wore a white, button down shirt and an open blue blazer over tan slacks. A computer case was slung over one shoulder. His hair was receding and graying, but still mostly dark despite his sixty-odd years.

They made eye contact when the big man reached the crest of the bridge and the man's face broke into a wide grin. They greeted each other warmly on the town side of the bridge.

"Mac, it's so good to see you again." The DDO embraced the smaller man in a bear-like hug and then stepped back and held him by the shoulders, examining him. "You look great–lean, mean, tanned and rested. What are you doing so far from home? Writing a book like so many of your other detached former colleagues?"

Dressed casually in blue jeans, a powder-blue polo shirt and running shoes, MacMurphy stood just under six feet tall. He had an athletic build, dark eyes, handsome chiseled features and short, prematurely gray hair, which made him appear older than his forty years.

"No, no exposés," he replied, grinning broadly. "I just love this place. Lots of old rocks and stones. This village has been here since the twelfth century, and I've been coming here regularly since my Paris assignment way back when. I rent a small condo in the village."

They walked slowly toward the center of town, chatting amicably. Mac pointed toward a hill on the far side of the town. "See that castle on the hill up there. It's the Chateau de Suze-la-Rousse. Built between the twelfth and fourteenth centuries and maintained in perfect condition. There's even a sixteenth century *jeu de paume* tennis court built for Catherine de Medicis and her son Charles IX. So much history here. The castle is now the home of the *L'Université de Vin* where sommeliers and just normal folk like you and me can learn about the great wines of the Drôme region."

The two colleagues continued to get reacquainted as they walked. The last time they had seen each other was at Wei-wei Ryan's funeral service at the Trinity church in McLean, Virginia, shortly after Mac had been separated from the Agency. At the time the DDO had reiterated to Mac what he had told him in Macau: that he would be calling on Mac from time to time to help out with some "sensitive, non-attributable things."

MacMurphy knew that Edwin Rothmann's visit to Suze-la-Rousse was not to chat about renaissance castles.

He was here on a mission.

CHAPTER SEVEN

They found a café in the village square next door to the ancient Chapel Saint-Sébastien. It was a sunny August day with a light breeze, and there were plenty of empty tables outside, but the two case officers opted for a banquette inside the restaurant where they would have more privacy.

"So, what mischief brings you to Suze-la-Rousse, Ed?" asked Mac-Murphy.

Edwin Rothmann was examining the menu. "First, let's get a glass of local wine—red for me. What do you suggest?"

Without looking at the menu, MacMurphy replied, "Let's get a bottle of the Domaine du Jaz. It's grown right here in the vineyards surrounding Suze-la-Rousse. Can't get much closer than that. You'll like it."

He motioned to a passing waiter carrying a tray and wearing a starched white shirt and black bow tie and ordered the wine. Then he turned his attention back to Edwin Rothmann. "I expect you're here to help me spend some of my ill-gotten wealth. Must be really important to bring you all the way out here."

Rothmann sat silently while the waiter brought the wine, popped the cork loudly and poured their glasses. When he set the bottle down and left, Rothmann pulled his bulk closer to MacMurphy and spoke in low gravelly tones. "I've got a problem in Thailand. Chiang Mai to be precise."

"You mean last week's attack against the consulate. It's all over the press."

"That's it." Rothmann took a sip from his glass, savoring the wine. "Yeah, Chiang Mai. What the papers didn't say was who was behind it. No one took responsibility for the attack. But we know that bastard Khun Ut did it. He's out of control. Killed one of our finest officers. Problem is, we're pretty impotent as a nation, and as an Agency, at the moment. Our ass-kissing DCI won't let us do anything about it. Zilch. They're all a bunch of scared pussies."

"I heard the FBI's been called in. Have they got the lead on this?"

"Yes, they do, and they're treating it like a crime, which of course it is, although an act of terrorism. Those Fibbies are swarming all over the place. They've even taken over our dead COB's office." The DDO shook his big head. "Bunch of arrogant bastards running around trying to uncover as much evidence as they can to link Khun Ut to the attack. Hell, we know he did it. We should just take him out. The sooner the better. That's the only way to handle a situation like this. That's what I suggested . . ."

He looked down at his wine, sighed, and took another sip from his glass. "The most the administration will agree to do is to exert more political pressure on the Thai government—to try to force them to take some military action against the guy. But we know it won't work. The Thais won't do anything because Khun Ut has everyone in his pocket. Bought and paid for."

"There's no question Khun Ut was behind the attack?"

"Absolutely. One of his wounded was left behind along with two dead. We got a confession from him and were able to trace all three back to Khun Ut."

The waiter returned and dropped a basket of sliced baguette on their table. He hovered over their table, twirling his tray, impatiently waiting to take their orders.

"What'll you have, Ed? Something to go with the wine?"

"You bet. I'm hungry. How about a nice *steak frites* medium rare?"

"You got it. I'll have the same."

Mac placed the orders in perfect French and when the waiter left he turned back to the DDO. "So you're frustrated. This Khun Ut guy is running amuck, the administration is treating it like a simple crime to be solved by the FBI, and without the help of the Thais nothing will be accomplished. Is that about it?"

"That's why I love you, Mac. You always cut right to the chase."

"What do you want me to do?"

Rothmann peered into his wine glass thoughtfully and then looked up.

"Let me tell you a story . . ."

CHAPTER EIGHT

ack in Vietnam in the late sixties, I was assigned as a liaison officer
to MACV-SOG. Ever hear of that outfit?"

"Sure. SOG, Army Special Operations Group, right?"

Rothmann smiled. "Well, you're half right. I keep forgetting how young you are or, I should say, how old I am. MACV-SOG stood for Military Assistance Command Vietnam—Studies and Observation Group, an outfit that conducted highly classified, deniable covert ops and sabotage missions behind enemy lines in Vietnam. The teams were made up of Army Special Forces, Air Force Air Commandos, and Navy Seals. They worked directly for the Joint Chiefs, and the commander at the time was a real smart Army guy named Jack Singlaub."

The waiter returned with their steaks and a heaping platter of chrispy *frites*. Rothmann speared a *frite* and held it up like a prize. "Jack was a colonel back then, already a legend due to his exploits in World War Two and Korea. He was one of the original OSS 'Jedburgs.' That's how he latched up with the Agency. He's worked closely with us ever since, and he's a real good friend of mine."

Mac said, "I've heard of Jack Singlaub. He commanded our troops in South Korea. He was a Major General at the time I believe."

The DDO sliced into his steak. "That's the guy. Anyway, Jack had this idea to lead the Viet Cong and the NVA to doubt the safety of their guns and ammunition—make their guns explode. He called the operation 'Project Eldest Son.' He came to us and we arranged for CIA ordnance experts to conduct a feasibility study, which we did. A few weeks later, Jack and I watched one of our techs slide a 7.62mm cartridge, loaded with high explosive rather than gunpowder, into a bench mounted AK-47. The explosive round blew up the receiver, projecting the bolt backwards. Jack whooped when he saw that. He said he could just imagine that bolt flying back into the face of some shitass VC."

Mac said, "Sounds like something that crusty old guy would say."

The DDO twirled his wine and emptied the glass. "Yep. So what the SOG teams did was to identify VC and NVA ammunition caches, mostly along the Ho Chi Minh Trail, break into them clandestinely, and replace a few of the 7.62mm rounds with substitute rounds provided by us. The explosive they used so resembled gunpowder it would pass inspection by anyone but an ordnance expert."

"You know, I have heard of that operation. From my dad. He was a Marine Gunny in Vietnam. He said it made the Marines wary of shooting AKs for fear they'd blow up in their face, and some of them preferred the AK to the M-16 before that came to light."

"That's right. Everyone feared using 7.62mm ammunition by the end of the war. By that time it was an open secret that the ammunition was tainted. Project Eldest Son was one of the most successful covert operations of the Vietnam War."

"That's a great story, Ed, but what's Project Eldest Son got to do with your visit? I don't get the connection between that and the attack on our consulate."

"Eldest Son . . . Just an idea I had." The DDO paused, then leaned forward and lowered his voice. "What would be the best way to take down Khun Ut? Think about it for a moment. Destroy his empire, break down his distribution network, and create havoc in his ranks. Make people fear using his narcotics." The big man sat back and gave Mac-Murphy time to let it all sink in.

The wheels spun in Mac's head. He looked up at his mentor and former boss. "You want to doctor Khun Ut's heroin. Make it unsafe to use. Then, if nobody buys his shit, his empire will crumble from the bottom up. Am I close?"

The DDO reached for the bottle and refilled both glasses. "You're on the right track. I'm thinking Project Eldest Son on steroids. I haven't discussed this with anyone but you. If we move ahead with this plan, it has to remain strictly between us. Agreed?"

"Of course, Ed. But whatever I do for you will have to involve my team—Culler and Maggie at the minimum. I'll have to brief them, right?"

The DDO pushed his plate away from him and then popped a last French fry into his mouth. "Culler and Maggie are fine, but strictly use the 'need to know' principle with anyone else you chose to enlist. The point is this—if we decide to proceed, there can be no blowbacks to the CIA. We're going to need complete deniability. Nothing can be traced back to the Agency. Understood?"

"Understood. And no one else in the Agency is aware of this?"

"Right. This is strictly between you and me, Mac. I'd never get approval for an operation of this sort in this day and age. Everyone is looking over their shoulders these days. That's why I came all this way to see you. If you're successful all fingers will naturally be pointed at the CIA."

"But you will have plausible denial," MacMurphy interjected.

"Yes, plausible denial. No links back to the CIA, unless someone is watching and recording us right now," the DDO gazed around the room and laughed.

"No chance of that, boss. Nobody comes to Suze-la-Rousse but me. And I know you made sure you weren't followed here."

"Right, I wrangled a boondoggle to Paris and then told the guys I wanted the day for some shopping and sightseeing. I hopped the bullet train to Montélimar and took a taxi to here. It took less than three hours." He glanced at his watch. "I've got to be back at the station in Montélimar by three-thirty to catch the train back to Paris, and we've still got some things to cover."

"I guess that means you won't get to see any more of my quaint little town while you're here."

"Next time, Mac. Now, why don't you get the check, my wealthy friend, and we can talk some more while you walk me back to the bridge."

"You bet. We need to figure out how to get to his stash and doctor it. It won't be easy."

MacMurphy signaled the waiter for the check and finished his wine. He paid with cash and the two men walked out into the warm summer air of Southern France. They strolled slowly back toward the ancient Roman bridge at the entrance of the village, enjoying the sun and summer breezes.

"Too bad you can't stay longer, boss. I'm disappointed."

"We'll have plenty of time to get together when this is over, plenty of time."

They crossed the main square and Rothmann looked back at the imposing Renaissance castle on the hill behind him. "That is a beautiful sight. I really will have to come back here some day. When this is all over."

"Yes indeed. You'll be my guest. I'd love to show you this part of France." They continued to walk while Mac thought about what he was being asked to do. Finally he asked, "So, how do we sabotage Khun Ut's heroin shipments?"

The DDO stopped and shook his head. "You're going to have to figure that one out for yourself, but I'll give you a couple of resources to help you come up with a plan. The first is a guy down in the Florida Keys. He's done some good work for me in the past. Bill Barker's his name. He's a bit of a rogue. An arms dealer who's always working on the fringes of the law. But he knows his shit. He'll fix you up with whatever you need in the way of weapons and get them safely delivered to Thailand. He's also a chemist. Knows everything there is to know about poisons. He can advise you on what you need to put into Khun Ut's shipments.

I'm thinking something that will make people who shoot up really, really sick. Kind of like Eldest Son."

Mac said, "What if the stuff we put in kills someone? Like Project Eldest Son."

"Collateral damage . . . can't help it. That's something we may have to struggle with."

"Okay, we'll cross that bridge if and when we come to it. But what about access?"

"You're going to have to be real careful with this one, Mac. There can be no connection to the Agency at all. That said, you're going to need a way to get access to Khun Ut's heroin in order to sabotage it. And I've given it a lot of thought. I don't see any way around it, so I'm going to put you in touch with our ACOB in Chiang Mai, Charly Blackburn. You may even remember her. She says she met you in Bangkok a couple of years ago. She was stationed there when you visited from Hong Kong to attend some sort of a narcotics conference."

"Of course, I remember her well. Real smart gal. Eurasian. Very pretty. An expert on the Golden Triangle heroin trade."

"That's Charly all right. I knew you'd never forget a beautiful face like that. Anyway, I named her the new acting chief in Chiang Mai after Sadosky was killed. She's a little young for the job, but I think she's up to it. Real bright and no one in the DDO knows more about that part of the world than she does. Speaks fluent Thai too, which is a big plus. Her mother was Thai. Dad was an Air Force officer. Bombardier on a B-52 out of U-Tapao, if memory serves. I hate to create a link to the Agency, but you're going to need some support. She'll be your contact in country—funnel intel to you. She's also got an asset who might be able to help get you access to Khun Ut's heroin shipments. Guard that connection with your life. She's totally loyal and reliable, the only other CIA employee who knows about you and me. That also makes her the weakest link in our little daisy chain, so be careful about meeting with her."

They reached the foot of the bridge and Rothmann stopped, reached into a pocket of his computer case, pulled out an envelope and handed it to MacMurphy. "This contains contact instructions for Barker and

Blackburn. Note that Barker only knows me as an arms buyer named Tom Willet. It's important we keep it that way. I vouched for you and told him you would be contacting him, so your bona fides is established, but I didn't give him a name. I assume you'll use an alias with him and, for that matter, for anything you do in Thailand. There's also a cell phone number you can use to reach me in an emergency. It's an untraceable throwaway phone. I suggest you get a similar phone. Make sure it's an international quad-band, so we can reach each other in an emergency."

"Okay, boss, I'll be in touch." They hugged each other warmly and said their goodbyes. MacMurphy watched the big man walk over the old Roman bridge, limping slightly with his signature swagger. On the other side of the bridge, Rothmann hailed a taxi, entered awkwardly and disappeard into the late afternoon traffic.

MacMurphy had his instructions, and funding for the operation was understood. It would come out of the stash sitting in MacMurphy's alias bank account in Bern. There would be no traceable connections back to the CIA. There would be total deniability.

CHAPTER NINE

AU: There is no CHAPTER NINE... WE HAVE RE-NUMBERED THE CHAPTERS FROM HERE?

FT. LAUDERDALE, FLORIDA

When Harry Stephan MacMurphy had separated from the CIA after thirteen years of service as an operations officer, he did two things right away. He moved to Ft. Lauderdale, Florida, and he rented a suite of offices on the eighth floor of a towering glass building overlooking the Intracoastal Waterway on Las Olas Boulevard. The sign he hung on the door read, "Global Strategic Reporting."

He financed GSR with the money he had taken from the Chinese embassy during his last gig with the CIA. Access to the account could only be gained by a U.S. citizen named Frederick Martin, and MacMurphy had the alias U.S. passport to show he was Martin.

Now he had a mission.

CHAPTER TEN

MacMurphy, Maggie Moore, and James "Culler" Santos sat huddled around a small marble conference table in the GSR offices. One wall of the conference room was glass from ceiling to floor; the view offered the sparkling Intracoastal Waterway, sprinkled with white yachts and marinas, and the office buildings and condominiums lining historic Las Olas Boulevard. Beyond spread the expansive blue waters of the Atlantic Ocean.

MacMurphy, dressed casually in jeans and a white, short-sleeved, button down shirt which accentuated his deep, Florida tan, was winding up his briefing on his meeting with the DDO in Suze-la-Rousse two days earlier.

"So that's about it. We've been given wide parameters to complete this job. Even Ed Rothmann doesn't know exactly how to accomplish it. He just gave us the goal and told us to run with it."

"How is this arms dealer down in the Keys going to fit in?" asked Santos in his slow, South Boston drawl. "We can find enough weapons in Northern Thailand to start a revolution. What do we need him for?"

Santos was a brute of a man. Not tall, he stood only about five foot seven or eight, but he weighed in at a solid two hundred pounds. Although he looked like a brawling lumberjack, he possessed two engineering degrees from MIT and was one of the CIA's best upcoming audio technicians until the fiasco in Paris left him and MacMurphy without jobs. He was wearing a dark polo shirt that accentuated his muscular frame.

"I was thinking the same thing," said Maggie, twiddling her pencil and leaning back in her chair. She was a career CIA officer "of a certain age," recently retired as one of the highest ranking women in the clandestine service. She had known and mentored MacMurphy almost since the day he entered the Agency. When Rothmann told Mac she had retired and was living in South Florida, Mac immediately contacted her and made her an offer she couldn't refuse. She sat at the head of the table, looking at them sternly through pale, wolf gray eyes over steel granny glasses. "If we bring him in on this, won't it just be one more person to worry about?"

MacMurphy flexed muscular arms behind his head, trying to relieve the tension in his shoulders and neck. "Right. You're both right. If we decide to use Bill Barker, he'll have to be compartmented from the rest of the operation. I agree we probably don't need him for guns and such, but it might be more convenient and secure if we don't have to go running all over Northern Thailand looking for illegal weapons. We certainly can't take them with us on the plane, and I wouldn't think about attempting any mission in the Golden Triangle without being armed like a Navy Seal."

"I guess the point here is that if Ed Rothmann thinks it's a good idea, then it probably is," said Santos. He massaged his temples and swiveled his chair to face Mac. "We don't need to tell him much, and Rothmann has already set everything up with him. And we can pay him in cash. He only needs to know that we need certain equipment to be delivered securely in Thailand. And he's got the connections to do that, right?"

"Yeah, that's about it," said MacMurphy. "But there's also the question of the way we sabotage the heroin. In Project Eldest Son, they substituted gun power for high explosive, so the guns would blow up when fired. The DDO is thinking along those same lines for this operation. That's part of the reason he wants us to see Bill Barker. Barker's also a chemist, and the DDO believes he'll be able to give us something to put into the heroin. We're going to have to explain this to him. That's a problem."

Maggie looked up at the ceiling, brought her hands up to her head and ran long, thin fingers through her graying, unruly auburn hair. She peered at them over her glasses. "Wait a minute, guys. Hold on. Yes, there is a problem here. When the AK-47s exploded and made the bad guys eat the bolts, it was a good thing for our troops because it killed enemies. But let's not kid ourselves. We're talking poison here, whether it makes the users sick or kills them, and I don't know how we're going to control that. The users are going to be the victims, not Khun Ut or any of his merry men. That's troubling to me. A lot. That's a problem."

"Good point," said Santos. He leaned forward thoughtfully and drummed his large fingers on the conference table. "There's an ethical question here, particularly if we end up killing some innocent person . . . But I'd like to point out that heroin users aren't exactly saints. It isn't like they're innocent kids puffing on a little pot, or some slick yuppie snorting a little cocaine in his Beemer with some hot little cutie. We're talking heroin here. People who use that shit are hard core druggies. They're shooting up in the ghettos before they go out and rape and pillage the world. So I say, screw them. What's the difference if we kill a couple of those worthless bastards?"

"Okay, okay, Culler, we get it," said Maggie, "We all know how you got your nickname. 'Culler,' the guy who wants to 'cull' the world of undesirables. Eliminate all the assholes and the world will be a better place. Right?"

"Yep. And it's true, too. He leaned back in his chair, satisfied that he had made his point, and then continued to pontificate. "And furthermore, that's the root problem with us Americans. We're always so damned concerned about collateral damage. That's why we're losing the war on terrorism. We're afraid to bomb the little fuckers when we have them dead in our sights because we might kill a couple kids or women along with the bad guys. Hell, do you think the Israelis worry about that shit? No way. They just pull the trigger when they get one of the bastards in their crosshairs and worry about the little kiddies and moms later."

MacMurphy chuckled. "Okay Culler, we know how you feel, but Maggie's right. We do have a bit of a conundrum here. But at this point we don't really know if it's even going to present a problem. So let's just get all of our facts together and decide what we will do and what we won't do later. I'm all for heading down south to the Keys tomorrow. We'll know a hell of a lot more after we meet with Bill Barker. What do you say?"

Culler nodded and Maggie said, "Fine, but I'll do some checking before you head on down there. I'll run the databases and see what I can come up with concerning his background. Then we can regroup and discuss it some more before you leave."

CHAPTER ELEVEN

The following morning Mac and Culler did their regular workout at the Ultima Fitness Center a block away from their office. Culler, beast that he was, worked out exclusively on the heavy weights, while Mac stretched, did a fast three-mile run along the quay bordering the Intracoastal Waterway, and finished up with light weights and some vicious beating on the heavy bag.

Mac had been a champion wrestler at Oklahoma State University and had been studying karate and mixed martial arts since he was three years old. His father, an amateur boxer and tough Marine gunnery sergeant, had pushed Mac hard ever since he was big enough to stand.

After their workout they returned to the office to check in with Maggie who was busy getting the weekly "CounterThreat" newsletter out to GSR's ever-growing client subscription base. It was a particularly important issue this week because it highlighted growing unrest and a deteriorating security situation in Algeria and Morocco, two places where GSR had an active client interest.

In the nine months since their departure from the Agency, the three of them had built a growing and somewhat lucrative small business. They published a weekly subscription "CounterThreat" newsletter which profiled the security situations in selected countries around the world and kept its corporate clients up to date on the world's hotspots—where they could go, where they shouldn't go, and what precautions to take if they must go. They also offered international consulting services—business intelligence and due diligence investigations for individual clients in the corporate sector.

They had hired two employees to work exclusively for GSR, a bright, recent college grad named Christy White as a receptionist and a middle-aged, bookish ex-journalist named Wilber Millstone to do the writing. Neither of them had a clue about the other, more clandestine, activities that Maggie, Culler and Mac were about to undertake. GSR, like the CIA, worked on a strict "need to know" compartmented policy.

The three former CIA officers jokingly called the undercover embedded company within GSR, "CIA Inc."

The trio gathered in MacMurphy's office and Culler shut the door. Maggie said, "I called Bill Barker on the blind line and made an appointment for you guys for later today. He sounds like a friendly guy and responded immediately when I mentioned the name Tom Willet. He said he was expecting our call and has assembled some gear he thinks you might need. I didn't go into it with him, but it sounds like the DDO may have already tipped him off about where you're going."

"Hmmmm," said Mac, flicking perspiration from his forehead, the after effects of his workout, "no telling what Ed may have told him. Never mind, we'll find out soon enough. When can he see us?"

"He said to arrive late in the day and plan to stay into the evening," said Maggie. "He wants to show you some night vision gear after it gets dark."

"Okay, let's figure on heading on down right after lunch then," suggested Santos. "That'll give us time to eat, get our alias docs together and rent a car at the airport."

"Always thinking about lunch, Culler," chided Mac. "Let's get some work done before we take off for the Keys. Have you got the address, Maggie?"

"It's just 'Islamorada, mile-marker seventy-two, turquoise gate, ocean side.' He says you can't miss it."

"Did you get a chance to check him out, Maggie?" asked Culler. "We'd kind of like to know what the guy's background is before we go traipsing down there."

"Sure did, Culler. He's got quite a reputation. And except for a lot of allegations of arms smuggling—nothing concrete, no arrests or convictions—which we already know, he's quite the marksman. He's got a ton of awards and certainly knows his weapons. It says here he's a founding member of the Fifty Caliber Shooters Association, and that he's a leading competitor in both regional and national 'extreme caliber' competitions, whatever that means."

She flipped through a stack of pages fresh from the printer. "Also, he seems to be persona grata with the Navy SEALs because he is an annual invitee at their Seal Team Eight .50 caliber qualification shoot at Camp Atterbury. They shoot out to twenty-five hundred meters at that match."

"Twenty-five hundred meters!" exclaimed MacMurphy. "That's like . . . what . . . a mile and a half!"

"That's what it says, and there's more. According to press reports he's a co-developer of the 'ceramic barrel' M2HB program, whatever that is, for the Defense Advanced Research Projects Agency."

"Pretty heavy stuff," said Santos. "That's a first-class outfit. High speed, low drag. I've worked with those DARPA guys a lot in the past."

Maggie pushed her glasses back up and continued: "He's also been a shooting instructor for several police departments, a range master, a legitimate automatic weapons procurement officer for the Colombian Secret Service, a consultant to the Naval Surface Warfare Center and to USSOCOM on combat assault rifles. Whew, the list goes on and on."

"Sounds like we've got a winner," said Mac. "I'm ready to rock 'n roll with this guy."

CHAPTER TWELVE

ISLAMORADA, FLORIDA KEYS

After a quick lunch with Maggie at their favorite sandwich shop, Culler and Mac rode together to the Ft. Lauderdale airport in Mac's new 6 series BMW coupe. They parked the car in the short-term parking and headed to the Avis counter in the terminal building and Mac used a Florida driver's license and Amex credit card in the alias Robert T. Humphrey to rent a car. If anyone spotted him meeting with Bill Barker and ran the plate on the vehicle, it would not lead back to MacMurphy.

The drive to Islamorada in the nondescript white Chevy Impala rental took a little over two hours. They drove west to the Ronald Reagan Turnpike, known in the state simply as Florida's Turnpike, and then south through Miami where the turnpike turned into US Route 1, running along the entire east coast all the way from Maine to Key West.

They drove through the Keys on a two-lane road that was often clogged with traffic and slowed by mom and pop campers, heavy trucks and trailers carrying large boats and yachts. Mac drove silently while Culler chilled out listening to classical music on his iPod.

It was just after three in the afternoon when they reached mile marker seventy-two on Islamorada Key. At a divided road, they took a u-turn and came back on the ocean side of the Key for a block until they reached the bright, turquoise gate.

They turned into the drive, honked, and the automatic gate slid open. They drove up the gravel drive to a sprawling flat roof, modern glass-and-stucco home, built typically high on concrete stilts to protect it from hurricane tides, and pulled into the shade on the south side of the house.

A big, heavy, middle-aged man—dressed in olive shorts and matching short-sleeved safari shirt—stood on the second level balcony waving down at the arrivals.

Bill Barker was once a powerful weightlifter, but now in his mid-fiftys he'd gone a bit soft. His hands were large and callused, with dirty, broken nails from working with weapons. The hands of a working man. He looked like a former Sumo wrestler and smelled faintly of gun powder and lubricating oil. He flashed a ready smile and spoke with a soft, slow South Florida drawl, not what Mac expected from a covert arms supplier.

Beside him stood his wife, a pleasant looking woman dressed in shorts and a tee shirt. She had short dark, wispy hair and a broad smile. Bill Barker greeted them warmly with friendly eyes. "How y'all doin' guys. This is my wife Ruth. Did y'all have any trouble findin' the place?" They mounted the stairs and he held out a large hand in greeting.

"None at all," said Mac. "We're the friends of Tom Willet you've been expecting. I'm Bob Humphrey and this is Ralph Callaway." They mounted the stairs and shook hands.

"Pleasure meetin' y'all." He turned to his wife, "Sweetpea, would you be so kind as to fetch us some of that fresh brewed tea of yours? These guys look parched." He turned back to Mac and Culler. "It's a lousy drive down here from Miami. Come on inside fellers. It's hot out here."

The back of the house was floor to ceiling glass with a wide porch that extended the length, overlooking the sparkling blue-green ocean beyond.

At a long, white rattan bar inside the living room, Ruth served tall glasses of iced tea with fresh key limes and then excused herself to leave the men to talk business.

"Tom didn't tell me very much other than I could trust you fellows and that you wanted to purchase some arms and other equipment for an operation in the jungles of Southeast Asia. That about it?"

"Yep, that's it," said Mac sipping his iced tea. "He spoke highly of you, too, saying we could trust your discretion one hundred percent. He also said you had a good contact in Northern Thailand who could receive the stuff we purchase and get it delivered to us securely in Thailand."

"Yep, sure can. Gotta fellow out there who used to be a police general. Very well connected. Knows just about everyone out there, including the drug dealers and smugglers and politicians. Works for a lot of them too, but one thing is for sure, he never crosses wires. If he does a job for you, he's yours—for that one job anyway." He laughed. "One hundred percent discretion. That's how he stays in business. So what is it exactly you guys are looking for?"

"We're going to be in the jungle up there for a few days, and there may be some bad guys in the same area. We need survival gear and weapons. Tom said you were one stop shopping. That true?" asked Mac.

"Oh yeah," replied Barker. "I can fix ya'll up with just about anything you need, top-of-the-line stuff. I don't deal in any crap. And every gun I sell I've personally sighted in and fired at least a hundred rounds through. A lot more on the automatic weapons. Now, Tom said you'd be paying in cash. If so, I can give you a good discount."

Mac nodded. "It'll be a cash deal. We can wire the money anywhere you like or give it to you in a sack. Whatever you want."

"Wire transfer will do just fine," Barker giggled in a high-pitched way that didn't fit his large frame. "I'll give you wire instructions for my bank in the Bahamas."

Santos, who had been sitting quietly at the bar nursing his iced tea during the conversation, asked bluntly, "I need a SAW. Can you get me a SAW?"

"Well, Ralph, you certainly look strong enough to lug a big, heavy Squad Automatic Weapon around in the jungle, but I wouldn't recommend it. How long have you been out of the military?"

"More than ten years. Army Special Forces."

"What about you, Bob?"

"Me? I led a Marine sniper platoon and later a Marine Security Guard detachment, but I've also been out a long time. Why do you ask?"

"Because a lot has changed in ten years. Sure, they still use SAWs in the conventional forces, and they still use the M40A1 sniper rifle, which is probably what you were trained on, Bob."

"Yeah, that's right, I love the M40. When fitted with a night vision scope and suppressor, it's absolutely deadly at night. I used one on an operation in Africa. It's sweet."

"Of course you love it. It's a great rifle, just like the SAW is still a great weapon, but I'm gonna show you fellers some guns that'll knock your socks off. Go ahead and fill up y'alls drinks and take 'em with you."

Barker led them into his ocean front office. The cluttered L-shaped desk faced sliding glass doors that led out to the porch. Barker pointed out three fishing pole racks loaded with poles and baited lines leading out to the ocean. "That's so I can fish and work at the same time. Life's laid back here in the Keys."

Barker sat behind his desk and motioned for Culler and Mac to take the two chairs in front of it. He leaned back in his executive chair and studied his large fingers. "Now I don't need to know exactly what you guys'll be up to there in Northern Thailand, but I do know that the Golden Triangle's up here. That's a pretty dangerous area, especially if you're goin' to be runnin' around in the jungle like you say. So, I'll give you my unsolicited philosophy about things like this—Go light, use the darkness, be silent and be invisible. If we can all agree to that, I'll fix y'all up real good."

Mac and Culler nodded their agreement.

"Now, Bob, you said you were a Marine sniper at one time, and you're familiar with the use of night vision gear and suppressors, right?"

"Yeah, that's right," said Mac.

"I am too," said Culler. "The Army Special Forces isn't that far behind the Marines." He glanced at Mac and smiled.

Barker pulled out a pen and yellow pad and slipped a pair of reading glasses low on his nose. "As long as we're on the same page, let's get started making a list of the gear you'll need for this here junket."

CHAPTER THIRTEEN

et's get y'all started with the simple stuff. Then we'll get into the guns.
You need to be invisible in the jungle, so you'll need Ghillie suits. I'd
go with the standard Marine sniper Ghillie which you can adapt when
you get in the field by adding some foliage and leaves and such. I'm sure
you guys are familiar with them." Barker glanced over at Culler Santos.
"We'll order one for you in extra wide, Ralph," he snickered.

"Yeah, about your size except wider in the chest and smaller in
the belly."

"Touché, touché." Barker laughed.

"Then y'all are going to need a couple of handheld GPS devices with
maps covering the Burma, Laos and Thailand area. And about a case of
granola bars and power bars. We don't want you to starve, but we also
don't want you to be pooping all over the place out in the jungle. You
guys know the drill, right? Leave nothin' behind and travel light. 'Spe-
cially if someone is lookin' for y'all. And I suspect that might just be the

case. I'll also throw in a couple cans of my special concoction that erases the odors of poop and pee. Use it faithfully and even a good hound dog won't catch the scent. Do y'all need boots?"

"No," said Mac. "We'll bring that kind of stuff with us. But we'll need a couple of Camelbacs and some purification pills just in case we run out of water."

"Of course." Barker looked over his glasses. "I was comin' to that. I wouldn't let y'all go into the jungle without plenty of water." He looked down at his yellow pad. "That's about it for the personal gear. I'll throw in some camping gear as well, shelter sheets and that sort of stuff to make y'all comfortable. Now let's git down to the important stuff."

He dropped his glasses on the desk, pulled himself out of his chair and walked across the room to a closet. Spreading open the bi-fold doors, he pushed hangers of shirts and jackets to each side and stepped into the closet. Once inside he unlatched a panel in the rear wall and revealed a hidden, four-foot by eight-foot room filled with racks of rifles and pistols and knives, boxes of ammunition, and a small desk loaded with gun cleaning gear.

Culler gave a low appreciative whistle. "You've got a bloody arsenal in there."

"Just a few of my favorite things, and this is my absolute favorite." He took a rifle from one of the gun racks and held it out to them, beaming. "It's a thing of beauty, a Noreen 338LM Lapua sniper rifle with an 8x32 variable power day/night scope. I can drop rounds in a four-inch bull at fifteen hundred meters with this baby. An average sniper can do it at one thousand meters. It's the finest sniper rifle ever made, and this model's a semi-automatic to boot. Never know when that might come in handy."

MacMurphy took the rifle and sighted it toward the ocean. "Fifteen hundred meters?"

"Sure, that's normal for the best snipers. Nothin' strange about that. She'll take out a target at twenty-five hundred meters. I mean, you can take a guy out at that range—a far cry from that old sniper rifle you're familiar with. Check out the sights." He held the gun out to MacMurphy. "You zero the gun with the 'day' eyepiece. At night you just push the release button on the eyepiece, pull it off and put on the light intensifying 'low light' eyepiece. Easy as one, two, three, and bingo, you've got night vision."

Culler said, "I've heard of those guns. The Delta teams and SEAL teams use them in Iraq and Afghanistan. They're even dribbling down to the Special Forces and Marines these days." Culler took the gun from Mac. "You ever shoot one of these, Bob?"

"No, never had the pleasure," said Mac. "I was long gone from the Marine Corps when these were introduced. But I've heard of them. And of course I've fired the .50 cal. Is it true they pack a punch like a .50 cal?"

"Sure can, with the right ammo," said Barker. "The .338 caliber is the first and only bullet designed specifically for sniping. The bullet will arrive at one thousand meters with enough energy to penetrate five layers of military body armor and still make the kill.

"Effective range is about sixteen hundred meters, that's about a mile, but under the right shooting conditions it'll reach out beyond the two thousand meter mark with no sweat."

"Unbelievable," said Mac, taking back the rifle from Culler, sighting it and caressing it admiringly. "I want this gun."

"We're not planning to be doing any sniping on this trip," Culler chided, "and we don't need to be carrying around any extra baggage."

Mac sighed. "You never know. Does it come with a suppressor, Bill?"

"Got one right here." Barker removed a Sierra suppressor from its box and screwed it onto the gun's barrel. "It fits on like this, easy. And like a lot of suppressors, it actually improves the ballistics of the rifle and the 'crack' sound becomes a soft 'poof.' I'll give ya'll a chance to try it out tonight with a little test firing in the dark."

"I sure do like that rifle. You sure we can't find some use for it on this trip, Ralph?" Mac joked.

Culler said, "You sniper dudes are all alike. You fall in love with your guns. Buy it if you want it, but I'm not carrying the sonofabitch."

CHAPTER FOURTEEN

Putting up the Lapua, Barker selected a short automatic rifle from one of the gun racks.

"This here is a POF 416. POF stands for Patriot Ordnance Factory. Fires a 5.56mm round and looks kinda like an M4 submachine gun, but it's a whole hell of a lot better. And it don't gunk up like the M16 and M4. I've put fifteen hundred rounds through it non-stop without any malfunction.

He handed the gun to Mac who examined it and passed it over to Culler.

"This is more to my liking," said Culler. "Short, light, and lots of firepower."

"That's because you can't hit anything, Ralph," chided MacMurphy. "You need to spray things like a garden hose."

"And if that's what you like to do, this is the weapon for you," said Barker. "The one you've got in your hand has a twelve-inch barrel. It also comes with a fourteen and a half inch barrel which will give you a little more accuracy, but this will definitely do the trick. The regular magazine holds thirty rounds, but I'll give you three Beta C-Mag drums for each gun. They hold a hundred rounds each, so you'll have plenty of firepower. One drum'll last you a long time."

As Culler was sighting the rifle in the direction of the ocean, Barker said, "It's got three separate sighting mechanisms on it. The sight on top is for shootin' in the daylight. It's the darling of the sandbox. See the red chevron in there? Well, no matter where the chevron is within the scope, when the tip of the chevron is on the target, that's where the bullet goes, every time. Very fast to acquire target. And over here is the built-in iron sight backup."

Both Culler and Mac paid close attention.

"Now, for night shootin' this is really neat. On the top of the grip's forearm is an infrared laser. It works with head mounted night vision which I'll give you. It's very, very effective. The laser beam is invisible at night unless you're wearing your head mounted night vision gear. But with that gear you see a green line of death. That's what the guys in the sandbox call it. And whatever the green line touches, fire the gun and bullets impact there—just like that garden hose of yours, Ralph. Unless the bad guys are equipped with similar night vision, they'll never know they've got death kissing their brows."

"Damn, that's cool," exclaimed Culler.

"And not only will they not see what is hitting them, they won't hear nothin' neither," said Barker with a big grin. "Here at the end of the muzzle we're going to screw on this here Gemtech suppressor. It'll add another seven and three-quarter inches to the length of the gun, but you'll be happy it's there when the shootin' starts. All they'll hear is a bunch of poofs, if anything."

"Okay, you've convinced me," said Mac. "We'll take a couple of these with all the accoutrements and six hundred rounds of ammo. You got any more stuff we should take with us? I want to talk to you about side arms and chemicals. Willett may have mentioned that we needed some chemical advice. He said you were a chemist."

"Yep, I am indeed, and Tom did mention somethin' about that to me. I've got just what the doctor ordered, I think. But first let's get through the gear you'll need, and then we'll get to that business. What about grenades? I've got some neat concussion and fragmentation grenades to show you if you want."

Mac shook his head. "We're not going to war out there. At least I hope not. We may have to use the automatic weapons, but I don't see any use for heavy artillery. We'll pass on the grenades, but we will need pistols and knives. I've got a good hunting knife at home and I carry a Kahr PM45 sidearm. Maybe you could just ship those out to Thailand for me." He turned to Culler. "We could ship your 9mm Glock out there as well."

Barker thought a moment and then responded. "As I understand it—and I don't need to know everything, just enough to get ya'll equipped properly—you're goin' to be out in the jungle doin' some suspicious stuff with a lot of bad guys runnin' around in the same general area. That about the size of it?"

"That's about it," said Culler. "If we need to shoot our way out of a bad situation, we'll need to be able to do that, but we're not going to be out looking for any trouble."

"Right," said Mac. "We need to be invisible and silent, but if someone steps on us we need to be able to strike back."

"Okay, got it. Then leave your Kahr at home, and that goes for the Glock as well. I don't go anywhere with less than a .45, but yours is too small for what you guys need. I mean, the PM45 only has a three-inch barrel and only holds five rounds. Great for concealment but no good for this. And the 9mm doesn't have enough hittin' power."

Barker went back to his closet and returned with a pistol in hand. "This here's a Heckler and Koch MK 23. Leave it to the Germans to make an awesome, offensive .45 caliber handgun."

"The .45s definitely pack a punch." said Culler.

"My favorite caliber too. This here gun was developed for U.S. Special Operations Command in the late nineties, probably after you left, Ralph. It's pretty big, certainly not the best for concealment, but you guys won't care much about that where you're goin'. And it'll shoot two-inch groups out to fifty yards. It's a mean sonofabitch."

"What about a suppressor?" asked Mac.

"Oh, yeah, you bet. It's a quick detach suppressor. On and off in an instant." He demonstrated. Mac and Culler nodded their heads in approval.

"One more thing. Wait'll you see this . . ." Barker walked back through the closet and returned with a sheathed knife in his hand. He pulled the knife from its sheath and held it out in front of him.

"It's a Russian made Spetsnaz Ballistic knife, a real good fighting knife under normal circumstances, but this one has a special character-istic. See here on the handle?" Culler and Mac moved closer. "That's a safety pin. And see here on the blade guard? That's a trigger. Now, if I remove the safety pin like this, and then press the trigger, the blade flies out. No shit, I mean it flies out with a lotta speed and energy. Damn accurate too. It'll penetrate a two-by-four at twelve feet but makes abso-lutely no sound. Great for takin' out a sentry real quiet like without havin' to get too close. Real nifty."

MacMurphy shook his head. "Amazing. Really amazing stuff. I want all of it. Go ahead and talley up the bill, pack everything up and get it shipped out to your guy in Thailand. I'll get your money transferred as soon as I get back home."

"You want me to include the Lapua and spotter gear?"

Mac glanced over at Culler with a longing look and then turned back to Barker. "Aw, what the hell, you never know. Go ahead and stick it in the box with the other stuff."

"Well then, let's join Ruthie at the bar for a cocktail or two before dinner. She and I are goin' to take you down the road a piece, so you can taste some of our local delicacies. Then we'll come back here after dark and I'll let you guys fire off those weapons you just bought. Best to have a little familiarization before you gotta use 'em for real."

CHAPTER FIFTEEN

It was dusk when they left the restaurant and headed back to Bill's place. Except for becoming more jovial and relaxed, Bill did not seem too impaired by the three martinis he had consumed. He drove two miles back home along the narrow, two-lane road without a waver.

Ruth busied herself brewing a pot of coffee and setting out cups and saucers and desert cookies on the bar while Bill Barker assembled the rifles and pistols. When he had everything together in his back yard, he joined the group at the bar and helped himself to a cup of coffee and a handful of cookies.

"Ruthie makes the best damn chocolate chip cookies this side of heaven, and her coffee's not too bad either."

Once back at the house, Barker sobered up completely and began to inventory all of the weapons and gear.

"Once I get this list together and the prices, how am I goin' to communicate with you fellers?" said Barker.

"Jot this down," said Mac. "RobertHumphrey123@hotmail.com. Send me an Email with a list of the gear and prices along with your wiring instructions. I'll get the money off to you right away. Also, don't forget to send me the contact instructions for your police general friend in Chiang Mai. Send everything air freight so we can pick it up within the next week or so."

"No problemo. I'll see how fast I can get everything out to you and let ya know."

Culler nudged Mac. "There was one more thing," he said.

CHAPTER SIXTEEN

Mac lowered his voice. "The chemist thing. You said you could give us something that would make people sick if they swallowed it. We need something untraceable, tasteless and odorless."

"That's right, I can cook you up just about anythin' ya want, but I'll need to know a little more about what you need it for before I can give you a good answer. I've got lots of concoctions that'll make people sick, if that's what you want to do, but a lot depends on what you want to put it in and how sick you want to make the people."

"How much did Tom Willett tell you?" asked Mac.

"Not much. He mentioned something colorless and odorless that could be put in something somehow that would kill or make seriously ill anyone who ingested it."

"And what did you say?" asked Mac.

"Told him ricin would do the job nicely. First thing that jumped to mind. I told him there were lots of things that could make people sick, but then they'd recover and wonder what made them sick and then go on about their business without thinking much more about it. But if what ya'll want to do is take down a couple a drug lords," he lowered his voice, "and that's what I suspect you want to do, then makin' some people a little sick won't do it for you."

"What then?" Mac asked.

"Then you need something stronger, like ricin. A little bit of that and, well, shit, they'd be dead, and then there'd be hell to pay. That would be the end of the drug lords who produced the shit that caused the deaths."

Culler said, "Ricin. That's what the KGB used to kill that guy on the bridge in London. Remember that Mac? They stabbed him in the leg with an umbrella."

"Georgi Markov. He was a Bulgarian defector," said Mac.

"Yep, that's the stuff. I know the story. It only takes five hundred milligrams to kill you. That's about the size of a half a grain of sand. Stuff's made from castor beans. You can buy them anywhere and I can mix you up a batch in no time at all, powder or liquid—your choice. Just depends on what you're gunna put it in."

Culler and Mac considered how much to tell Barker, though Barker had clearly figured out what they wanted to do. Maybe Rothmann had told him more than he would admit. In any event, if they were to succeed, they would need Barker's help.

Sensing their dilemma, Baker decided to jump in with both feet. "Look guys, I'm here to help y'all. I think I got a pretty good idea of what y'all want to do out there, and I can tell you straight out there ain't no half measures in this business. Either go big or stay home. That's what my ole daddy used to say. Do it right the first time or don't do it at all. Y'all look like good guys to me, and Tom and I go back a long way. You're on the right side and that's the side I'm on, too. We all wear the same color hats. You want to fuck up the drug lords and turn their own people against them. That's a good thing. I'd like to have a part in that. Just tell me what you want to do and I'll help you do it."

Santos glanced at Mac and nodded.

"Okay, you're right, of course," said Mac. "You've figured it out. We're planning on getting into to a shipment of heroin bricks and salting it with something that will make the users never want to buy any of the druggie's shit again."

Barker nodded, "Yep, figured."

"And if they get sick enough, they will turn on the pushers and eventually on the drug lords themselves—right up the ladder until the entire network is disrupted. That's our goal."

"Yep, well then, ricin's what y'all need." Barker took a theatrical sip of his coffee. "Untraceable and easy to make. Only problem is you'll kill anyone who ingests even a tiny bit of it. But that'll sure as hell get their attention."

"And Tom seemed okay with that?" asked Mac.

"Yep, suspect so."

Culler looked over at Mac. "Can't say as I disagree with him, and if the goal is to get their attention, that's the way to do it."

"If we decide to go that route, how would you get it into the heroin bricks?" asked Mac.

"Well, I'd probably use a liquid form and either pour it on the bricks and let it soak in or, if they're wrapped up in paper or something, y'all could use a syringe and inject the ricin through the packing to the center of the brick. The heroin would absorb the ricin nicely."

Barker scratched his head. "Heroin bricks are much like cocaine bricks. They're a chalky substance and weigh about a kilo each when they come out of the hills. The bricks are actually made up of morphine hydrochloride, a fine white powder that they press and dry in the sun before they take it out for more processing where they have real chemists. That'd be Hong Kong in that part of the world."

Culler and Mac exchanged glances. Anyone using the tainted heroin would die, and many of the users would be innocent people. Well, maybe not so innocent. They were contributing to the drug trade, but they weren't actually profiting from the drug trade. They were simply users. Could they afford this kind of collateral damage, and if not, was there an alternative—one that would still allow the operation to succeed? They were on the horns of a dilemma.

Mac broke the silence. "I don't know if we can afford to do this. We'll be killing a lot of innocent people. Isn't there a better alternative?"

"None that I can see." Barker was leaning over the bar toward them, studying his nearly empty coffee cup. "Not if y'all want to succeed in this."

"You know my thoughts on the subject," Culler said to Mac. "This is war and in war you've got to accept some collateral damage, and anyone dumb enough to be shooting up on heroin doesn't deserve to live anyway."

"Okay, okay," said Mac. "Tell you what. Bill, go ahead and mix up a batch of ricin for us. Fill up a dozen or so syringes for injection, so we can put a couple cc's into each kilo brick. Then put 'em into our shipment with the other stuff. We can decide later whether to use them or not."

"I can certainly do that. But I'd better dilute the ricin a bit so it can absorb better into the bricks. If we put only a couple of cc's into each brick, it might not saturate enough of the brick to do the job. How about I make up about fifty syringes of about ten cc's each? If you inject five cc's into each brick in two or three places, it should do the trick nicely and be totally unnoticeable. After all, the shit is going to have to go through another refining process anyway when it gets to the chemists. That ought to spread out the ricin really good."

Mac looked over at the unperturbed Santos and said, "Okay, let's go with it. Go ahead and assemble all of the gear and the ricin and get it ready for shipment to your contact in Thailand. Now we've got to hit the road."

"Don't ya want to shoot them weapons and check out the night vision gear." Barker was clearly disappointed.

"I'm sure everything will work just as advertised. We should get back," said Mac.

Barker called to Ruth who was watching TV in another room. She joined them at the bar and they said their goodbyes.

Culler and Mac spoke very little on the drive back to Ft. Lauderdale. Culler dozed in the passenger seat listening to his music on his iPod, while Mac was left alone with his thoughts. Knowing Maggie would not approve of what was being planned, he was not looking forward to the inevitable confrontation.

CHAPTER SEVENTEEN

It was after midnight when they got back home to Ft. Lauderdale. Mac dropped off Culler at his apartment and drove east toward home. He entered the access code at the entrance of a new gated community a few blocks from the ocean and drove through the gates down a tree-lined winding road to the two-story Mediterranean town home he had purchased shortly after his separation from the Agency.

The house was dark and lonely. He turned on the TV for noise, showered, brushed his teeth and went straight to bed. He didn't like to sleep alone, but being single meant he did it a lot. The scent of his most recent girlfriend, Cindy Keskiner, a bright, attractive psychiatric nurse at Ft. Lauderdale General Hospital, was still on the sheets and pillow. He wished she were there now and thought of their last night together in that bed while inhaling the scent of her familiar soap and shampoo. He had thought about calling her after he dropped off Culler, but knew it was too late and she would already be in bed.

MacMurphy knew it was about time to settle down with one woman and start raising a family, but his career in the Agency had always precluded that. He recalled one of his instructors down at The Farm telling a group of students that if CIA case officers devoted too much time to their careers, their family life would suffer, and if they devoted too much time to their families, their careers would suffer, and if they tried to do both, both family and career would suffer.

For now he satisfied himself with cyclical affairs with local women and with colleagues in the CIA and State Department. He was an attractive, exciting and charming man with an exceptionally strong libido, who never had trouble finding attractive and exciting women to join him in bed. He moved easily from one woman to another, and frequently back again, as he moved from post to post within the CIA.

The closest he had ever come to marrying and settling down was with Wei-wei Ryan. They had been together, off and on, for more than ten years. MacMurphy first met Wei-wei when he was assigned as a case officer to Udorn Base in Northeast Thailand, and she was a branch secretary at the CIA's station in Bangkok.

Their romance progressed through subsequent overseas posts in Paris, Tokyo and back again to Paris with Wei-wei attempting to follow him wherever he was posted. But the Agency finally put its foot down when Mac was posted to Hong Kong as chief of station and Wei-wei tried to follow him. Rules were rules, and the Agency was not about to permit the wife or girlfriend of any COS to work with him in the same station. That would give "the appearance of impropriety," in Agency lingo.

When Wei-wei couldn't follow Mac to Hong Kong, she requested to be assigned back to Paris where she had lived as a child and became fluent in the French language. Her request was granted and she landed the much-coveted job of secretary to the COS.

When Mac showed up in Paris on temporary duty a year later to run the operation against the Chinese embassy, their relationship was rekindled. But when the operation went bad and Wei-wei Ryan became the victim of Lim's rage, and Mac was forced into early retirement, Mac moved to Ft. Lauderdale alone

Mac should have protected her. He was wracked with guilt over the mess he had caused. He should have kept her out of the operation. He should have married her. She would still be alive now and would be with him now in Florida. But for some reason he did neither. He had always put career and duty ahead of his personal life, and so, more out of habit than anything else, he moved on once again.

Soon the events of the last few days, beginning with Rothmann's visit which cut his vacation short in Suze-la-Rousse, took over his thoughts.

He was excited about being back in the game with Culler Santos at his side, but worried about the ethical aspects of what he and Culler were planning to do. Mostly he worried about what Maggie Moore would think. She had the reputation of being a straight-shooter in the Agency, and had kept many a young case officer from making egregious errors in operational judgment. Being torn between Edwin Rothmann and Maggie Moore was not a good place to be.

CHAPTER EIGHTEEN

MacMurphy awakened early. He had slept fitfully during the night, his mind churning with ideas, possibilities, different approaches, arguments. He drove to the airport, turned in his rental car, and retrieved his BMW from the parking lot. He called Santos and they agreed to meet for breakfast before heading to the office. Mac wanted to go over the events of the previous day one more time before briefing Maggie.

"She's not going to go for it, Culler. I can't lie to her, and I don't know how to do this without her."

Culler surprised Mac with compassion. "There's no way around it, Mac. You've got to tell her the truth. She'll never accept some cockamamie story about making people sick. She's too smart. And I agree, you can't lie to her. Actually, she probably already knows that the only way to do this is to kill a few people in the process. You've just got to convince her that a little collateral damage is worth it."

"I know, I know. But what if she doesn't go along? What if she puts up a stink?"

"She won't. Anyway, we don't really know how this is going to play out until we get there. Tell her what might happen, that some people might die, but leave everything kind of open to adjustment depending upon what happens when we get out there."

MacMurphy was silent for a long while and then he looked up at his friend. "Yeah, good advice. I'll be as smooth as I can, but I'll tell you what I think. I think if we get an opportunity to poison some of Khun Ut's heroin, we're going to do it.

Culler pushed his chair back and hit Mac on the shoulder. "That's what I like to hear, Mac."

CHAPTER NINETEEN

CHIANG MAI, THAILAND

The discussion with Maggie had not gone well. She acquiesced only after Mac appealed to her loyalty to Edwin Rothmann and asked her to reserve judgment until after he got on the ground in Thailand and got a better feel for the situation. She had no compunctions about taking down Khun Ut and his empire, only about the collateral damage that would inevitably result.

So it was with mixed emotions that MacMurphy landed at the rural airport in Chiang Mai, Thailand, with Santos.

Culler had been a rock for MacMurphy ever since they met at the CIA's covert training base, The Farm. Santos was one of the smartest and toughest men Mac had ever known. Trained as an electrical engineer at MIT, he was a mathematical genius and a skilled artist locked in the body of a brute.

His sensitivities to those around him astounded MacMurphy. Always calm and unflappable, he had a knack for relieving tensions and cooling things down when tempers rose. But if confronted, he would destroy anyone who threatened him or those he cared about.

Mac had seen Culler erupt only once. They had been hanging out with a small group of Farm students at a nearby bar called the Tumble Inn. Everyone was feeling mellow, and the beer and camaraderie were flowing freely when one of the female students slapped one of the townies who was slobbering all over her.

The townies hated the CIA students. The whole town knew that the facility was a CIA training base, despite the CIA's futile efforts to maintain its cover. They considered the students pompous interlopers on their territory.

The townie was a huge, pot-bellied, tattooed beast accustomed to bullying people in "his" bar, and he was surrounded by an entourage of similar low-lifes who egged him on.

Culler had calmly stepped between his female colleague and the townie, politely asking the townie to leave his friend alone and take his smelly group of pig farmers to the other side of the room.

The townie responded by smacking Santos in the face with a beer bottle, splitting open his lip. The blow had not seemed to faze Culler. He had stepped back away with his left foot, crossed his right foot over in front and brought it up and around to meet the townie's right cheek with such force that teeth and cheek bone shattered, sending the huge man careening across the room and into la-la land. Without missing a beat, he had turned on the others, swiftly taking out two of them with rapid-fire, vicious kicks and punches while the remaining thugs beat a hasty retreat toward the door.

Mac was reminded of this fight every time he saw the angry scar on Culler's upper lip. Santos was the meanest, toughest guy MacMurphy had ever known, and he was totally loyal to Mac and Maggie and Edwin Rothmann.

CHAPTER TWENTY

At the Avis counter at Chiang Mai airport Mac rented a dark Toyota Corolla in the alias Bob Humphrey. He and Culler drove north to Chiang Rai along a newly paved, four-lane highway. On the way they stopped at a roadside local restaurant and had a lunch of Mac's favorite Thai *gueyteow lad na* noodles with sauce, pork, and vegetables as well as a couple of local Kloster beers.

They arrived at the center of the town less than an hour later and pulled up in front of the modern Wangcome Hotel. Again using their aliases, they checked into adjourning rooms on the tenth floor overlooking the bustling city.

Mac recalled Chiang Rai as the Thai city closest to the famed Golden Triangle, formed by the confluence of the Mekong and Ruak rivers where Burma, Laos and Thailand came together. The town was infested with people involved in one way or another in the drug trade. A modern day Dodge City, much like Medellian in Colombia. It was equally infested with police—some who were not even on the take.

The tourist business was also booming in Chiang Rai, with excursions to the surrounding ancient temples, mountain villages and the poppy fields, and an abundance of first class hotels. There were also hundreds of low cost hostels frequented by hippies and youth interested in trekking and hanging out and sampling Thai *gunsha*—the best marijuana in the world. There was also an abundance of heroin in all forms, and earthier Oriental delights.

Culler and Mac chose to pitch up in one of the first-class hotels for reasons other than just comfort. These hotels offered better security and fit well with their use of tourist cover.

Once they had settled into their hotel rooms, Mac used his non-attributable cell phone to call Bill Barker's Thai contact, retired policeman General Sawat Ruchupan.

While not perfect security, prepaid cell phones could not be traced back to owners, and cell phone records were not kept by the companies because there was no billing. MacMurphy knew that all security was a tradeoff with efficiency, and the convenience in this case outweighed more stringent security measures.

Since it was getting late in the day, General Sawat suggested they meet at his villa in Chiang Mai the following morning. He informed Mac the shipment of gear had arrived and was awaiting opening and inspection.

Tired and jet-lagged, Culler and Mac had an early dinner at the hotel, took two melatonin each to assist in getting over the jet-lag, and retired for the evening.

CHAPTER TWENTY-ONE

Mac and Culler arose early, had a light breakfast at the hotel and headed south for Chiang Mai. They easily found Sawat's spacious villa overlooking the Gymkhana golf course in a beautiful residential section of Chiang Mai, located in the posh southeast quarter. From the looks of his palatial villa, General Sawat Ruchupan was clearly a man of some means.

A thin, balding man in his mid-seventies, he met Culler and Mac at the door. Dressed impeccably in long white trousers and a long-sleeved, white shirt, he bowed deeply in the traditional Thai *wai* with his palms pressed together in a prayer-like fashion, showing respect to his visitors. "*Sawatdee khrap*," he said.

Both Culler and Mac returned the *wai* and spoke the *sawatdee khrap* greeting in unison. They removed their shoes at the door and left them on the threshold. The general led them through the hotel-like foyer, padding barefoot over the polished teak floor, through sliding glass doors at the back of the house and onto a patio pool deck beyond.

They took seats around a white patio table shaded with an umbrella to shield them from the morning sun. A tanned, bikini-clad young Thai woman was lounging by the pool nursing a yapping Shih Tzu at the obviously augmented breasts that threatened to burst out of her bikini top.

"Quiet Ling Ling," she chastised the mutt, "these are *farangs* from America. They won't hurt you my baby." But the dog continued to yap incessantly, regarding the interlopers with canine disdain.

"Noi, my darling, this is Mr. Humphrey and Mr. Callaway." The dog continued to yap as they greeted one another with *wai*'s across the pool deck. "*Sawatdee kha,*" she said in a sweet, little-girl voice, "happy to meet you."

An elderly Thai servant arrived to take their drink orders and then disappeared back into the house. After lighting a local *Krong Thip* cigarette, the general blew a lungful of foul smelling smoke up into the air. He didn't bother to offer one to his *farang* guests, assuming all Americans were health nuts who distained smoking. It was just one more thing he could not understand about these strange foreigners, but their money was good.

Returning with a large pitcher of lemonade, glasses, and cookies on a silver tray, the servant quietly placed them on the table in front of them. He poured the glasses and, without asking, he poured one for Noi and brought it and a cookie on a napkin to her by the edge of the pool where he served her with a bow. She fed the dog a piece of her cookie and the mutt finally settled down in her lap contentedly.

The general took a long, last pull on his *Krong Thip* cigarette and crushed it out in his cookie dish. He spoke in excellent American accented English with smoke oozing from his mouth and nostrils. "Your shipment arrived two days ago. I have not opened it but I have seen the manifest. It appears you fellows are going on a hunting expedition—hunting men, from the description of the automatic weapons in the box."

He smiled knowingly, lit another rancid *Krong Thip* and continued. "I hope I can be of further service to you in that regard. Mr. Barker surely must have told you that I stand ready to offer a wide range of discreet services to my clients. I am more than just an arms merchant."

Culler, wearing a short-sleeved Hawaiian shirt, placed his hands behind his head and stretched, displaying massive biceps and forearms. "Can you get us transportation, like, maybe an airplane?"

"That can be arranged easily," said the general. "I am a pilot and I own a small Cessna 172 four seater. It is a very reliable plane for, shall I say, surveillance of certain places in the area." He smiled knowingly.

Mac didn't know how far he could take this but decided the general could be useful in leading him to Khun Ut's heroin. "What about a helicopter? Can you fly one of those as well?"

"Yes, of course. I have part interest in a Bell Ranger which has room for four people and some luggage. Very reliable. We use it mostly for tours up and down the Mekong and around the native hill tribe villages.

"That's good to know," said Mac. "Bill said you were both trustworthy and resourceful. It appears that he was right on both counts."

"It goes without saying that all of this has to be held in the strictest confidence," said Culler. "We don't want anyone else knowing our business. No one."

"Understood. You will not have to worry about me. It is like the American saying, 'Whatever happens in Vegas, stays in Vegas.'" The general laughed loudly at his own joke, displaying a mouthful of nicotine stained teeth and gold.

"Okay," said Mac, standing, "Now that we've got that out of the way, let's go see what Bill Barker sent us."

CHAPTER TWENTY-TWO

The three men padded in their stocking feet back across the polished teak floor of the foyer to the general's study in the front of the house.

The general opened ornately carved teak double doors to reveal a warm, paneled room with masculine leather couches and chairs. A huge, beautifully carved partner's desk dominated the center of the room. The room was impeccably organized, but it reeked of stale cigarette smoke. In one corner, two wooden shipping boxes were stacked neatly.

"The larger box contains the weapons and other gear," said the general, reading from the manifest, "and the smaller one contains the ammunition. I am sure that both can't be shipped in the same container." He handed the manifest to MacMurphy. "Please check to see that everything is in order while I open the boxes."

Santos walked over to help the general. After he picked up a claw hammer and the general grabbed a crowbar, they went to work on the boxes.

They inventoried the gear, examined each piece of equipment and found that everything had arrived as planned and paid for.

Sawat puffed on another *Krong Thip*. "That is quite an arsenal you've got there, gentlemen. Those automatic weapons are beautiful. I don't think I have ever seen anything like them. May I see one?"

Culler handed him one of the rifles.

The general set down his cigarette, caressed the rifle and sighted down the barrel. "Very nice," he said.

"It's a POF 416 5.56 mm assault rifle. State of the art. Treat us right and we'll leave one behind for you when we leave."

"Oh," said the general amidst a gust of smoke, "I will treat you right. No doubt about that. I would not want you coming after me. Not with those weapons."

Mac grabbed an armful of the gear and headed towards the door. "Let's start moving this stuff to the car," he said over his shoulder to Culler, "but leave the H&K pistols and a couple boxes of the .45 mag ammo out. We should keep them close from now on."

Culler removed the two H&K pistols and suppressors from their boxes and set them aside. He found the correct ammo and set a couple of boxes of those aside as well. Hunting for the holsters, he found that Barker had sent two holsters for each gun. One was a thigh holster suitable for carrying openly on military type missions, and the second was a mid-back, belt clip-on holster for concealment under a long shirt.

Barker had thoughtfully included two green military duffle bags in the shipment. They placed the loose weapons and gear into the bags before carrying everything to the trunk of the car.

The general watched intently from the door as Culler and Mac loaded the rental car. Noi padded across the foyer on bare feet about half-way through the loading operation. She was wearing a diaphanous top unbuttoned over her bikini and was still clutching Ling Ling at her breast. Her tanned skin shone from suntan lotion, and she smelled like cocoa butter. She regarded the activities with bored disdain.

"Daddy," she said kissing the general on the cheek and snuggling his arm, "I'm going upstairs to shower and change for lunch. I won't be long."

Culler appeared and the dog began to yap frantically. He glared at the mutt until Noi and the dog disappeared at the top of the stairs. "Can't stand yappy mutts," he muttered to Mac. "But I do love lazy, floppy-eared dogs. You know, the kind that sit at your feet and look up at you adoringly. I like my women that way too . . ."

"You wish," said Mac, "You wish."

CHAPTER
TWENTY-THREE

Mac drove while Culler busied himself with loading ammo into the pistol magazines, wiping down the guns and breaking in the waist holsters by sliding the guns in and out of the form fitting, hard leather. He popped a loaded magazine into each gun and placed one next to Mac and kept the other for himself.

About half way back to Chiang Rai, Mac grabbed his cell phone. "We should call to set up a meeting with Charly Blackburn." He had earlier programmed the blind cell numbers of Culler, Charly, Maggie and Edwin Rothmann into his phone and had added the general's number that morning.

He pressed the speed dial for Charly Blackburn, but her phone went immediately into voice mail. "Hi," he said, "This is Bob. We're in Chiang Rai staying at the Wangcome Hotel. We can meet anytime after work in room 1048. Please give me a call and let me know what time you can meet. Thanks. Talk to you later."

Mac had decided to meet in Chiang Rai rather than in Chiang Mai because Charly was well known as a consulate official in Chiang Mai. He knew the weakest link in any operation was usually the officially covered case officer. They were the most likely to be under surveillance by the opposition.

Security was never perfect, but he thought it would be good enough under these circumstances.

Charly Blackburn called a little over an hour later and left a short message on his phone. "Hi Bob. Good to hear from you. See you at nine. Okay? Ciao."

CHAPTER TWENTY-FOUR

At eight-thirty Mac sent Culler Santos down to the hotel's lobby to provide counter-surveillance for the meeting. In the lobby bar, Culler selected a bar stool with a good view of the revolving doors at the front entrance.

At eight fifty-six a woman who met the description of Charly Blackburn spun through the revolving door and hurried purposefully toward the elevators at the rear of the lobby. Her shoulder-length, black hair was pulled back away from her face and tied at the nape of her neck. She wore a black, short-sleeved, silk blouse, black slacks, and black pumps. She carried a large black leather shoulder bag.

The ninja lady, he thought as she breezed through the lobby in front of him. She entered an empty elevator and disappeared from his view.

His eyes moved back to the revolving doors at the entrance. Only moments behind her, a harried looking, balding Thai in a wrinkled white shirt, dark slacks and old tennis shoes entered the lobby through the revolving doors and stopped, frantically looking around the lobby for something or someone. *Bingo, that's the surveillance*, thought Culler.

Culler watched the man move through the lobby, eyes darting about and clearly anxious. The man dropped into a comfortable armchair in the middle of the lobby and made a call on his cell phone. He spoke into it while still rubber necking around the lobby.

CHAPTER TWENTY-FIVE

The knock on the door of room 1048 came at exactly nine o'clock. Mac greeted Charly at the door and quickly ushered her into the room. After glancing up and down the hall to make sure no one observed her entering the room, he shut the door and bolted it. When he turned to face her, he caught the hard slap on the side of his face.

"You bastard!"

He stood rubbing the sting out of his cheek with his left hand and holding his right up in front of him as if to say she had made her point. When it was clear there would be no follow-up strikes, he reached out to her. She slipped into his arms and they hugged tightly for a long time, rocking back and forth without saying a word.

They had first met almost ten years earlier. She had just finished her training at the top of her class at The Farm and had been assigned to Bangkok Station as a junior case officer.

He was visiting Bangkok on temporary duty to attend a narcotics conference. She followed him back to his hotel after a dinner party at the home of the Bangkok station chief, and that was the start of an on-again, off-again affair that lasted until Mac rotated out of Hong Kong and dropped completely off of her radar screen. He made no attempt to contact her after that.

Charly Blackburn was known as a "comer" in the Agency. Although her initial interest in Thailand was due mostly to her heritage, she honed that interest by majoring in Far Eastern History, earning a masters degree in the subject in her home state at the University of Oklahoma.

Her thesis on the history of the drug trade emanating from the Golden Triangle was widely published and received kudos from the academic community. The thesis was also the deciding factor in her selection into the elite clandestine service of the CIA, and in her subsequent posting to Thailand.

But it wasn't just her academic achievements that helped to advance her budding career in the CIA's clandestine service. She was blessed with native fluency in the Thai language and oriental good looks which allowed her to move gracefully throughout the Thai community as well as on the diplomatic scene.

And she never missed an opportunity to use these God-given feminine charms to advance her career. Ever since that night after the senior prom in Midwest City, Oklahoma, when she finally agreed to give Bobby Jack Spencer her virginity in the parking lot behind the Baptist church, she knew how to manipulate and control men. And she thoroughly enjoyed that power.

She learned to use that newfound power over men to advance her career in the insular community of the CIA. Indeed, the CIA management encouraged its officers to link up with one another. Better to sleep with the good guys than the bad guys. This was the philosophy. Keeping affairs in-house kept things more secure.

So she slept her way through the ranks of the CIA's East Asia Division management and picked up a number of influential supporters along the way. Her targeting of MacMurphy was one such effort, but she ended up falling for the guy. Not what she had planned at all.

CHAPTER TWENTY-SIX

Seeing her again brought back emotions and memories that Mac had long buried. She was as beautiful as ever, despite the black eye and angry red scar closed with a butterfly bandage on her forehead, wounds she received when slammed against the wall during the explosion.

The feel of her in his arms again aroused him. His hands began to explore first her hips and then further down. He kissed away her tears and she raised her face to meet his. They kissed deeply and longingly.

Memories of past trysts flooded their minds, and their hips pressed together hotly.

His cell phone rang, interrupting the moment.

They broke apart and he answered. "Hey . . . Okay . . . You're certain? Okay . . . Good idea . . . Okay, but make it look like a robbery if it comes to that. Don't do anything that that will bring attention back to us. . . . Right . . . Okay . . . Stay there and keep an eye on him. We'll be about an hour . . . Right, I'll call when she leaves . . . Okay, bye."

Charly was still breathing heavily, regarding him with misty, lustful eyes. "What's wrong? What was that all about?"

"You were followed."

"Impossible!"

"No, it's pretty clear. He came in right after you, but you had already disappeared into an elevator. He knows you're in the hotel. Santos is keeping an eye on him in the lobby."

"They must have picked me up on the outskirts of Chiang Rai. There's no way anyone could have followed me from Chiang Mai to here. I had the pedal to the metal all the way."

"That's it. They probably lost you on the highway and called ahead. There's only one road between Chiang Mai and here. Where'd you park?"

"In a garage about three blocks from here."

MacMurphy turned away from her and walked to the other end of the room where a bottle of Pino Grigio was chilling in an ice bucket on a coffee table sitting between two chairs. He busied himself opening the wine. "Sit down and let's think for a moment." He poured two glasses of wine and sat beside her.

"There's only one way out of here, and that's back through the lobby." He was thinking out loud and his mood was all case officer now. "So, let's figure this out. They know you're meeting someone here. They just don't know who. They may also have someone else staking out your car in the lot. But then again, they've already gotten as much as they'll get out of this surveillance. They probably suspect you're having an important meeting here, otherwise you wouldn't have attempted to lose the surveillance, but they have no idea who that might be. So they've failed in that regard. The surveillance is already a bust. It's lucky you got into that elevator so quickly."

She took a long drink of her wine, sat back and crossed her legs. "I guess I blew it. Sorry Mac."

"Happens to everyone at some time or another. Let's just deal with it. My main concern is maintaining the integrity of the operation, and our connection with you is our weakest link. We've just got to get you out of here safely and make sure they don't find out who you were meeting here."

She held out her glass and gave him a sorrowful look. He refilled their glasses and continued. "Actually, when you think about it, there's no need for them to surveil you any longer. They know you'll be leaving here and going back home to Chiang Mai sooner or later. They know you're meeting someone but don't know who. It could be anything, a clandestine meeting with an asset or just a simple tryst. I just don't want them to do anything stupid to you. These guys play for keeps."

She lowered her head and looked up at him with her most sultry look. "Can we make it later rather than sooner?"

He reached over and caressed her cheek pushing her silky black hair away from her face. "Not tonight, Charly. You've got to get out of here as soon as possible. Culler is downstairs watching your surveillant, and he'll make sure you get back on the road safely. And you're armed, right?"

"Got my trusty PPK right here." She tapped her shoulder bag. "And this little 'ole Oklahoma gal definitely knows how to use it."

"I know you do. Just keep it close when you leave here. In your hand would be good."

"I'm just happy you're so concerned about my safety. I hope that's a personal concern and not just a professional one."

He smiled, looked her over from head to foot, and took a slow drink from his wine glass. "You're a piece of work Charly. A real piece of work. Now let's get down to business. We've got a lot to cover in a very short time."

CHAPTER
TWENTY-SEVEN

M ac pulled a pen and yellow pad out of a briefcase next to his chair. "As you know, without going into any great detail, we're here to neutralize Khun Ut and bust up his heroin network. How we go about doing that depends greatly on the assistance we can count on from you."

She leaned forward, all business now. "I handle an asset I recruited nine months ago. We use him to track Khun Ut's heroin shipments from his jungle refineries to his main warehouse north of here in Mae Chan.

"Yes, Ed told me. Do you know the exact location of the warehouse?"

"Sure do. My guy has been there many times. I have the exact coordinates. But it's heavily guarded, and those guys are a trigger happy bunch of thugs."

"But it's the logical place to start, the warehouse I mean, don't you agree?"

"Depends on what you want to do."

"We want to get into one of Khun Ut's shipments of heroin. All we need is a few minutes. The warehouse where the heroin is stored would be the best place, right?"

"Well, that's where the heroin is stored, lots of it, and tons of marijuana all stacked up in neat bales." She took another long drink from her wine glass, re-crossed her legs, and continued.

"The opium is harvested in the mountain villages and then brought to movable refineries in the jungle and in the highlands where they turn it into white, chalky one-kilogram bricks of low grade heroin.

"The bricks are then assembled in a small warehouse near Khun Ut's mansion on the outskirts of Ban Hin Taek, an Akha village in the highlands where Khun Sa—Khun Ut's father, of course—used to have his headquarters.

"From there the heroin bricks are loaded onto donkeys and sent by caravan down through the hills on narrow trails through the jungle to Khun Ut's main warehouse on the outskirts Mae Chan, a few kilometers north of Chiang Rai. As you would expect, the warehouse is heavily guarded at all times with the guards living on the premises. The heroin is trucked, mostly concealed in shipments of charcoal, to the seaports in southern Thailand. There it's concealed in shipments of one thing or another and loaded unto ships bound for Hong Kong for further, final refinement. Once the refining process is complete it's smuggled to the United States and other parts of the world."

Mac said, "We need to get access to it at some point after it has been turned into the one kilogram bricks but before it's concealed and loaded onto ships bound for Hong Kong."

"What are you going to do with it when you get your hands on it?" she asked.

"We're going to poison it."

She smiled admiringly. "You are a treacherous son of a bitch, aren't you? Whose idea was that, yours or Edwin Rothmann's?"

"Ed's. That's why he's the DDO. The idea came from an operation he was involved in during the Vietnam War. He got into VC and NVA arms caches clandestinely and salted the 7.62 ammo boxes with rounds filled with high explosives rather than gunpowder."

"I heard of that op at The Farm. The AK-47s exploded in the enemies' faces when one of the explosive rounds was chambered. It was very effective as I recall."

"Sure was. Made the VC afraid to use its own weapons and ammo."

"And once you kill a few people using Khun Ut's heroin, the word will get out that he's selling bad shit, and people will stop buying it. His distribution network comes tumbling down, is that about it?"

"That's about it. Got a problem with that? The collateral damage, I mean?"

She shook her head and chuckled. "Not at all. Sounds like a great plan to me."

"So who's the treacherous one, you or me?"

"That's why I love you, Mac. We're cut from the same cloth." She ran her tongue over her lips.

"Knock it off Charly. We've got serious work to do and I need your help. We can't risk any more meetings, not until this is over at least. You're under Khun Ut's microscope; if anyone makes the connection between you and me, all of the DDO's 'plausible denial' will dissolve into mist. This can't be a CIA op. That's the whole point. You understand that, right?"

She put on her most doleful look and gave him a deep *wai*, with her prayerful hands touching high on her forehead, and replied with resignation. "I know. I get it. Don't worry. Rothmann needs to deny any connection between this operation and the CIA, and I'm the weakest link in that plan. You can count on me, Mac. Just tell me what you need and I'll deliver it."

"Okay, now we're on the same page. Tell me about this asset of yours."

CHAPTER
TWENTY-EIGHT

S he collected her thoughts, took another swallow of her wine and proceeded to brief him.

"He's a low-level security guy who works for Khun Ut and the Cambodian. He and a team of armed guards accompany the heroin shipments from Khun Ut's collection point in Ban Hin Taek down through the jungle to the main warehouse near Mae Chan. He's a Hmong tribesman who fought alongside of General Vang Pao and the CIA's Bill Lair in Laos during the Vietnam conflict. He's a wily old cuss—smart, tough as nails, and totally loyal to the United States, thanks in large part to the rapport he had with his case officer, Bill Lair. And this is despite the fact that the U.S. abandoned the Hmong tribesmen after the war.

"What a disgrace. Anyway, I met him through his son, a bright graduate student at Chiang Mai University. The kid serves as a spotter for us among the academic community in Thailand. Spotting his dad was by far his crowning achievement. It paid for his education."

Mac was taking notes furiously on his yellow pad. "So he's been to both warehouses and knows the routes between them."

"Right. The information the guy has given us has been invaluable. It was instrumental in our recent crackdowns on Khun Ut, which of course led to his retaliatory attack on our consulate in Chiang Mai."

"And you have casings of the warehouses and have mapped the donkey routes." "The warehouse casings are not a problem." She dug down into her large black bag, pulled out a folder and handed it to him. "Here they are. I Xeroxed them on water-soluble paper so you can flush them after you study them. I also included Khun Ut's villa in Ban Hin Taek and GPS coordinates for all three locations."

"That's terrific, Charly. You're way out in front of me."

"I usually am. Anyway, when you read them you won't be so pleased. The security around all three locations is tight. They're surrounded by guards armed with automatic weapons. They've also got a couple of Huey gunships with mini guns to protect them. You can't get within a thousand meters of any of them.

"The donkey routes are less clear. There's no one route they take each time. They just wander down through the jungle on animal trails. I solved that problem by giving VANGUISH—that's his cryptonym, you don't need to know his name—a stainless steel Rolex watch with a GPS built into it. Pretty neat, eh?"

"Very neat. Go on."

"Well, actually we had his son give it to him. He needed to be able to explain how he got such an expensive item. So now we can track his every move through the jungle, in real time, from Ban Hin Taek to Mae Chan." She sat back, proud of herself, and drained her glass.

"Good work. Excellent. That must have taken some convincing on your part." He refilled their glasses. "How did you get him to agree to all that? How'd you recruit the guy?"

"Truth be told, it wasn't hard at all. I was just lucky to find him. He's a brave old cuss who sees his cooperation with me and the Agency as an extension of what he did with Bill Lair and the Hmong hill tribes in Laos way back when. You've heard of Bill Lair, right?"

"Of course. Met him once right after I joined the Agency. He spoke to us down at The Farm. We had a reception for him afterward. A good 'ole Texas boy who married into Thai royalty and spent most of his career in Thailand, a true legend in the CIA."

"Yes, and his legend lives on in Vanguish."

"Fitting. Did you pick out that cryptonym?"

"I did indeed."

"Nice touch. So, you think we should stay clear of the warehouses and concentrate on the donkey trails."

"That's the way I see it. The only way to get to the warehouses is to bomb them, but we can't get the Thais to agree to that. But if you can intercept one of the donkey caravans . . . well, that's probably your best shot, and Vanguish and I can help with that."

"One more thing and then I've got to get you back on your way to Chiang Mai. Tell me what you know about General Sawat Ruchupan."

"How do you know about him?"

"Well, it's kind of a long story. Rothmann put us in touch with an arms dealer down in the Florida Keys, the guy who outfitted us with our weapons and the chemicals.

"He in turn put us in touch with the general, the one who received the shipment. He turned the stuff over to us yesterday and offered his services in other ways as well. He's a pilot. Has a helicopter and a plane. I thought he could be useful to us because we have no support structure out here."

"I'd be very careful when dealing with General Sawat. He profited greatly from the drug trade under Khun Sa. He was known at the time as one of the most corrupt police generals in Thailand, and—believe me—that's saying something.

"Then, when General Prem Tinsulanonda took over as Prime Minister, back in the early nineteen-eighties, things changed rapidly. Prem and the DEA decided they had had enough and decided to push Khun Sa out of Thailand. By then, Khun Sa had built up his empire to the point where it was providing more than seventy per cent of the heroin consumed in the U.S.

"So Prem leaned on General Sawat and persuaded him to change sides. Sawat did and the rest is history. The Thai army and police attacked Khun Sa's headquarters in Ban Hin Taek with tanks and planes and, after several days of violent fighting, managed to force Khun Sa and his SUA army to retreat across the border into Burma. That ended Khun Sa's rule in the Golden Triangle."

"So how's the relationship between Khun Ut and General Sawat today?"

"Not great, but word has it that the general still benefits from Khun Ut's drug trade, despite the fact that he's retired now and out of the chain of command. They've apparently reached some sort of a *modus vivendi*."

"Damn . . . so he's not trustworthy."

"No, I didn't say that. To the extent that any former corrupt police general can be trusted, General Sawat has the reputation of being a straight shooter. He works for anyone who will pay him. The word is he keeps his clients compartmented and tries not to cross wires."

"So we should trust, but verify, in the words of Ronald Reagan."

She laughed. "Something like that."

"Okay Charly, you've got to get out of here. You've been here over an hour already."

"Time flies when you're having fun. Are you sure we can't stretch this out just a little bit longer?" She gave him a look that promised everything.

He shook his head. "I'd love to, Charly, and I mean that. Just keep your phone handy in case I need some more of your help on this. Okay?" He grabbed his cell phone and punched in Culler's number.

She stood up and flipped her hair back from her face. "Okay Mac, I'll stand by the phone. Just like the old days."

MacMurphy spoke into his phone. "She's on her way down."

She gathered her things and Mac walked her to the door, but before he could open it she put her hand on his outstretched arm and stopped him. She turned and took his face in her hands, brushing his lips with hers.

He hesitated. "No, Charly, you've got to leave."

She pulled open the door and was halfway into the hall when she turned back to him and uttered, "You really are a mean bastard."

CHAPTER TWENTY-NINE

S antos dropped a one hundred baht note on the bar and prepared to leave. He was dressed in jeans, tennis shoes and a blue, short-sleeved Thai silk shirt that barely covered the large Heckler and Koch .45 caliber handgun holstered in the small of his back.

The Thai surveillant sat awkwardly in the same chair in the middle of the lobby. He pretended to read a magazine, but his eyes never left the elevator banks at the rear of the lobby.

Exiting the elevator, Charly briskly crossed the lobby between Santos and the surprised surveillant, her high heels clacking rhythmically on the marble floor.

The surveillant fumbled with his magazine, dropped it on the floor, lurched out of his chair, and fell in behind her, stuffing his cell phone in his pocket as he hurried to keep up.

She pushed through the revolving door and headed out into the night with the Thai close behind her, and Santos close behind him.

One behind the other, the three of them hurried through the city streets of Chiang Rai until they reached the two-story parking garage where Charly had left her car.

Two blocks off of the main strip made a huge difference in both foot and vehicular traffic. Aside from the well-lit parking garage, the surrounding streets were quiet and dark. She stopped at the kiosk at the garage entrance, paid her bill, and one of the valets went running up the ramp for her car.

The surveillant stepped into the shadows at the corner of the garage and watched. When she had finished paying and moved to the waiting area, he darted across the dark street toward a lone black, beat-up old Toyota parked illegally in a fire zone a half block down the road across from the garage entrance.

A red and white, official-looking permit was visible on the dashboard. Santos guessed it gave the owner permission to park in restricted zones. *Incipient corruption,* he thought.

Santos figured that, since the surveillant had made no effort to use his cell phone to alert anyone else to Charly's movements, he was probably alone on the job. That was a good thing. He only had to worry about neutralizing one person.

Santos circled around and darted across the dark, tree-lined street behind the surveillant. He moved quietly but rapidly in a low crouch and came up behind the unsuspecting Thai just as he rounded the car on the curbside and was about to put his key in the car's door.

The surveillant was so intent on keeping his *rabbit* and the garage in sight that he never noticed the big *farang* moving up behind him.

The surveillant leaned toward the car, fumbling in the dark intently focused on trying to fit his key in the door. Santos slipped up behind him and brought both hands out and around and cuffed him on both ears in a powerful clap. The surveillant went down like a stone.

Santos stood motionless for several moments and surveyed the area around him. The attendant in the parking kiosk looked up momentarily and went back to reading his magazine. Two young Thai strollers, walking hand in hand further down the street, looked back in the direction of the sound but, seeing nothing, continued on their way. A car drove by, illuminating the empty street.

Santos kneeled down in the shadow of the car and quickly removed the surveillant's watch and wallet. He pulled a money clip with about five hundred baht in small bills out of one front pocket and his cell phone from the other. He stuffed everything into the side pocket of his shirt.

He rolled the unconscious man off of the curb down into the gutter, partially under the car. Spotting the car keys laying in the gutter, he put these in his pocket as well.

Santos reached down and felt the jugular vein for a pulse. *Well, you're alive you little fucker,* he thought, *but you're going to have one hell of a headache when you wake up, and your ears will be ringing like a Christmas string quartet for a month.*

Santos stood up, watched Blackburn's car exit the garage and turn south, took another look around him, and casually strolled back to the Wangcome Hotel. He walked straight through the lobby to the elevator bank, up to MacMurphy's room, and knocked quietly on the door.

Opening the door, Mac saw Santos standing there with a big, shit-eating grin. His big outstretched hands contained the surveillant's belongings. "Brought you a present, Mac," he said.

"Pretty good haul for your first mugging, Culler. Now get in here before you get arrested. Tell me all about it, and then I'll brief you on my meeting with Charly Blackburn."

CHAPTER THIRTY

The next morning Mac called General Sawat and arranged for an airplane tour of the Golden Triangle. He wanted to get a feel for the topography of the area and a look at the two warehouses and Khun Ut's headquarters from the air. They agreed to meet at the restaurant of the general aviation section of the Chiang Mai airport at noon.

Noi met them at the entrance of the restaurant, greeting them with a respectful *wai*, revealing her deep cleavage. "*Sawatdee kha*," she purred.

The men returned the *wai* and greeted her in Thai, "*Sawatdee khrap.*"

She spoke to one of the waiters who led them to a table at a window overlooking the airstrip. The table was already set with a tray of Thai appetizers, *gueyteow* noodles, assorted satays and a pot of tea. She served them with typical Thai grace while Ling Ling, peeking out of the top of Noi's oversized bag, yapped at Culler, who glared back at the mutt. "General Sawat will join us shortly," she said. "He is preparing the plane for our tour."

The dog continued to yap at Culler and Noi muzzled the mutt with her hand, quieting the obnoxious animal momentarily.

"Will little Ling Ling be joining us on our little tour of the Golden Triangle?" Santos asked.

"Of course Ling Ling will join us," she purred, clucking at the dog. "She is my baby." She snuggled the dog, kissed it on the snout, and fed it a piece of spring roll from her dish. "Aren't you, my little sweetie?" she said.

Santos forced himself to smile, leaned toward her, and said in a calm, controlled voice, "But, my dear, if you can't control little Ling Ling's incessant yapping, I will personally wring her neck, skin her and eat her for dinner."

Noi's eyes widened and the dog whimpered as she squeezed it tightly to her breast, muzzling it with a hand to protect it from the huge *farang* monster.

Mac looked over at Culler with a combination of disapproval and admiration. Santos had echoed his thoughts precisely, but MacMurphy would never be so confrontational in a situation like this. He needed Noi as an ally, or at least neutral. If she turned on them, she could turn the general against them, and that would not be good for the mission.

The tension of the moment was broken with the arrival of the general.

He approached the table with a spring in his step, greeting them with a *wai* and in a jovial voice, "My friends, I am happy to see you are enjoying your lunch. I hope you enjoy the food. This is not the finest restaurant in Northern Thailand, but I have selected items from the menu that are within the chef's capabilities.

"The plane has been prepped and is ready to go whenever you are, but first let us finish our lunch. I have an excellent tour mapped out for you."

If he noticed the pout on Noi's face, he didn't react to it at all.

They finished eating, with Noi only picking at her food, and followed the general down the tarmac to the aircraft. The general did a final inspection and removed the chocks from the wheels and the tethers from the wings. Then they all began to climb aboard the aircraft.

Sawat said, "Noi, you and Ling Ling sit in the back with Mr. Ralph. Bob, you come up front with me. It is a beautiful day for a tour of the mighty Mekong and the Golden Triangle."

Seeing the expression of shock and discomfort on Noi's face, Mac smiled and suggested that he and "Ralph" sit in the back, with Noi and Ling Ling up front next to the general.

Visibly relieved at the new seating arrangements, she bowed deeply to Mac. The general was oblivious to the whole act being played out before him.

CHAPTER THIRTY-ONE

O nce inside with the doors closed, it rapidly grew hot in the cabin. Rivulets of sweat ran down Culler's face and off his chin onto his Thai silk shirt. As the propeller caught, the engine revved and the cooling system cut in; they finally began to cool off.

The general maneuvered the howling Cessna 172 out onto the taxiway and then to the end of the runway, where he did a final check of his instruments and received permission from the control tower to take off. They raced down the runway and up into the air.

Banking right he took the plane due east toward the Mekong River. They climbed to an altitude of fifteen hundred feet and leveled off over thick triple-canopy jungle interspersed with villages and farms. Soon the meandering, wide, brown swath of the mighty Mekong came into view. He banked left and they followed the river north toward the Golden Triangle.

The general kept up a steady stream of commentary on the landscape and history of the land below them, shouting over his shoulder to be heard above the wailing engine.

They reached the Golden Triangle, and Culler and Mac could see plainly how the place got its name. The Mekong flowed north to south, dividing Burma to the west and Laos to the east. The Ruak River flowed from the west to the east separating Burma from Thailand, its neighbor to the south, until it curved south and joined the Mekong in a perfect triangle, joining Burma, Laos and Thailand.

The general circled the Golden Triangle while continuing to enlighten them on the jaded history of the area over the roar of the plane. He banked south beyond Doi Mae Salong and headed back into the mountains of Northern Thailand until he reached the village of Ban Hin Taek, securely nestled deep in a long finger valley in the shadow of Doi Tung, the highest mountain in the region.

"There it is," the general shouted. "The notorious Ban Hin Taek— easy to get to by air, but by land it is a very different story. See that road over there? It starts at Bap Basang on route 110 between Chiang Rai and Mae Sai, winding up that mountain to Doi Mae Salong. From there it continues as a dirt road heading north toward the Burmese border to Ban Hin Taek. It's the same road the Thai Army took when they attacked Khun Sa. Many trucks loaded with men—armed with assault rifles, grenade launchers, recoilless rifles and rocket launchers—drove all night to surprise Khun Sa. And they succeeded. Khun Sa never thought they would do it. Or if they did, he figured he would have plenty of warning from his many paid informants. He never thought such a thing could happen with all the money he spread around the area."

"I'm surprised no one warned him," said Mac.

"Frankly, I would have warned him if I could have, but the raid was such a closely guarded secret that even the Thai Army and Border Patrol soldiers didn't know where they were going until after they got there.

"It is not as small a village as you might think, either. Even during Khun Sa's days, it was thriving. Khun Sa first came to Ban Hin Taek in the mid-sixties. He lived here for about a year and fell in love with the place. So, about ten years later he returned with his wife and children. He made the village his base of operations for his Shan United Army and for his associated drug trade. At its peak the SUA had twenty thousand heavily armed soldiers totally devoted to him, and seventy percent of the heroin consumed in the United States came from his organization."

The general brought the Cessna lower and buzzed the village. "See that large villa there at the base of that mountain? That was Khun Sa's home and headquarters. It was very modern, beautifully furnished with expensive furniture and artwork. It had a television in every room, an elaborate stereo system, an Olympic sized swimming pool and a tennis court that doubled as a helicopter landing pad."

"Pretty nice digs," said Mac.

"Yes, the officers and chemists in Khun Sa's narcotics army also lived in spacious, modern villas with manicured lawns. You can see some of them over there, lining the base of the hill next to Khun Sa's place."

Mac leaned forward and shouted a question at the general. "If that's the only road leading to Ban Hin Taek, how did the Thai Army flush him out of there?"

"Yes, good question. Ban Hin Taek was a heavily fortified mountain stronghold. Khun Sa felt very secure there surrounded by two thousand soldiers. The actual battle was like a shootout in one of your cowboy movies: street by street and house by house. Vicious.

"The battle for the village, back in 1982, lasted three long days. The Thai soldiers and Border Patrol took up battle lines along the east side of the main street, over there. Ten meters away, on the other side of the street, stood the surprised drug traffickers, many of them rousted from their beds and still in their underwear, but heavily armed with automatic weapons and not afraid to use them.

"When asked to surrender, the bedraggled line of scruffy soldiers, many of them high on marijuana, just opened fire. The fighting was close quarters and bitter, but the Thais had them outgunned and the element of surprise in their favor. The Thai Army was supported by aircraft that strafed the dense surrounding jungle and the SUA positions.

"In the end, fifty-one of the SUA mercenaries, including Khun Sa's natural son, lay dead alongside of sixteen Thai soldiers. The rest of the opium mercenaries fled with Khun Sa to safety over the border into Burma. Khun Sa never returned. Thailand had finally had enough of him."

"What supports the village now?" asked MacMurphy. "The same old drug trade but with Khun Ut in charge?"

"No, although there are certainly similarities, the trade is much more disbursed under Khun Ut. It certainly continues to bring a lot of revenue to the village, but tourism actually brings in more."

Mac leaned forward and shouted over the engine. "Tourism? You've got to be joking. People drive all the way up here on that little dirt road to tour the village?"

"Yes sir. Khun Sa's old town villa, the one I told you about, is now a museum for the drug trade. People drive all the way up here to see how he lived. And we also get our share of trekkers who walk all the way up here just to sample the opium in one of the many native huts that will sell them a pipe or two."

The general paused to clear his throat, which was becoming sore from shouting over the engine. "But it's not over. Far from it. The destruction of Khun Sa's army disrupted the heroin flow for awhile, but the opium war is far from over. The syndicate is gaining momentum once again under the leadership of Khun Ut, who is, as I am sure you know, Khun Sa's adopted son.

"See that mountain aerie about halfway up that hill over there?" He pointed to a sprawling lodge nestled in the woods directly across the village from the towering Doi Tung Mountain. "That villa was used by Khun Sa as a mountain retreat back in the old days and is now the headquarters and home of Khun Ut. I cannot take you too close to it, or they will shoot at us. It is very heavily guarded. Just like the good old days, or maybe not so good old days. No one can get close to Khun Ut's house. It is a fortress."

Mac leaned forward and shouted into the general's ear. "Take us over Ban Mae Chan, will you? We would like to see Khun Ut's warehouse."

Startled, the general asked over his shoulder. "Mae Chan. What do you know about Mae Chan?"

"Why don't you tell me?"

Turning in her seat, Noi regarded Mac and Culler in disbelief.

"Well, you already know Khun Ut has a warehouse there. Actually, it's his main storage depot. But you can't get close to it. He has got security tighter than a virgin's twat. That's a good one, eh? I learned that expression in California."

Noi rolled her eyes and cuddled Ling Ling closer to her breast, as if to shield the dog's ears from the general's crude words.

"That warehouse is the last stop for the heroin before it is shipped out of Thailand. Most of it goes to Hong Kong where it is put through the final refining process by Chinese chemists. The mountain refineries in the hills around here are very primitive and have to be moved around constantly to avoid detection. The heroin bricks that are produced here cannot be used for very much the way they are."

"Let's go see it," said Santos.

Noi gave the general a frightened look, but he seemed unconcerned. The general banked the small plane to the left and headed in a southeasterly direction away from Ban Hin Taek. "Okay, it's off the normal tourist routes of the Golden Triangle, Ban Hin Taek and the Mekong, but I will take you as close as I can get without alerting Khun Ut's security team. That is not something any of us would want to do, and they know me and my plane very well."

CHAPTER THIRTY-TWO

MacMurphy had traveled to Ban Mae Chan when he was stationed in Udorn. The town was located on Route One at the end of a high plateau extending south into Thailand from the Burmese border. It was in the heart of the opium growing region twenty-two miles north of Chiang Rai, mid-way between Chiang Rai and Ban Mae Sai on the Burmese border. Traditionally the town was a trading post for the Akha and Yao hill tribes to sell their goods and purchase manufactured items. Now it was all about tourism and opium.

They were flying at one thousand feet when they came upon the town from the north. "There it is," said the general, pointing ahead and to the right of the plane. "It is not much to see. Just another little hill village turned into a tourist trap. In front of us to the south, you will see where the plateau comes to a point and falls into a deep jungle ravine. At the edge of that ravine in those woods you will see . . . there it is—see that shiny tin roof there in the woods? That is the warehouse."

Both Culler and Mac strained to see, as the general banked the plane first to the right and then to the left for each of them to get a clear view of the terrain below.

Sawat said, "This is as close as we dare to get. We will have to fly around it and continue south towards Chiang Rai. But at least you know where it is. You certainly don't want to go asking directions for it in the village." The general laughed heartily at his joke while Noi stared at him with wide, disapproving eyes.

Culler and Mac settled back into their seats in the rear of the plane thinking the same thing. This was going to be a bitch! They had studied the casings Charly had provided, but actually seeing the facility from the air gave them an entirely new perspective.

They needed to break into the facility, inject the ricin into as many of the heroin bricks as possible, and get out without being detected, or—if they were detected—make it look like they were attempting to rob the place. Stealing a few kilos of heroin would be good cover for the operation as long as it allowed them to get in and out and do their thing.

The casings showed that the bales of marijuana were stacked around the perimeter of the warehouse's ground floor, with the pallets of heroin bricks near the center. They could possibly get through a back door or a window, maybe even cut a hole in the wall.

It seemed unlikely they would be able to gain access to the interior any other way. Not with all the security around, and not without having to kill the guards they would inevitably encounter along the way.

Maybe they could quietly take out a few of the guards on the warehouse's rear—the apparently less guarded side facing the ravine. That would be a possibility. But it would mean a steep climb from the jungle floor to the ridge of the plateau: a tough job, but not impossible.

CHAPTER THIRTY-THREE

While Santos and MacMurphy were flying over Ban Hin Taek and Ban Mae Chan, Khun Ut and Ung Chea were meeting in Khun Ut's mountain lodge in Ban Hin Taek.

Impeccably dressed in a tan, starched safari suit, Khun Ut leaned back in his leather executive chair. His feet were propped up on the corner of an oversized, ornately carved antique teak desk that had once belonged to his father. He watched as the smoke wafted from his cheroot.

"What makes you think it was anything more than a mugging?" he asked. "After all, Chiang Rai is a rough neighborhood, and he was robbed of everything of any value he had on him."

"Just a feeling," said the Cambodian. He had plopped himself down in a chair across the desk from Khun Ut and was absentmindedly tracing the jagged scar on his cheek with a thumb. "Things don't match up, boss. She drives all the way to Chiang Rai, parks her car, walks straight to the Wangcome Hotel, through the lobby to the elevators and disappears upstairs for over an hour. Surely she was meeting someone in one of the

129

rooms. A clandestine meeting of some sort, and I do not think it was about sex. She would not come all that way for a quickie."

"But that is her job, right? She is a CIA officer. She was probably meeting one of her agents."

"Of course she was. But why would she come to Chiang Rai for an agent meeting? She almost never comes here. And then the mugging . . ."

"I would understand it, Ung Chea, if she had counter-surveillance, but no CIA counter-surveillance team would ever be so bold as to do that to a surveillant. Not unless they thought her life was in danger."

"Maybe they did. I mean, our attack on their consulate . . . well, maybe they finally decided to get revenge. It is possible, no? Considering what we just did to them."

Khun Ut spun out of his chair and walked to the expanse of windows across the front of the room. He studied the village below and then lifted his gaze toward the towering Doi Tung Mountain on the other side.

He thought back to the first time he had played in this room as a small boy with Khun Sa's son.

Khun Ut was born Duangdee Khemmawongse in Ban Hin Taek. His father was pure Akha, and his mother was half-Chinese, half-Akha. His family lived on the outskirts of the village, in a thatched roof hut with a dirt floor, among the pigs and chickens. As long as he could remember, they had worked in one capacity or another in the opium trade.

As is the custom in Thailand, he was given a nickname shortly after his birth. While most Thai nicknames reflect what the baby looked like at birth, his parents chose Ut, which had no particular meaning. They just liked the sound of the name.

Ut had a vague recollection of the time when Khun Sa first arrived in Ban Hin Taek. He remembered Khun Sa as a handsome, charismatic man who gave the dirt poor villagers hope of better times in the future: a future where opium would be more than just a remedy for their ills and an escape from their troubles, but one which would bring them heretofore unimaginable wealth and prosperity.

Khun Sa came to the village with his wife and three children, one of whom was a three-year-old boy, the same age as Ut. The boys quickly became inseparable, and they grew up as brothers while Khun Sa built up his opium empire and brought prosperity to the small village.

By the time the boys reached the age of thirteen, they were constantly at his side, collecting opium from farmers and delivering it to refineries deep in the jungle.

And as Khun Sa's empire expanded, the boys took on ever increasing responsibility, and their power and wealth increased commensurately.

Ut, the smarter boy by far, reveled in his newfound status and soon began to overshadow Khun Sa's natural son, much to the chagrin of Khun Sa at first, but soon with the resignation that the two boys complimented each other and would always be together at his side.

When the forces of the Thai army and border patrol attacked Khun Sa's Ban Hin Taek stronghold, Khun Sa lost many of his men, including his son, in the fighting. He also lost guns and ammunition worth more than two million dollars.

Ut was badly wounded in the right leg by shrapnel, making it impossible for him to retreat with Khun Sa. The injury left him with a permanent limp and the resolve to recover his former lifestyle and climb back to the top of the heap, with or without Khun Sa.

By then Ut was twenty-one years, a seasoned veteran of the opium trade. While Khun Sa roamed the hills of Burma trying to avoid capture with the remnants of his SUA army, Ut remained in Ban Hin Taek and quietly began to rebuild Khun Sa's empire.

He adopted the name Khun Ut and took up permanent residence in Khun Sa's mountain retreat overlooking Ban Hin Taek. No one challenged his right to be there.

Khun Sa remained on the run, hounded by Burmese authorities, for the next ten years. He finally surrendered in 1996 and was held in house arrest in Rangoon until his death in 2001.

The drug trade under the direction of Khun Ut was by this time restored to the point where it was once again becoming a nuisance to the

Thai and Burmese governments, and a particular menace to the U.S. government. It had reached a point where its production amounted to forty-five percent of the U.S. heroin supply, rivaled only by Afghanistan.

Under pressure from the U.S., the Burmese started shelling the border region around Ban Hin Taek and made preparations for an invasion to wipe out the drug trade. But the Thai government protested the invasion of its territory vigorously, forcing the Burmese to call it off and leaving Khun Ut to manage his revived drug empire with minimum resistance.

Ut shook himself out of his reverie and returned to the moment. *That is the answer. She was meeting with some outside CIA people. That is why she didn't meet with them at the consulate in Chiang Mai. It is an outside team. Maybe paramilitary.*

He turned to face the Cambodian and gestured with his cheroot. "The filthy maggots sent a team in to get us. But the Thais will not help them this time, and they can not do anything without the consent of the Thai government. They must respect Thai sovereignty. Double up on the surveillance of Blackburn and the other suspected CIA officers at the consulate." He pumped his cheroot at the Cambodian. "And get me a list of everyone registered at the Wangcome Hotel on the night of the incident. I will bet you a million Baht that if we concentrate on registrations of single, non-Thai *farangs* we will find our CIA team."

The Cambodian smiled broadly, which only made him look more grotesque. He dug into his pocket and unfolded two sheets of paper. "I anticipated your request. Eleven rooms are occupied by single male *farangs*. Five of them are Americans."

"Good work, Ung Chea. You know what to do next."

CHAPTER THIRTY-FOUR

Santos and MacMurphy returned to their hotel to consider their next move. They showered and changed out of their sweaty clothes and spent the remainder of the afternoon going over the maps and casings of Khun Ut's warehouse and headquarters.

They discussed possible operational approaches and agreed that whatever approach they decided to take would, regrettably, have to exclude the use of Charly Blackburn and her Hmong asset, Vanquish.

Using Vanquish would clearly be the easiest and best route to take, but it risked exposing Charly and the CIA hand. Since Edwin Rothmann had made it clear that he did not want any connection to the CIA, they would have to do it without her.

Charly Blackburn could only be used as a conduit for information. No more personal meetings would be held, if they could be avoided. Their one face-to-face meeting had already demonstrated the risks involved in meeting with her.

They were up against a ruthless adversary, but one that was also astute and professional.

Efficiency gives way to security to some degree in clandestine tradecraft. It was like a child's seesaw. When security was highest, efficiency was lowest and vice versa. They would err on the side of caution and security for the time being.

By six o'clock their brains were saturated with studying maps and photos and casings. Mac decided he needed a drink, so they made their way down to the bar before heading out to dinner. Both men wore short-sleeved, untucked shirts to conceal the .45 caliber H&K weapons they carried in the small of their backs.

Santos nursed a frosty Kloster beer while MacMurphy downed two vodka martinis on the rocks. Santos had decided he had had enough spicy Thai food for awhile and suggested they grab a steak someplace. He explained that he needed the fortification that only red meat would bring him for the day that lay ahead of them.

They got directions from the bartender to an American-style steakhouse on the south end of the city and headed down to the garage to retrieve their car. Culler drove and Mac, feeling relaxed with the effects of the two martinis, did not object.

On their way to the Texas Steakhouse, Culler asked Mac if tomorrow was too soon to launch their operation at the Mae Chan warehouse.

Mac replied, "Everything we need is in the back of this car and there's nothing more we can do in Chiang Rai, so I guess tomorrow's as good a day as any, unless you want to sleep in."

"Yeah, right. I'm not the one who sleeps like a teenager."

MacMurphy leaned back in his seat and massaged his temples. He gazed out the window as they sped past bicycles, Honda 50cc motorbikes with whole families aboard, and thatched roof shacks on bamboo stilts lining the side of the road. "Sleep is good for the soul, my friend. Perhaps you should get more of it. Maybe then you wouldn't be so cranky."

"There it is," said Culler. "Up there on the right. The Texas Steakhouse. Finally we're going to get some real sustenance."

Aside from the exterior surroundings, the interior of the Texas Steakhouse looked like something you would find anywhere from Tysons Corner to SoHo—dark paneled walls lined with burgundy banquets under racks of wine bottles. A stuffed Angus bull guarded the entrance.

Culler Santos devoured a bloody, sixteen-ounce New York Strip steak and sipped on another bottle of the local Kloster beer while Mac picked on a six-ounce filet mignon with pepper sauce and quashed it down with most of a sixty dollar bottle of French Bordeaux wine.

Both shunned the desert cart, but Mac selected a chunk of ripe Camembert cheese from the cheese cart to accompany the remainder of the Bordeaux. Then he ordered a cognac to settle everything down. Santos topped off his meal with a sweet cappuccino coffee.

Mac was quite mellow by now, relaxed and talkative, while Culler mostly listened and observed his surroundings. When he responded to a question from Mac, he noticed that Mac seemed distracted, swirling the cognac in his glass.

"I can see you're sorry you sent Charly back," Culler said.

"That obvious?"

"Finish the drink and let's head back before you talk me into chasing women."

On the drive back to their hotel, they agreed to check out of the Wangcome in the morning, not too early so Mac could get his beauty sleep, and drive up Route One toward Ban Mae Chan and Khun Sa's warehouse.

They had selected a spot on the map where they could drive in, cache the car and enter the jungle. The spot was at the edge of the ravine along an old logging trail about four miles south of Ban Mae Chan. From there they planned to make their way north on foot until they hit the bottom edge of the ravine. Then they would make the steep climb up to the warehouse. After that they would have to wing it.

CHAPTER THIRTY-FIVE

MacMurphy slept like the dead. The martinis, wine and cognac put him out as soon as his head touched the pillow. Santos was a different story. He tossed and turned and listened to the street noises and planned the next day in his mind. When he finally did fall asleep, he slept fitfully.

At one forty-seven in the morning, Santos heard loud pounding at the door of the room directly above him, then muffled voices, then louder voices and then the sounds of a struggle and then a thud. The thud brought him fully awake, and he reached for his pistol on the nightstand. The silencer was already attached.

The muffled sounds of a struggle and shouted commands continued overhead. It sounded like someone had been rousted from his bed and was being interrogated. He could not hear what was being said, but it was clearly in English.

Santos's mind raced. He quietly slipped out of bed and padded across the room to the doors which separated his room from Mac's. He opened the door on his side and knocked softly. He could hear Mac's snoring coming from inside. He called to Mac in hushed tones through the door but the snoring continued.

Cellphone, he thought, and darted back across the room to the nightstand. He picked up his phone and punched Mac's number on the speed dial. He heard the door to the room above him slam shut and the noises stopped. He returned to the adjoining door and listened for ringing, but heard nothing but Mac's continued snoring.

CHAPTER THIRTY-SIX

The Cambodian exited room 1150 with his two broad-shouldered cohorts, slamming the door in frustration behind him. The thugs were dressed alike in black slacks and tee-shirts with SECURITY written across the back. Both looked like weight lifters with bulging biceps, although one of them had gone to seed and wore his pot belly like a proud pregnancy.

The Cambodian whispered into his lapel microphone. "This is base. It is not Levine either, but he put up a struggle. He thought we were busting him. He is just another long-haired, hippy pot-head here to smoke our *gunsha*. Definitely not a CIA operative."

He pulled a slip of paper from his shirt pocket and read from it. "There are two more Americans in rooms 1048 and 1050 below. We are heading down there to check them out now. You check out room 922. That will be the lot of them. Over."

Ung Chea and his cohorts took the stairs down one flight to the tenth floor. The hall was quiet as they made their way down the carpeted hall.

When they reached the rooms, the Cambodian stood back and motioned
to the heavier of the two men with his 9mm pistol. "Udom, take the door
on the right. Boon-Nam, you take the door on the left."

The two thugs, each holding a .357 caliber Smith and Wesson
revolver at the ready, listened at the two doors. Udom spoke first. "Someone is inside 1048; I can hear snoring."

The smaller man, ear pinned to the other door, said, "I cannot hear
anything here. No sound."

"Okay," whispered Ung Chea, "Take the snorer first."

The Cambodian joined Udom and Boon-Nam at the door of room
1048 and quietly inserted a key card into the lock. He pushed it all the
way in carefully and then withdrew it. The lights on the lock beeped and
signaled green, and he pushed down on the door handle, opening the
door a crack. With the door partially open, he stepped back into the
hallway to let Udom at the door.

Udom put his ear to the crack and, hearing the continued snoring,
signaled okay to the others. He stuck his .357 in his ankle holster and
inserted a wire tool into the opening, running it up the crack until it hit
the security chain. He closed the door as far as it would go and manipu-
lated the tool up against the security chain until the chain dropped free
and clanged against the door.

Ung Chea and Boon-Nam stepped back, pistols at the ready, and
leveled at the door as Udom unholstered his revolver, held it up at the
ready position and pushed the door open with the back of his arm
and shoulder.

At that instant the three of them heard the muffled *phifft* of a silenced
bullet exiting the suppressor of Santos's .45 caliber H&K handgun.

The heavy round hit Udom under the right armpit, mushroomed
through ribs and lungs, and exited through his chest on the other side,
slamming him against the door. He fell dead halfway inside the room,
but not before he reflexively fired off one booming .357 round into
the floor.

That awakened the sleeping man inside.

Ung Chea and Boon-Nam stood frozen for a moment and then turned in shocked unison toward the direction of the shot. They saw with wide-eyed disbelief a huge *farang* dressed only in checkered boxer shorts in a crouched shooting position with a long pistol leveled at them.

Another *phifft* and the huge gun jumped in the *farang's* hand. The round crashed into Boon-Nam's chest just above the solar plexis, picked him up and sent him flying backwards down the hall. He hit the floor dead, arms flung wide.

The Cambodian brought his 9mm around and leveled it at the big *farang*.

CHAPTER THIRTY-SEVEN

The booming report of the .357 magnum handgun finally blasted MacMurphy out of his drunken reverie. He swiped his silenced H&K off of the nightstand and rolled out of bed onto the floor, coming up with the gun at the ready.

The door to his room was wide open with a motionless man sprawled across the threshold halfway into the room. On the other side of the door in the hallway stood two more men holding pistols aimed down the hall.

MacMurphy's mind spun. What was happening? Someone obviously tried to break into his room, but he was dead on the threshold. The other two must be his cohorts. They must be aiming at the shooter. Culler!

At that instant the closest gunman flew backwards, revealing the other man. Mac immediately recognized the scarred face and the nub of an ear of the Cambodian.

Ung Chea turned toward Mac and their eyes locked for an instant. The Cambodian had a shocked, wide-eyed expression of fear as he reflexively brought his gun around to meet this new threat through the open door.

Mac snapped off a quick shot from his rolling prone position on the floor, aiming for center mass, but pulling it low and to the right. Nevertheless, he saw his target spin from the impact of the heavy bullet, bounce off the wall behind him and take off running down the hall.

And then Santos was filling his doorway, standing over the dead man and wearing boxer shorts, his long, silenced H&K hanging loosely in his hand at his side.

"About time you woke up."

Mac got to his feet rubbing his eyes with his left hand and holding his own pistol in his right. He was naked and completely sober. "What the fuck is going on?"

"Later. Let's get these goons out of sight before anyone sees them. Get this guy inside while I get the other one. The sound of that shot will wake up the hotel."

Mac, fully awake now, grabbed an arm of the thug in his doorway and pulled him all the way into the room. He grabbed his boxer shorts and pulled them on as he ran out into the hall to help Culler with the other one. Together they pulled him into Mac's room, leaving a visible trail of blood, and laid him beside the other gunman.

A door opened down the hall and then another and another. Heads popped out of the rooms into the hallway. Culler leaned out of the doorway to Mac's room, still in his underwear, and motioned to the people that everything was okay and that they should go back to bed. The heads retreated into the rooms and the doors closed.

Santos closed the door behind him, locked it and set the security chain. "Okay, we've bought some time, but we gotta get out of here fast. Grab your gear and bring it into my room. That blood trail will lead them right here."

They worked swiftly and silently, moving all of Mac's belongings into Culler's adjourning room and locking the doors between the rooms.

While they were dressing and packing up their gear, a couple of the hotel's security staff arrived and knocked loudly on the door of Mac's room. When they got no response, they used the hotel master key card to open the door, but were denied entry by the privacy chain. They called into the room in Thai and English through the crack in the partially opened door. Finally, one of them was sent downstairs for a bolt cutter to cut the chain.

Culler and Mac were dressed, packed and ready to leave, but they waited until the man with the bolt cutter returned and had snipped the chain. The group had entered the room, chattering loudly at what they found, before they darted out of the room, ran down the hallway and into the stairway.

They hurried down the stairs all the way to the garage, tossed their bags into the back seat of the Toyota and drove rapidly out of Chiang Rai in the direction of Chiang Mai to the south.

They breathed a combined sigh of relief when they determined no one was following them. They were out of danger for the moment, but things were definitely heating up.

CHAPTER THIRTY-EIGHT

Santos drove, maneuvering deftly through the dark city streets on the way to the four-lane highway that connected Chiang Mai to Chiang Rai. "Glad you finally woke up when you did. Do you always sleep like that? Like the dead? Which you almost were, I might add."

"Yeah, sorry about that. Guess I drank a little too much."

"A little? Yeah, I guess you could say that. You were snoring like a banshee too. You always snore like that? Must be a bitch for your girlfriends."

"Yeah, I get that complaint a lot when I drink. Forces them right to the couch. It's a bitch."

"Well, I don't want to preach to you, but it almost cost you your life tonight. I couldn't wake you by knocking and calling through the door, so I called your cell phone and the bloody thing didn't ring. Why'd you turn it off?"

"I didn't . . . I . . . I had it on vibrate."

"Vibrate! Why'd you have the fucking thing on vibrate for, for God's sake?"

"I don't like it ringing when I'm in public places, so I leave it on vibrate. I can feel it and hear it buzz when it's in my pocket, and I can hear it vibrate against the wood of the nightstand when it's next to my bed. Usually, that is."

Santos rolled his eyes. "For God's sake turn the bloody ringer on and leave it on from now on. Okay?"

MacMurphy took the phone out of his pocket and turned the ringer on. "Happy now?"

"Yes, very. I'm very happy now. Thank you . . ."

"So, how did you get behind them?"

"I left the room and ran down the hall, away from the elevator and stairs, and ducked into the ice vending machine room. The three of them came out of the stairs and went directly to our rooms and listened at the doors. I could see they were armed, and when it was clear they were going to break into your room, I shot them—well, two of them anyway."

"Well, I'm damn glad you did. Sorry about the Cambodian getting away though."

"Yeah, it would've been better if we'd killed him. But I'll tell you one thing, Mac, you sure scared the shit out of him. You must have hit him in the side the way he spun and hit that wall. I should've shot him as he was running down the hall, but everything happened so fast."

"So I'm not the only fuck-up on this team . . ."

"Yeah, you could say that. Never could shoot at a running deer either."

They were quiet for several minutes when Mac straightened in his seat and turned to Santos. "Why are we heading to Chiang Mai?"

"I don't know. Where else could we go? I didn't give it any thought. Just wanted to get out of Dodge. We've got to regroup, right?"

MacMurphy was thoughful. "They know who we are by now. At least they know our aliases and what we look like. They must have been checking the rooms to find out who Charly was visiting. Now they know for certain."

The wheels spun in Mac's head. Looking straight ahead through the windshield at the landscape rushing by, he said. "We're burned. No doubt about it. Our covers are blown. And this car was rented in the Humphrey alias. We're going to have to get rid of it right away. But we're going to need wheels."

"It's the middle of the night. Where are we going to get another car at this hour?"

"We'll have to steal one or buy one. Another rental is out. But first we're going to have to ditch this one. So . . . let's . . . let's continue on to Chiang Mai. It's a big city, easier to get lost in. Maybe we can get a couple hours of shut-eye, pick up another vehicle, and then head back north to Ban Mae Chan to do what we set out to do."

CHAPTER THIRTY-NINE

The Cambodian rendezvoused with the remaining two members of his team on the ninth floor. His white Thai shirt was stained with blood. He held his left side and was clearly in a great deal of pain. He spoke to them in excited, stuttering tones.

"This is bad. Very bad. Udom and Boon-Nam are dead. Shot by those CIA guys. They almost killed me too. We got to get out of here fast. Khun Ut is going to be really pissed when he hears about this."

He raised his bloodied shirt and looked down at his side. There was a deep, four-inch, ugly gash where the heavy slug had grazed him. The sight of it made him ill and he began to feel faint from the loss of blood. He leaned on one of his men, while the other called for the elevator, and the three of them rode down to the lobby. They exited the elevator, scurried across the lobby and out the front door, one black shirted security guard on each side of the Cambodian, holding him up like a drunk.

Outside they climbed into a white van and headed straight for Khun Ut's warehouse in Ban Mae Chan. In the backseat one of the men used a first aid kit to bandage Ung Chea's side, while the other drove and called ahead for medical assistance to meet them at the warehouse. The Cambodian dozed during the twenty minute drive and thought about what he was going to say to Khun Ut in the morning.

But he didn't have to wait until morning.

The Cambodian and the two security guards were met by Khun Ut when they pulled into the warehouse compound. Although it was the middle of the night, Khun Ut was impeccably dressed in a dark blue safari suit and polished Wellington boots. His longish black hair was slicked back, and he was smoking a long, thin cigar. He smelled of liquor and was slurring his words, which indicated he had come directly to the warehouse from one of the local nightspots.

Khun Ut took immediate command of the situation. "Get him upstairs to my office and put him on the couch." Motioning with his cigar to a man in a white lab coat standing next to him, he added, "Dr. Vikorn, sew him up. He looks like he has lost a lot of blood."

While the doctor was dressing his wound, Ung Chea nervously related the events of the evening. "Just as we pushed the door open this big *farang* came out of nowhere and started shooting. He blasted Udom and Boon-Nam before I could react, and then the guy in the room shot me and I had to get the hell out of there fast or I wouldn't be here to tell you about it.

"Boss, believe me, those guys were good. Really good. They had silencers too. They are professionals. Definitely the guys we were looking for."

Khun Ut pushed back in his chair and put his polished boots up on his desk. He thought for a moment and exhaled a long stream of smoke toward the ceiling. "So now we have their names and descriptions. You can give me a description of them, right?"

The Cambodian grimaced as the doctor went about cleaning and stitching up his side. It was clear that Khun Ut's disapproval weighed heavier on him than the wound in his side. The welling tears were not just from the physical pain. "Well, er, I think so. I mean, it all happened very fast. They were *farangs*. One was a big guy. Heavy. Muscular. He came out of nowhere, dressed in his undershorts. He carried a long pistol—silenced, like the Japanese Yakuza use. And, and, so did the other guy.

"I didn't get a good look at the other guy. He was lying on the floor in the room with his long gun aimed right at me. He looked me right in the eye. He was aiming right at me. Scared the shit out of me, boss. He is the one who shot me. The big guy shot Udom and Boon-Nam. Bang, bang, both gone. Just like that. I was lucky to get out of there alive. I did my best, boss, really I did . . ."

"Calm down Ung Chea, calm down." Although Khun Ut hated that the operation had gone terribly awry, he enjoyed being in charge—in control when everyone else was panicking. "Let us figure out where we are and what we are going to do next. We lost a battle but we did not lose the war. Those guys will pay for what they did. We know who they are now. We will find them and kill them."

Ung Chea was reassured and the doctor was almost finished stitching him up. Soon he could rest. He took a deep breath and said, "Their names are Robert Humphrey and Ralph Callaway. I think Callaway is the big guy registered in room 1050, and Humphrey is the guy that shot me from the room next door, 1048. But I am sure we will not find them there any longer."

"Yes indeed," said Khun Ut, thinking out loud. "You can bet they have beat it out of there. Those are probably not their real names either. But they showed passports when they registered so they have documentation in those aliases. They are professionals all right. They must have rented a car in one of those names as well."

"That is right. They did." Ung Chea brightened. "The hotel clerk told me they had paid for parking in the hotel garage, so they definitely have a car."

"Okay, we will check all the rental car agencies in the vicinity of Chiang Mai and Chiang Rai in the morning. We will find out what they are driving, and we will nail them that way. Divert all of our surveillance teams to scour both cities and every place in between to find that vehicle. Start at the airport. We will find them, Ung Chea, and then you can have them."

CHAPTER FORTY

Santos and MacMurphy spotted a small business class hotel named the Orchid Lodge on the northern outskirts of Chiang Mai and pulled into the parking lot behind it.

It was almost four in the morning, and they were exhausted from lack of sleep and the adrenaline flow they had experienced earlier that evening. They grabbed a couple of well deserved hours of sleep in the car and then went into the hotel to freshen up and eat breakfast.

"Maybe we should reef our sails a bit," said Santos. They were drinking coffee after having ordered huge American breakfasts of ham and eggs, home fries, fruit and juice.

"What's that, one of your New England expressions?" MacMurphy was already feeling better.

"Yes, and it's a good one too. That's what you do when the seas get too rough. You slow down and ride out the storm. Maybe we should go to the mattresses and wait until things quiet down a bit."

"Go to the mattresses? That's what the Mafia does when they want to hide out, right? You're just a font of esoteric, useless knowledge."

Santos toasted him with his coffee cup and a large grin. "Right. That's what we should do. Slow down, regroup and strike when we're ready."

"We're ready now. We just need to get a clean car, transfer our gear and head for the jungle below Ban Mae Chan."

"Maybe Charly or the General can get us a car. We also need a place to stay. We can't use these aliases in any more hotels. Humphrey and Callahan are blown."

"Yeah, you're right. And that's the only set of alias docs we have with us, so I guess that means no more hotel rooms or rental cars."

Culler was thoughtful. "Hmmm, we could steal a car. That won't be a big problem. I can hotwire anything on wheels. But we'll need to use the General or Charly to find us a place to stay, a safehouse or something."

"I'd rather not use the General or Charly any more than we absolutely have to." MacMurphy paused and then said, "See that couple sitting over there?" He nodded at a young American couple sitting a couple of tables away from them. They were eating breakfast and planning their day's sightseeing activities with maps and brochures spread out on the table.

"Yeah, what about them?"

"I've been watching them. They're American tourists. Maybe honeymooners. They probably don't have a lot of money; otherwise they would be staying in one of the four-star hotels, not a cheap business one like this. And I'll bet they also have a rental car, because it looks like they are on their own."

"So, what does that mean? You want to steal their rental car? We could probably do that."

"No, they would scream and report it. The cops would be looking for the car and we'd be right back where we are now. I think maybe we could buy their car."

Culler shook his head. "You think you can buy their rental car from them? Why would they want to do that?"

"Persuasion and charm, Mr. Santos, something you techies have very little of. And, of course, money."

MacMurphy got up and went over to their table. "You guys are Americans, right? I overheard you talking. I'm also American. Where are you from? Are you touring this little corner of paradise?" He was friendly and non-threatening and offered them a big, beaming smile that nobody could refuse.

She was cute, in a plain sort of way, with light brown hair in a bob. She wore hiking boots, knee-length khaki shorts, and a sleeveless yellow shirt. He was tall and skinny with longish unkempt brown hair. He was dressed in jeans, boots and a light blue, Disney World tee-shirt with Mickey Mouse on the front. They appeared to be in their early twenties.

Culler watched admiringly as his friend worked his case officer magic on the couple. Within minutes they were laughing and shaking hands like old friends. Mac pulled a chair up to their table, and they chatted and laughed as they looked at the maps.

Ten minutes later Mac paid their bill, and they all got up together and started heading for the front entrance. Mac excused himself for a moment to return to his table where Culler Santos was sitting.

He winked at Culler. "Okay, it's all arranged. Pay the bill and join us outside. We're going to switch cars."

Santos's jaw dropped and he started to say something but Mac was gone, following the young couple out the door. *Case officers*, he thought, shaking his head. *They are indeed a unique bunch, all charm and persuason.*

Santos suspected the case officer had probably just seduced the young American couple into lending him their car.

He found them outside in the parking lot at the side of the building. They were standing beside a small, white Toyota RAV4 SUV with an Avis sticker on the left rear bumper.

Mac introduced him to the couple. "Ralph, meet Linda and Sam Peoples. Linda and Sam, meet my associate Ralph Callahan." They all shook hands and did their greetings while Mac announced that they had agreed to swap cars for a few days.

He explained: "Linda and Sam really don't need a 4WD vehicle and we do, and rather than us having to go back to the Avis counter at the airport and taking the chance that they don't have one available, they kindly agreed to swap the 4WD for our Toyota Corolla. Wasn't that nice of them, Ralph? It'll save us a ton of time."

"Yeah, that's great," replied Santos, puzzled.

"Would you bring our car around so we can swap out the suitcases?"

"You bet. And . . . thanks guys, really," he said to the couple.

Fishing the keys out of his pocket, Culler jogged around to the back of the building. When he returned he parked their Corolla next to the RAV4.

The Peoples had very little in the way of personal effects in their car. Most of their things were up in their hotel room. But their eyes widened at the sight of Culler Santos and Mac moving all of their gear, including two long, heavy duffle bags into the back of the RAV.

Mac dug into one of the bags, located an envelope full of one hundred dollar bills and counted out five thousand dollars. He handed the stack of bills to Sam Peoples who quickly dropped the wad into Linda's large handbag.

"Now you guys enjoy the rest of your vacation," Mac said, "and don't worry about returning your car. We'll take care of that. And remember, when you get ready to depart just leave the Corolla in the parking lot of the hotel, and take the shuttle bus to the airport. Leave the keys with the bellman and tell him to call Avis to come pick up the car. We'll do the same with the RAV4 when we're done with it."

Linda and Sam were delighted. "Thanks Mr. Humphrey," said Sam. "This is really going to make our vacation. The Lord was smiling on us today."

"He certainly was," said Linda with a beaming smile. "God bless you. God bless you both."

CHAPTER FORTY-ONE

Culler drove and they waved back at the young couple as they pulled out of the Orchid Lodge parking lot and turned south toward the heart of Chiang Mai.

Culler was still shaking his head in amazement over what Mac had just accomplished. "How'd you know what buttons to push with that couple?"

"Well, it's really pretty simple." Mac adjusted the seat back and got comfortable. "First I put 'em at ease, showed 'em I wasn't a threat. Then I elicited information about them, like the fact they were almost broke, and had to pay extra for a 4WD vehicle they didn't want in the first place, and how they got hassled at the Avis rental counter. You know, stuff like that. Then I just made up a story that fit with their story."

"What story was that?"

"Well, I told them you were my father and you were sick and . . ."

"Bullshit! What did you really tell them?"

Mac laughed. "I said we had a mission to accomplish up north on the border. I told them I didn't know if we were going to make it in time because we were already late, and the roads up there are so bad that our two-wheel drive car that the same rental car agency gave us may not make it. I commiserated with them and said we had ordered a 4WD vehicle, but they didn't have any when we picked up the vehicle."

"And then you asked them if they would be willing to switch vehicles with you for five thousand dollars?"

"A little smoother than that, but you're right, that's about it. The exchange fulfilled all their needs: money, they got rid of the bumpy vehicle and there was no downside to the deal."

"They weren't the least bit suspicious?" asked Culler incredulously.

"Well, maybe a little bit at first, but then I explained that we were with Interpol and that's why we could be so generous with the money. And when I reiterated about there being no downside, I mean they would have our car and the money and all, well, they just bought it."

"And we didn't have to steal one."

"Right, if we had to steal one we'd just have the cops on our tail along with Khun Ut's crew. Double trouble."

Culler thought for a moment. "But what about those kids? Khun Ut is looking for us and it won't take him long to figure out what car we were driving. Aren't we placing them in serious danger now? What happens when he finds the car with them in it?"

"Well, hopefully Khun Ut won't find them. And if he does, well, he'll find out quickly enough that it's not us. I mean, maybe he'll question them and find out what happened, learn about the switch and all."

Both men were thoughtful, considering the possible consequences for the innocent young couple.

Santos broke the silence. "Well, you certainly bought us some time, but those kids are going to be in deep kimchee if the Cambodian gets a hold of them and decides to . . . well, I don't want to think about it."

"Yeah," said Mac, "I really hope that doesn't happen."

Mac sat up abruptly and looked around him. They were entering the city traffic of Chiang Mai. "Where are we going?"

"Chiang Mai. Isn't that where we want to go?"

"Hell no! Not now. We've got a new car. That's all we wanted. We've got nothing further to do in Chiang Mai. Our job is in Ban Mae Chan. Turn around and let's do what we came here to do."

CHAPTER FORTY-TWO

L ater that evening, Khun Ut was enjoying dinner, surrounded by friends at the expensive Chao Phraya restaurant, when his cell phone rang.

He dug the phone out of his pocket and glanced at the caller ID. With an annoyed expression, he announced to his guests, four lovely young women dressed in traditional long Thai silk sarongs and three men in business suits, that he had to take the call.

He walked away from the noisy heart of the restaurant into the foyer and spoke into the phone. "What is the problem?" He knew there had to be a problem or the Cambodian would never interrupt his dinner.

"Actually, there is no problem, Boss. You always think there has to be a problem for me to call you. This time it is good news. I thought you would want to hear it right away."

"Okay, what news is good enough to tear me away from Toi, Daeng and their beautiful friends?"

"Our guys found the car. They got it staked out right now. It is parked behind the Orchid Lodge, a small business hotel on the north side of Chiang Mai."

"Are you sure it is them?"

"One hundred percent. We got the make and registration number from the Avis agent at the airport. Plates match and it has an Avis sticker on the rear bumper. No doubt about it, Boss."

Khun Ut was excited. He paced back and forth in the foyer, careful not to be overheard by other guests entering and leaving by the front door. "Did you check to see if they are registered at the hotel?"

Yes, but their names did not show up. They probably registered under different names. One of the hotel staff thought he saw two guys that matched their description having breakfast there this morning."

"Okay, okay, that is good enough. Good work, Ung Chea. Tell your guys not to spook them."

His mind was suddenly spinning with ideas. Should they wait in ambush and get them when they get back into their car? Should they try to find them in the hotel and get them in their rooms? No, he had a better idea.

"Keep an eye on the vehicle and make sure they don't leave. If they try to leave, take them out. Let me see, it is almost ten now so they probably will not be going anywhere tonight, right?"

"That is what I think, Boss. They are probably in for the night. They are definitely not in any of the public areas of the hotel, not in the bar or restaurant or anyplace like that. We checked all those places."

"Okay, listen, call Sunthon right away. Tell him to get over there right away and wire the car. We will blow the bastards to hell when they start the car in the morning. Make sure you are there to witness it, and make sure there are no survivors. Got it?"

"Got it, Boss. Great idea."

CHAPTER FORTY-THREE

Culler and Mac drove back in the direction of Ban Mae Chan. They turned off the main highway when their GPS showed them to be at the bottom end of the valley that ended at the precipice at the southern end of Ban Mae Chan, the location of Khun Ut's warehouse.

They followed the GPS map along a narrow, paved road that ended abruptly at an old dump at the jungle's edge. They circled around the dump and continued slowly in four-wheel drive over a rutted and unmarked logging trail that took them deep into the jungle until the road ran out.

They pulled into the underbrush and piled branches on and around the vehicle to hide it from view. With the car sufficiently camouflaged, they dressed for the day-long hike through the jungle.

They pulled on Ghillie-suits and filled their backpacks with extra ammo, granola and power bars, dry clothes and socks, hammocks, shelter sheets, sleeping gear, and other personal items.

GPS devices, commo gear and night vision headgear went into separate pockets on the outside of the backpacks. Camelbaks filled with water went under the backpacks.

Over his shoulder, Culler carried a small, extra bag that contained two dozen, twelve cubic centimeter vials of ricin packed in Styrofoam.

They unpacked their short POF automatic weapons, screwed on the suppressors, checked the day and night vision sights and popped in a 100-round drum of ammo for each weapon.

Last, they put their suppressed H&K sidearms in thigh holsters, belted their fighting knives, and prepared to leave. The last thing they did was apply camouflage paint to their faces. With the paint and Ghillie suits, they would be nearly invisible in the jungle, day or night.

They checked their GPS devices, entered the current coordinates for the return trip and selected coordinates for their destination.

"We're all set, Culler. Let's do it."

They hefted on their backpacks, slung their assault weapons and headed in a northwesterly direction through the triple-canopy jungle on their way toward Ban Mae Chan.

They figured the roughly five-mile hike over the rough terrain would take most of the day. They moved slowly and silently, like hunters stalking a deer, with Mac in the lead. They were in no hurry and stayed close enough together to use hand signals to communicate. The only sounds came from scurrying animals, birds and screaming monkeys.

The backpacks, Camelbaks, weapons and ammo weighed almost forty pounds, and the uneven, slippery terrain through the wet jungle made the going even slower than expected.

Soon they were sweating profusely and sucking heavily from the tubes on their Camelbaks. The rainy season had just begun so mosquitoes were an added problem, forcing them to continually douse themselves with mosquito repellent.

It was dark when they reached the base of the butte that led up at a thirty degree angle to the back of the warehouse. The sky was cloudy, threatening an evening shower, and blurring the stars and moon intermittently.

They could barely see the reflection of lights above them through the almost impenetrable triple canopy. Without the help of their night vision gear, they would have been blind.

They decided to rest and regroup. They sat close together among the winding roots of a huge banyan tree.

Mac whispered, "This is a good place to dump our packs. Let's mark it on our GPS's. The climb is going to be a bitch, and we need to be as light and mobile as possible."

"Good idea. I'm bushed already." The sweat poured off Culler's face and down his nose. "Let's eat a couple of granola bars and re-hydrate a bit before we tackle the hill."

They ate, drank and rested for two hours before Mac nudged Culler and whispered, "Let's go. It's almost midnight and it's going to take us an hour or two to get up this hill. Move slowly and quietly, and watch out for sensors or tripwires. I don't think their security is going to be that hi-tech, but you never know."

Culler said, "Let's use the commo gear. It won't hurt to have a backup in case we get separated up there."

"Good idea."

They inserted their ear pieces, adjusted their volume controls down to minimum, clipped the microphones to their collars and tested them.

Mac led the way up the slope. The climbing was tough due to the slippery ground from the recent rains. They followed animal trails which meandered up the hill, using branches and trees to help pull them along whenever they could grab on to something.

As before, they climbed in silence but maintained visual contact with each other.

About half way up the slope, they paused to rest. It began to pour and they hovered close to a tree, wishing they had brought a shelter sheet. By now they could see the reflection from the lights above them. The rain lasted only a few minutes, and they continued their climb. The jungle thinned out as they approached the highlands surrounding Ban Mae Chan. They could hear no sounds coming from above other than the rustling of branches in the breeze and the occasional squealing of monkeys.

They still had no idea how they would get into the warehouse once they got up there, but they were confident that a plan would emerge when they could lay eyes on the place and evaluate the situation firsthand.

They stopped frequently to rest as they continued their climb up the slope of the ridge. The night vision headgear they wore covered their left eyes only, leaving their right eyes open to normal vision. Both scanned the ground in front of them continuously for sensors or tripwires.

Finally, at roughly one thousand meters from the top, they began hearing faint sounds from above. First they heard a dog barking in the distance. Then, further up, they heard the muffled sounds of men talking. They looked at each other to make sure each of them had heard the sounds, adjusted their gear, checked their weapons one more time and continued up the hill, even more slowly and cautiously now.

CHAPTER FORTY-FOUR

The Cambodian watched the old black pickup truck turn into the parking lot behind the Orchid Lodge. He stepped out of the darkness of a row of parked cars and approached the pickup from the front, illuminated by the headlights, and waved the driver to stop.

"*Sawatdee khrap,* Sunthon. Pull over there in that row of cars and cut your lights." The Cambodian's fingers barely touched in front of his face when he offered Sunthon an offhand *wei.*

The driver, a short, stocky man dressed in dirty mechanic's overalls, did as he was told and stepped out of the pickup. He carried a package about the size of a motorcycle battery which he respectfully offered to the Cambodian with a bow.

"*Sawatdee khrap.* I got it right here, Ung Chea. Sorry I am a little late, but I had to put everything together."

"*Mai pen rai,* no matter. We have plenty of time. The car is over there. That dark Toyota Corolla in the middle there." He pointed to the car near the end of a row. "How long will this take?"

"Not long, Ung Chea. Please watch out for me while I am under there."

The Cambodian signaled two other members of the surveillance team. They were staked out in the darkness at separate corners of the parking lot. He pointed to his own eyes with two fingers and then to the Corolla to indicate he wanted them to watch closely while Sunthon was under the car.

Sunthon selected a handful of tools and a roll of duct tape from the back of his pickup and walked to the Corolla. He looked around one final time, ducked down between the Corolla and the car next to it, and slid on his back under the engine compartment.

He worked silently for several minutes and then emerged without the package.

He walked back to the Cambodian. "All done Ung Chea. You want me to hang around for the fireworks?"

"No, go back home to your family. We will take it from here."

The Cambodian and the two other members of his team settled in to wait for the morning.

By ten o'clock in the morning, the parking lot had thinned out considerably due to departing guests, but no one approached the Corolla and no one matching the description of Robert Humphrey and Ralph Callaway exited the building.

The surveillance team saw, but took no particular interest in, a young *farang* couple who exited the rear door of the building, stood on the steps for a moment discussing something. Then they saw the woman shake her head and reenter the hotel, while the man headed toward the parking lot.

It wasn't until they saw him point his key remote in the direction of the Corolla and the car beep open that they realized the wrong person was entering the car.

They all stood there with mouths agape and did nothing while the young man inserted his key in the ignition and turned it and the Toyota Corolla exploded in a huge fireball before their eyes.

CHAPTER FORTY-FIVE

Culler and Mac reached a point about twenty feet below the edge of the precipice. They could see the illumination of the security floodlights above them. Both were soaked with sweat and needed a bit of rest. After a few minutes to catch their breath, they checked their commo gear one more time and exchanged final words before moving to the top.

"Okay, it's a little after two. Everyone but the guards should be asleep. How are you feeling, Culler?"

"I'm good. Glad there weren't any tripwires and hope we didn't set off any sensors we didn't notice."

"Doesn't look like it, but we're not there yet. Be real careful going over the ledge. The back of the warehouse is about fifteen meters back from there, so it's going to be tight if they have any roving security. If we have to take anyone out, let's do it as quietly as possible. We're only going to get one crack at this place, so let's make it good."

Both men were outwardly calm and determined, but Mac, for one, had butterflies flying around in his stomach. It always happened to him in situations like this. He struggled to bring his breathing down and to display no outward signs of nervousness.

Whenever he was faced with a dangerous situation, he used techniques learned from years of martial arts training. His senses were sharp; he was ready—nervous as a cat ready to spring. Everything appeared to be in slow motion, but his reactions would be quick and determined.

They checked their weapons and night vision gear one last time, took deep breaths, and crawled up the final steps to the edge. The climb was even steeper now, and they had to pull themselves along using branches and roots to gain purchase on the ground. They were about ten feet apart when their heads peeked above the ridge.

They had a clear view of the back of the warehouse. There were five windows across the second floor and four along the ground floor with double doors in the middle. All appeared closed.

One security guard with an AK-47 on his lap sat on a chair in front of the double doors. He was awake and smoking a cigarette, blowing smoke up into the sky. No other security was visible, although they knew others were present.

Mac signaled Culler to wait and adjusted his night vision lens down over his left eye, then he clicked on the infrared laser located on the top of the forearm of the grip of his assault rifle. The laser's green line of death shot out in front of the gun.

The green line was invisible to anyone not wearing night vision gear, and whatever that green line touched when he pulled the trigger would be hit dead on.

He gently brought the gun out and over the ridge, set it to fire on semi-automatic and placed the deadly green line directly on the unsuspecting security guard's forehead. He held it there, waiting for the guard to relax and exhale another lung full of smoke into the sky, and slowly squeezed the trigger.

The gun spat out a single 5.56mm round with an almost inaudible *phifft,* and the security guard's head snapped back into the doors with an audible thud; he slid off the chair onto the ground in a heap.

MacMurphy and Santos leaped over the ridge in tandem and raced to opposite corners of the building where they stopped with their backs to the wall, guns at the ready. Both set their weapons on full automatic with the infrared lasers activated.

Mac signaled Culler to hold his position and returned to the center of the building. He leaned over the dead security guard and checked the knobs on both doors but they were locked. *You never know*, he thought. He shrugged at Culler and returned to his position at the side of the building, signaling Santos to move out along his side.

They kept in the shadows close to the wall, moving silently toward the front of the building, green lasers scanning the terrain in front of them.

Mac heard voices. He stopped, dropped to one knee, and pressed his back to the wall. He heard muffled laughter and talking coming from the interior of the building on the other side of the wall and above him on the second floor. It sounded like several men chatting together, maybe playing cards or mahjong or some other game. He looked up and saw light coming from the second floor window.

He whispered into his lapel microphone. "Hold it. I'm about halfway down the building and can hear a group of men talking inside above me. They may be off duty security guards or maybe on-duty guards goofing off. Maybe some good luck for us. Meet you at the end of the building."

Santos was in the shadows of the building close to the wall when Mac broke the silence. "Got it. Hang on a minute. Someone's coming this way."

He dropped to the ground in a prone position, invisible in his Ghillie-suit, and aimed his rifle down the wall toward the front of the building.

Santos's night vision gear illuminated a security guard, an AK-47 slung over his shoulder, heading in his direction. *Maybe a relief for the guy we killed behind us*, he thought, *or maybe a rover*. He set the green line on the unsuspecting guard's chest and watched the poor fool continue in his direction.

He waited, and waited, and waited until the man was less than fifteen feet in front of him, then he pressed the trigger once. Three rounds spat out of the gun. The first hit the guard in the solar plexus, the second in the center of his chest and the third two inches higher and slightly to the right. The guard's heart exploded and he was knocked backwards, dead before he hit the ground.

The only sounds heard were the three consecutive *phiffts* of the rounds leaving the suppresser and the rattle of the AK-47 when it hit the ground. Culler was up and standing over him seconds later, his weapon pointed down range searching for another target. "Got him," he said into his lapel mic. "All clear on this side."

"Clear here," came the response. "Meet you up front."

Keeping to the shadows close to the wall, Mac moved silently to the end of the building and peeked around the corner. He saw three men gathered next to a pickup truck at the front of the parking lot directly across from the entrance to the warehouse. Illuminated by the bright floodlights, they were smoking cigarettes and chatting animatedly.

All carried AK-47 assault rifles slung over their shoulders and were oblivious to what was happening around them.

The shock of the floodlights illuminating the front of the building and parking lot affected Mac's night vision gear by causing light blooms. Blinking his eyes, he backed up into the shadows, flipped up the night vision eyepiece and turned off the infrared laser.

He brought the rifle to his shoulder and sighted through the riflescope to make sure everything was working perfectly before again peeking around the corner of the building and setting the red chevron of his scope on the three guards.

But Santos got there before him.

Mac watched all three guards go down in a hail of silent 5.56mm rounds plinking into the surrounding vehicles. In the next instant Santos was standing over them. One guard groaned and Culler put a double-tap through his head. And then there was silence.

Culler ducked down into the shadows of the vehicles beside the dead guards and turned his attention to the front of the building. There was a large roll-up garage door in the center of the warehouse and two smaller pedestrian doors on each side. Five windows ran across the second floor as in the rear. All of the windows were dark.

He surveyed the entire area around him but saw no movement other than Mac running out of the shadows at the corner of the building and taking up a position at his side of the parking lot behind one of the vehicles. Both men concentrated on the front entrances of the warehouse.

Mac pulled his lapel microphone up close to his lips and whispered into it. "That's five of them. Good shooting. That's it for the outside, but there are still a few more inside. You try the door on the right and I'll try the left."

"Roger that."

Keeping low, both men ran to the doors and flattened themselves against the building. They listened intently for any sounds coming from the interior and then gently tried the doorknobs.

"Locked," whispered Culler.

"Mine too."

"What now?"

"Don't know. Wait for someone to come out? What do you think?"

"Naw, that won't work. There must be another way into this building."

"Didn't see any, aside from the back door. Did you?"

"Nope, and the corrugated walls look pretty strong, and there are no windows along this side at all."

Mac was silent for a few moments. "Do you think we should knock?"

CHAPTER FORTY-SIX

The four off-duty security guards were wrapping up their card game in the break room on the second floor. They were dressed alike in military style camouflage trousers and boots and black "security" tee-shirts. Pistols hung from their web belts, and their AK-47s stood stacked in the corner of the room.

Anon, the heavyset leader of the shift, glanced at his watch. "Hey, it's after two-thirty and Michai hasn't checked in yet. Sano, go out back and kick the sonofabitch in the ass. This is the last time for him. I am tired of warning the lazy bastard. Check on the other guys too. Make sure they are not standing around with their thumbs up their butts lying about the whores they screwed. I want to hear about it if they are not doing their rounds. Then we can all get some sleep."

"Yes sir." Sano grabbed his cap, slung his assault rifle over his shoulder and pushed the door open. The door led to a catwalk that extended the length of the building and provided access to the rooms and offices on the second floor. At each end of the catwalk were stairs leading down the ground floor.

He turned left and headed down the catwalk to the stairs that would take him down to the rear entrance. *Poor Michai*, he thought, *all he has to do on this job is stay awake and he cannot even do that. Now he will be out of a job and will have the Cambodian to contend with as well. The Cambodian will smack the crap out of him. I would hate to be in his shoes.*

Sano reached the double doors and called through them in a hushed voice. "Hey, Michai, open up. It's me, Sano." There was no response. He called again, louder this time, and tried opening the door. The door opened a few inches and bumped up against something. "Wake up Michai." He put his shoulder to the door and pushed harder, forcing the door open a few more inches.

Then he saw the blood and the body; he knew his friend was dead.

Sano pulled the door shut and called out. "Anon, Anon. Michai is dead. Hurry up. Someone killed Michai."

CHAPTER FORTY-SEVEN

Moments earlier, Santos whispered into his lapel mic. "Don't you dare knock on that door. Look, there are rooms on the second floor on your side of the building, but I don't think there is a second floor on my side. No windows at all. So come over here and we'll shoot the lock out of this door and enter from this side."

"I was just screwing with you," said Mac. "Sounds like a good plan to me. I'm on my way."

Mac joined Culler on his side of the warehouse. He leaned close and whispered, "It's going to be dark inside, so let's go back to night vision and lasers."

They changed the settings on their rifles and flipped down their night vision gear over their left eyes. "We've got plenty of ammo. At least we don't have to worry about that."

"One more thing," Mac whispered. "Let's not forget why we're here. Once we get inside, you concentrate on injecting the ricin into as many of those heroin bricks as you can, and I'll take care of the rest of the guards. And if we have to skedaddle, make sure we get a couple of those bricks to make it look like we're thieves. That'll give us at least a bit of a fig leaf for why we were here."

"Okay, okay. I got it. We're thieves. Now stand back while I blast the door."

Santos brought the POF up to his hip, put the green line above the bolt of the lock and hit the trigger. As five silent 5.56mm rounds leaped out of the muzzle and splintered the wood around the lock and door jam, the door opened with a gentle tug.

Santos slipped into the warehouse and turned right toward the side of the building. He saw two pallets of heroin bricks sitting in front of bales of stacked marijuana. MacMurphy followed, pulling the door closed behind him and flattening himself against the wall on the other side of the door.

His eyes quickly surveyed the interior of the dark warehouse and caught the sight of one of the guards at the other end of the building pushing at the double doors and calling softly to someone on the other side. He saw the guard push the door open wide enough for him to see his dead colleague laying on the ground, and all hell broke loose.

The guard turned and started yelling up to the second floor. Mac already had the green line on him, and he touched the trigger, slamming the guy back into the doors and down in a heap.

Mac glanced over at Santos who was standing with his back to a pallet of heroin bricks looking up toward the second floor. A heavy-set security guard came running out of one of the rooms yelling something in Thai to others behind him.

Culler was already aiming in that direction, and when the guard hit the catwalk he brought the green line to bear on the running man and hit the trigger, sending him sprawling to the floor, his AK-47 assault rifle flying out of his hands, over the ledge and clattering onto the concrete floor below.

An alarm blared, echoing through the warehouse in a cacophony of noise. Other doors flew open on the second floor level, and men ran out onto the catwalk in their boxer shorts.

Mac fired at the guards in short bursts, alternating back and forth as they came out onto the catwalk. Two went down immediately, but one of them returned fire with his AK-47, adding to the noise, before Mac cut him down in a hail of 5.56mm rounds.

Other guards came out of the rooms on their bellies and started to return fire from over the edge of the catwalk. The noise of the AK-47s joined the mind-numbing yells, shouts and the incessant wailing alarm.

Mac continued to rake the catwalk with his assault rifle, but the odds were not looking good for them. "We're fucked," he shouted. "Get the shit and let's get the hell out of here." Glancing over at Culler, he saw the big man stuffing a heroin brick into the sack carrying the ricin.

They both concentrated their fire along the second floor catwalk, keeping the guards at bay as best they could, but the guards continued to return blind fire over the edge in the general direction of Culler and Mac. Bullets pinged into the corrugated steel wall behind them as they dove for the door and darted out into the relative safety of the night.

"Are you okay?" asked Mac.

"Where did those fuckers come from all of a sudden?" Culler replied with wide eyes. "So much for stealth and clandestinity. Let's blow this popsicle stand."

They were at the far corner of the building heading toward the rear when Mac stopped abruptly. "Wait a minute," he said into his lapel mic. "You go ahead and watch the back door. I'll slow them down from this end. Let's try to keep them inside for as long as we can, or they're gonna be on our asses all the way to town."

Running to the edge of the parking lot, Mac set up behind a black pickup truck. The area was well lit, so he switched off his laser sight, flipped up the night vision monocular over his left eye and sighted his rifle on the front entrance. The door nearest to him flew open, and two men dressed only in their undershorts came running out only to be met with a hail of fire from Mac's assault rifle. Three of them went down in the doorway and none followed.

The far door opened a second later. Mac sighted the assault rifle; two more men were met with another hail of silent 5.56mm bullets.

Figuring that would stop them for the time being, Mac left his position behind the truck and took off running down the side of the warehouse to join Culler at the far end. "I'm on my way. Don't shoot me," he called into his mic as he ran.

He met up with Culler, who was standing with his back to the ravine with his rifle leveled at the back doors of the warehouse, and shouted: "Rake the doors and let's bug out of here."

Culler stitched the doors back and forth at waist high and then joined Mac over the ledge, sliding down on their butts through the mud and foliage toward the bottom.

CHAPTER FORTY-EIGHT

Chaos reigned in the warehouse. Anon hit the alarm to warn the others of the intrusion, and sleeping guards baled out of their racks.

He hit the speed-dial of his cell phone to call the Cambodian. The call was answered on the second ring by an angry, groggy voice.

Anon sputtered into the phone: "Boss, we have . . . an intrusion . . . at the warehouse. We need . . . help immediately."

The Cambodian leaped out of bed and struggled to pull his pants on while holding his cell phone up to his good ear with his shoulder. "How many? What is going on?"

"I don't know yet. I don't know. We have at least one guard, Michai, dead at the rear of the building. That's all I know. I'm going out to see what is going on now, but you better get over here."

"I'm on my way." The Cambodian cut the connection.

Anon grabbed his AK-47 and charged out of the door directly into a hail of gunfire from below.

CHAPTER FORTY-NINE

Culler and Mac were half-sliding, half-running down the steep slope of the ravine, holding their weapons high out in front of them to keep them clean. They reached the base of the huge banyan tree where they had rested on the way up and stopped for a moment to retrieve their backpacks and listen.

"I don't think anyone followed us. Do you?" said Mac.

"I can't hear a damn thing with that siren blaring up there, but I'll bet the little fuckers won't come out of there too soon."

"But eventually they will, so let's haul ass out of here before they realize we're gone and start sending out search parties."

"Yeah, let's go back to night vision. We'll move faster that way," said Culler, knocking mud from the back of his Ghillie-suit.

"We already covered more ground in one minute than we did in thirty going up. At this rate we'll be down at the bottom and out of range in no time."

"Sure, but once we get done sliding on our asses we'll be at the bottom and the long march begins. And they're definitely going to be looking for us."

Mac saddled up and glanced back up towards the top of the ridge. The siren was still blaring but there didn't appear to be any other movement at the ridge's edge. "Okay, let's move out as fast as we can. I'll lead the way so try not to tumble into me."

"Yeah, make a nice smooth trough in the mud with your ass, and I'll slide down behind you nice and easy."

They slipped and slid their way toward the bottom of the ravine. The sound of the incessant wailing siren became dimmer and dimmer. Occasional bursts of AK-47 fire and shouts could be heard, an indication that the trigger-happy guards were now outside of the building and searching the perimeter.

By the time they reached the flat bottom, their Ghillie-suits and boots were covered in mud. They paused for a few minutes to catch their breath and scrape off as much of the gunk as they could. They rinsed off their hands, took long drinks of water from their Camelbaks and munched granola bars for energy. Then they were on their way again, moving at a fast walk with Mac in the lead.

They moved rapidly and silently through the triple canopy jungle, pausing only to glance at the GPS occasionally to establish their position. Twenty-six minutes had passed since they went over the ledge. Going down was a hell of a lot faster than going up.

Suddenly they heard the sound of a helicopter landing in the distance behind them, and then the wailing siren went silent.

CHAPTER FIFTY

U ng Chea and a dozen of his men began jumping out of the Vietnam vintage Huey helicopter before it settled onto the tarmac of the parking lot. All but the Cambodian were dressed in boots and security uniforms. They all carried AK-47 assault rifles.

The Cambodian wore blue jeans, tennis shoes and an untucked, short-sleeved orange shirt. He held a 9mm pistol.

The men spread out in front of him and advanced toward the warehouse. Ung Chea followed closely behind, spewing out a steady stream of orders to the leader of the group.

The Cambodian surveyed the damage. Three men lay dead in a tangled heap amid bullet ridden cars at the edge of the parking lot, and more men lay dead in both open doorways to the warehouse.

Approaching one of the guards standing at the front of the building, he asked, "Where is Anan? What happened here?"

The quivering guard responded in a squeaky voice, bowing deeply with his fingertips touching his forehead in a deep *wei*, and almost dropping his AK-47 in the process. "I, I do not know, sir. It happened so very fast. So many dead. Anan dead. Michai dead. Sano dead. Many dead."

The Cambodian's scarred face burned red and his eyes spit hatred. "How many were there? Where did they come from?"

The guard continued to *wei* repeatedly and cringe in fear. "I do not know, sir. Everything happened so fast. I think they were many. They killed so many."

The Cambodian brushed the slobbering guard aside and yelled, "Does anyone know what happened here?" Stepping over three bloody bodies, he entered the warehouse. He glanced around the interior and, without emotion, took in the sight of the still bodies of several guards lying sprawled on the catwalk and on the floor of the building.

A tall, young security guard with an AK-47 slung over his shoulder stepped forward and addressed the Cambodian in a soft voice. "Sir, my name is Phao. I was with Anan and the others when we were first alerted that something was wrong. I was the one who set off the alarm."

He related the story of how Sano found Michai dead at his post, and two men with silenced automatic weapons broke into the building through one of the front doors and started shooting everyone in sight. "And then, when the alarm went off and we began to return fire, they left through the same door they entered."

Ung Chea stared up at the young guard and then motioned around the room with his 9mm pistol. "Two men? You said two men did all this? What about the guys outside? Who killed them?"

Phao dropped his head respectfully and answered quietly. "I only saw two men, Ung Chea, only two. And, oh yes, they were both *farangs*."

The remaining security guards focused their attention on the Cambodian standing just inside the door amid three of their dead colleagues.

Ung Chea could only remember one other time in his life when he had experienced as much anger, fear and trepidation as he was feeling at the moment.

He was six years old living in the northeast Cambodian border town of Anlong Veng when the Khmer Rouge seized power and changed the country's name to Democratic Kampuchea. Ta Mok, the most brutal Khmer Rouge general, nicknamed "The Butcher," arrived to take charge of the army in the northern zone.

The killing of intellectuals and the wealthy class began immediately after Ta Mok's arrival. Ung Chea's father, a wealthy merchant engaged in trade across the border with Thailand, was one of the first to be hacked to death with hoes by Ta Mok's vicious Khmer Rouge.

His mother, an educated nurse, pretended to be a simple peasant to escape certain death, but her family and friends knew that it would be only a matter of time before her secret would get out and Ta Moc's thugs would see to it that she would meet the same fate as her husband.

The fear of losing his mother after witnessing the horrible death of his father was unbearable for the young Ung Chea. Several days went by and he couldn't keep anything in his stomach. He spent his days and nights quivering in his bed, unable to eat or sleep, paralyzed by fear and foreboding.

Ung Chea felt the same squeamish pangs in his stomach today. He felt like he was going to retch.

Fortunately, Ung Chea's luck changed abruptly on the day Ta Mok was carried back home on a stretcher following a skirmish with Vietnamese forces in the surrounding Dangrek mountains. His right leg had been blown off below the knee by a land mine, and he was near death from loss of blood and shock.

The call went out for anyone with medical experience to help their beloved leader, and Ung Chea's mother, despite her fears, stepped forward.

Ung Chea and his mother were moved into Ta Moc's huge three-story villa where she nursed Ta Moc back to health with hidden medical supplies and precious antibiotics.

By the time Ta Mok had recovered enough to screw on a peg leg and get back to fighting the Vietnamese, he had fallen in love with his nurse.

Needing the security and support Ta Moc provided, she became his mistress and the six-year-old Ung Chea was adopted and trained to be a guerilla fighter alongside his legendary adoptive father.

Ung Chea shook out of his reverie and began shouting orders to his troops. "Everyone outside," he commanded.

When the men had assembled at the front of the building, he addressed them. "I know exactly who is responsible for this. They are *farangs* and we have their names and descriptions. They appear to be American CIA agents. We have been searching for them for days. Now everyone fan out and search the woods around us. They are on the run and we must find them. Now get moving and shoot them on sight."

CHAPTER FIFTY-ONE

Khun Ut was soundly sleeping beside his favorite mistress when he received the call from the Cambodian. At first he was annoyed at being awakened in the middle of the night, but as soon as he heard what the Cambodian had to report, he was wide awake, furious and ready to take action.

He shouted into the phone. "Get everyone on it. You have got to find the bastards. They must be on foot so it should not be too difficult. Get more men if you need them. Just find them and kill them. Get another helicopter if you need it. Dogs. Get some dogs if you want. Scour the jungle and the woods. They are out there somewhere."

He was out of bed pacing with the phone to his ear. His mistress was wide awake now, sitting up and looking at him with frightened eyes, the sheet pulled up to her chin.

In a calmer voice he continued. "Oh, I almost forgot to tell you. The last report from the police is that they still have not found the RAV4 they are now driving. I've got everyone, including the police who want them for questioning about the bombing of their car, scouring the area between here and Chiang Mai for it."

He paused a moment, thinking about what he had just said and putting things together in his head. "Oh my God," he said, thinking out loud. "The car is there. It's got to be somewhere fairly close to the warehouse. You have got to find the car, Ung Chea. That is where they are headed. Use the Hueys to find the car. They must have dropped it off someplace on the edge of the jungle and walked in. Find the car and you will find them."

His next call was to his police contact.

CHAPTER FIFTY-TWO

The five-mile trek back down to the car was going considerably faster than the long, cautious walk in. Santos and MacMurphy were humping it as fast as they could, moving at slightly less than a jogger's pace through the jungle back to where they had left their vehicle.

Mac stopped to check their location on his GPS, and Culler looked over his shoulder. "Let's keep to this side of the stream where the going is a bit easier and keep humping it as fast as we can until it branches off to the right. That'll be about a mile from the car. Then we can cut off in a more easterly direction and make a beeline for the car."

Culler nodded his head, sending rivulets of sweat careening down his face and off his nose. He sucked heavily from the tube on his Camelbak. "Fast is good. Let's put as much distance between them and us as we can. What a goat rope this turned out to be."

"Can't argue that. Let's get moving."

"Wait. Let's toss this kilo of heroin. I don't like carrying it around. We stole it—that's enough. Let's just toss it in the stream."

MacMurphy thought a moment and then his face broke into a large grin. "No, let's leave it here on the trail where they can find it. But first empty one of those ricin vials into it and hope they find it and keep it. It's worth a lot of money. That'll help us take out a few more of those drug-dealing bastards."

"Now you're thinking." Santos took out the brick, unwrapped it and laid it on the ground in front of them. He removed one of the vials of ricin and injected it one cc at a time into several places around the chalky brick until the vial was empty. Then, being careful not to get any of the ricin on his hands from the tip of the needle, he flipped the empty vial into the stream like a disgusting bug.

At that moment the familiar sound of a Huey helicopter could be heard lifting off in the distance behind them.

Mac looked back in the direction of the noise and then up at the triple canopy above him. "They'll have a hell of a job seeing us from up there, and they sure as hell can't hear us, so let's get a move on. If they find the RAV before we do, we'll really be screwed."

CHAPTER FIFTY-THREE

The Cambodian's men scoured the perimeter of the warehouse with flashlights, looking for tracks and other signs that would indicate the direction in which the two *farangs* had fled. One of his men called out from the rear of the building. "Over here. They went down the ledge over here. I can see where they slid down the slope."

Ung Chea ran to the rear and looked over the ledge. "You are right," he exclaimed. "They went down this way." He called to one of his team leaders. "Paiboon, take your men down here and follow their trail. They will be moving fast, not covering their tracks. Get going. I will leave a few behind to guard the warehouse and take the rest in the Huey."

"Yes sir," said Paiboon, saluting. He quickly selected five of the youngest and most athletic of his men, eschewing the older, overweight guards. He led them to the edge and commanded, "Follow me." And over the ledge he went with the others close behind like parachutists leaving the door of a plane.

Ung Chea and the rest of his men ran back to the Huey, which was idling in the parking lot. They climbed aboard and the helicopter lifted off noisily. When it reached altitude, it banked south toward the rear of the warehouse and the jungle beyond.

Once they were airborne the Cambodian keyed his walkie-talkie and called Paiboon. "This is base calling One. Come in, One."

Paiboon answered in a breathless voice. "Base, this is One. We have their trail. They are moving fast. It is tough going here." He stumbled and cursed as one of his men slammed into him from the rear, forcing him to stop transmitting for a moment. "Base, can I call you back when we reach the bottom? We are slipping and sliding all over the place here."

"Okay, One. Call when you get straightened out. We will continue searching from above. They are moving south so, until you say otherwise, that is where we will continue to search."

The triple canopy made it impossible to view the ground below from the helicopter, so Ung Chea ordered it to cover the western perimeter of the swath of jungle that ran from the precipice behind the warehouse for almost thirty miles, until it ended at the outskirts of Chiang Rai. He called for his other Huey to join the search and ordered it to search the eastern side of the jungle swath.

Ung Chea moved up to the front of the Huey and stood behind the pilot and co-pilot. "They are on foot and moving through thick jungle, so they cannot move that fast," he instructed the pilots, shouting over the wail of the turbo engine. "But they have got to come out of there at some point so keep on the perimeter. We'll box them in until Paiboon's men can catch up to them."

CHAPTER FIFTY-FOUR

uller and Mac walked rapidly along an animal trail alongside the stream. Their Ghillie-suits were soaked through with sweat and mud.

Both men were familiar with a jungle environment. They had gone through survival school together in the jungles of Panama as a part of their CIA junior officer training, and they were at least thankful for the absence of Black Palm trees in the jungles of Thailand. They recalled being pierced frequently by the sharp black palm needles after each slip and fall in Panama, having to deal with the puss-filled, infected sores the needles left afterwards. Black Palm was worse than mosquitoes and leaches combined.

A Huey helicopter flew noisily overhead, its powerful searchlight arching back and forth over the trees above them. Protected by the triple canopy, they were not afraid of being seen from above. The searchlight could not penetrate all the foliage to the ground, but just the same they quickened their pace as the adrenalin coursed through their veins. The

Huey continued heading south, waving the searchlight from side to side over the tops of the trees.

Mac estimated they had less than two miles to go to find the hidden RAV4. At this rate they would be there in about twenty minutes. He prayed the camouflage would protect it from detection by the helicopter.

The first signs of daylight could be viewed occasionally through breaks in the canopy above them, but the jungle floor remained dark. Their night vision gear illuminated the way in front of them and permitted them to continue to move swiftly through the jungle.

Occasionally they would startle a bird or animal that would go scurrying out in front of them, but otherwise the monotonous chirping and wailing sounds of the jungle remained constant.

CHAPTER FIFTY-FIVE

Paiboon was in the lead, swinging a powerful searchlight back and forth in front of him. His men were strung out behind. All of them carried flashlights. Their beams swayed and bounced about in front of them. The trail was fresh and not difficult to follow, but the men slipped and fell constantly as they struggled to keep up with Paiboon.

Paiboon's walkie-talkie squawked and he replied. "This is One."

"One, this is base. What is your situation?"

"Base, we have reached the jungle floor and are following. They are heading almost due south, and so far their trail is not too difficult to follow. We are moving as fast as we can."

"I can see your lights, One. We are looking for their vehicle. We think they are headed for it. Keep the pressure on them, and we will try to keep you in sight from up here. Base out."

The flashlights did not work as well as night vision gear because the lights cast deep shadows wherever their beams were cast, and the shadows concealed depressions and roots which were constantly tripping up the pursuing security guards.

Because of this Paiboon walked right past the heroin brick lying in the middle of the trail near the stream.

But the next man in line, Kaset, stumbled on it and stopped abruptly, causing the next man in line to bump into him.

"Paiboon," Kaset called out. "Stop. Look what they dropped."

Paiboon shined his searchlight on the brick. *"Mai pen rai,* leave it there. We can come back for it later. Keep moving. We must catch them." He turned and continued following the trail and the others followed.

Kaset thought for a moment, his flashlight illuminating the precious heroin brick, and stepped aside to let the others pass him. He licked his lips and reached down to scrape off a thumbnail-sized flake of the heroin to taste. Satisfied, he crumbled it between his fingers and snorted it up his nose.

That will give me energy, he thought, smiling at his good fortune as he slipped back into the line and continued following the trail.

The heroin kicked in almost immediately, giving Kaset a burst of energy and a feeling of euphoria. He edged past the guards who had passed him and took up his position directly behind Paiboon.

But minutes later the potent toxin ricin began to trigger allergic reactions and inhibit protein synthesis throughout his body. His throat and nasal passages began to swell and he felt nauseous. His stomach began to rumble, and the first urges of diarrhea began to trouble him.

He tried to shrug off the debilitating effects of the poison that was now coursing through his body, aided by the pounding of his heart caused by the severe exertion of the forced march through the jungle.

Mai sabai, what is wrong? he thought, just before his entire body seized up in shock, and his legs ceased to move on command. He pitched forward into the mud, eyes wide open and swollen tongue hanging from his open mouth.

The guard following behind tripped over him and joined him on the ground. "Paiboon, stop! Kaset is sick," he called.

Paiboon stopped and dropped to one knee beside Kaset's body, while the others stood around gaping at the convulsing figure on the ground. "Must be a heart attack," he said. He grabbed the nearest guard by the sleeve. "Stay here with him. If he can walk, take him back. If not, stay here with him and I will send help."

He stood up and motioned to the three remaining guards. "Come, we must hurry or they will get away."

CHAPTER FIFTY-SIX

Culler and Mac reached the cutoff point where they left the stream and turned east for the final mile and, hopefully, the RAV4. They had stopped momentarily at the stream to shoot another azimuth on the GPS and drink heavily from their Camelbaks, but now they were charging through the underbrush as fast as they could manage. They tried to move as quietly as they could, but it was not always possible. Speed was their main concern at this point.

The Huey buzzed over their heads, blades thumping loudly and causing the foliage to rustle in the downdraft. It was flying low coming south to north, the searchlight moving incessantly, attempting to probe into the depths of the jungle. Another circled far to the west of them. They knew they were nearing the edge of the jungle where they would be most vulnerable, and they figured that was where the helicopters were concentrating their surveillance.

Mac stopped to check his GPS. Both men were breathing heavily. Culler was bent over with his hands on his knees trying to catch his breath.

Between gulps of breath and water, Culler broke the silence. "Almost there?"

"Almost . . . it's about another quarter of a mile. We're doin' good."

"Then I think we should slow it down a bit." Santos took long, deep breaths to re-oxygenate his body. "We need to be rested in case we have to fight our way out of here, and we need to keep the noise down to a minimum from now on."

Mac responded between long gulps from his Camelbak. "Good point. You sound like a bull elephant thrashing through the under-brush . . ."

"Me? What about you? You're no Goddamn gazelle."

"Okay, it's starting to get light out there, too, so you're right, let's take it a little easy. But not too easy. Wait . . . hang on . . . Listen . . . I hear something." Putting his hands to his ears, Mac turned around to listen behind him. He concentrated on his hearing while both men held their breaths and remained motionless. Maybe it was just the rustling of the leaves or an animal.

Culler said, "I don't hear anything."

"Maybe not . . . I know they're behind us, so maybe I'm just imagin-ing things. We need to get to the car before they catch up to us."

Culler adjusted his gear and took a deep breath. "Okay, let's move out."

They proceeded more quietly now, choosing each step with care not to snap twigs or rustle branches. Their ears were focused in front of them, listening for signs of people near the RAV4. The Huey buzzed over their heads once again, this time coming from north to south.

Eleven minutes later Mac stopped to check the GPS one last time. They were less than one thousand meters from the spot where they had left the camouflaged vehicle. Mac thought he heard something. They squatted down and listened intently, holding their breaths.

Then they heard it—the unmistakable sound of a car engine in low gear whining, growling, and struggling to maneuver along the same rutted logging road they had used to enter the jungle. They looked at one another with wide eyes and muttered "Shit!" in unison.

"Let's move out," said Mac. They ran toward the spot where they had left the car. The jungle was thinning, making it easier to move, but the underbrush was still fairly thick. Despite their efforts to keep the noise down, they sounded like two large deer charging through the woods.

They almost overran the RAV4. Culler saw it first, nestled in a small clearing and covered with branches. They doubled back and set up in a position between the RAV4 and the oncoming car.

They could now clearly hear the car heading up the trail directly toward them.

The morning light cut through the trees on the edge of the jungle, forcing them to switch off their night vision gear. They were each down on one knee with their weapons pointing toward the sound of the oncoming car.

Mac spoke softly, "There's only one way in and out of this place, and it won't take a Davy Crockett to follow those tire tracks right to our vehicle. We're gonna have to neutralize whoever's coming up that trail before we can get out of here.

"Okay," said Culler, hefting up his gear and checking his rifle. "Let's go get 'em. I'll take the left side of the trail and you take the right."

They moved out quietly at a fast walk, occasionally darting from one concealed location to another, keeping in the shadows on each side of the trail. The recent ruts left behind by the RAV4 were unmistakable. The distinct sounds of a vehicle struggling up the trail toward them were also unmistakable.

And then the sounds of the vehicle changed. It was stuck in the mud, or getting stuck. The whine of spinning wheels increased and then stopped completely. Moments later they heard the sound of doors slamming and men talking.

Mac signaled Culler by pointing to his ears and then toward the vehicle. Culler acknowledged with a nod. Moments later they had the car in sight. It was stuck in the middle of the trail with two men standing beside it trying to decide what to do next.

It was a police cruiser, and both men were uniformed police officers.

Mac went down on one knee behind some brush and whispered into his lapel mic. "There're cops. Whatever you do don't shoot 'em. We can't kill these guys."

"Yeah, I know. We're going to have to stop them though, and fast. How do you figure on doing that?"

"Hell, I don't know. Hit 'em over the head or something. Let's get closer and we'll figure it out."

They moved through the underbrush on each side of the trail until they were within a few meters on each side of the police car. One cop was behind the wheel, and the other was trying to push from the rear. The left rear wheel spun, spraying mud and grass up behind it, splattering the cop who was pushing.

He yelled something in Thai that probably meant stop. The driver took his foot off of the accelerator and the engine stopped screaming.

But the muddy cop in the road did not. He ran around to the driver's side and continued to yell at the driver. Seizing the opportunity, Mac ran up behind him and swung the butt of his rifle up an around and smacked the screaming cop hard on the side of the head.

The cop went down in a heap and Mac shoved the barrel of his rifle through the open window. He jammed the muzzle into the side of the driver's head and the driver froze.

"Hands where I can see them," commanded Mac. He pulled the door open, grabbed the cop by the shirt and jerked him out of the car, shouting, "Out, out, out."

The cop hit the ground hard and Mac butt-stroked him on the side of the head. He lay still in a heap next to his buddy.

"Need any help?" asked Culler, who had run up and was standing on the other side of the car, rifle at the ready.

"Naw, got it under control. Why don't you just take a nap under that tree over there while I take care of things here?"

"Great idea!"

Mac took a deep breath and thought a moment, surveying the situation. "Look, those other guys aren't far behind us so we don't have much time. You get these guys off to the side and immobilize them and I'll go bring the RAV around."

"Got it." Culler removed the pistols and walkie-talkies from each cop and threw them in the backseat of the cruiser. He dragged each of the cops by their collars, one in each hand, back away from the trail. Once in the brush he removed their handcuffs from their belts and cuffed them together with their arms linked behind them. He tossed the keys far into the underbrush. Neither cop budged. Both were in la-la land.

Moments later Mac returned with the RAV4 and pulled up to the police cruiser. "I've got an idea," he said.

"Uh oh, we're in trouble again."

"Why don't you take the cruiser and follow me like you're a cop on my tail? That will give us a little cover and maybe buy us a little more time to get the hell out of here. I'll give you a push to get it unstuck."

"Sounds like a plan. Let's do it."

CHAPTER FIFTY-SEVEN

Paiboon put up his hand to signal his men to stop. They had strung out so far that the last one was almost fifty meters back. "Did you hear that?" he asked the guard behind him.

Breathing heavily and soaked in sweat, the exhausted guard replied, "What?"

"Listen, shhhhh. Sounds like a car."

"*Mai sabai.* The blood is pounding in my ears. I cannot hear anything."

The other two caught up and the four of them huddled together, listening intently.

"There it goes again," said Paiboon. But they all shook their heads.

"*Mai pen rai*, no matter. I heard a car from over there. No question about it. You are all so badly out of shape, huffing and puffing like old women, you cannot hear anything. Spread out and be careful. It must be them. And turn off your flashlights. If you screw this up, the Cambodian will make curry stew out of you."

Dawn was setting in but it was still quite dark under the canopy of the jungle, slowing them down considerably as they picked their way through the underbrush.

When they got nearer to the clearing, Paiboon heard the unmistakable sounds of a four-wheel drive vehicle spinning and clawing in low gear ahead of them. Paiboon pointed to his ears and in the direction of the noise and signaled them to fan out and to hurry up.

He estimated the sound was coming from about one hundred meters in front of them. He was exhausted from his hike, so he stopped and drank heavily from his canteen before charging off in the direction of the sounds. The combination of the ground mist and the darkness caused him to trip on a root and he fell heavily on his face in the mud, cursing.

The others were out in front of him by the time he recovered and cleaned himself off enough to resume the chase. Another one of his men tumbled in the underbrush and cursed. Now he wanted to tell them all to slow down because they were nearing the edge of the jungle. Suddenly it became much lighter as the morning sun penetrated the dwindling canopy above them.

The guard to his left was the first to break through the edge of the jungle. When he did he immediately brought his AK-47 up and began firing in short, staccato bursts.

CHAPTER FIFTY-EIGHT

Mac had returned to the police cruiser with the 4WD vehicle. The two vehicles were nose to nose on the narrow trail. Culler got into the cruiser and put it in reverse. The wheels spun in the mud of the trail while Mac nudged it backwards with the RAV4.

Finally the spinning wheels of the cruiser gained traction and Culler took off weaving down the trail in reverse, one hand on the wheel and the other on the backrest of the passenger seat, looking out through the rear window.

When the cruiser hit firm ground, Culler gunned it, hit the brakes hard and spun the wheel, executing a perfect mud slinging reverse one-eighty. Then he was off, careening down the narrow trail with his rear end fishtailing in the dirt and mud.

Mac watched closely in the RAV4, admiring Culler's driving ability. Defensive driving was something all CIA case officers learned down at The Farm. *Things are looking up,* he thought.

The unmistabable staccato sound of an AK-47 shocked him, and then the plinking sound of the rounds impacting the left rear side of the RAV4 frightened him.

He popped the gearshift lever into neutral, grabbed his assault rifle and hit the door hard with his shoulder, tumbling out of the vehicle and rolling. He came up in a low shooting position behind and to the rear of the right rear wheel.

He spotted the shooter standing behind a tree by the edge of the woods, still firing short bursts at his vehicle.

Mac put the red chevron on the assailant's chest and pulled the trigger, firing off a silent burst from his POF. Seven 5.56mm rounds stitched the tree and the assailant at chest level, sending bark and gun flying, and spinning the hapless guard hard around and down with four rounds in his chest and arm.

Still in a prone shooting position, Mac used the scope to scan the tree line to the northwest where they had exited the jungle. He spotted another guard running through the brush toward the logging trail, carrying his AK-47 at port arms.

Mac touched the trigger, sending three deadly rounds into the man's gut. The man went down with a crash in the underbrush.

Mac's earpiece came alive. "Nice shooting, Mac. Now let's get the hell out of here before any more of those guys come out of the woods. Are you okay?"

"I'm fine. See if you can get that police cruiser moving a little faster while I cover us from here."

"I'm working on it. Don't want to get too far from you. Just get your ass over here."

Mac took a last long look through his scope and, seeing nothing, bolted up and back into the RAV4. He pulled the gear shift lever back into drive and floored it, spraying mud and dirt behind him from all four wheels.

Then it came again. The pop, pop, pop, sound of an AK-47 rattled off a long burst, and the rear of the RAV absorbed the 7.62mm rounds in a staccato plink, plink, plink. One of the rounds ricocheted through the back of his seat and creased his left hip, causing him to wince in pain.

Santos yelled into his lapel mic. "Are you okay? Are you hit?"

"Shit, shit, shit! I caught one in the butt. Stings like a sonofabitch. I'm on my way."

"Me too. I'm moving out."

"I can see you. I'm right behind you."

The two cars careened down the narrow logging trail. Soon they were out of sight of their pursuers and the automatic weapons fire ceased.

CHAPTER FIFTY-NINE

Paiboon cursed as the vehicle sped out of sight down the trail. He stood up from his kneeling shooting position, exchanged the empty magazine for a full one and slung the hot assault rifle over his shoulder. His remaining security guard was huffing and puffing toward him.

"They are gone," he said to no one in particular. "But they cannot get far."

He keyed his walkie-talkie. "Base, this is One."

The Cambodian answered from the helicopter. "This is Base. Go ahead, One."

"They are heading east on a trail which leads into this strip of jungle, approximately eight or nine kilometers south of our warehouse. They are in two vehicles, a police cruiser and a small jeep, and they are moving fast."

"Talk us in, One. We are turning around and heading for your position now. Did you say one of the vehicles was a police cruiser? How did they get a police cruiser?"

"I don't know, sir, but the two vehicles left together and I saw no police around."

The Cambodian thought for a moment before answering.

"The police have been searching for them. Khun Ut notified them. They must have killed the police and taken their cruiser, so their bodies must be around there someplace. Find them and I will notify the police to be on the lookout for a police cruiser as well as their vehicle."

"Yes sir. I hear your helicopter coming this way . . . I see you now . . . Keep coming. Keep coming . . . Left about thirty degrees . . . Good, keep coming and you will pass directly over my position . . . Okay, now turn due west and you will be directly over the trail. It must head out to a road."

"Good work, One. We can see the trail. Base out."

CHAPTER SIXTY

The two vehicles careened down the logging trail as fast as possible, but it wasn't fast enough. Mac heard the sound of the helicopter first. "Uh-oh, we've got company again."

"I hear it," Culler replied.

The helicopter passed directly overhead and continued in a westerly direction. "I think they missed us," said Mac. "The tree cover is still pretty good along this strip of road. It'll be hard for them to find us from the air until we hit the road, but not impossible. What do you think?"

Culler fought the wheel of the police cruiser, trying to keep up his speed but being thrown from one side of the trail to the other by the deep muddy ruts left by logging trucks.

"I don't think anyone's following us from behind any longer, so let's pull over into some cover the next chance we get and try to wait them out. That helicopter's been in the air since before dawn. They'll have to refuel sooner or later, so if we can hide till then . . ."

"Good idea. Let's ditch the RAV4 as well. Everyone's looking for it and it's riddled with bullet holes. But the police cruiser looks like every other police car in Thailand. And this is as good a place as any. Hold on, I'm going to pull off into that brush over there to my right."

Mac pulled off the trail and ran the vehicle deep the underbrush beneath a thicket of fichus trees. Culler stopped the cruiser and backed up to get as close as he could to the RAV4.

Stripping off his gear and Ghillie-suit, Santos said, "We better get out of this camouflage shit, so we don't look like a couple of jungle monsters." He opened the trunk of the cruiser and tossed his gear into it. He was now dressed in a sweat soaked white tee-shirt and blue jeans.

Mac followed suit. His Ghillie-suit and jeans were torn and bloodied from the ricochet. He turned to help Culler, who was busy emptying the RAV and loading their gear into the back of the cruiser. They decided to keep their rifles and pistols beside them in the cab.

Culler surveyed the back and side of the RAV. "You sure did get shot up. How's your butt?"

Mac looked down at a three-inch tear in his jeans high on his hip between the pocket and belt. The tear was coated in blood. "Stings like a bitch but it's not too deep. I'll live. We'll get it fixed up later."

The helicopter returned from the west and thump-thumped over their position, rustling the trees and bushes in its powerful downdraft. They could barely see the helicopter through the trees as it passed overhead. "We've still got pretty good cover on this trail," said Mac. "What do you think?"

Culler threw the last of the gear into the cruiser and slammed the trunk. He looked up through the trees and assessed their situation. "We're most vulnerable out on the trail. The helicopter can see it from up there. I think our best bet is to move as fast as we can down the trail and dash for cover whenever we hear the bastards approaching."

"Good idea. I don't want to hang out around here any longer than we have to, and if we can get out on the road with the cruiser, we'll be able to blend in better."

"And thank God for those tinted windows. People won't be able to see our big *farang* faces peering out at them."

"Yeah," said Mac, "got to avoid being seen. Leaving the trail for the highway will be tricky. That'll have to be timed just right. But they'll be looking for two vehicles, not just one, which is a good thing."

Mac thought for a moment. "Wait a minute. What about the police? Surely they're out looking for their guys, too. And what if Khun Ut's men in the helicopter have communicated with them about this? Damn, Culler, we need to get the hell out of here *tout de suite* before the whole goddamned world converges on this trail."

CHAPTER SIXTY-ONE

The Cambodian cursed into his walkie-talkie. "This is bullshit. *Mai sabai*. How long ago did they leave? We cannot see them from up here."

"They left not more than ten minutes ago. I called you immediately. I hit the jeep as they were leaving. Maybe I got one of them."

"Then why did you stop following them? We cannot see the ground from here."

"*Phom mai khao jai khrap*, we could not follow, Ung Chea. There are only two of us left, and they are in vehicles and we are on foot."

"Why are there only two of you left? *Mai pen rai*, you are incompetent. Have you found the bodies of the police officers yet?"

"Yes, Ung Chea, we just found them. They are unconscious but not dead."

"*Dee mak*, thank you. Stay with them until the police arrive. They are on their way. We will continue to search from here."

CHAPTER SIXTY-TWO

Culler and Mac piled into the cruiser. Culler drove and Mac sat in the passenger seat with his POF across his knees. His left hip burned like hell, and he tried to keep it from rubbing on the seat. Culler hit the gas and the cruiser leapt forward down the narrow trail.

"Keep going like this and don't touch the brakes," said Mac. "We don't want any lights flashing for them to see. Damn, it's hot in here." He put the A/C on high and opened his window to listen for the surveilling helicopter above.

The trail improved as they progressed toward the road, and Culler pushed it faster. As the trail widened a bit, Mac heard the sound of the returning helicopter behind them. "Quick, pull over to the side as far as you can, but don't hit the brakes. The helicopter is returning."

The Huey flew low overhead while Culler hugged the side of the road and slowed down by downshifting.

"Good job," said Mac. "Now let's hang out here for a moment until he turns around and then let's make a dash for it."

Culler pushed the gear lever into neutral, and the car slowed to a stop as far over under the cover of the trees as he could get. Moments later the gunship circled wide and came back toward them, low as before and thrashing the trees above them under the prop blast.

Then it was gone behind them and Mac hit the dash with his fist. "Let's go."

Culler slammed the car into drive and pushed the accelerator to the floor. The rear wheels spun and he cut the wheel to the left and bounced over the ruts and back to the middle of the trail. The speedometer reached thirty as the car lurched in and out of the deep ruts and spun haphazardly down the logging trail.

Finally they careened out onto the pavement of the macadam road leading to the highway, and the car accelerated again. It was almost seven in the morning.

Mac studied the GPS. "Keep heading straight until you hit the highway, then turn right, south, and go for about a thousand meters and then branch off to a dirt road on the left. Then you can slow down. But for now we need to get away from that Huey."

Culler concentrated on his driving. "Got it."

They skidded and bumped up unto the highway, and Culler hit the gas again. Ahead of them they saw a police cruiser speeding their way with sirens blaring and lights flashing.

Mac leaned forward and hit the lights and siren switch on their cruiser.

Culler screamed, "What the hell are you doing?"

"Just drive. I've got an idea. As soon as we pass the cruiser, spin around and follow it north. They'll think we're one of theirs— maybe . . ."

The police cruiser flashed past and Culler spun their car around on the shoulder of the road, spraying gravel and dirt, and came up behind the other cruiser. Their police radio squawked and something was said in Thai.

Mac listened intently to the radio. "My Thai isn't good enough to get the whole thing but it sounds like they are calling all units to look for the RAV4. Maybe they don't know we're in one of their cruisers."

"That would be a really good thing," said Santos.

They reached the road that led to the trail that had brought them out of the jungle and the police cruiser they were following turned into it. "Keep going straight," said Mac.

The Huey circled above them menacingly for several more minutes but then broke off and headed back east.

"Let's put as much distance between us as possible," said Mac, studying his GPS. "There's a secondary road coming up on the right. Take it east and follow it for about twelve miles. There it will intersect with another north-south secondary road. Take it south past Chiang Rai and follow it all the way to Chiang Mai."

"We need to stay away from the main highway. That's where they'll be looking for us."

Culler turned right onto the secondary road heading west and hit the button for the lights and siren. "We don't need those any more."

"Right, but keep the speed up. We need to put some distance between us and them. Once we hit the north-south road, we can slow it down a bit and try to blend in."

"Then what?"

"Then we find a place to ditch the cruiser and regroup." Mac thought a bit before continuing. "We're gonna need support. We're too hot to handle this on our own."

"Well, that means either the general or Charly Blackburn. Take your pick."

Mac pushed back into his seat and massaged his temples. "Hell, I don't know. Neither one's a good choice. We can't trust the general, and it's risky to get Charly too far involved. We've got to keep that connection secure. Otherwise denial goes down the drain. We can't do that to the DDO, not to Ed Rothmann."

"The way I see it, we're going to need Charly and her Hmong tribesman. Without them we're dead in the water. We're not going to accomplish anything. Trying to go it alone is turning into a goat rope."

"And we're not out of it yet. You're right, of course. We're going to need Charly to get us out of this mess and back on track to complete the mission. I'll call her and tell her we're on our way."

CHAPTER SIXTY-THREE

C harly Blackburn was eating a breakfast of fresh mango, sticky rice, and assorted fruits on the veranda of her villa when her "non-attributable" cell phone rang. She scrambled to find it in the bottom of her cluttered purse, and her heart jumped when she recognized the number on the caller ID.

She shooed her servant away with a wave of the hand and the woman bowed deeply and shuffled back into the house on calloused bare feet. "Hey, what's up?" she said into the phone, trying to act casual.

The sound of her voice reassured Mac. Charly was a rock. She would know how to get them out of this situation. They were exhausted from the physical exertion and the adrenaline rush of the previous twelve hours. And they had left their Camelbaks and granola bars in the trunk and were afraid to stop the car to retrieve them for fear of being seen, so now they were hungry and thirsty as well.

"The short story is we've commandeered a police cruiser. Right now we're northeast of Chiang Rai heading south through a village named . . . Ban Lao, I think. The whole country is out searching for us, and pretty soon they're going to know we're in a police cruiser. Got any bright ideas?"

"Yeah, stay off the main roads and don't let anyone see your ugly *farang* faces."

"Thanks, I needed that . . ."

Charly smiled and popped a grape into her mouth. She liked having the upper hand over MacMurphy. But she liked helping him even more. She was tired of flitting from one case officer to another, and the job was getting to her. She was also tired of fighting a losing battle with the drug lords, and she was especially tired of sex without romance.

She wanted Mac, but he was, after all, Mac . . . *Life sucks*, she thought. *It really sucks.*

Her mind spun. How could she get him out of this mess? There was only so much she could do. The rest would be up to them, but they were resourceful guys.

"Okay, keep coming south on the back roads. Head southeast toward a town named Ban Huai Kang near the Lao border, and then turn southwest toward Ban Khai then Ban Pa Kha. Have you got that?"

"Yeah, I'm writing. Keep going."

"When you get to Ban Pa Kha, turn west toward Chiang Mai. Just before you get to Chiang Mai, you'll go through a small village called San Sai. That's where I'll meet you. In San Sai. Got it?"

"Okay, that's great, Charly. We really appreciate this. But be careful you're not followed, and . . ."

"Don't lecture me about security. I'll be clean when I get there and I'll have a clean vehicle. Just get there in one piece, hopefully without a dozen police cars on your tail.

"By the way, in case you haven't heard, your exploits at the Orchid Lodge and the Wangcome Hotel are all over the news, and whatever you did at the warehouse in Mae Chan is soon to follow. That's already in our channels."

Mac was confused. "What happened at the Orchid Lodge?"

She looked around to make sure her maid was out of earshot before answering. "Your rental car was blown to bits in the parking lot with an American tourist inside."

"Oh my God. I didn't know. You said 'a' tourist. How many people were in the car?"

"Just one, a man. His wife was the one who told the police about you and Culler and the vehicle trade."

Mac cast Culler a nauseated look. "Sonofabitch. I'm really sorry about that."

"Of course you are. Now just concentrate on getting to San Sai safely. It should take you about three hours over those roads. When you get near the center of town—it's not very big so keep your eyes open—you will see a long tree-lined driveway on your left. It leads to a burned out, abandoned charcoal factory. You can't miss it. Go down that driveway and pull around back of the building. I'll be waiting for you."

CHAPTER SIXTY-FOUR

don't know about you, Mac, but I've got to take a leak and we've got to get our Camelbaks and power bars out of the trunk. I can't last another hour without food and water."

"Me neither. Let's find a secluded place to pull over and take care of our animal needs and cravings."

They found a spot on a lonely stretch of the road on the outskirts of Ban Lao. There were woods to their left and fields to their right. They got out, stretched, and each selected a tire upon which to relieve themselves.

Mac popped the trunk and rummaged around looking for the Camelbaks and granola bars. He pulled them out and slammed the trunk shut just as a jeep drove by coming from the other direction. The jeep slowed and the two men in the front seat craned their necks in the direction of the police cruiser.

Culler and Mac tried to shield their faces as best they could by turning away and putting their hands up to their heads. They did not look back as the jeep passed them.

They hurried back into the cruiser and slammed the doors shut. Culler pulled the vehicle back onto the road.

Then Mac broke the silence. In a philosophical tone he said, "It never ceases to amaze me. You can be in the most remote spot in Asia, and as soon as you stop to take a leak someone comes out of nowhere to watch. It's definitely a third world kind of thing."

"Do you think they noticed us?"

"Hell, I don't know. But it's not good. We've got every cop and druggie in north Thailand out looking for us, and those idiots have to drive by while we're outside of the car taking a piss on the side of the road. If we didn't have bad luck, we wouldn't have any luck at all."

"Mind if I go a little faster?"

"Just don't get a ticket."

Culler drove as fast as he could over the narrow back roads. They slowed as they passed through the little village of Ban Huai Kang and then headed southeast toward Ban Khai. There was very little traffic on the road, but when they did meet an oncoming vehicle they had to slow to a near stop and pull over to the side to let the other vehicle past.

The trucks were the worst. They hogged the road and drove way too fast, the drivers not caring one bit whether they drove the oncoming vehicles off the road. Mac wondered what would happen if two trucks met at a curve. But he knew the answer.

Truck accidents were the bane of Thailand. The drivers were often unlicensed and overworked, resorting to drugs to stay awake on their long hauls. And when an accident did occur, the drivers would simply disappear from the scene, leaving the injured and dead behind them, and going on to the next truck driving job.

The two men munched on granola bars and drank heavily from their Camelbaks. The road ran through heavy woods broken by fields and scrub brush, wild elephant country years ago.

They were feeling better and the police radio remained relatively silent, probably because reception was so bad in the hills, which was a good thing.

They passed through Ban Pa Kha at a crawl due to the gaggle of people and animals walking on the road. The people regarded the cruiser with mild curiosity, but the heavily tinted windows did not permit them to see inside.

They turned west on an improved, two-lane macadam road to Chiang Mai. They were thirty-three kilometers from their rendezvous with Charly Blackburn.

They arrived in San Sai at a few minutes before eleven in the morning, almost exactly three hours after speaking to Charly on the phone.

Mac said, "Look at that. Right on time. Charly sure does know this part of the world. She said it would take us about three hours to get here and here we are."

"And I do believe that's the tree-lined driveway we're looking for. Up there on the left, in that field."

They crept through the village of San Sai. It was larger than many of the others they had passed through, more like a small town. The road was lined with shops and open restaurants with cars parked in front along both sides of the road. People, dogs, goats and pigs milled about.

"My, my," said Mac, "I do believe we have reached the suburbs."

Culler turned the cruiser into the tree lined drive and headed toward the burned out charcoal factory. Everything was exactly as Charly had described it.

CHAPTER SIXTY-FIVE

Charly Blackburn stood behind the factory where she said she would be, leaning up against a white Toyota Land Cruiser.

She was wearing tan slacks and a matching tan safari style blouse. Her rich black hair was pulled back into a pony tail. She looked crisp and fresh. She tilted her sunglasses down and peered over them as the men approached.

Culler pulled the police cruiser in behind the Toyota. Mac jumped out and hurried over to her. Grinning broadly, he embraced her and whispered in her ear, "God, you look great."

Winking, she whispered back, "You stink like a horse, and what happed to your ass?"

"It's not my ass. It's my hip. See, right here."

"Doesn't look too bad."

"That's easy for you to say. It hurts like hell."

Culler approached them from the other side of the car. He held his hand out to her, and she took it in both of hers. "So I finally get to meet the famous Culler Santos."

"It's all my pleasure, Charly. I've heard a lot about you, too. Thanks for getting us out of this jam."

She smiled and put her hands on her hips. "That's my job, keeping people like Santos and MacMurphy out of trouble. But you're not out of the woods—or jungle—yet, boys."

Then she was all business. "Okay, guys, let's get your gear into the back of the Land Cruiser. Pull the police car over there, Culler, close behind the building by that door where it can't be seen from the road. Then let's get the hell out of here. These villagers notice everything, absolutely everything."

Charly drove and Mac sat next to her in the front seat while Culler stretched out in the back. She drove rapidly the last few kilometers into Chiang Mai, briefing them on the arrangements she had made for them.

"You can keep this car for as long as you need it. It was leased in alias by one of our most trusted Thai support assets. It's as close to clean as we can get. When we get to Chiang Mai, I'll drop you off at an unused safehouse. It's a two-bedroom apartment in a nice neighborhood, not too far from the consulate. Lot's of *farangs* live around there, so you won't stand out too much if someone sees you. It was leased in alias by an American retired Navy Chief and used only once, for the debriefing of a Hong Kong station journalist asset, so it's as clean as we can expect. It's also quite comfortable. The Chief's alias name is Harold Moscowitz, just in case anyone asks."

"You're the best, Charly," said Mac. "Rest and food and a stiff drink, not necessarily in that order. That's what we need most right now."

Charly glanced over at him and then at Culler in the back seat, and pinched her nose with her fingers. "And a bath, boys—a long hot soak. You guys are ripe!"

Culler and Mac responded with sheepish and knowing nods.

"Oh yeah, I almost forgot, I brought some light disguises for you guys as well. They are in that blue sports bag in the back, Culler. They're nothing great, but quick and easy to use and enough to blur your appearances. The good guys and the bad guys are all out looking for you, and they have your descriptions."

Culler rummaged through the bag, examining the items she had brought, while she continued talking.

"You'll see I brought a selection of different mustaches, two longish wigs, a couple of different caps for you to wear, an assortment of sunglasses and regular glasses that are big enough to hide your eyebrows. And, oh yes, some hair dye for you, Mac. That is unless you want to wear one of the hippy wigs I brought."

"Hair dye? You want me to color this distinguished gray hair of mine?"

"Don't worry, handsome, it's not permanent. It'll wash out over a week or two, and you'll be back to your old, extinguished–I mean distinguished–self once again . . . and alive. That's the most important thing."

She drove into the outskirts of the city and soon pulled up to the underground garage entrance of a four-story, sand colored, brick and stucco apartment building on a quiet, tree-lined street. She pressed a remote above her sun visor and the door rolled open.

She pulled into the garage and parked in slot number 222.

"This is your space. Don't park anywhere else, or the manager will come knocking on your door. People are very protective of their parking spaces in this building."

The garage was almost deserted. Only about a quarter of the spaces were occupied with cars. She said, "Most of the residents are at work during the day, so if you have to come and go, this is a good time to do it."

They grabbed their gear out of the trunk, leaving behind the heavy boxes of ammo and the assault weapons. "Don't forget those two bags of groceries," she said. "You guys must be hungry, and I came prepared to give you a pasta fix."

She led them to an elevator near the middle of the garage and hit the call button. When the elevator arrived, she pushed the button for the fourth floor. Thus far their arrival was unnoticed.

Soon they would be home free and out of sight inside the safehouse apartment.

When the elevator stopped on the ground floor to let in a Filipina maid dressed in a white uniform pushing a baby stroller, Culler and Mac shuffled to the back of the cab and tried not to make eye contact with the woman. The woman pushed the stroller and child into the elevator cab and turned it around, facing the door with her back to Culler and Mac.

She pushed the button for the second floor and the doors closed. No one spoke on the ride up to the second floor, but the woman made sniffing sounds and glanced around her on the floor for the source of the odor. When the elevator reached the second floor, she exited rapidly without looking behind her.

When the door closed, Mac broke the silence. "Murphy's law. Do you think she'll remember us?"

Charly frowned at him like he had lost his mind. "Oh yeah, she'll remember you all right. No doubt about that."

CHAPTER SIXTY-SIX

Charly gave them a quick tour of the apartment and directed them to their respective rooms and showers. She found some Neosporin salve and bandages in one of the medicine cabinets and handed them to Mac. "Okay, clean yourselves up and slip into something more comfortable while I get started on fixing you something to eat."

Mac pecked her on the cheek. "Thanks Charly. I'll call you when I'm clean so you can dress my wound, okay? By the way, you didn't by any chance bring us something to drink to go along with that pasta, did you?"

"Of course I did. Knowing your love of vodka and wine, I brought both. But you can't have anything until you are shaved and clean. Then I'll fix your scratch and you can have a drink."

She busied herself in the kitchen, unpacking the groceries and preparing to cook the pasta. When she heard the water from the showers shut off, she grabbed three glasses from the cupboard, filled them with ice, sliced a lime and prepared three strong vodka tonics.

Mac padded into the kitchen barefoot, wearing gym shorts and a tee-shirt. He smelled of soap and shampoo, and his wet hair was neatly parted and slicked down. She offered him one of the vodka tonics and took another. "Cheers," she said, clinking his glass with her own.

"Cheers!" He took a long satisfying drink, exhaled and then put his arm around her, pulling her to him. "This is manna from heaven."

She moved into him and put both hands around him, being careful not to spill her drink. He looked down at her, deep into her eyes, and stroked her hip with his free hand. His breathing quickened.

"Am I interrupting something?" said Culler, entering the room.

She pushed Mac away and blushed. "Not at all. Here, I fixed you a drink." She handed him the vodka tonic, and the three of them clinked glasses in a toast.

"To better days ahead," said Culler.

"Hear, hear," said Mac. "Now will you dress my wound? It really hurts, damn it."

Culler laughed. "Go fix his ass, Charly. I'm tired of hearing him complain about it."

Charly took Mac into the bathroom, slathered the four-inch long wound with Neosporin and bandaged it lightly. "It looks like a burn from a poker," she said. "You'll live. You don't need any stitches. Just keep the Neosporin on it, so it doesn't get infected. You'll be okay."

Later, Mac and Culler sat at the small kitchen table drinking their cocktails, while Charly busied herself preparing the meal. They filled her in on what had transpired over the past few days, and she briefed them on what had been reported in the local press and in Agency cable traffic.

"So the bottom line is they—and I'm talking about the police and Khun Ut—have your descriptions and know your alias names. They also know you escaped in a police cruiser, and as soon as they find it behind the charcoal factory in San Sai, which won't take long, they'll know you're probably in Chiang Mai. That's about it. There's very little in Agency or State traffic, only a little reporting about the killing of an

American tourist in a car bombing and some internecine fighting among the drug lords. As far as I can tell, no one at Headquarters knows you guys are here, other than Edwin Rothmann, of course. So I think you're okay on that score."

Mac got up to make refills. "We tried to do this without any support from you or the Chiang Mai Base, and the reasoning behind that decision was sound. Problem is we failed. We got a lot of people killed, including that young American kid—that really hurts—and didn't accomplish anything other than to raise the ire of Khun Ut and his people."

"Yep," said Culler, "I expect we managed to piss them off real bad."

"Well," said Charly, "You've just got to be more careful from now on. You need to do what you've got to do, then leave."

Mac took a long drink of his vodka tonic. He was feeling human again and the alcohol helped him to relax. "Tell me again about General Sawat. How much can we trust him?"

"The only person in Thailand you can fully trust is me, Mac, and I think you know that. But if you keep Sawat on a short leash and use him on a strict 'need to know' basis, I think he's about as good as you can get around here. He won't just decide to turn you in or blow your cover, but if Khun Ut puts the screws to him, he'll squeal like a pig."

"What about his ever present mistress, Noi?" asked Culler. "He takes her everywhere, her and that yappy mutt."

Charly turned the heat down on the pasta and turned to face them, gesturing with a long wooden spoon. "She's definitely a problem. Sawat bought her out of a massage parlor three or four years ago, when she was about seventeen. Her family is from northeast Thailand, around Loei, I think. A very depressed area. Her father sold her to the massage parlor in Chiang Mai. It's a pretty common thing in these parts, a huge source of income for the impoverished. Now that she's set with the general, I'm sure they receive some sort of a monthly stipend from him. Word is she's very doting on him and extremely loyal."

"But she's basically a hooker, and you can't trust hookers, right?" said Mac.

Charly raised her eyebrows. "Of course, she's in it for the money, and if she gets a better offer she'll take it. She's clearly a weak link."

"But they're a package," said Culler. "The two of them and that obnoxious mutt."

"That's right," said Charly, "so be extra careful if you feel you have to use him again. I wouldn't be surprised if Khun Ut or the Cambodian has tapped into her to keep tabs on the general.

"Anyway, pop open that wine, will you, Culler? Then let's eat. You guys must be famished and the pasta is done."

Charly watched them devour a huge bowl of spaghetti with meat sauce, a loaf of Italian bread, large green salads with tomatoes, onions and hard boiled eggs topped with a creamy Italian dressing, and a bottle of Chianti Classico.

It was almost five in the afternoon when they pushed back from the table. Charly began clearing the table, rinsing the dishes and placing them in the dishwasher. "I brought coffee as well. Shall I make a pot?" she asked.

They both shook their heads. "Not me," said Mac. "I don't want anything to keep me awake."

"Me neither," said Culler. "Just point me toward the bedroom."

"Well, I should get back to the office and check the afternoon cable traffic. I'll check in with you guys in the morning."

"Do you need a lift back?" asked Mac.

"No way, I don't want to be seen with you guys. I'll take a taxi."

Mac stood and took both of her hands in his. "Take care of your business and let us crash. Tomorrow morning we'll decide what to do next. Right now I'm too tired to think."

She hugged him and then Culler. At the door she turned and looked back at them. "Sleep well, my beauties. I'll check in with you in the morning."

CHAPTER SIXTY-SEVEN

It was almost nine o'clock when Charly returned to the apartment and gently rapped on the door. Mac, who was puttering around in the kitchen dressed only in boxer shorts, opened it.

She reached out her hand and placed it on his chest as if to say *don't come any closer*, but then she moved her fingers gently through the hair and caressed him before slipping easily into his arms.

He pushed the door closed and succumbed to the smell and feel of her. They embraced and kissed deeply standing in the doorway, and he could feel the heat rising between them.

But it was she who pushed back this time. Then she leaned forward, nibbled his earlobe and whispered, "I'm crazy about you and want you more than anything, but I'm not going to fuck you in this apartment at nine o'clock in the morning with Culler Santos in the next room. Got it?"

"Got it," he replied. They glanced down at his growing erection. "I'd better go get some pants on," he said, hurrying into his bedroom.

When he returned in gym shorts and a tee-shirt, he found her in the kitchen making coffee. She was dressed in a pale green sundress which clung tightly to the curves of her hips. "Is Culler up?" she asked.

"I heard the water running in there. He should be out shortly."

She turned toward him, hands on hips, serious. "I told you you couldn't get into that warehouse."

"I know, I know . . . don't rub it in, we had to try. I don't like having to involve you in this. The DDO wanted plausible denial, and with you we risk losing that."

"Rothmann knew that I would have to be a part of this. That's why he put us together in the first place. Otherwise, he would have sent you out here on your own with only General Sawat to support you."

"You're probably right."

"I am right."

Culler entered the kitchen, also dressed in gym shorts and a tee-shirt, but wearing one of the longish wigs, a drooping Fu Man Chu moustache and large eyeglasses. "How do I look?"

Charly grinned. "If it weren't for your ripped physique, I wouldn't recognize you."

He plopped down in a chair at the table, removed the wig, moustache and glasses, and sniffed the air. "That coffee smells great, Charly."

"And it's ready." She poured the coffee and served them orange juice, muffins and bagels.

Mac said, "It's nice to have a galley slave to take care of us."

"Don't get used to it, sailor. Now listen up—the reason for my early morning visit . . ."

"You mean it's not just to see that we get fed?" asked Culler.

"In your dreams. We need to do some planning. I got a message from Vanquish last night. He's back in his village and wants to meet in the morning. I think you guys should come with me. You should meet him and chat about doing your thing without blowing his cover."

"This is the Hmong who used to work with Bill Lair. Security guy for their donkey trains, right?" asked Culler.

"That's him. He's a highly compartmented agent. No other case officer has ever met him. He's your best hope to get access to one of Khun Ut's shipments. They bring the stuff down from Ban Hin Taek to the warehouse in Mae Chan, the one you guys shot up the other day."

"Oh yeah, that one," said Mac.

"His village is a couple kilometers east of Ban Hin Taek. It's called Ban Rai, near where you guys were when you were on the run. I meet him on a trail in the woods near his village. He comes to the meetings on horseback."

"What time's the meet?" asked Mac.

"Oh seven hundred."

"How are we going to get there?" asked Culler.

"I'll take you, but we should probably take your car. It's the cleanest one we have in the base inventory."

Mac calculated. "Then you'd better stay here tonight. What time will we have to leave? Around four AM, right?"

"That's right. It's close to a three-hour drive. Staying here probably wouldn't be a bad idea. Tell you what, I'll come back this evening with some steaks, and we can have dinner together. I can bunk right out there on that couch in the living room. How's that sound?"

"Sounds like a plan," said Mac. Culler nodded his approval.

"It's set then. I'll see you back here after work, around six or seven. Dress comfortably for the trip, and do something about your appearances. That disguise you had on looks great, Culler. Mac, use the hair color and change your appearance as well. If anything goes wrong . . . well, see you around seven. Okay?"

She was already at the door when they replied in unison. "Okay."

CHAPTER SIXTY-EIGHT

She returned at seven, carrying a bag of groceries. Mac surprised her at the door with a new head of freshly dyed, light brown hair.

The men had spent the day cleaning and reloading their weapons, watching cable TV, preparing their disguises, napping and generally hanging out.

Except for one trip down to the garage to retrieve the automatic weapons and ammo, they stayed out of sight in the apartment. They had already started cocktail hour and were sitting at the kitchen table drinking vodka tonics when she arrived.

Culler relieved her of the groceries and placed the bag on the counter. Mac greeted her with a hug and kisses on both sides of her face in the European style.

"You look ten years younger without that grey hair, but not quite as distinguished. And I see you've already started cocktail hour. Who's the bartender tonight?"

"I am," said Mac. "We have vodka and vodka. Which would you prefer?"

"I think I'd like a glass of red wine. There are two bottles of Bordeaux in the grocery bag."

Mac opened the wine while Culler emptied the groceries and laid out the three steaks on a plate. "How are we going to cook these?" he asked.

Charly rolled her eyes. "I'll take care of them. Have you ever heard of a broiler?"

"Nope, I only know how to use an outdoor barbeque grill."

"Of course, I should have guessed."

When they were finished eating, they sat around the table for another hour leisurely finishing off the wine and going over the planning for the meeting with Vanquish in the morning.

They studied a map of the region surrounding Ban Hin Taek and discussed the possible routes the caravans could take from there down to Mae Chan. Charly traced the routes with her index finger.

"The entire trip is made off the roads through the forests of the highlands here, and down through the jungle, here, to Mae Chan. And they rarely take the same route twice. Here's where we'll meet up with Vanquish. There's a meadow right here off route 1234. It's a dirt road at this point."

It was almost nine o'clock and the wine was gone. Charly stood up. "Okay guys, time for beddy-bye. You guys hit the sack while I clean up this mess and do the same. Mac, would you grab a couple of sheets and a pillow out of the linen closet in the hall and drop them on the couch? Then I'll see you all in the morning. Three-thirty will come early."

The men said good night and retired. Charly cleaned the kitchen and readied a pot of coffee so that all she would have to do was flip the switch in the morning. She brushed her teeth in the hall bathroom, undressed and crawled between the sheets on the couch.

She lay there quietly, eyes open looking up at the ceiling, thinking of the day ahead—and of Mac in the next room.

She glanced at her wrist watch. It was a little after ten. Except for the occasional car and street sounds, and the humming of the air conditioner, it was quiet. She wondered if they were asleep. She turned on her side and continued to think of Mac. *Would he come out and join her on the couch? No, he wouldn't do that. He was probably already asleep. Probably, but . . . but what if he was waiting for her? Probably not. They had to get up very early in the morning, in less than six hours. Mac was always so damn mission oriented. Damn him.*

It was warm and she threw back the sheet. Her body glowed in the moonlight. She wore only bikini panties. She caressed her breasts and let her hand wander down lower and felt the heat and wetness. She stroked and pushed and . . . *damn it!*

She sat up and looked for several moments at Mac's door. Then she stood up and walked quietly to the door. It was ajar. She pushed it gently. *He did that on purpose,* she thought. She pushed the door open just wide enough to slide in and gently pushed it closed behind her. She stood there, staring at the bed, letting her eyes become accustomed to the darkness.

"What took you so long?" he said.

CHAPTER SIXTY-NINE

They were awakened by the beep, beep, beep of her wristwatch alarm. She bolted out of his bed, scooped up her panties from the floor, and hurried back to the couch where she grabbed a sheet, wrapped it around her and darted into the hall bathroom, thankful that Culler did not see her exit Mac's bedroom.

The three of them were on the road, coffee mugs in hand, thirty minutes later. Mac had chosen a baseball cap and pair of sunglasses to go with his newly colored hair; Culler was wearing sunglasses, a longish wig and matching Fu Man Chu moustache.

Both men were dressed in tennis shoes, jeans and untucked polo shirts to cover the concealed H&K weapons. Charly was dressed similarly in jeans and tennis shoes and a white blouse. Her PPK was in an ankle holster.

Charly knew the streets of Chiang Mai well. She drove rapidly but cautiously. When she hit the intersection of Route 109, she turned onto the highway and headed toward Chiang Rai.

Culler lay dozing across the back seat, while Charly and Mac chatted quietly in the front.

They made good time on the highway. Traffic was light in the early morning hours, and the only hazards were the speeding trucks coming south, inevitably driving in the middle of the road, forcing oncoming traffic to take evasive action. Trucks ruled the highways and the drivers made their point every time they drove a smaller vehicle onto the shoulder of the road.

They passed quickly through Chiang Rai and headed due north on Route 110 toward Mae Chan. They passed the road Mac and Culler had taken to enter the jungle and begin their assault on Khun Ut's warehouse. Mac pointed it out and said, "That's the road we took in and out of there. Pretty hairy experience and I've got the wounds to prove it."

"Are you still bitching about that little scratch on your butt?"

"A little sympathy would be in order."

"And that's all you're going to get from me—a little sympathy, very little."

"You are a cold-hearted wench."

"That's what I've been told."

CHAPTER SEVENTY

The day before, at a little before noon, Khun Ut, Ung Chea and Paiboon met at the Mae Chan warehouse to discuss what had happened there. They walked the perimeter of the building, and Paiboon briefed the other two on his analysis of what had transpired.

"Here is where the two *farangs* climbed up the side of the ridge and began their assault on our warehouse," said Paiboon, indicating the edge of the ridge and the rear of the warehouse. "They began their assault by sneaking through the jungle from that direction, from where we found their car, and climbing up from there. Then they surprised Michai who was posted over by those doors."

"Was he sleeping?" asked Khun Ut.

"We don't know. Maybe . . . but they were wearing jungle camouflage and using silent weapons. Maybe he just didn't see them. They shot him in the head? Very good marksmen."

Ung Chea said, "They were very well equipped, boss. They used 5.56mm assault weapons equipped with suppressors, and we think night vision as well. They were very accurate and silent—like Ninjas."

"*Mai pen rai*," said Khun Ut. "The point is these *farangs* are definitely not amateurs. They are well trained and well equipped. We need to find out why they were here and, more importantly, who sent them."

"They stole a brick of heroin, Khun Ut. We chased them away before they could steal more. Maybe they were just thieves," said Paiboon.

"Maybe, maybe not. But I don't think so. By the way, you said you recovered the brick."

"Yes sir, they dropped it during their escape. We found it on the trail and recovered it. Kaset snorted some of it before he had a heart attack and died."

"What an idiot. Kaset got what he deserved. Heroin and exertion do not mix well. That is what gave him the heart attack. Good work on getting it back, Paiboon. If they were thieves, they got away empty handed."

The Cambodian was unconcerned about the demise of Kaset, but he was very concerned about the two *farangs*. "I don't think they were thieves. I think they were CIA, boss. I have believed that from the start. I am certain they are the same guys we met in the Wancome Hotel. Only the CIA has the capability and motive to come after us like this."

"*Mai, mai.* Absolutely not. The CIA is impotent. This is not the same CIA that chased my father across the border into Burma. I know the CIA very well. I have studied this enemy very hard. It used to be strong but is now just another weak bureaucracy in Washington. They have had their nuts cut off by their own Congress. They would never authorize an operation like this. With all that killing? Never."

"But the CIA lady, Charly Blackburn, was at the Wangcome Hotel where the two *farangs* were staying. Remember? She must have been meeting with them. It could have been a coincidence that they were all there at the same time, but I really don't believe this was a coincidence."

The three of them walked leisurely toward the front of the warehouse. Khun Ut was reflective. He paused and blew a long stream of smoke from his cheroot. "You are right, of course, Ung Chea. I had forgotten about that. There must be some connection to the CIA, but still . . . maybe they are mercenaries. They must be mercenaries."

"Maybe mercenaries hired by the CIA?"

"I cannot imagine that. I have studied the CIA. Someone would have to authorize an attack like this. And even if that happened, they would not hire mercenaries. They require strict command and control over their operations and would be too afraid of what the congress and the press would say if it got out."

"Not even after what we did to their consulate?"

"You must understand, Ung Chea, the CIA is still very good at collecting information. That is true. They, along with the DEA, were hurting us very badly by exposing our operations and disrupting our distribution networks. It is for this reason that we attacked them at their heart, their Chiang Mai Base. Our attack has set back their operations against us for years. It instilled confidence in our allies that we are strong and fear in our potential competitors and enemies like the CIA, DEA, and the Thai government. We needed to strike and strike hard, and we did. The CIA's only possible response is to back off and try to convince the Thais to take action against us. That will not happen in my lifetime."

"Then who sent these mercenaries, Khun Ut? And why would they be meeting with Blackburn, a known CIA operative? We control all drug trafficking in this part of the world. We have no rivals, no competition."

Khun Ut stopped at the front of the warehouse and turned to face the Cambodian and Paiboon. He took a deep drag on his cheroot and expelled a lungful of smoke. "There are three people here in Thailand who can answer that question, the two *farangs* and Charly Blackburn. We will just have to ask one of them."

CHAPTER SEVENTY-ONE

Charly turned the Land Cruiser off of Route 110 at the little village of Bap Basang and headed west up into the mountains on rural Route 1130 toward Doi Mae Salong.

All of the roads this far north were unpaved and full of potholes. Small villages were scattered among the hills along the route.

She shifted the Land Cruiser down into four-wheel-drive as they climbed higher up into the mountains. Soon she turned off onto a small dirt road heading due north toward the Burmese border.

"This will take us up all the way to Ban Hin Taek, but we aren't going to go quite that far. About eight or ten kilometers up this road, there will be a logging trail heading off to the right. Keep your eyes peeled for it. Our meeting with Vanquish is in a small meadow about two clicks up that trail. A pretty deserted location."

The Land Cruiser bounced and churned and whined its way along the rutted road up higher and higher into the mountains. Culler was awake now. He leaned forward and placed his folded arms on the front backrests. "Well, at least we know we don't have any surveillance."

"No, you've got that right . . . except for the stray villager or hunter, we're not going to run into anyone up this far," said Charly.

"And Vanquish is arriving at seven?" asked Mac.

"He's never on time. I've waited for well over an hour at times, but he always shows up and—anyway—I can track him on my GPS."

"Does he know that watch he's wearing contains a GPS?"

"No, and don't tell him either. He never takes the watch off. It was supposedly a gift from his son. I told you the story, didn't I?"

"Yes, you did. This is a great op you put together, Charly. A real professional job. You should get a medal for this one."

"Speaking of medals, Harry MacMurphy, tell me how you got your Intelligence Star. I've heard lots of rumors, but no one seems to know the full story. No one I've talked to anyway."

Mac and Culler looked at one another and laughed. "Yeah," said Culler. "He got the medal, the same day he got fired."

"Yeah, I heard that too. I also heard you followed him out the door, Culler."

"Indeed I did."

"Well, I want to hear the story, the whole story. I also heard you are richer than God. Is that true also?"

Mac laughed. "Now that last part, that's real classified. Only a small handful of people know about that. Where did you hear that?"

"You know how it is in the clandestine service. We're a small, incestuous group of professional intelligence officers. It's our business to know stuff. Now, how can you do something important enough to deserve a medal, get fired for it, and end up with a bundle of money?"

"It's a long story."

"Don't give me that crap. I've got plenty of time. Tell me what happened."

"I will, but not now. I think you just drove past that trail you were looking for."

CHAPTER SEVENTY-TWO

Charly hit the brakes, cussed, and backed the Land Cruiser down the narrow road to the entrance of the trail. Once on the trail, she concentrated on her driving.

The trail was narrow and overgrown. Trees along the way scratched the bottom and sides of the vehicle. She drove cautiously until they reached a small meadow. The grass in the clearing was covered in dew, and a light morning mist rolled over it. She pulled out into the clearing, turned the heavy Land Cruiser around and headed it back into the trail. There she parked it for a quick and easy departure.

"Now we wait for Vanquish," she said. "He'll be coming from over there, on the other side of the meadow." She indicated a spot about fifty meters ahead where the trail continued north. "His village is a couple of miles northeast of us."

Culler glanced at his watch. "You timed this well, Charly. It's exactly nine minutes to seven."

"Well, I've done this a few times before. I keep trying to get him to vary our meeting locations and times, but he's very stubborn. He feels safe here and it fits in with his morning routine. His morning rides are a passion for him, and he rarely misses a day."

"Where is he now?" asked Mac.

She pulled her GPS out of her bag and turned it on. They looked over her shoulder as she zeroed in on their location and then expanded the map to show an area ten kilometers around them. The pulsating blip emanating from Vanquish's stainless steel Rolex appeared about two kilometers away.

"There he is and here we are. He's on his way. His village is over here, in this clearing. Ban Hin Taek is in this direction about fifteen kilometers from us in this valley." She expanded the map further so they could see. "He'll be here in about fifteen minutes."

"You want me to get the assault rifles out of the back seat for some extra security?" asked Culler.

"Sure, if you like. But I can assure you, we're safe here. We weren't followed. The only way they could find us is if Vanquish is compromised, and I'd bet my life on him."

Mac looked at her and then down the trail. "You already have, Charly."

CHAPTER
SEVENTY-THREE

Vanquish rode out of the morning mist from the north end of the trail, sitting tall and stern in the saddle aboard a large palomino mare. He wore colorful native Hmong dress with bright blue Chinese style baggy trousers and a gray wool vest with silver buttons.

His only concession to modern civilization was the broad-brimmed, black cowboy hat he wore. The hat's crown was decorated with a chain of native silver ornaments. He wore it pushed back on his head away from his tanned face. His skin resembled overcooked meat, but his penetrating grey eyes, surrounded by deep wrinkles from years of squinting into the sun, showed wisdom. He was of indeterminate age—maybe sixty, maybe eighty. He rode like he was joined with the horse.

When he spotted the two *farangs* standing by the Land Cruiser next to Charly, he jerked the reigns as if considering whether to flee, charge or stand firm. Charly waved him over with broad gestures of her arm, indicating everything was alright.

Vanquish trotted across the clearing toward them but remained sitting erect in the saddle after he reigned in the mare. As his aloof and penetrating stare fixed on the two *farangs*, Charly approached and reached her hand up to him. His pale eyes darted from one *farang* to the other in a suspicious, disapproving way.

"Don't worry," she said, taking his hand in both of hers, "these men are my friends and colleagues. I won't introduce you because none of you need to know each other's name. They have heard of your exploits with Bill Lair and Tony Po."

Culler and Mac approached and reached up to shake hands with Vanquish, who remained on his horse. "You know Bill and Tony?" he asked. When he reached down to shake hands with them, the saddle squeaked and the scent of leather enveloped him.

Mac said, "I met Bill Lair once many years ago when I was in training, and I met Tony Po up in Udorn shortly before he died. It was in the mid-90's. I was assigned there."

Vanquish looked down and asked, "How many fingers did Tony Po have on his right hand?"

Mac smiled knowingly. "Three. His middle and ring fingers were blown off while he was screwing around with explosives. He used to order four beers with his two outside fingers sticking up in the air like this." He held up his hand with pinky and index fingers extended.

Vanquish laughed, breaking the tension and showing yellow stained but straight teeth. "That is Tony." He swung down from the saddle and stood facing Mac, who was surprised at his shortness. "He was quite a character. Crazy, daring and indestructible. The Japanese on Iwo Jima tried to kill him, and the North Koreans tried at the Chosen Reservoir, and then the North Vietnamese and Viet Cong and Pathet Lao could not kill him in Southeast Asia, but all those beers and many gallons of Mekong whisky . . . that finally did him in."

Mac shook his head and laughed. "You're right, he was a legendary figure. He lived one hell of a life. And when he died he had a liver like a hockey puck."

"So you guys are SKY?"

Mac considered his response carefully. He knew that SKY was the cryptonym used by the Lao Resistance, including the Hmong, to refer to the CIA. Rather than go into details of their present situation, he figured it was best just to agree with the man. "Yes, we are. We are all colleagues. We are all SKY."

"Good, then we can get started." He wrapped the horse's reigns loosely over the rearview mirror of the Land Cruiser and turned to Charly. "Do you have the map?"

She unfolded a 1:50000 map of Northern Thailand and laid it out on the hood of the vehicle. Vanquish put on an old pair of yellowed reading glasses and set his gnarled index finger on the map.

"You know all of this Charly, but I will repeat it for the new guys. The opium is assembled in various movable refineries around here, here and here." He indicated areas along the border north of Mae Sai at Wan Ping, Tachilek and Wan Lom in Burma, proud to display his knowledge to his newfound SKY compatriots.

"There it is cooked in large pots and filtered through burlap bags and turned into a thick, dark paste. The places where the cooking is done are moved around on an almost daily basis to avoid detection by the CIA's surveillance planes. After the initial refining is done, the paste is dried in the sun and turned into something like putty. The places where the drying occurs are changed regularly as well."

Mac asked, "Do you have anything to do with that part of the operation?"

"No, all of that takes place in the hills near where the opium is collected from the farmers. There are others who bring the opium putty by donkey down to the warehouse in Mae Sai. That is where the next stage of the refining is done. It is very close to Ban Hin Taek.

"They cook it again in large drums and add lime to the solution. That turns it into a brown sludge which is scooped out and reheated and then they add ammonium chloride. After that it is filtered again and dried into a coffee-colored powder morphine base."

Culler said, "But the bricks we saw were white, not coffee colored."

"Yes, you are right. There is another step in the process. It is a bit more complicated and done at the warehouse with more sophisticated equipment, not in the movable jungle refineries. I do not know exactly how it is done. But I know they dissolve the morphine base in acid and then add charcoal and heat it again before filtering it through fine cloth several times until they have a fine, white powder. The powder is then pressed into one kilogram bricks. That is what you saw."

"And that's the end of it? That's pure heroin?" asked Culler.

Vanquish smiled. "No, not at all. The final refining process is much more complicated. It takes real chemists for that part."

Charly explained. "He takes over after the bricks are pressed at the Mae Sai warehouse. It's his job to get the bricks from Mae Sai down to the Mae Chan warehouse. The bricks are loaded onto donkeys, and he guides them down by caravan through the jungle. That's his job."

"And we never use the exact same route twice. We stay off the trails and meander down through the jungle until we reach our destination." He drew his ten fingers down the map from Mai Sai to Mai Chan to show the many possible routes he would take.

"Okay," said Charly to Mac and Culler. "That's your background briefing. Now let's get down to new business. We can't keep him here all day. It's best to keep our meetings as short as possible."

CHAPTER
SEVENTY-FOUR

Charly spent the next ten minutes debriefing Vanquish on the route he had taken on his most recent trip and the number of heroin bricks he transported.

His caravan was made up of eight donkeys carrying forty kilograms each for a total of 320 kilograms of heroin. He had been accompanied by two other men on horseback, all carrying AK-47 assault rifles and sidearms. He had hugged the Burmese border all the way to Wan La-ba, then cut almost due south through the jungle to Salong Noi before turning southeast to Mae Chan.

The trip took almost five days down to Mae Chan and two days back to Mae Sai, direct and empty. It was uneventful, hot, mosquito-infested, boring work.

When Charly was finished, she asked, "What about your next trip down?"

"We have another load going down the day after tomorrow: eight monkeys with about forty bricks each, the same team of three on horseback."

"Our colleagues would like to examine the shipment. Can that be arranged?"

He looked suspiciously at Culler and Mac. "How close?"

"Pretty close," she replied quietly.

Mac said, "We need to get close enough to take samples of the heroin. Scrapings."

The old man rubbed the stubble on his chin with a gnarled hand. "How much time will you need to take your . . . scrapings?" He emphasized the word *scrapings*.

Mac replied, "Ten, fifteen minutes at the most. Can you arrange that?"

Vanquish studied the map. "You will have to do it at night, when I am on guard duty and the other two are asleep. It will be risky. If you are detected we will have to kill you. Is this really necessary?"

Mac nodded his head. "It's extremely important. We won't take long and will do it silently. We'll just have to work out some signals between us. Give us a time and an exact location, as well as some sort of signal, and we'll be in and out without disturbing anyone."

Vanquish looked over at Mac and then Culler and then Charly. Finally he spoke. "I can give you an exact location on our first night out. There is one spot by a stream where we like to camp. After that it is hard to tell where we will be."

"Show me," said Mac.

"Here," he pointed to the map and tapped his finger on a location, "about two kilometers east of Wan Hsenta-na on the Burmese side of the border. This stream runs north and south. See where it bends like a horseshoe here? That is where we will camp on our first night out, on the inside of the bend of the stream—right here."

Mac jotted down the coordinates. "How will we know everything is clear and the others are asleep?" Charly and Culler were silently attentive.

"We will have a small campfire on the bank of the stream here, on the south end of the clearing. That is where my two companions will be sleeping. We will corral the donkeys and horses on the north side of this horseshoe. The donkey packs with the heroin bricks will be stacked here, in the middle."

"That's awfully close," said Charly.

"Yes, very close. The area in the horseshoe is not large. It is our job to guard each shipment with our lives. That is why it is never far from us. Whoever is on guard, in this case me, will be sitting on top of the packs while the others sleep. You must be very careful not to disturb the animals or the other two guards. If you do, you will wake everyone."

Culler and Charly looked at Mac, who was deep in thought. "What's the best route for us to take in?" he said.

"You can drive to Wan La-baon the Thai side of the border. Then you must walk north across the border for about one kilometer and then turn west for about four or five kilometers. The jungle is not too dense in that area, so you can make pretty good time on foot. I would suggest you circle around our campsite to the north and enter from the west. That way you will not come splashing across the stream right next to us."

The three of them smiled. "Good advice," said Mac. "What time?"

"I will volunteer for the midnight-to-four shift. No one wants that shift, so I will be sure to get it. I will also bring a bottle of Mekong whiskey with me for the boys. They should be out by the time you arrive."

"What's the best time for them to get there?" asked Charly.

"Between three and four, say three-thirty, after they have been asleep for awhile. They will sleep soundly, especially with their bellies full of Mekong. The horses and donkeys will be your biggest problem, but they know me, so when you get there I can try to comfort them while you do your . . . *scraping.*"

"Okay," said Mac. "How will you signal us that all is clear?"

"I will be sitting on top of the packs with my rifle across my lap. As soon as I see you, I will take off my hat and wipe the inside of sweatband. Like this. Then, when I think it is okay for you to come in, I will put my hat back on, get up, sling my rifle, and walk over to the corral, leaving the packs unattended.

"If I do not move off of the packs, you must stay out of sight. If I go anywhere other than the corral, you must stay out of sight."

"Understood," said Mac. The others nodded in agreement. "We'll see you in two days, at oh-three-thirty."

CHAPTER SEVENTY-FIVE

K hun Ut climbed out of the pool at his mountain retreat in Ban Hin Taek and limped toward a row of lounges. Two bikini clad, darkly tanned Thai women met him with towels and patted him dry before he plopped himself awkwardly on one of the lounges and lifted his stiff, mangled leg onto the lounge using both hands.

He had just completed his regular morning swim and was feeling invigorated. Now he was ready to get down to business.

Reaching for his cell phone, he pressed the speed dial. "Come over to the lodge, Ung Chea, and bring Paiboon with you. Now that Paiboon has inherited the responsibility for security at the warehouse, we should include him in our discussions. I am by the pool. It is a beautiful day. We will have breakfast at poolside before it gets too hot."

Pointing to a barefoot waiter dressed in starched white shorts and shirt, Khun Ut ordered him to set a table in the shade for breakfast for three. Thirty minutes later Paiboon and Ung Chea were escorted to the table by another servant. They bowed deeply and exchanged *wais* with

Khun Ut before sitting at the table. The waiter shook open starched napkins and placed them on their laps.

Paiboon was decidedly uncomfortable in such opulent surroundings. It was his first visit to Khun Ut's mountain villa.

Khun Ut, still dressed in a bathing suit with a towel tossed over his shoulders, toasted the two men with a tall glass of iced green tea.

"Welcome to my home, gentlemen, and congratulations to you, Paiboon, on your well deserved promotion. Ung Chea holds you in high esteem, and therefore I do as well. I am sure you will do very well in your new position."

Paiboon blushed and gave Khun Ut a deep *wai*. "Thank you, sir, for your confidence. *Khrap khun ma khrap.*"

Ung Chea was amused at Paiboon's discomfort.

When the waiter departed, Khun Ut asked, "What is the status of the surveillance on the CIA woman?"

Ung Chea pushed back from the table and turned to face Khun Ut.

"Well, um, let me start from the beginning. We, the police actually, found the police cruiser two days ago behind an abandoned charcoal factory in San Sai. That is a little town just east of Chiang Mai.

"I spoke with one of our police contacts from the district, and he told me that a villager had seen a large white SUV drive up and park behind the factory where the police cruiser was found. They suspect that the SUV picked up the two *farangs* there, where they left the cruiser, and took them away. The SUV headed in the direction of Chiang Mai."

"Did the villager get the license plate number of the SUV or the make of the vehicle?"

"No. He just described it as a big, white SUV. That is all he knows."

Paiboon, less intimidated now, volunteered, "I can go down there myself and talk to the villagers, sir. Maybe I can get a better description, or maybe the tire tracks will tell me something."

Khun Ut shook his head. "Good idea, Paiboon, but your job is here. It is better if we let the police do their own police work. We certainly pay them enough."

The Cambodian nodded. "I will speak directly with the constable responsible for that town. Perhaps he can get a better description for us. I will also suggest he look at the tire tracks to see if that helps. This country is full of white SUVs."

"But it is helpful information just the same," said Khun Ut. "At least it narrows our search. The *farangs* are probably holed up in Chiang Mai where it is easier for a *farang* to blend in, and they are probably driving a white SUV. That is something, anyway. Now tell me about the woman."

The Cambodian absentmindedly stroked the scar on his cheek with his thumb. "Yes, the CIA woman. She is very difficult to follow, Khun Ut. We cannot stake out too close to the consulate because the police have tripled their security there. The same goes for her residence. Security is heavy all over the place.

"She is also very good at avoiding our surveillance. We think maybe she comes and goes from the consulate during the day in cars other than her own. I think she hides in other people's cars going in and out. Then she may take taxis for her meetings. At least we never see her go anywhere during the day."

"So you do not know what she does during the day, but you do know that she goes to work in the morning and returns home at night. Is that all you can tell me?"

"Basically, yes, that is correct. Except for last night. She did not return home last night, and her car remained parked at the consulate. The surveillance team does not know where she is."

Khun Ut thought and massaged his knee. "I will bet you this magnificent mountain lodge that my father built that she is now with the two *farangs* in the white SUV. They are up to some sort of mischief, but they will be back. At least she will be back. You can count on that."

He turned to the Cambodian and spoke forcefully. "And when she returns I want you to grab her and bring her here to me. Intercept her between her home and the consulate. That is one route we can be certain that she will take. Set up an ambush and bring her to me. I have questions to ask her."

CHAPTER SEVENTY-SIX

harly, Culler and Mac drove back to Chiang Mai, but on their way they made one slight detour. They drove southwest along the border to the village of Wan La-ba to case for a good place to drop off Culler and Mac.

They found a spot on the northern outskirts of the village behind an old abandoned petrol station and junk yard. The far end of the junk yard, filled with rusting cars and trucks, was at the edge of the jungle. It was a perfect place for Charly to drop them off and pick them up with a minimal chance of being observed.

They arrived back in Chiang Mai in the late afternoon. Charly dropped the two men off at the safehouse—where they showered, shaved and cleaned up—while she drove to a nearby grocery store to pick up more provisions.

The men were happy to remove their disguises and were relaxing in tee-shirts and shorts when Charly returned. They fixed cocktails and sat around the kitchen table chatting before beginning to prepare dinner.

When the topic turned to planning, Mac took a long pull from his vodka-tonic before speaking.

"This whole God-forsaken country is out looking for us: police, Khun Ut's men, good guys, bad guys. It's only a matter of time before somebody spots us, disguise or no disguise, or they figure out we're driving that Land Cruiser."

He turned to Charly and placed his hand on hers. "And I'm especially concerned about you, Charly. There's no doubt they know who you are, and we have to believe that they have figured out that you're a link to us."

"Maybe, maybe not," she said, "but I agree we need to tighten up our tradecraft."

"And that means staying as far away from you as possible, Charly," said Culler. "We're placing you in jeopardy just by being here. You did a great job setting everything for us, with Vanquish and all, but we've got to cut the cord."

"I know, I know. I understand. I really do." She looked up at them with pleading eyes. She wanted to remain a part of the operation, and she wanted to remain close to Mac. "But you still need me to get you up there and back, and then you may need my help to get out of the country."

"I agree with Culler. I think it's becoming too risky. Why don't we use General Sawat to get us up to Wan La-ba and back?"

"You can't trust him, Mac. You know that. I told you. He's one of the most corrupt police generals in the country."

Culler said, "Everything's a tradeoff. Like the proverbial security-efficiency teeter-totter. He's been okay with us so far. Except for that yappy mutt and his ever-present bimbo, that is."

Mac laughed. "How about I give him a call and ask him what he can do. Maybe he's got a driver or a taxi or something. Then we could leave the Land Cruiser here and keep this place secure. We're going to need a place to come back to, and we certainly can't pitch up in a hotel any longer."

Charly stood up, downed the last of her white wine and set the empty glass down on the table.

"Well then, if you don't need me for anything else, I'll get dinner started. I picked up some pasta for us. Figured you would need a carb load before embarking on your adventure—without me."

She reached down to her bag and dug out her GPS unit. "You'll need this to keep track of Vanquish. Don't lose it and don't forget to return it when you get back. It's the only one we have to track him."

Starting to the kitchen, Charly turned back to the men.

"I just don't want to go home tonight. I want to stay here, with both of you. I have a bad feeling about this."

CHAPTER SEVENTY-SEVEN

Charly cooked a delicious dinner of pasta and salad. When they finished eating, Culler stood up, offered a fake yawn, excused himself and retired for the evening.

They all seemed to catch Charly's feelings of foreboding—or perhaps it was just normal pre-operational jitters—but something hung heavy in the air.

Charly and Mac made love slowly and passionately, with an intensity and a feeling of apprehension they had never experienced before. Afterward, they lay in each other's arms quietly for a long time, caressing one another. Neither wanted to sleep. Neither wanted the night to end.

Charly left early in the morning and took a taxi directly to the consulate where she had left her car. She had a full day at the office in front of her, having been away from her desk for the past few days; the cable traffic was piled high on her desk.

Mac called General Sawat who agreed to pick them up on the third level near the "D" elevators in the parking garage at Chiang Mai International Airport. The meeting was arranged for eight that evening, after dark and when the airport was still fairly busy with flight activity.

Mac planned to park the Land Cruiser somewhere near the pickup point and to haul whatever they needed in the two green duffel bags. They decided to dress casually in blue jeans, running shoes, short-sleeved shirts and, of course, their light disguises.

General Sawat was alerted that he may not recognize them at first, though that did not concern him in the least. He agreed to park his car, which he described as a black late-model Mercedes sedan, next to the elevator bank and wait for a knock on his window at exactly eight o'clock.

Culler urged Mac to ask the general to leave Noi and Ling Ling at home, but Mac demurred, citing the need for rapport with the general over Culler's sensitivities. When Culler argued that it would be more secure if Noi and the dog did not come along, Mac replied, "It is what it is," adding that the general might leave them at home anyway, since they would be driving half the night.

They spent their day organizing their gear, packing and re-cleaning and checking and reloading their weapons, and resting and watching the local news on TV. The police were still looking for the two Americans, Humphrey and Callaway, who had shot up the Wangcome Hotel in Chiang Rai and had rented the car that was blown up in Chiang Rai, although the reportage was far less frequent than before. There was still no mention of the shoot-out in the warehouse in Mae Chan.

CHAPTER
SEVENTY-EIGHT

They fortified themselves with an early dinner, put on their light disguises, loaded the two duffle bags into the back of the Land Cruiser and headed for the airport.

They parked their vehicle on the second level of the main parking garage, close to the "D" elevators, waited until one minute before eight, grabbed their bags and took the elevator up to the third level. The black Mercedes was waiting for them at the curb.

"*Sawatdee khrap*," said the General as Mac and Culler piled into the back seat with their bags. He giggled, "You look different than before."

"*Sawatdee khrap*," they replied. The car was filled with the strong scent of Noi, who was sitting in the front seat with Ling Ling at her breast.

"*Sawatdee Ka. Sabai dee mai?*" Noi said with a *wai*. The dog barked when she saw Culler.

"*Sabai dee*," said Mac.

"We're fine," said Culler, who barked back at the dog.

The doors slammed shut and the General hit the gas. "Where are we headed, gentlemen? The border maybe? You fellows are quite famous, you know."

"Yes, we know," said Mac. "But we're not leaving quite yet. We have another small job to do. Head north toward Chiang Rai and I'll direct you from there." Mac passed him an envelope. "This is for a round trip up north. I hope it is satisfactory."

The general drove with one hand while stuffing the envelope in his shirt pocket. "It feels very thick. I am sure it is quite generous. What do I have to do for this?"

"Just get us safely up north. I'll direct as we go, and then we will need you to pick us up in a day or two and bring us back here," said Mac.

"You are not going to Mae Chan by any chance, are you? Maybe shoot the place up again?"

Mac and Culler glanced at one another in the back seat. "What did you hear about Mae Chan?" asked Mac.

The General cackled. "*Mai pen rai.* I hear about everything, my friend. I knew it was you two guys the minute I heard about it. Khun Ut knows it was you as well. But trust me, I did not tell him. He figured it out for himself."

"What else did he figure out?" asked Mac.

"From what I have heard—and I have very good sources, you know—he knows you two guys are out to get him, but he can not figure why. He thinks maybe you are CIA. Are you CIA?"

Leaning forward, Culler put his hand on Sawat's shoulder. "Let's just hold off on all the speculation. Let's just say we're the good guys and they're the bad guys and leave it at that. Okay?"

"Okay, okay . . . no problem. I was just asking."

Culler spoke forcefully, but quietly. "That's the point, General Sawat, don't ask. You came recommended to us as a person of some integrity. Someone who would respect the privacy of his clients. Someone who would not play both sides at the same time. If that's true, we will all get along just fine. You will make money and be safe. If not, well, let's just say there will be severe consequences."

Noi looked at him with wide eyes and squeezed the dog closer to her chest, making the mutt whine.

Sawat pulled out onto the highway and floored the Mercedes, as if to say, *I'm getting the hell out of here before this guy loses it.* "Do not worry about a thing," he said. "Your secrets are safe with me."

"I certainly hope so," said Santos, leaning back into the soft leather cushions of the Mercedes.

Mac broke the tension. "Keep driving north through Chiang Rai and then head for the border town of Wan La Ba. Do you know it?"

"Yes, of course. I know it quite well. How fast do you want to get there? This car is equipped with blue police lights and a siren. We can go very fast if you want."

"No, no," Mac shook his head. "Just get us there safely and quietly, without drawing attention to ourselves. We're not in any great hurry."

CHAPTER
SEVENTY-NINE

They pulled into Wan La-ba almost three hours later. Mac directed the general to the abandoned filling station. The bright half moon in the star-filled sky illuminated the area, showing it to be quiet and deserted.

The Mercedes pulled slowly to the rear of the gas station, its tires crunching on the gravel, and stopped out of sight of the road.

General Sawat cut the engine and lights. "Okay, what next?"

Noi whined, "I'm scared, Daddy, and so is Ling Ling. I do not want to stay here. It is too scary and dark. *Mai sabai.*"

"*Mai pen rai.* It is okay, baby, we will not be here long. We are just dropping off our friends."

Mac and Culler grabbed their duffel bags and stepped out of the car. "We're good," said Mac. "We will be calling for a pickup in about thirty-six hours. Thanks for the lift. Please keep close to your cell phone, and be prepared to pick us up right here."

"You call and I will be here. You can count on it," said the general.

"We'll count on it, that's for sure," said Culler with a menacing glare.

They slammed the doors shut and took off at a trot for the edge of the jungle, duffel bags slung over their shoulders. Sawat slammed the Mercedes in reverse and hit the gas. Then he reversed gears and spun out onto the road, spitting gravel behind him. He hit the switch for the blue police lights and was gone, zooming back to Chiang Mai.

Once inside of the tree line, Culler and Mac slowed to a walk and let their eyes adjust to the darkness. Mac checked his GPS while Culler looked over his shoulder.

"Let's find a good spot about a kilometer from here to hide our bags and civvies and change into boots and Ghillie-suits. After we cache our gear, we should turn almost due west to this point here, by the bend in the stream. That's where we'll look for a good spot to wait for Vanquish and his caravan. We'll have lots of time to reconnoiter the area."

He set the way-points in on the GPS, hefted his duffle bag up on his shoulder, and headed down into the jungle. Culler followed close behind, stuffing his disguise moustache, wig and glasses into his shirt pocket.

After they found a spot to cache their bags near the base of a huge banyan tree, they changed, snacked on a couple of power bars, drank some water and checked their weapons one last time before heading west toward the rendezvous point with Vanquish.

They moved silently and slowly, using their night vision gear to pick their way through the heavy undergrowth. They figured it would take them about five hours to travel the five kilometers to reach the rendezvous point ahead of them. They were in no hurry. They would sleep when they got there around dawn.

CHAPTER EIGHTY

Paiboon was excited. It was the first time the Cambodian had trusted him enough to allow him to do anything other than routine guard duty. He was tired of being stuck doing boring security rounds at the warehouse or one of the other installations owned by Khun Ut.

The only time he had ever experienced any excitement in his job was during the attack on the warehouse by the two *farangs*. That attack had fortuitously resulted in his promotion to chief of security at the warehouse and, now this, his first stakeout: his first real operational job.

He was sorry about the unfortunate deaths of his colleagues, but he wouldn't have gotten to his current position if the attack hadn't happened.

He was now on the fast track in Khun Ut's organization, and he was most certainly getting an adrenaline rush on this job, even though he had been sitting there at the side of the road with the motor running for more than an hour already.

He sat at the wheel of a long, black stretch limo, wearing a shirt and tie, dark suit and chauffeur's cap. He had an important job—maybe the most important job of the entire mission.

The Cambodian had given him very specific instructions. He was to sit patiently at the side of the narrow, wooded road in the residential neighborhood, ostensibly waiting for someone, until signaled by the Cambodian to pull out onto the road and block it. The stretch limo would easily block both lanes of traffic.

Once the road was blocked, he would exit the vehicle, raise the hood and stand by the side of the road with his cell phone at his ear pretending to call for help. The Cambodian and the other guys would take care of the rest.

While sitting there alone in the limo in the early morning hours, he reflected on his conversation with the Cambodian at the warehouse earlier in the day. It was the conversation that had stimulated the Cambodian to invite him on this mission.

He had told the Cambodian about the birthday party he had attended with his family over the weekend. During the party his sister had told him that one of her girlfriends, the mistress of retired police General Sawat, was upset about the visit of two *farangs* to their villa. The girlfriend had complained bitterly about one of the *farangs*, a large muscular man, who had threatened her precious little dog.

The Cambodian had listened intently to Paiboon's story, congratulating him on his ability to recognize the importance of such a seemingly innocuous story.

"So," the Cambodian had said, nodding his head approvingly, "General Sawat is helping the two *farangs*. That is important information, Paiboon. I want you to find out more from your sister, and we will pay her generously for her cooperation. I will inform Khun Ut about this immediately." He embraced Paiboon, the first time he had ever done that.

Paiboon's earpiece squawked, jerking him out of his reverie. "She's up. The lights just went on. Stand by." It was the voice of the Cambodian.

CHAPTER EIGHTY-ONE

The alarm didn't startle Charly Blackburn. She had been watching the clock on and off all night. Her mind was spinning. She was worried about Mac and Culler, and she was concerned about her agent, Vanquish.

The fact that she had renewed her affair with Mac also troubled her. She was falling for him again, but when this operation was done he would probably move on again, like he had always done in the past. *Damn*, she thought, *why can't I ever get a break?*

Too much was going on in her head to sleep, so she was glad when it was finally six-thirty in the morning and time to get ready for work.

She pulled herself out of bed, turned on the lights and padded nude into the bathroom. She planned to get to the office a little early this morning. Her desk would be pilled high with stacks of cable traffic that had accumulated over the past few days while she was out of the office, and she wanted to plunge back into her normal routine. She needed to take her mind off all the stuff that was causing her stomach to churn and flutter. It was making her sick.

She showered, dressed in a cool, bright ensemble of print slacks and blouse and slipped into matching sandals. The last thing she did before heading downstairs for breakfast was to strap on her ankle holster.

Her maid had set the table with a healthy breakfast of juice, fresh fruit, mangos and sticky rice, yoghurt and coffee. She ate in silence on the veranda while reading the morning edition of the *Bangkok Post*.

The sun was already warming the morning when she tucked her unfinished *Bangkok Post* under her arm, grabbed her bag and headed for the garage and her silver Toyota 4Runner.

A uniformed Thai security guard swung open the gate to her compound, and she pulled out onto the narrow residential street that would take her past the Galse Shopping Center to the busy Charoen Prathet Road and north along the Mae Ping River to the consulate.

It was cool in the early morning hours, and the air smelled fresh. Rolling her front windows down to take advantage of the morning air, she concentrated on all that she needed to do when she got to her office, but not so much that she didn't notice the green pickup truck that pulled out of a neighboring driveway and dropped in a few car lengths behind her.

Something was not right. The road was practically deserted, which was not unusual for this time in the morning, but that pickup truck behind her was curious. She could see in her rear view mirrors two men in the front seat. Maybe they were workers coming from one of the homes in the neighborhood.

They had pulled out of one of the driveways beyond her villa, but what were workers doing there so early? And even if they were workers, why were they leaving at this hour? Shouldn't they be arriving?

She sped up and the pickup did the same to stay directly behind her, a bit too closely. She slowed down to let the pickup pass, but it slowed as well, keeping the same distance between them. As a car passed coming from the other direction, she became nervous. Maybe she was getting paranoid, but she was a professional—she could not ignore the signs.

She should get off the narrow residential road. The Galse Shopping Center was about a kilometer up ahead. Even at this hour there would be people at the shopping center—shopkeepers opening up for the day and deliverymen. She decided to pull in there. Maybe the pickup would not follow her into the parking lot.

She dug into her bag, pulled out her cell phone and placed it between her legs, ready to call security at the consulate, if necessary. She also removed the PPK from her ankle holster and pushed it under her right thigh where it would be handy.

Near the entrance to the shopping center the road curved sharply to the right, she turned into the curve with the pickup close behind her. Then she saw it.

Approximately one hundred meters in front of the entrance to the shopping center was a stretch limousine with the hood up, completely blocking the road in front of her. The limo's chauffeur was standing by the front of the vehicle, looking directly at her and talking into his cell phone.

Oh shit, she thought. *This can't be happening.* Her mind spun and her defensive driving training kicked in. She took a deep breath and blew it out slowly. She was calm now. She was in a bad situation, and she needed to get out of it.

She slowed down almost to a stop and dropped the 4Runner down into four wheel drive and low gear, then she lined up her left front fender with the left rear fender of the limo and floored it.

The 4Runner crossed the median of the road, engine wailing, and crashed into the rear of the limo, spinning it sideways and knocking the chauffeur off of his feet and into the ditch. She held the accelerator to the floor and bulldozed the rear of the limo out of the way, its tires screeching along the pavement.

Her rear wheels spun in the dirt at the side of the road, and then she was through and free. She jammed the gearshift up into drive, sped through the wreckage and skidded back onto the road. She popped the gearshift out of four-wheel drive to gain speed and floored it again.

The pickup followed her through the wreckage, its rear wheels spinning in the dirt at the side of the road and almost sliding into the ditch.

Then the shooting began.

The traffic on the other side of the shopping center's entrance was heavier due to the workers arriving from the more populated side of Chiang Mai. But she kept the accelerator to the floor. She passed one car after another, swerving to get back into her lane and to avoid cars coming from the other direction.

She could hear the bullets striking the rear of her vehicle, and she hunched low over the wheel to present as small a target as possible.

She wanted to reach the relative safety of Charoen Prathet Road, where rush hour traffic would already be moderately heavy.

She grabbed her cell phone and hit the speed dial for the Marine Security Guard Detachment at the consulate. The Marine on duty answered after two rings, and she screamed into the phone: "This is Charly Blackburn. I've been ambushed near the entrance to the Galse Shopping Center. I'm heading east toward Charoen Prathet Road and being pursued by a green pickup with two men who are shooting at me. Send help now! Please hurry. Now!"

She tossed the cell phone on the seat beside her without waiting for a response and pulled the PPK out from under her thigh.

Two bullets punctured her rear window and exited through the front windshield, making her wince and forcing her to drive faster. She sped through the light traffic, weaving in and out, with the pickup close behind.

She snapped off a couple of rounds out the window in the direction of the pickup behind her but held little hope of them hitting anything. Getting away was her main concern, but why not frighten them a bit, letting them know she was armed and dangerous?

She hit the entrance to Charoen Prathet Road, but it was backed up with traffic at the red light. She spun around the traffic on the shoulder of the entrance ramp, ran the red light and careened onto the main road. The pickup hesitated for a moment but then followed her around the stalled traffic, through the red light and up the ramp onto the road.

Blaring her horn to get people to move, she wove back and forth through the traffic with the pickup close behind her. *Why won't they drop off?* Three more rounds punctured the window, one dangerously close to her head.

They were still five kilometers from the consulate when she saw the Marine Security Humvee speeding toward her from the other direction, lights flashing and siren blasting. It passed her in a blur and then, as the driver recognized her and the green pickup, spun off the side of the road and reversed direction. The pickup was now between Charly and the swiftly closing Marines.

She continued to weave through traffic as rapidly as possible, heading for the safety of the consulate, while the security vehicle was gaining on the pickup. She heard the distinct sound of automatic M-16 fire behind her and gleefully thought, *Now the bastards will know what it feels like to be in the sights of U.S. Marines.*

The men in the pickup evidently did not want to mess with the Marines. They broke off the chase and exited the highway heading west.

As soon as she saw the pickup exit the highway, she eased her foot off of the accelerator. The Marines caught up to her and pulled alongside. They gave her the thumbs up sign and signaled her to follow them. She blew them a kiss and pulled in behind.

CHAPTER EIGHTY-TWO

She did what? You let her get away? This was supposed to be a simple operation." Khun Ut was furious. He was standing behind his desk in the Ban Hin Taek mountain villa, dressed in a tailored, eggshell-colored safari suit, jamming his cheroot at the Cambodian.

Ung Chea was not intimidated by Khun Ut's rant, but he was ashamed. "She is very good, sir. She drove through Paiboon's limousine like it was a movie prop. I never saw anything like it."

"Of course she is good. I told you that in the first place. She is CIA. You should have taken more men to do a proper ambush. The three of you were clearly not enough."

Ung Chea was not used to being berated by anyone, including Khun Ut, whom he considered to be a friend as well as a boss.

"I am sorry, Khun Ut. If I were Japanese I would commit suicide right here and now, in front of your desk."

"Okay, okay. Enough." Khun Ut collapsed in his chair and swung his good leg up on his desk. "Let us not dwell on the past. We screwed up. All of us. We should have used more people. We underestimated her. Now what can we do to get things back on track?"

The Cambodian dropped heavily into one of the chairs in front of Khun Ut's desk and massaged the nub of his missing ear, trying to get his mind around what had just happened.

"I think we are done with the girl. If she ever leaves the consulate again, we can be sure it will be with armed guards. If she does go back to her home, she will take plenty of protection with her. She will be out of reach for us, at least for the time being."

Khun Ut took a long drag from his cheroot and exhaled a stream of smoke toward the ceiling. "Maybe, maybe not. But . . . damn, she was key. She was the one with information on the two *farangs*, all the information. She was the only one who could tell us everything—what they are up to, who sent them and what their next move will be. *Mai pen rai*, we have to move on."

He thought, toying with his cheroot. "What about Paiboon's source? You know who I mean, the one you told me about who is close to Sawat's whore?"

"I was thinking the same thing, sir."

CHAPTER
EIGHTY-THREE

Mac and Culler reached the rendezvous point before daybreak, with a whole day to kill before the arrival of Vanquish and his heroin-laden donkey caravan. They checked his progress on the GPS regularly, noting the wristwatch Charly had given him was working perfectly. They would not be surprised by his arrival.

They found a comfortable spot, ate a snack of granola bars and water, doused themselves with mosquito repellent, and made themselves comfortable. They slept or just rested for most of the day.

"Come on, Mac, let's get moving. It's almost four o'clock. We've only got another couple of hours of sunlight left."

"Yeah, yeah, I know. I was having a great dream, though." Mac sat up, rubbing his eyes.

"I never met a person older than a teenager who could sleep like you can. How do you do it?"

"Practice, my friend, practice."

They scouted the area and found a good location about one hundred-fifty meters west of where Vanquish would set up his camp. An outcropping of rocks would give them good concealment from the camp, and there was a place where they could burrow into the undergrowth in case they needed to hide from anyone searching the area.

They stood side by side at the base of the boulders. Looking up, Mac said, "This is as good a place as any for us to wait for them. We can lay up there on the top of the rocks tonight and get a good view of their campsite. Now let's reconnoiter the area around here and take another look at the layout of their campsite."

They stood in the middle of the campsite area and looked around them, trying to reconstruct what Vanquish had told them during their meeting.

"The guy is really good," said Mac. "See how the stream circles the place like a horseshoe? Over there to the south is where they will have their fire and sleep. See the remains of their last campfire? Surely that's where they'll camp tonight."

"Yep, that's what he said they would do."

"And here, about where we're standing now, is where the packs of heroin bricks will be stacked. That means the donkeys and horses will be tethered over there to the north."

They walked to the spot and Mac pointed out signs of hoof prints and manure as indications the animals had been there before. "You know it's actually a pretty nice campsite. It's no wonder Vanquish didn't think he'd have any problem convincing them to return here for their first night."

"You're pretty good at reading animal shit. You must be part Indian. Let's find the spot where they crossed the stream the last time. I believe he said . . . I can't remember. Did he mention it?"

"No, he didn't, and we forgot to ask him. Damn. We don't want them crossing anywhere near the spot we picked out to observe them. Let's find it."

It didn't take them long to find the crossing spot. It was at the shallowest part of the stream, right in the middle of the bend of the horseshoe where the stream widened to make the curve.

"That's perfect," said Mac. "Now let's go back and wait for them. We can get another couple hours of rest."

"Is that all you can think about? Sleep? Getting your beauty rest?"

"No, it's not all I think about."

Culler rolled his eyes.

CHAPTER
EIGHTY-FOUR

I f Vanquish was making an effort to move stealthily through the jungle, he certainly didn't act like it. It was dusk and Culler and Mac were lying prone, side by side on the top of the boulders, when they heard the first sounds of Vanquish and his caravan moving toward them through the jungle.

"What's that?" asked Mac.

"What? I can't hear anything."

"That's because you've had far too many explosions going off too close to your head. You're half deaf. Listen."

"Sounds like animals. Do you think that's them?"

"Maybe. Or maybe it's a herd of elephants."

Twenty minutes later the caravan reached the stream, and they could hear voices and splashing as the animals crossed over to the campsite. They still could not see them clearly through the thick underbrush.

"Stay here and keep me covered while I try to get closer," said Mac. "We need to find out exactly what we're up against while there's still some light."

Mac slid off the rocks, checked his rifle and ammunition drum, and moved stealthily through the underbrush toward the campsite. Culler watched the man in the Ghillie-suit blend into the undergrowth and become practically invisible.

Culler surveyed the area with binoculars, but, aside from the occasional rustling of bushes as Mac moved closer to the campsite, he couldn't see anything.

The foliage thinned and the voices and the braying of the donkeys became clearer as Mac crept closer to the edge of the clearing. He dropped into a prone position and pushed himself deep into the underbrush. He lay motionless and surveyed the campsite through his binoculars.

Vanquish, clearly distinguishable with his broad-brimmed black cowboy hat, directed the activities. There were three men, including Vanquish. One wore a dirty white bandana on his head and looked to be about middle aged, and the other was much younger, maybe a teenager or early twenties. He wore a faded blue baseball cap. Both men deferred to Vanquish.

Vanquish and the older man busied themselves setting up a temporary rope corral for the three houses and eight donkeys, while the young man set up their sleeping area at the southern end of the campsite. The boy spread out a large tarp on the ground and strung a shelter sheet above it from surrounding trees, and then he went about collecting twigs and branches for a campfire.

Once the corral was complete at the north end, the two older men unsaddled the horses and unloaded the heavy packs from the donkeys. Carrying the saddles and packs to the middle of the campsite, they stacked them in a neat pile.

At one point just before dark, the boy, in search of twigs and branches for the fire, came dangerously close to Mac's hiding place.

Mac watched the boy approach and thought, *I've set up too close to the campsite. God don't let him spot me.* But he didn't, and Mac breathed a huge sigh of relief as the boy walked away from his position carrying an armful of branches back to the camp fire.

Mac lay motionless, as only a trained sniper can do, for the next four hours, observing every movement through his night vision binoculars.

Vanquish and the bandana guy ate their dinner and smoked by the fire while the boy took his dinner back to his post on the pile of packs.

After dinner the Hmong dug the bottle of Mekong whisky out of his saddle bag and presented it to the others, who were delighted at the unexpected treat.

They passed the bottle among them. The boy was on duty so he did not drink at all, and Vanquish drank very little, while bandana guy was happy to guzzle most of the bottle.

When the bottle was empty, bandana guy stood up on unsteady legs and stumbled to the bank of the stream where he took a long, wobbly pee. Then he wove his way back to the sleeping area, fell unto the tarp and passed out.

The Hmong flipped his cigarette into the fire, checked on the boy one last time and joined the bandana guy on the tarp to get a couple hours of rest before his midnight shift.

Mac remained where he was until he saw the boy climb off the packs, walk over to the Hmong and shake him awake. The boy and the Hmong exchanged places, the boy on the tarp and Vanquish on the pile of packs. The Hmong lit a cigarette, took a deep drag, and settled in for the rest of the evening.

Mac gently backed out of his position and quietly returned to the boulders where Culler was waiting. "It's about time you got back here," said Culler. "You missed dinner."

"What? You ate without me? Shows what kind of a friend you are."

"Okay, tell me what happened out there while I was laying in the dark on this God forsaken rock protecting your sorry ass."

Mac briefed him while munching on a granola bar and drinking from his Camelbac. He suggested they try to get some rest before heading for the campsite at zero three-thirty.

CHAPTER
EIGHTY-FIVE

They dozed, but neither one of them could sleep. They were actually relieved when three-fifteen finally rolled around. They were anxious to get on with it.

They left everything behind with the exception of their weapons, night vision gear and the vials of ricin. The night was cloudy with a half-moon, and the only sounds were created by the light breeze rustling through the branches and the occasional scream of a monkey.

The night vision gear illuminated their way, and the "green line of death" of their assault rifles danced in front of them. They moved stealthily in the direction of the campsite with Mac in the lead.

When they reached a spot near where Mac had done his earlier observations, they dropped into the prone position, side by side and surveyed the campsite. Vanquish was sitting on the packs smoking a cigarette.

"There's the campsite," whispered Mac, indicating the area at the south end where a small campfire was burning and the tarps were strung.

They could see the two guards sleeping and could clearly hear the drunken snores from the older man.

"Sounds like that bottle of Mekong was put to good use," whispered Culler.

"I like Vanquish. He's bold, resourceful . . . a terrific asset. Charly got herself a real good one this time. Let's make sure we pull this off without a hitch. I wouldn't want anything to happen to him."

Culler turned his attention to the makeshift corral where the horses and donkeys were tethered. "Things look pretty quiet on the other end as well. The animals make less noise than that drunk over there."

They laid there quietly for a few more minutes, observing the campsite and waiting for their watches to slowly tick down to three-thirty.

Vanquish did the same and at exactly three-thirty he took one more long look in both directions and then removed his hat in a sweeping, theatrical motion and wiped the inside of the sweatband. He replaced the hat on his head in another sweeping motion and stood up stiffly by the side of the pile of packs.

They watched him for another few moments while he squinted in their direction, clearly not seeing anything.

Mac nudged Culler and they stood up quietly, advancing slowly toward Vanquish, weapons at the ready with green infrared laser lines, visible only to them, bouncing around the site.

They spread out and approached Vanquish from two sides. With the darkness of the trees behind them, he did not notice them until they were less than fifteen feet away from him.

When he finally saw the two shadows moving toward him, he jumped back and shouted a startled whisper at them: "Damn, where did you guys come from? Whew, you are like a couple of ghosts."

Holding up a hand, Mac moved closer to him and whispered. "It's okay. We got your signal. Everything looks great. The other guys are asleep, and it looks like one of them is going to have a huge hangover in the morning. Good work."

Culler waved at him, gave him the 'okay' sign making a circle with his thumb and index finger, and moved silently to the pile of packs and dropped to his knees. Sliding the pack containing the boxes of vials from his shoulder, he looked up at Mac and Vanquish.

Mac put his arm around the Hmong's shoulders and guided him back toward the corral area. "Let's go over there so the animals can get used to us and let him do his work in private."

"Scrapings, right?" said Vanquish with a smirk.

"Right. Scrapings."

Culler worked rapidly and methodically. The heroin bricks were individually sealed in a heavy plastic wrap. They were then wrapped, twenty bricks to a pack, in heavy burlap-like plastic material. Each donkey carried two packs, one on each side, in a heavy leather saddlebag-like sling which fit over the donkey's back.

While Vanquish and Mac chatted quietly near the corral, Culler began sliding the packs up and out of the saddlebags one by one to prepare them for their injections.

Moving to the first pack of twenty kilos, he began injecting each of the ten bricks on the outer side with one cc each of the ricin. He plunged the needle through the outer plastic burlap wrap and through the heavy individual plastic wrap deep into the center of each chalky brick to allow the poison ample room to be absorbed without a trace.

He worked rapidly, emptying one ten-cc syringe in the outer ten bricks of the first pack and placing the empty syringe carefully back into its Styrofoam container.

He decided it would be quicker to do only the outer bricks; after all, the entire shipment of heroin would be sent to Hong Kong where the chemists would mix it in exacting proportions with acetic anhydride and ethyl alcohol in vats to turn it into pure heroin base. He slid the first pack back into its saddlebag pouch and reached for another, repeating the process with the next pack.

At first the needle slid easily through the heavy plastic burlap outer covering and through the plastic wrap deep into each brick, but while he was working on the third pack the needle almost broke off while he was trying to push it through the thick burlap-like outer packing.

He cursed under his breath. His greatest fear was to break off a needle and spew the highly toxic ricin on his hands. He remedied the situation by taking out his knife and poking a small hole in the outer wrapping with the point. The needle then slid easily into the center of the chalky heroin brick.

Santos continued to work silently and methodically, using his knife to open a tiny slit in the outer burlap-like wrapping before injecting the ricin into the bricks, while MacMurphy kept the Hmong occupied in light conversation while petting the horses at the edge of the corral.

No one noticed when the heavy snoring stopped.

CHAPTER
EIGHTY-SIX

Khun Ut and the Cambodian listened intently while Paiboon briefed them in the dimly lit local restaurant. They were drinking cool Amarit beer served in frosted mugs and enjoying a light lunch of *Tom-yan* soup, sticky rice and *Phat-Thai* noodles with assorted curries.

Paiboon had hardly touched his food but Khun Ut and Ung Chea ate ravenously as they listened, shoveling the aromatic spicy food into their mouths by the spoonful and guzzling their beers.

Paiboon gestured with his spoon. "Noi hates the *farangs*, that is why she is so talkative. We can use that to our advantage." He thought a moment. "Actually, to be more precise, she only hates one of them. She described him as a big brute with a scar on his lip that turns red when he snarls, which is often, she said."

"She actually likes the other guy. She said he is polite and speaks some Thai and knows Thai customs very well. She said he is taller and slimmer than the other guy and handsome for a *farang*, with grey hair which makes him look older than he is. He is the one who is in charge. He acts like the boss."

"What is General Sawat to them?" asked the Cambodian between loud slurps of his *Tom-yan* soup.

"He is like some kind of liaison. They picked up heavy boxes of guns and ammunition and other military type gear at Sawat's villa in Chiang Mai. All that stuff was shipped ahead to General Sawat. That was the first time Noi met them."

Khun Ut pushed back from the table and lit a cheroot. "So that is where they got their fancy weapons, through Sawat. Hmmm. What else?"

"The next day Sawat took them on a tour of the Golden Triangle in his plane. They flew over Ban Hin Taek and our warehouse in Mae Chan."

"How does she know that?" asked Khun Ut.

"She was with them. The General takes her everywhere. She is always at his side, along with her Shih Tzu named Ling Ling. That is why she hates the big *farang*. He threatened to kill her dog."

The Cambodian laughed. "I've seen that yappy mutt. I understand why he would want to wring its scrawny neck."

Paiboon said, "She is very attached to her dog."

The Cambodian nodded, "Yeah, she suckles it at her breast like an infant. Disgusting."

"What else?" asked Khun Ut.

"This is the best part. The General and Noi met them at the airport last night and drove them up to a small village on the Burmese border named Wan La-ba. They dropped them off behind an old junkyard and they walked into the jungle carrying their gear in duffle bags."

"That means they are up to something right now," said the Cambodian. "What could they be doing up there?"

Khun Ut shook his head and blew out a long stream of smoke in exasperation. "I know Wan La-ba. I had an aunt who used to live up there. It is in the middle of nowhere. Not close to anything. What could they be doing way up there?"

Ung Chea massaged his scar in thought. "Could they be hunting? You are right, there is nothing up there."

Khun Ut's eyes widened. "Oh yes there is. They are hunting all right. They are hunting for one of our heroin shipments. They go right through that area on their way down to Mae Chan."

CHAPTER EIGHTY-SEVEN

Phom sia jai, khrap. What you doing?" said bandana guy. He stood over Culler Santos, not ten feet away, with his assault rifle at his hip, leveled.

Culler looked up startled, straight into the muzzle of the AK-47. His own rifle was out of reach at the edge of the packs. He had the knife in his hand and instinctively pointed it toward his assailant in a defensive posture.

Bandana guy blinked his bleary eyes and shook his head. "You gonna get me scared with that little knife?"

Then Culler remembered the kind of knife he held. He brought his other hand up to the round metal handle of the Spetsnaz and removed the round safety pin with his thumb. He raised the knife out in front of him, holding it with both hands and pointing it directly at bandana guy.

The bandana guy looked at him quizzically. "That knife do you no good, asshole. Put down, stand up and get away from packs."

Culler pressed the trigger button in the handle. The blade shot out and hit bandana guy square in the middle of his chest, piercing his breastbone, penetrating his heart and knocking him backward with the force of a karate punch. He let out a surprised grunt and hit the ground dead with a thud.

"Holy shit!" muttered MacMurphy, hurrying toward Santos, the Hmong close at his heals.

The trio huddled around the dead bandana guy, looking down at him in astonishment. "That is some knife you got there," whispered Vanquish.

"Never bring a knife to a gunfight, unless its one of those . . ." whispered Mac to no one in particular. He turned to Vanquish, placed his hand gently on his shoulder and whispered, "Please go check on the kid while we try and figure out what to do next."

The Hmong walked to the campfire and looked down at the boy. The kid was curled up in a fetal position hugging his pillow and breathing heavily, deep in sleep. When he returned he found Santos quickly finishing his job of injecting the remaining vials of ricin into as many heroin bricks as he could readily access. Santos did not try to hide his actions. He didn't even look up.

MacMurphy walked over to the dead man, pulled the Spetsnaz blade out of the man's chest and wiped it clean on the man's shirt. He turned to Vanquish and asked, "What are we going to do now? How are we going to cover this up and protect you?"

The Hmong looked over at the body and pulled a pack of cigarettes from his pocket. Seemingly in no hurry to respond, he shook a cigarette from the pack and lit it. He inhaled deeply and blew out the smoke in a long sigh.

"Well, I very happy you did not shoot him. That be very, very hard to explain. A knife wound is different. He was fighter and a drunk. Maybe I tell them he got out of control and we fought and I had to kill him, or maybe he fell on his own knife during our struggle, or something like that . . ."

"What about the boy?"

"Yes, the boy. He did not see nothing. He was sleeping. And, well, he is my nephew. He will say anything I tell him to say."

Culler stood up and joined them. "That's it. We're done. Now what are we going to do about bandana guy over there?"

"We were just discussing that," said Mac.

Vanquish took another deep drag on his cigarette. "I take care of this." He walked over to the body and removed the man's knife from its scabbard. He glanced back at the two *farangs* momentarily and bent over, plunging the knife deep into the man's chest at the exact spot where Mac had removed the Spetznaz knife. Then he kicked the body over onto its stomach.

"That should do it. Now you guys better get out of here before my nephew wakes up. Seeing two *farangs* standing here would not be good thing. I will take care of everything here. Do not worry . . ."

CHAPTER EIGHTY-EIGHT

Santos and MacMurphy shook hands with Vanquish and vanished into the jungle undergrowth. They flipped down their night vision goggles and moved rapidly back to their staging area by the rocks, retrieved their packs, checked their GPS and headed off toward the place where they had cached their duffle bags and clothing

They stopped only long enough to bury the Styrofoam boxes of empty syringes. While they were scraping out a hole with their knives, Culler said, "I sure hope what we just did won't harm any innocent people."

Mac stopped digging and looked up at him. "I know. That would be too bad. But we've got to expect some collateral damage. It's inevitable. We can't control the results . . . But I do know one thing."

"What's that?"

"Whoever touches this stuff—this heroin—is not innocent. There may be degrees of innocence or guilt, but no one using this shit is totally innocent. People who play with this kind of fire are bound to get burned."

"That may be true, but still . . ."

"No buts about it, Culler, this operation has the potential to bring Khun Ut and his entire drug syndicate down. That's a good thing. No doubt about it. And no one is going to die who doesn't first shoot some of this shit into his veins. That's also a good thing."

"Yeah, I know you're right. I just wish we could control the outcome a little better . . ."

"Can't believe you of all people are going soft on me . . ."

They finished burying the boxes in silence and when they were done and satisfied that the spot was well camouflaged, Culler asked, "You got any of Barker's anti-animal stuff with you? We don't want anything digging up this stuff."

"Right, good idea." Mac sprinkled the area thoroughly and, satisfied that no one would ever find evidence of what they had done, they took off into the night, rapidly heading east in the direction of Wan La-ba.

CHAPTER
EIGHTY-NINE

The next morning, the Cambodian was sitting across from General
Sawat on the veranda of the general's villa when Sawat's cell phone
rang. The questioning had not yet gotten nasty.

They were having breakfast. Noi was still upstairs in her bedroom,
putting on makeup and dressing. Two of the Cambodian's husky body-
guards stood with arms crossed, backs against the double entrance doors
that led to the pool deck and veranda.

Sawat glanced at the number on the caller ID and repelled. He tried
to regain his composure but knew the Cambodian had seen his reaction.

"Who was it?" the Cambodian asked.

"Um, no one," replied Sawat, rejecting the call and putting the phone
back into his pocket.

"Who was it?" the Cambodian repeated, more forcefully now, staring menacingly at Sawat.

The General stuttered, "It is nothing. Nothing. A client. It can wait.
Would you like some more coffee?"

Ung Chea took advantage of the moment. "It is them, isn't it? Those two *farangs* you have been helping. They want you to pick them up somewhere around Wan La-ba, where you dropped them off. Isn't that right?"

The general's eyes grew wide. He fidgeted, his palms were sweaty and his mind raced. *How much does the bastard know? I must remain calm. I can talk myself out of this, but I must find out how much he knows. How could he know about the farangs?*

"Yes, I dropped off two *farangs* near Wan La-ba the night before last. They paid me well for the lift. But I have no idea who they are or what they are up to. It is my business not to ask questions."

The sudden backfist knocked Sawat off his chair. Coffee, croissants and dishes crashed across the pool deck.

The Cambodian jerked the old man to his feet by the front of his shirt, righted the toppled chair with his other hand and slammed him back into it.

"What about the guns you delivered to them? What about the plane ride to Ban Hin Taek and Mae Chan? Tell me you don't know anything about these things."

He crashed another fist into the old man's solar plexus, knocking the air from his lungs. He followed up with a left cross to the side of the head which sent the old man sprawling to the floor once again.

Noi came running and screaming down the stairs and out onto the veranda, the dog yapping in her arms. Ung Chea motioned the guards to stay where they were and stopped her before she could reach the General. He ripped the dog from her arms by the back of its neck and tossed it high across the veranda and into the pool. Then he hit her with an open handed slap that sent her sprawling as well.

Ung Chea was breathing heavily from the exertion, but pleased at the results. He took a deep, calming breath. "Now everyone sit down quietly and listen to what will happen to you if you do not tell me the whole story and cooperate fully with me from now on."

CHAPTER NINETY

S antos and MacMurphy were relaxing out of sight at the edge of the jungle when the general returned Mac's call. They had changed back into jeans and tee shirts, but kept their assault weapons close at hand.

"Hello. This is Sawat. I am sorry I missed your call. Is this Mr. Humphrey?"

"Yes," said Mac. "Is everything okay?"

"Everything is fine. Just fine. Are you ready to be picked up?"

"Yes, as soon as possible. Can you use the chopper? It'll be faster."

"The chopper? No problem. Are you in the same place?"

"Yes, at the old petrol station. You can take us back to the airport. Okay?"

"Okay, I will leave right away. I should be there a little before noon. Is that alright?"

"Sure, as early as possible. We'll be waiting. See you then. Bye."

"Good bye Mr. Humphrey."

Santos watched Mac closely during the conversation. "Is everything okay?" he asked.

"I don't know. He seemed . . . I don't know . . . frightened . . . nervous maybe. He certainly wasn't his jovial old self, and I don't like the way he cut me off when I called the first time. That was strange . . ."

Culler thought for a moment. "What was it old Bert used to say while we were in training down on The Farm? 'If it doesn't taste good, spit it out.' Something like that. Remember Bert?"

"Oh yeah, I remember him—huge guy who taught jungle survival. He's the one who showed us how to catch monkeys, snakes and all that good stuff to eat."

"That's him. He was referring to plants when he made that remark. He said there were lots of good things to eat in the jungle, but you had to be careful because some things could poison you."

Mac chuckled, "So he told us to taste first and if it tastes bitter or rotten to spit it out. He said your tongue was put in your mouth for a reason—to stop things that might kill you going past it down into your stomach."

Culler pulled at his ear. "So what do you think? Should we spit this one out?"

"Yep, I do. I really do. Let's not hang around here and wait to get ambushed by Khun Ut's men. I don't want another shootout. Let's just get the hell out of Dodge on our own."

CHAPTER
NINETY-ONE

Fuller and Mac gathered up their gear, put their assault rifles and Ghillie-suits out of sight in their duffle bags and donned their hats and light disguises. They carried their handguns concealed under their shirts in the small of their backs.

They walked out of the jungle, across the junk yard and stopped at the abandoned filling station by the side of the road.

"What do you think?" asked MacMurphy. "Do we hitch a ride, steal a car, what?"

"I don't see any cars around here to steal. We could walk back towards the town. There must be something we could grab in town."

An old pickup truck rounded the curve and rattled toward them. Mac dropped his bag and hurried to the side of the road and put his thumb out. The driver, an elderly man with a woman sitting beside him, started to slow down but when he saw the two of them he sped up and made a wide circle around them.

"I think we look too threatening," said Mac, watching the rear of the vehicle disappear down the road. "Why don't you take the bags and get out of sight behind the garage. Maybe it'll be easier to get someone to stop if there is only one of us."

Two more cars passed without stopping. Mac glanced at his watch. Almost an hour had passed since they spoke with General Sawat. They were running out of time. They had to get out of there and on their way pretty soon or they were going to end up fighting Khun Ut's men again.

Then he had an idea . . .

He ran back to where Culler was hiding with the bags and opened his duffle bag.

"What are you doing?" Culler asked.

"Getting some money," Mac replied. He pulled a wad of $100 bills out of the bag and hurried back toward the road.

He waited and waited, sweating and pacing up and down the side of the road, glancing at his watch every few moments. They had to get moving.

He heard it before he saw it—a large truck growling and grinding gears was heading toward them from the north. He stepped out into the middle of the road and held out a fan of green $100 bills and waved them at the driver.

The truck, loaded with burlap bags full of charcoal, rounded the curve and the driver dropped it down a gear and hit the accelerator. Mac barred his way, waving both hands for him to stop and holding the money up high so the driver could see.

At first it appeared the truck was going to run him down, but then Mac could see the driver's eyes widen when he saw the money.

The driver hit the brakes and brought the truck to a screeching halt in the middle of the road inches in front of Mac.

Mac walked around to the driver's side, still holding the money in his hand in front of him and waving it at the driver. "*Sawatdee khrap,*" said Mac with a deep *wai*.

The puzzled driver, covered in charcoal dust, replied, "*Sawatdee khrap*," and returned the *wai* hesitatingly.

In halting Thai and with gestures, Mac indicated he needed a lift south and handed the driver one of the hundred dollar bills. The driver took the bill with wide eyes and nodded while regarding the remaining bills in Mac's hand quizzically.

Mac called to Culller who came running toward them carrying both duffle bags. When the driver flinched, he removed another one of the bills and handed it to the driver. The driver was catching on. He gave Mac a grateful *wei* and said, "*Khrap khoon khrap.*"

"*Mai pen rai, khrap,*" said Mac.

Culler and Mac climbed onto the dusty long wooden bench that served as a front seat for the old truck and slid in next to the driver. They stowed their duffle bags under their feet and the driver pulled out, gears grinding, heading south. They were glad to be on their way out of Wan La-ba.

The driver drove like a maniac, hogging the middle of the road and forcing oncoming traffic off onto the shoulders of the road to avoid him.

Like most Thai truck drivers, he chewed the mildly narcotic betel nut to help keep him awake and to relieve the boredom of driving. He spat the brown betel nut juice out his window like a cowboy.

The spray annoyed Culler but he said nothing, happy to have finally gotten a lift out of Wan La-ba.

Mac used his limited Thai vocabulary to engage the driver in polite conversation while they careened down the highway. The driver was surprised and happy to chat with a *farang* in Thai. He smiled broadly showing a mouthful of teeth blackened by years of betel nut.

Mac learned that the driver was headed for *Krung Thep*—Bangkok—with a load of charcoal collected from northern villages. That was good news. It meant he would be driving straight through Chiang Mai. The driver agreed to drop them off at the airport in Chiang Mai on his way.

Mac rewarded him with another $100 bill. The driver beamed and thanked him profusely. He was holding more money in his hand than he had seen in his entire life. He was deeply grateful for the luck he was experiencing today. The driver reached up and rubbed the belly of the jade Buddha which dangled from his rear-view mirror.

CHAPTER NINETY-TWO

It was close to noon when the charcoal truck reached the outskirts of Chiang Rai. Culler and Mac slouched down in the uncomfortable hardwood bench which doubled as a front seat, trying to keep out of sight. Soon they would be at the airport in Chiang Mai. They could not relax until they had retrieved their vehicle and were safely back at their safehouse apartment.

The driver was making good time, contentedly chewing his betel and keeping the accelerator of the old truck to the floor. They prayed they would get there safely without an accident. They didn't want anything else going wrong.

Mac's cell phone rang, jolting him out of his reverie. He glanced at the caller ID and recognized the Sawat's number. He looked over at Culler, giving him a slight nod, and answered, "Hello."

"Hello Mr. Humphrey. This is General Sawat. I am here at the petrol station but I do not see you."

Mac could hear the sound of the helicopter's prop churning and the nervousness in the general's voice. "I'm very sorry, General Sawat. We're on our way but we've had a slight mishap. Mr. Callaway has injured his ankle and it's taking us longer than we expected to get out of here. Please wait for us. We should be there within the hour. I'm very sorry to keep you waiting."

There was a long pause before the general answered, "Okay, okay, Mr. Humphrey. I will wait for you here." Then another pause and, "You are in the jungle, correct? And will be coming out at the same spot . . ."

"Of course. Just stay there and wait for us. We're moving slowly because, well, it looks like Mr. Callaway has broken his ankle. He's in great pain and can't move very fast. We'll be there shortly. Please be patient and wait for us. We're on our way. Okay?"

"Okay, Mr. Humphrey. I will wait for you right here. Goodbye."

"Thank you General Sawat. See you soon. Goodbye."

Mac glanced over at the driver for any indication he had understood anything that was said. There was none. The driver's bleary eyes were fixed on the road ahead of him. All of his attention was focused on getting his truck to Bangkok as soon as possible so he could begin celebrating with his newfound wealth.

Mac leaned close to Culler and spoke in hushed tones. "That should buy us enough time to get to the airport, collect the Land Cruiser and get out of there before he realizes we've tricked him."

"I certainly hope so, because if he's betrayed us, he knows our ultimate destination. You told Sawat you wanted him to take us back to the airport and you can bet the farm he conveyed that information to Khun Ut."

"You're right. Shit. No doubt about it."

The words were no sooner out of his mouth when the truck's right front tire blew and the wide-eyed driver nursed the wobbling old wreck to the side of the road and rolled to a stop.

CHAPTER NINETY-THREE

Tell me exactly what he said." The Cambodian, sat next to General Sawat in the front seat of the helicopter, rotor chomping the air above them. He emphasized the word "exactly."

"He said they are running behind schedule. The big one broke his ankle and they are moving slowly but are on their way."

"Do you believe that?"

"Yes, of course. Why should I not believe them? They know nothing about you. They will come out of the woods right here where they said they would. They will not get lost. This is where they went in, and this is where they will come out."

The Cambodian stared at Sawat for a long time, looking for a sign of duplicity. But there was none.

Sawat was a beaten, humbled man. It hadn't taken much to turn him. Only a few hard blows and the threat of a painful death—and that he would slice off Noi's gorgeous breasts and feed them to him, fried with sticky rice and curry sauce, for his last meal.

"Okay, turn this thing off and stay here where they can see you when they come out of the woods. And don't do anything stupid, old man, my men have you and this whole area surrounded, and you will be the first to die if you betray us."

The general cut the engine and sat back in his seat to wait. Ung Chea jumped down and slammed the door shut behind him. He pulled his walkie-talkie from his belt and spoke into it as he jogged out of sight around the front of the filling station.

"Okay, settle in and stay out of sight. They are running late. Keep your eyes open and do not fire until they are out in the open and you have a clear shot. And make sure you get both of them. They will exit from the north behind the junk yard and head toward the helicopter. You will have plenty of time so don't rush things. Be patient and stay down and out of sight."

One by one his men responded in acknowledgement.

He sat down on the ground in a doorway and lit a cigarette. After collecting his thoughts, he called Khun Ut and relayed what had happened.

" . . . so I have eight men deployed around the area. They are well concealed around the edge of the woods and will cut the *farangs* down when they come out into the open. Sawat is in his helicopter in plain view as a decoy, but they will never get that far."

"Are you sure they are still in the jungle?"

"Sir, um, I think so. I heard Sawat speaking to them. I mean, that is what they said. They are just delayed because the big one broke his ankle."

"Maybe, but then again, maybe not. Do not believe everything people tell you, Ung Chea, especially those guys. They can be very tricky. Are you certain they do not suspect anything? Did Sawat act completely normal while he was talking to them?"

"I, I think so, sir. Maybe he was a little nervous and out of breath because I had to smack him around a bit, but nothing he said was out of the normal. I guess it's possible they could be tipped off, but, I don't know . . ."

"I hope you didn't knock him around too much. General Sawat is a wily old fox and when he is cornered he will tell the truth—maybe not the whole truth, but the truth just the same. I owe him a lot."

"No sir, I did not know. What could you possibly be in his debt for?"

"He saved my father's life. Twice, actually."

"Twice? Really? How did he do that?"

"The first time happened in the early eighties when the new Thai Prime Minister, General Prem, and the CIA got together to launch a secret bombing raid on my father's headquarters in Ban Hin Taek. It was planned in such secrecy that even the pilots thought they were going on a routine live fire training mission. They had no idea what they were about to do. Not until they were in the air were they given the coordinates of my father's house and told to destroy it.

"But Sawat—he was a police colonel in charge of the Northern Thailand District at the time—heard the order to divert the bombers and immediately informed Khun Sa, who managed to escape only moments before the bombs began to land."

"Wow! Yes, I heard about that raid, but I did not know it was Sawat who tipped off Khun Sa. I am sorry I had to rough him up."

"Yes, it was Sawat. He saved my father again two years later when another Thai Prime Minister, General Chavalit, tried a similar secret raid on my father's headquarters. Sawat's tip saved my father once again. Very few people know that it was Sawat who gave us those tips. So I owe the man a lot."

"Yes, now I understand, Khun Ut."

"But do not worry, Ung Chea, you did the right thing. Just do not overdo it with the old man. Loyalty is of great value to me and it works both ways. I do not consider that Sawat has been disloyal. Not yet anyway. He just works for those who pay him . . . but that said, you may be correct in thinking he has tipped them off. Inadvertently or on purpose. So . . . maybe we should alert the police to the possibility that they may have made their own way to the airport, if that is where they are headed."

"Yes sir. Good idea. That is where Sawat picked them up and that is where they said they wanted to return. Maybe they are taking a flight out of there."

"Or maybe they have a car parked there or maybe they have someone waiting to pick them up. Anyway, I'll alert the police at Chiang Mai International Airport to be on the lookout for them. They are wanted criminals and the police will welcome the tip. I'll also send a couple of our guys from Chiang Mai to look for them. It may be unnecessary, but better to be on the safe side."

"Thanks, boss. I'll keep you posted on what is going on here."

CHAPTER NINETY-FOUR

Fuck!" said Santos, pounding his fist on the dashboard. "Fucking Murphy's Law. if something can go wrong, it will. Let's get the fucking tire changed. Quick. He's got a spare, right? Please tell me he's got a spare."

Mac spoke with the driver, who shook his head, and then turned to Culler. "Sorry, no spare . . ."

"Got any other great ideas?"

"We need to hitch another ride."

They were on the outskirts of Chiang Rai when the tire blew. The highway was lined with small, one story shops and noodle restaurants with corrugated steel roofs and flaking paint. It was lunchtime and a number of cars and trucks were parked in front of the businesses near the side of the road.

One restaurant near them had a large neon sign over the door spelling out the name "Pak Essan." It appeared to be more upscale than the rest and several cars were parked directly in front of it.

They recognized the area immediately. The Orchid Lodge, where they had stayed and met the young American couple, was a few hundred meters down the road.

The three of them jumped out of the truck and stood looking disgustedly down at the flat tire. Mac said, "This place brings back bad memories."

"You got that right. Let's get out of here *tout de suite* before someone recognizes us. I'm sure every last one of these people has heard about the car that blew up at the Orchid Lodge and the two *farangs* who were involved."

Mac glanced around him and his eyes fell on the Pak Essan Restaurant. "I've got an idea."

He turned to the driver, held out another one hundred dollar bill, and in halting Thai said, "Please go into that restaurant and ask if anyone would be interested in taking your two friends to Chiang Mai while you fix your truck. We will pay one hundred dollars for the ride, but we must leave immediately."

The driver happily pocketed the one hundred dollar bill and took off at a trot for the restaurant.

"Those hundred dollar bills sure work magic, don't they?" said Culler.

"Money is the best weapon there is—far better than guns and intimidation. But we'll see in a minute just how magical those Ben Franklins are. Try to stay out of sight and keep your fingers crossed."

A few moments later a middle-aged, thin man dressed neatly in dark slacks, a short sleeved white shirt and skinny dark tie came out of the restaurant with the driver. They walked to where Culler and Mac were standing by the truck.

The man put his hands together and bowed in greeting. "Hello," he said in good English, "my name is Sophon. I understand you want to go to Chiang Mai." They shook hands and exchanged respectful *wais*.

"Yes, Khun Sophon, and we are in a bit of a hurry because we do not want to miss our flight. We need to get to Chiang Mai International

Airport. Can you help us? We can pay for the ride." Mac held out a hundred dollar bill. "But we need to leave now or we will be late."

Sophon eyed the bill suspiciously. "That is very generous. I just arrived from Chiang Mai and am heading north, I do not know if . . ."

Mac pulled another one hundred dollar bill from his pocket and held out two hundred dollars. "We need to leave right away or we will miss our flight. If you can not take us we will have to ask someone else."

Sophon smiled and took the bills. "Okay, *mai pen rai*, I can be a little late today. Come with me."

Culler and Mac grabbed their bags, thanked the truck driver and followed Sophon to a sixties vintage, but well maintained, black Chevy Impala sedan. They threw their duffel bags in the back seat and Mac climbed in after them. Culler, fidgeting with his wig and false moustache which was becoming uncomfortable and unstuck in the heat, climbed in next to the driver.

Santos asked, "How fast does this thing go? I used to have one just like it. Mine was a convertible. That V-8 engine under the hood used to push it pretty fast."

Sophon smiled knowingly and gunned the old Impala up onto the highway and then south in the direction of Chiang Mai. "Then you appreciate the old American cars as I do, my friend. American cars ruled the roads all over the world in those days, now you can not find an American automobile outside of the United States. What happened?"

Culler said, "Corporate arrogance, greedy unions, high manufacturing costs and poor quality. That's what killed the American automobile industry. But thankfully a few of these old beauties still remain to remind us of the way things were."

Sophon laughed. "Yes, I admire all things American. I would like to visit some day. I have relatives in San José. They have invited me to visit, but I have to sell a lot of auto parts before I can afford the trip. And, well now I have a rather large family that depends upon me. So that is another problem."

Mac chimed in from the back seat. "Save your money, Khun Sophon, and send one of your children to school in the U.S. Then you will build your own ties and the rest of you can follow later."

"Yes, you are right. My oldest will be ready for university in two years. He hopes to get a scholarship and attend school in California near my relatives. That is his dream, and mine."

"Get us to the airport in one piece and without being stopped and another one of these one hundred dollar bills will be your tip—think of it as a kind of advance on your son's education," said Mac.

"Can do," said Sophon, pressing his foot on the gas.

CHAPTER NINETY-FIVE

Khun Ut had tipped off the the Chiang Mai airport police and municipal police to be on the lookout for the two Americans wanted for
questioning in the car bombing at the Orchid Lodge and the shooting
death of two men at the Wangcome Hotel in Chiang Rai.

The alert flashed their descriptions and spelled out their names—
Callaway and Humphrey. Police all over Thailand, and especially in the
north, were well familiar with the descriptions of the two, by now infamous, *farangs*.

Instructions were given to set up check points at the two main
entrances of the airport. Cars were to be stopped and the passengers
visually inspected. Those vehicles with *farangs* aboard were to be pulled
over and detained. The papers of all adult males would be inspected, and
all suspects matching the descriptions of the two suspects would be
detained for further questioning.

Police were warned that the two *farangs* were armed and extremely
dangerous.

Roving patrols of municipal police and airport security were instructed to cover the departure gates, both foreign and domestic, and the parking garages as well as all entrances and exits.

Seven of Khun Ut's men were sent to the airport to do their own independent surveillance. They were in plain clothes, armed and led by Paiboon. They were instructed to remain on the periphery and not interfere with the police, but to monitor closely the police checks at the exits and entrances.

The police were scrambling to set up checkpoints at the entrances to the airport when the old black four-door Impala carrying the two *farang* passengers drove past them and entered the airport unchallenged.

CHAPTER NINETY-SIX

T wo police cars with sirens wailing and lights flashing came toward
the black Chevy as it pulled into the main entrance of the airport.

"Whoa! What's that all about?" said Santos. The two cars sped
past and blocked the entrance behind them.

Sophon watched the two police cruisers in his rear-view mirror while
the two *farangs* reflexively slumped lower into their seats. "They are
blocking the entrance to the airport. Setting up a checkpoint. They do
that when there is a security alert of some kind."

"Hmmm," said Mac with a glance at Santos. "They're probably
looking for terrorists."

He knew exactly what the commotion was all about, and said a silent
prayer of thanks to God for getting them there when He did, before the
roadblock was set up.

Santos responded with a wide-eyed look and a nod that conveyed he
was in total agreement with his friend.

Mac said, "Take the entrance to the main garage over there, where it says long-term parking."

Sophon pulled into the garage, stopped at the automatic gate and took a ticket. The bar raised and they entered. "Now continue driving up the ramp through the garage toward the upper levels until I tell you to stop."

They passed the A, B, C, and D elevator banks on the lower level and then circled up to the second level where they repeated the process, passing the A, B, and C elevator banks.

They passed the Land Cruiser just beyond the C elevator bank. When they reached the end of the ramp near the D elevator bank they spotted two vacant spaces.

"Pull in there. In that space," ordered Mac, pointing in the direction of the nearest space. Sophon did as he was told. Thus far they had not seen any security in the garage. "Now lock the car and come with us." Mac pulled another one hundred dollar bill from his pocket and handed it to Sophon. "There is one more thing I need you to do for us."

Culler looked quizzically at Mac, eyebrows raised, but said nothing. Mac gave him a reassuring glance with a slight nod in return.

They unloaded the car and walked together back toward the Land Cruiser. When they reached it Mac unlocked the doors with the remote and they threw their duffle bags in the back. Then he turned and handed Sophon the keys.

Mac said, "I want you to drive us out of here, Sophon. I don't know who the police are looking for, but I have a hunch they are looking for a couple of *farang* drug dealers. Not us, but I heard something about it on the radio earlier today and I don't want us to be stopped and questioned. Will you help us?"

"Of course," said Sophon, clearly worried. "But I thought you were taking a flight out of here."

"We're too late." Mac glanced at his watch. "Our flight leaves in ten minutes. We will have to come back tomorrow. We tried, but didn't make it here on time."

Sophon's face showed disbelief, but all he said was: "Okay, but how will I get back to my car?"

"We'll drop you at a taxi stand in town and you can take a cab back, Okay?"

Culler and Mac crawled into the back seat of the Land Cruiser. Mac slid his H&K pistol from the holster at the small of his back and indicated to Culler to do the same. The gesture was unnecessary, as Culler already had his pistol out and by his leg. They kept the weapons low and out of sight but at the ready.

"We're going to slouch down on the floor so no one sees us," said Mac. "The parking ticket is in the ashtray in front of you. Just get us out of here safely."

Mac pulled a one thousand baht note out of his pocket and held it out over Sophon's shoulder in the front seat. "Here, this should cover the parking charges. Keep the change."

Sophon nervously stuffed the ticket and the one thousand baht note into his shirt pocket, backed out of the parking space and headed down toward the garage exit. When they reached the first floor of the garage they passed two airport police officers walking up on either side of the ramp. Sophon slowed and waved at them and they stepped aside and waved the Land Cruiser past after noting only a lone Thai driver in the car.

When they reached the garage exit one of the two toll booths was closed and the remaining one had two cars backed up in front of them waiting to pay. Sophon spoke softly over his shoulder to the men in the back. "There is only one attendant on duty. Only one booth open. Two police officers are inspecting the car that is paying at the booth."

Culler and Mac were down low on the floor, pistols at the ready. Mac, who was directly behind the driver whispered to Sophon. "Keep all of the windows up until you reach the booth. The Land Cruiser is high, so they won't be able to see us unless they get very close and look directly inside and down. Act natural and friendly and let us know if they decide to look into the back seat."

All Santos could think of at the moment was that he wished he had taken the suppressors for the .45 caliber pistols out of the bags before they got into the backseat. If they had to shoot their way out of this mess they were going to make a hell of a lot of noise, and that wouldn't help matters at all.

The first car finished paying and pulled away and the car immediately in front of the Land Cruiser pulled up to the booth.

CHAPTER
NINETY-SEVEN

Paiboon was stationed at the side of the road about forty feet from the exit of the garage. Another one of his men was stationed directly across the street from him. Both were dressed casually in dark slacks and light, untucked short sleeved shirts. Their weapons were concealed under the shirts. They intently monitored the police checking the cars exiting the garage.

Paiboon felt a rush as the big white Land Cruiser pulled up to the booth. There appeared to be only one person in the vehicle—a Thai driver—but something spooked him. Something was not right.

He watched the driver pay the attendant through the open window and wait for his change while the two police officers casually walked the length of the Land Cruiser on either side from front to back, looking disinterestedly through the windows.

What is it? His mind raced back in time. *What is it about that vehicle?*

The driver collected his change, rolled up the window and pulled out onto the airport exit road.

Then it dawned on him. *The two farangs had used a large white SUV in their escape. This was the type of vehicle that the villagers in San Sai said had picked them up behind the abandoned charcoal factory on the outskirts of Chiang Mai.*

Paiboon stepped off the curb out onto the street and started jogging toward the slowly moving vehicle, waving his hand and shouting for it to stop. His eyes locked on the driver's and he saw pure, unadulterated wide-eyed fear.

Paiboon reached the side of the SUV just at the moment the driver swerved and gunned the engine, almost knocking Paiboon off of his feet.

The SUV sped down the exit ramp and headed out onto the highway.

Paiboon screamed at the two police officers. "That is their car. They are in that Land Cruiser. You did not check the inside. Alert the police to go after them."

The nearest police officer glanced at his partner in disbelief and then turned toward Paiboon. "We did check. There was only one person in the vehicle. And if you continue shouting at us I will personally arrest you right here. Now shut up and let us do our job."

Paiboon stood in the middle of the road, speechless, and watched the white Land Cruiser disappear from sight.

CHAPTER
NINETY-EIGHT

Sophon pulled out onto the highway with his eyes fixed on the rear view mirror. He was relieved not to see anyone following him. He was still shaken by the crazy man who ran at him at the airport exit. "*Phom sia jai, khrap.* I am sorry. I almost run over that guy."

Culler and Mac straightened up from their cramped positions on the floor and sat up in the back seat. "You did great," said Mac. "Now continue heading into Chiang Mai until you spot a taxi stand and we'll drop you off."

Sophon wanted nothing more than to end this odyssey, collect his money and get as far away from those crazy *farangs* as he could. "Amarin Hotel is up on left. I could get taxi there. Is that okay?"

Mac said, "That would be perfect, Sophon. Pull in and we'll drop you off at the entrance. Maybe you could grab a nice, leisurely lunch inside the hotel before heading back for your car as well. That would put even more distance between us." Mac pulled the remaining three one hundred dollar bills out of his pocket and passed them up to Sophon.

"Take this for your extra time and trouble—and please don't say a word about this to anyone."

Sophon stuffed the bills into his shirt pocket. "Please do not worry about me. I go back and collect my car and be on my way. I will not say nothing. You very generous and I thank Buddha you are safe."

They pulled into the drive leading to the hotel and Santos said, "Don't go all the way to the entrance. Pull over here where we can turn around and avoid the congestion at the front door."

Sophon did as he was told and jumped down out of the vehicle, leaving the keys in the ignition and the motor running. He exchanged a deep, respectful *wei* with Mac as they exchanged places and Mac climbed behind the wheel.

"Khawp khoon ma khrap," he said, "I wish you both good luck and good fortune. May Buddha smile on you." And then he was gone, hurrying toward the front entrance of the hotel, glad to be out of there.

"Do you think he'll really keep quiet about this?" asked Culler, heaving himself into the front passenger seat.

Mac pulled the Land Cruiser around and headed back onto the highway toward the center of Chiang Mai. "I think so, for awhile anyway. By the time he has to explain where he got all of his newfound wealth and figures out who we are we'll be long gone."

Culler pushed back in his seat and took a deep, cleansing breath. "Okay, we made it safely this far, but before we can declare mission accomplished we're going to have to get out of this God forsaken country. How are we going to do that with every cop in Thailand on our trail?"

"I've been giving it a lot of thought. I think we should first go back to the safehouse to get cleaned up and rest a bit and get rid of all these alias docs, guns and military crap we've been lugging around. We can leave the excess gear behind and Charly can get the stuff out of the safehouse after we're gone. Then, with our civilian gear and true-name passports, we'll drive across the country to Nong Khai like a couple of tourists. Nong Khai is on the border with Laos. There's a new bridge there, the Thai-Lao Friendship Bridge. We can cross the Mekong over to Vientiane, and fly back home without having to go through Thai customs."

Culler frowned skeptically. "Won't we have to go through Thai customs in Nong Khai? It's a border crossing point, right? Same as an airport?"

"Same, but not same-same, as the bar girls often say. They certainly do chop people in and out, but it's a border town and not as sophisticated as say, Bangkok or Chiang Mai. They don't have the on-line computer hook-ups like those major cities. And then . . . well, I have some good contacts there. They will be able to help us get across the river safely. Once we're in Laos we'll be home free."

A police car sped toward them with lights flashing and siren wailing, causing them to stiffen, but it passed and disappeared in their rear-view mirror, and they relaxed once again.

"Is that where you were posted way back when? Nong Khai?"

"No, but close. I was in Udorn, about fifty kilometers south of there. That was back in the late nineties. The base is in Udorn."

Mac slowed the Land Cruiser and turned onto the tree lined street leading to the safehouse apartment.

CHAPTER

NINETY-NINE

W orking silently, they unloaded the Land Cruiser in the garage and carried the duffel bags up to the apartment. There they sorted out their gear, showered, cleaned out the refrigerator of all of the leftovers, and took a long nap.

Mac made two brief calls on his throwaway cell phone. The first was to Charly Blackburn to tell her of their plan to leave the country via Nong Khai and to alert her that their gear and alias documents would be left behind in the safehouse; the second was to Maggie in Fort Lauderdale to tell her they had accomplished their mission and were on their way back home.

Maggie in turn informed Edwin Rothmann of their plans and mission success.

They waited until dark before leaving the apartment. They were refreshed, rested, cleaned up and well fed. They dressed casually in jeans and light, short sleeved shirts. They carried their true name passports and wallets and several hundred dollars in cash. The rest of the remaining cash, approximately twenty thousand dollars, was concealed in the lining of MacMurphy's travel bag.

They discussed leaving their side-arms behind as well, but agreed that they would be better off with them during their approximate ten hour drive across the mostly deserted Thai countryside to Nong Khai.

MacMurphy suggested they could give the H&K pistols to his police contact in Nong Khai as a gift for helping them across the border. The police contact could also make secure arrangements for the return of the Land Cruiser.

Everything would be neatly wrapped up and all traces of Bob Humphrey and Ralph Callaway would be gone.

Santos climbed behind the wheel of the Land Cruiser and MacMurphy climbed in beside him with his GPS and a Thai roadmap spread out on his lap. "Let's roll," said Mac.

They reached Nong Khai early the following morning. After a huge breakfast at one of Mac's favorite floating restaurants on the bank of the Mekong River, they drove to the home of Police Colonel Chatchai Sunthonwet to make arrangements to cross the border into Laos.

The Colonel was already at work when they arrived, but his wife remembered MacMurphy fondly and invited them in for tea while she called her husband.

After a brief meeting where Mac and the Colonel became reacquainted, Colonel Sunthonwet personally escorted Culler and Mac to the border, supervised their passage through Thai customs, and drove them in the Land Cruiser across the Friendship Bridge into Laos. He dropped them off at the beautiful French colonial Settha Palace Hotel in the center of Vientiane, and returned to Thailand in the Land Cruiser with two .45 caliber H&K pistols, suppressors and holsters, and $1000 in U.S. currency in his pocket.

CHAPTER
ONE HUNDRED

FT. LAUDERDALE

M aggie met them at the airport in Ft. Lauderdale and drove them back to the offices of Global Strategic Reporting on Las Olas Boulevard. They briefed Maggie on what happened in Thailand—for security reasons, the rest of the GSR staff was kept entirely out of the loop. The briefing was complete with screw-ups, anecdotes, warts and accomplishments, but without, of course, any mention of Mac's trysts with Charly Blackburn.

Maggie in turn briefed them on her conversations with Edwin Rothmann. The DDO was effusive in his praise for what they accomplished, but fearful of reprisals by Khun Ut, particularly regarding Charly Blackburn, who was laying low on his orders.

She informed them the front company was beginning to pay for itself and subscriptions to GSR's "CounterThreat" publication were continuing to rise.

Back in Northern Thailand, Vanquish and the kid delivered the tainted shipment of heroin bricks to the warehouse in Mae Chan along with the body of bandana guy tied across the back of one of the donkeys.

Vanquish's explanation of the cause of death was accepted by a simple shake of the head and a tongue clucking "tut-tut" by Ung Chea.

A few days later the three hundred and twenty kilogram shipment of tainted heroin was included in a five hundred kilogram shipment that moved by truck, secreted in the midst of a load of bagged charcoal, from the warehouse in Mae Chan to Samut Sakon, a small fishing port in the Gulf of Thailand, south of Bangkok. From there the heroin bricks were loaded onto a small coastal freighter where it made its way to Ho Chi Minh City, Vietnam.

In Ho Chi Minh City the shipment was secreted in a concealed compartment in the bilge of a Hong Kong registered nineteen hundred ton bulk grain carrier named the Ruaha. The ship was pumped full to the gunnels with rice from the Mekong Delta and sent on a three day voyage to the port of Hong Kong.

In Hong Kong the heroin bricks were transferred in a mini-bus to a state of the art refinery located in the basement of an old colonial mansion in the hills overlooking Tsim Sha Tsui and Hong Kong harbor.

There the ricin laced heroin bricks went through the most delicate fourth and final refining process, turning the heroin base into heroin hydrochloride, a fine white powder, ready for packing and shipping to distributers in cities around the world. The process also had the affect of spreading the deadly ricin equally throughout the five hundred kilogram batch.

The bags of white powder were then secreted in a container load of rough cut teak lumber destined for The Decorator's Furniture Warehouse in North Carolina. Several of the four inch by six inch solid teak planks had been carefully split, hollowed out and glued back together with the bags of pure heroin filling the void inside. The concealment was unnoticeable to all but the most trained eye.

A huge Mersk Line container ship carried the teak lumber to the Port of Miami, arriving on the third of September. From there the lumber container was shipped by rail to Fayetteville, North Carolina and unloaded at The Decorator's Furniture Warehouse three weeks later. By that time the pure white heroin had a street value of $175 per gram.

The ricin laced heroin was cut further and repackaged at the furniture factory. It began hitting the streets in cities along the entire southeast coast of the United States by mid-October.

CHAPTER
ONE HUNDRED-ONE

S antos and MacMurphy slipped back into the routine of life in sunny Ft. Lauderdale.

They worked out in the mornings, Santos mostly in the weight room and MacMurphy with long runs along the Intracoastal and ocean. The rest of their days were spent in the GSR offices, working to turn the company into a profitable business to enhance its cover.

Mac, Culler and Maggie continued to debate the ethics of the operation in the Golden Triangle, but they tried not to let the disagreement affect their business relationship. As weeks turned to months, Khun Ut and Ung Chea and Charly Blackburn and Northern Thailand seemed very far away.

As part of their daily work, under the cover of doing research on the effects of drug overdose on heroin users for a large government "think-tank" customer, Maggie had put the whole GSR research team to work digging up statistics on the subject of heroin overdose.

They found that across the country drug overdoses killed about thirty-five thousand people a year, making it the second leading cause of accidental death, right behind motor vehicle accidents and ahead of deaths caused by firearms.

But some of the information they uncovered through confidential interviews with coroners gave them pause. It indicated deaths caused by poisoning might be masked, and falsely attributed to simple heroin overdose. Whenever a coroner's autopsy detected any kind of illegal drugs in the body of a corpse, the autopsy was usually stopped right there, and the death was declared to be caused by an accidental overdose.

So their concern was, if people started dying from the ricin laced heroin, and their deaths were attributed to simple drug overdose, the results of their operation could be in jeopardy. If no one found out that the heroin was poisoned, then there would be no blow-back on Khun Ut and the trail of suppliers between him and the local street pushers.

They worried about this, and reported their fears back to Rothmann, who did not appear to be overly concerned. He just told them to wait and keep researching—something would happen.

But nothing did.

By early November their research began to show a definite rise in heroin related deaths in the southeastern United States, but no one outside of GSR seemed to notice, and not a word was written about ricin or any other related reason for the deaths.

All of the deaths appeared to be individual overdoses. Some were caused by inhalation (snorting), others by injection. And all of them were of known heroin addicts.

And then, finally, it happened.

On Thanksgiving Day, the Palm Beach Post ran a headline story about eight members of the violent Palm Beach County Haitian gang, *Top 6*, dying from an apparent heroin overdose in a run-down smack-house on Sappodilla Avenue in West Palm Beach.

With so many deaths occurring at the same time, police suspected foul play and immediately jumped to the conclusion that the deaths were somehow related to reprisals by a rival gang. The *Top 6* gang controlled a corridor of territory that ran roughly along the railroad tracks from Riviera Beach to Boynton Beach, but another Haitian gang called the *Tru Haitian Boyz* had recently been infringing on its territory. They became the main suspects.

The police collected syringes, spoons and heroin residue from the scene, and when the toxicology and autopsy reports came back they showed clear evidence that the heroin was tainted with ricin poison.

Two days after the press published the news of the ricin poisonings, two well-known drug dealers, twenty-three-year-old Berno Chalemond and twenty-five-year-old Tite Sufra, were shot execution style in the back of the head on Southwest Second Street in Boynton Beach.

Two suspects, identified by eyewitnesses as eighteen-year-old Jeriah "Plug" Woody and twenty-five-year-old Jesse Cesar, were arrested a day later. Under interrogation they admitted they had killed the two drug dealers because they had supplied the ricin-laced heroin that had killed their eight *Top 6* brothers.

Aware now of the possibility of ricin tainted heroin, toxicologists began reporting an epidemic of apparent overdose deaths caused by ricin tainted heroin spreading throughout the gang controlled areas of Palm Beach County, Florida.

These deaths were followed by other assassinations of known drug suppliers in *Folk Nation* territory in Boca Raton, *Latin Kings* territory in Belle Glade, and *Bloods* and *Crips* territory in Jupiter and Palm Beach Gardens.

The epidemic of gangland killings and deaths by ricin-laced heroin caught the attention of the national media, which fueled the frenzied killing of heroin suppliers across the entire southeast coast of the United States.

CHAPTER
ONE HUNDRED-TWO

Culler Santos tossed the newspaper across the conference table to Mac-Murphy. "It couldn't happen to a better bunch of lowlife. Talk about culling society of its undesirable elements! I couldn't have done it better myself."

Maggie looked at him crossly across the table. "You did do it, Culler. Have you already forgotten?"

"No, I haven't forgotten, but as much as I love you, Maggie, I can't understand your stance on this issue. The world is a better place without those assholes . . ."

"The ends don't justify the means, Culler. Never. And what about the collateral damage? What about the innocents who will die?"

"I haven't seen any evidence of that. At least not yet I haven't . . ."

Mac stood up and stretched. "Okay, okay. No more squabbling. What's done is done. The moving hand, having writ, moves on . . . as the poet says. We can't go on worrying about things we can't control. These animals know nothing more than swift retribution. And that's a good thing. Let'em keep on killing each other. Culler's right about that. The world will be a better place without them."

Maggie stood up and walked to the door. She pulled the door open and turned back to face them, legs apart and breathing heavily, chest rising and falling under her light blouse. "Until the first innocent kid, or father or mother dies. Will it be worth it then? I don't think so . . ." She slammed the door behind her.

Mac sat back down at the table. "I don't know, Culler. I don't know."

Culler said, "I'm sorry she feels that way, but this isn't going to stop any time soon. It'll travel all the way up the daisy chain to Khun Ut and his cohorts. Those who aren't killed in the fury of mass retribution will go broke and be put out of business. Now that it's in the press the entire heroin trade in the U.S. will suffer. Looks like our version of Operation Eldest Son has been a resounding success. It's what we wanted to happen and it's happening. And that's a fact and I'm happy about it."

Mac stood up. "You're right of course. The operation worked." He reached out his hand to Santos and they embraced, shoulder to shoulder. "But hell," he snickered, "people will now probably just switch to cocaine. We may have just done the Colombian and Mexican cartels a huge favor."

CHAPTER
ONE HUNDRED-THREE

Cindy and Mac were awakened early the next morning by the ringing of Mac's throwaway cell phone.

"Sorry to bother you so early, Mac, but I managed to wrangle a trip down to Miami to meet with the station and I wondered if we could meet for a few minutes while I'm in the area."

Mac recognized Rothmann's deep, gravely voice immediately and sat up straight in bed. "Sure, just tell me when and where and I'll be there."

"I'm leaving for the airport now. Should be done with business by about three o'clock. Pick me up in front of the Borders Book Store on San Lorenzo Avenue in Coral Gables at exactly three forty-five. *Ça va?*"

"Okay, three forty-five, Borders, Coral Gables. Got it. I'll be there."

"Good . . ." The phone went dead.

They were both fully awake and sitting straight up in their bed. Cindy rubbed the sleep out of her eyes and regarded him with a wide

questioning look. The sheet had dropped down to her lap revealing lus-
cious breasts and capturing Mac's gaze. "Who was that?" she asked.

"Potential client," he lied, "He wants to meet later this afternoon."
He reached out and caressed the nearest breast with the back of his
fingers, causing the nipple to harden.

"Stop it!" she giggled, brushing his hand away.

He moved toward her and nuzzled her neck and whispered into her
ear. "Now that we're awake, can you think of anything to do?"

She slid into his arms and pulled him down on top of her. "I'm sure
we can think of something." His hand moved over her hip and around
the soft inner part of her thigh and then up . . .

CHAPTER
ONE HUNDRED-FOUR

The Borders Book Store was located only a few blocks from the CIA's Miami station.

Edwin Rothmann's interest in books was legendary in the Agency. Wherever he went he always visited the local bookstores. He had a voracious appetite for reading and usually read two or three books at a time. Although history was his passion, historical novels, as long as they were accurate, were his second love.

So it was not unusual when Rothmann broke off his meetings with the station staff and announced that he was going to take a short walk over to the Borders Bookstore before heading back to Washington DC.

It was a bright, sunny day in southern Florida—just another day in paradise, as the natives would constantly remind the snowbirds from the north. A refreshing November breeze coming off the ocean rustled through the palm trees while the big man strolled the shady tree-lined streets, blue blazer thrown casually over his shoulder, limping slightly.

361

He arrived at the bookstore about ten minutes early and went inside to browse a bit before his pick-up by MacMurphy. At precisely three forty-five he walked briskly outside and jumped into the beige Cadillac that pulled up to the curb. He glanced at his watch. "Right on time, as always. But where did you get this car? I thought you told me you bought a BMW when you 'retired.'"

"I did. This is a rental. In alias, of course. What would you expect me to do when meeting with the DDO?"

"Of course. Never slack up on the tradecraft, Mac. You never know . . ."

"Don't worry, sir, I won't."

"I know, I know. Glad to see you back in one piece, Mac. It got a little hairy out there, didn't it?"

"Yes, it did. We had a couple of close calls, but it looks like everything worked out as planned in the end."

The big man shifted his weight in the seat and turned toward Mac. "That's why I'm here, Mac. Khun Ut has gone berserk again. He's totally lost it this time. Yesterday morning he and his men assaulted Charly Blackburn's compound, killed the guards and grabbed Charly. He's also got her Hmong asset. Intercepts tell us they're both being held in the basement of his villa in Ban Hin Taek."

Mac pulled the car over to the side of the road and stopped. He pounded his fist on the steering wheel. "Holy shit! You've got to be kidding . . ."

"No, I'm not kidding. And we've got to assume that Khun Ut now knows for certain what happened in the jungle that night when you guys injected that ricin into his shipment of heroin. Otherwise he wouldn't have grabbed Vanquish."

Mac rubbed his temples. "The fucking butcher! We've got to get Charly out of there. Won't the Thais do anything?"

Two men dressed in business suits walked past their car on the sidewalk and one of them glanced back over his shoulder at them. "We'd better keep moving," said Mac, pulling back onto the road.

"Good idea. To answer your question, the Thais only know that Charly has been kidnapped. We've told them who we suspect is behind it and they agree, but they won't take any action until they have completed their own investigation. That could take weeks, and then . . . who knows. They're not very cooperative these days. I wish General Chavalit was back in charge. The current leadership is made up of a bunch of pussies."

Mac drove aimlessly through the residential streets of Coral Gables while they talked. "We can't leave her with that maniac for that long. They'll kill her."

Rothmann pushed his bulk back into the seat, adjusted his seat belt over his girth and stretched out his bum leg. "That's what I'm concerned about. That's why I'm here."

"You want us to go back." It was a statement, not a question.

"Yes, go back there and put eyes on Khun Ut's mountain villa. If you get the opportunity, take him out. You know how to do that. His empire is crumbling and with him gone we might be able to save Charly and Vanquish. But we've got to act fast."

"Son of a bitch . . ."

"Yeah, my sentiments exactly. By the way, before she was picked up Charly cleaned out the safehouse of all your gear. It's being held at the base. How do you want me to get it to you?"

Mac's mind was spinning. "Damn, I don't know. Is there anyone else? We can't use General Sawat any longer . . ."

Rothmann shook his big head. "And we can't risk exposing any more base personnel to you. You guys are toxic." He scratched his head in thought. "But I can have someone drop it off someplace for you."

"You're right, Ed. How about bringing the stuff back to the old safehouse? If it's still clean, we can stay there and avoid having to check into a hotel."

"As far as I know it is. That's not a bad idea. There's one guy in the base I would trust to do this. He was close to Charly. A base communicator—big lanky, good ole boy Texan named Gene Garrett. I can chat with him securely offline through the communicator's work link without alerting anyone else. That might work."

"If he could bring the gear to the safehouse and leave the key someplace, maybe taped above the door jam, we'd be in business."

"Okay. Good idea. That way you guys will never have to meet. I'll tell Garrett to deliver the gear to the safehouse and leave the key taped above the door jam. I'll also tell our new acting chief of base to stay away from that safehouse until further notice. I'll give him some excuse like it may be blown or something like that. That'll give you some privacy."

"Okay, we'll leave tomorrow. I think we'll go back through Vientiane and cross into Thailand from there. That's the way we got out. Colonel Sunthonwet can get us in and out without any problems."

"Sunthonwet's a good guy. Corrupt as hell, but still a good guy. Hell, they're all corrupt out there. Especially around Nong Khai. The cops pay a lot of money to get assigned to border crossing spots like Nong Khai. They make a fortune in graft from all of the commerce going back and forth across the border."

"You can drop me off here. I can walk back to the station."

"Okay, boss." Mac pulled off to the side of the road and the big man heaved his bulk out of the car.

Rothmann leaned back through the car window and the two shook hands. "I'll be in touch . . . and good luck, Mac. Sorry I can't help you more. Keep your phone on and I'll keep you updated on the situation. If there are any changes I'll let you know. You've got to get Charly out of there . . ."

"I know, boss. I know . . ."

CHAPTER
ONE HUNDRED-FIVE

MacMurphy dropped off the rental car and drove back to the office
to brief Maggie and Santos. It was after five when he got there and
the staff had left for the day. Mac stopped in front of Santos's office
and poked his head inside. Santos was hunched over his computer screen
answering emails.

"Got a minute?" said Mac.

Santos pecked a few more words and pushed back from his desk.
"You bet. Can't wait . . ."

Culler followed Mac down the hall to Maggie's office. They found
her behind her desk, deep in thought editing an article for GSR's CounterThreat publication. She wore reading glasses down low on her nose
and was scratching her graying head with a pencil.

Mac waited for Culler to enter and then closed the door behind him.
They plopped into comfortable chairs in front of her desk. She removed
her glasses, tossed them aside and put her elbows on her desk. "Shoot,"
she said. "What did the boss have to say?"

"Not good . . . Khun Ut has gone on another rampage. He's feeling the pressure and wants to know what's behind it. He grabbed Charly and Vanquish and is holding them in his mountain villa in Ban Hin Taek. The DDO's got some intercepts to confirm that's where they're being held."

Maggie threw her head back and stared at him, mouth agape, wide eyed, unable to speak. Santos uttered: "Son . . . of . . . a . . . bitch . . ." Punctuating each word.

"So he wants you back there," said Maggie.

"Yes, right away."

"You're going to miss Christmas," she groaned.

"It's not even December yet. We'll be back in plenty of time for Christmas."

"Let me get this straight. He wants you to go out there and rescue them—just the two of you—without any help from the Company or the Thais or anyone else. How the hell are you going to do that?"

Mac didn't know how to respond. Finally he said, "This isn't about Charly Blackburn or Vanquish. It's about cutting the head off the snake. It's about stopping Khun Ut. Ed Rothmann believes that if Khun Ut is gone the rest of his organization will dissolve—his men will desert him like rats deserting a sinking ship. And I agree with him . . ."

"And how do you intend to 'cut the head off the snake,' as you so aptly put it? Do you have a plan?"

Santos felt like he was watching a tennis match, his head turning from him to her.

Mac took a deep breath, exhaled, and said, "Look, right now chaos reigns in Khun Ut's dirty little empire. Pushers and buyers are at each others' throats. People who have lost loved ones due to the tainted heroin are going after the local pushers, and the pushers are going after the local distributors, and they're going after the regional distributors. This is happening all the way up the line to Khun Ut himself. I'm not telling you anything you don't already know. Buyers are shunning his product. His distribution networks are crumbling. This is what we intended to happen. The problem is he suspects the CIA is behind it and if he has any luck with his interrogations of Charly and Vanquish—and I don't doubt that he will—he'll know for sure. That's what we're dealing with."

Santos's head turned to Maggie.

She nervously finger-combed her hair back away from her face and leaned forward.

"So now you are going to add assassination to your list of misdeeds. How many people are you going to kill before this is over? Mac, you're a case officer. You're both intelligence officers. Intelligence officers don't do these kinds of things. Our country doesn't do these kinds of things."

Santos's head swung back to MacMurphy.

Mac didn't want to argue with her, but tensions were elevating and he felt himself getting sucked in.

"Oh yeah, right. What about all of those Predator and Reaper drones in Afghanistan and Iraq? Tell me the difference between a bullet from a sniper rifle and a Hellfire missile from a drone. The answer is: there is no difference."

Santos's head swung back to Maggie.

"You know very well that political assassination was outlawed by the Agency way back in the seventies when everyone found out we tried to take out Castro with poison and an exploding cigar. The drones are different." She sat back in her chair in a display of finality, as if to say, *This argument is over.*

Santos stood up and excused himself.

Mac stood up and started to leave with Culler, but he turned back to her and said, "The answer is yes. I would follow Edwin Rothmann to the gates of hell and back. We're going to finish this. I don't know how we are going to do it, but we're not going to give up now and leave Charly swinging in the wind. We owe that to him. And her."

Santos turned to Maggie. "I'm sorry, Maggie. Mac's right. We've got to try. We'll be careful, but we have to try. It's more than just the DDO now. Khun Ut has two of our people and we can't abandon them. We've got to do something. I'm sorry . . ."

She shook her head. "Go ahead, get yourselves killed. I can't stop you. But I've got a bad feeling about this. A real bad feeling . . ."

CHAPTER
ONE HUNDRED-SIX

Santos and MacMurphy met at the gym early the next morning. They both worked out in the weight room and then Santos spent the next forty-five minutes working out on the heavy bag while Mac went for a leisurely, five-mile run on the quay along the Intracoastal Waterway.

After their workouts, they indulged in a large breakfast of ham, eggs, hash brown potatoes, toast and coffee at the Denny's across the street from the gym.

Filled with trepidation about their impending trip back to Thailand, they did not talk much about what they planned to do once they got there. They knew how they were going to get into the country—with the help of Colonel Sunthonwet over the Thai-Lao Friendship Bridge—but they didn't really have a plan beyond that.

This bothered Mac more than it did Santos. MacMurphy liked to plan everything down to the minutest detail before embarking on a mission. Although he possessed that special case officer trait of being able to "wing it" whenever necessary, he never went into an operation intending to just "wing it" or "play it by ear."

He believed that precise planning for every possible eventuality was the key to success in any operation. But in this case he had yet to figure out what he was going to do when he got to Thailand, and this concerned him a lot.

What he did know is that they would fly to Vientiane via Hong Kong and cross into Thailand black, with the help of Colonel Sunthonwet. From there they would get a car and drive back to the mountains surrounding Ban Hin Taek where they would find a place to observe Khun Ut's mountain retreat.

Long periods of observation had worked for him before, helping him to devise a plan in his head based on what he saw, but this time he knew he would not have time for any long-term observation.

Once he got there he hoped a plan of some sort would begin to emerge in his mind. He knew that storming the place would be out of the question. The Thai army had tried that once before when Khun Sa was ruling the drug trade and the firefight that ensued lasted for several days and dozens of men lay dead at the conclusion of the fight. As with Khun Sa, Khun Ut had the total support of his mercenary army and the townspeople.

This attack would have to be surgical in nature. And for that, he was happy that Bill Barker had urged him to bring along the Lapua sniper rifle. But taking out Khun Ut from a distance with the rifle was one thing; getting Charly Blackburn and Vanquish out of there safely was another matter. That was what he couldn't get his head around.

CHAPTER
ONE HUNDRED-SEVEN

VIENTIANE, LAOS

They booked seats in business class on a direct Cathy Pacific Airways flight from Miami International Airport to Hong Kong, with a connecting flight to Vientiane, Laos. The flight left Miami at seven in the evening.

MacMurphy hated flying. Ever since the advent of the terrorist, flying had become increasingly distasteful—too much ridiculous, inefficient and ineffectual security, all in the name of political correctness.

But once he boarded the aircraft and settled into his comfortable business class seat, it was a good as it could be for the fourteen hour hop to Hong Kong.

He was dressed in his usual traveling garb—dark blue Hickey-Freeman blazer, blue button-down Brooks Brothers shirt, Levi 501 jeans and cordovan penny loafers.

Santos was also dressed casually in a brown and tan checked sport jacket, jeans (relaxed fit to cover his muscular thighs), white sport shirt and loafers. Their carry-on luggage contained everything they would need to sustain them for a week. They did not check any luggage—one less hassle for international travel.

After cocktails, a fair dinner consisting of small, four-ounce beef fillets with roasted potatoes and vegetables, washed down with glasses of an unknown but decent French Bordeaux wine, followed by an assortment of cheeses and more wine, they were ready to sleep. They each popped a couple of Melatonin pills to help them sleep and adjust to the jet lag, and settled in for the night.

In Hong Kong they had a two hour and forty-five minute layover before connecting for the short hop across the South China Sea and Vietnam to Vientiane. They relaxed in the Cathy Pacific business lounge where they checked emails on their laptops and freshened up before boarding the flight to their final destination.

In Vientiane they took a cab directly to the Settha Palace Hotel. For security reasons they had not made reservations, but the hotel was not full and the desk clerk remembered them from their previous visit in August.

They had been traveling for more than eighteen hours and it was one o'clock in the morning in Vientiane. They checked in, took some more melatonin to help with the jet lag, and crashed for the evening.

The next morning MacMurphy was up early and used the hotel lobby phone to call police Colonel Sunthonwet at his home in Nong Khai. Sunthonwet's wife answered and promised to pass a message on to her husband that Mac and his friend were at the Settha Palace Hotel and would like to meet as soon as possible.

Colonel Sunthonwet pulled up in front of the Settha Palace hotel in his police cruiser one hour and twenty minutes later. He left his car parked conspicuously in the driveway and strolled through the lobby of the hotel in full police uniform, eliciting glances from hotel patrons and staff along the way.

He found Santos and MacMurphy lingering over breakfast in the hotel coffee shop and joined them at their table.

"I did not expect to see you back so soon," said Sunthonwet. "What a pleasure. How can I be of service to you?"

After exchanging pleasantries, MacMurphy said, "We need to get back to Thailand but don't want to get chopped in through Thai customs. Ummmm . . . we would rather not have our names appear on any Thai visitor list. You understand . . . and we will need transportation for a week or so . . . and, ummm . . . well, we would rather not rent a car through a rental agency. You understand . . ."

He paused and exchanged glances with Santos. "And, if you still have those two H&K pistols, we would like to borrow them back as well. Can you arrange that for us?"

There was never a question that Colonel Sunthonwet would be well rewarded for filling MacMurphy's requests, and there was no doubt in MacMurphy's mind that all of his requests were doable and would be fulfilled by Sunthonwet with the utmost discretion.

"Certainly," said Sunthonwet with a wave of the hand. "No problem. No problem at all." He leaned forward and lowered his voice. "You should know that there are outstanding warrants for the arrest of two renegade *farangs* named Humphrey and Callaway. I would not want anyone to confuse those two vicious murderers with you two upstanding representatives of your country." He winked and settled back in his chair, knowing that his comment would most likely raise the amount of the stipend he would receive for his cooperation and assistance.

Neither Santos nor MacMurphy reacted to the colonel's statement. A deadpan stare was all he received. They did not take his remark as a threat, only that the colonel wanted to show that he knew the score and the risks involved in helping them, and that he expected to be generously rewarded for the risks he would be taking on their behalf. It was just business . . .

"When can we leave?" said Santos.

"As soon as you are ready."

CHAPTER
ONE HUNDRED-EIGHT

They returned to their rooms, grabbed their bags and checked out of the hotel at the front desk. Colonel Sunthonwet was waiting for them in the lobby, pacing back and forth in front of the teak trimmed revolving doors at the entrance.

They followed him to his police cruiser and loaded the bags in the trunk. The drive to the Lao-Thai Friendship Bridge took a little over twenty minutes.

The police cruiser was waved through the Lao customs check-point on the north side of the bridge and they crossed into Thailand. When they reached the Thai check-point on the south side of the bridge Colonel Sunthonwet rolled down his window and summoned one of the uniformed customs police officers to the car. They exchanged words and, after glancing into the car, the customs officer waved them past.

Sunthonwet drove them back to his villa in Nong Khai, located high on the banks overlooking the Mekong. They stood chatting, looking down at the mighty river from a sunny day room thirty feet above the water. A maid brought them a frosty pitcher of lemonade and a plate of cookies and poured three glasses.

The rainy season had ended in Thailand, but the river was still swollen from the earlier monsoon rains. Despite the swift currents at this time of year, children were happily swimming near the banks and diving into the muddy water from Sunthonwet's boat dock below them.

The weather had begun to cool and it was a sunny and pleasant day. November through February were indeed the best months to visit Thailand. It was far too hot from March through July, and the monsoon rains of August through October only brought added humidity to the region.

Colonel Sunthonwet toasted them with his glass of lemonade and welcomed them back to Thailand. Then, remembering something, he raised a finger in the air, set his glass down and excused himself. Moments later he returned with the H&K pistols, suppressors, and two holsters—concealment and leg—for each gun.

"These guns are a dream," he said. "I fired them at the range and was the envy of my colleagues. They are clean, loaded and ready to go."

MacMurphy said, "I really appreciate this, Colonel. I assure you, you will get them back when we leave."

"And when might that be? I do not wish to pry into your affairs, but for planning purposes . . ."

"We shouldn't be gone for more than a week or so . . . We just . . . have to tie up a few loose ends. I'll call you here at your home to give you some warning before we arrive. Then you can have these two beautiful pistols back."

"Not a problem. Except for a day trip or two to Bangkok, I do not plan to go anywhere. I will be here for you. Is there anything else you need? You said you will need transportation . . ."

"Yes, we need a car. Not the Land Cruiser we left with you, a different vehicle."

"Oh yes, I left your Land Cruiser parked in the middle of town on Sa Dei Road near the train station. After a few days one of my officers reported it abandoned and had it towed to the police lot. We did a registration check and contacted the owner in Bangkok who declared it had been stolen and came to retrieve it. So the Land Cruiser is out of the question anyway."

Mac exchanged glances with Santos. "Good, that's one loose end we don't have to worry about. Do you have something we could use? We would rather not rent one from an agency for obvious reasons."

"Not a problem. Not a problem. I will lend you one of my cars. It is a Range Rover. Only two years old. Very comfortable and will go anywhere you want. My wife drives it, so it is like new."

"That would be perfect, Colonel. We'll take very good care of it." Mac glanced over at Santos who rolled his eyes.

"I am sure you will. It is my pleasure. Before I left the office I also prepared something special for you." Beaming from ear to ear, he handed MacMurphy a red, pocked-sized folio with a police seal on the cover. MacMurphy unfolded it with Santos looking over his shoulder. It looked very official with stamps and a bold signature at the bottom, but Mac's limited Thai did not permit him to read it.

"Looks great, but what does it say?"

"It is basically, hum . . . how do you say it, a get out of jail free card. It says you are under my personal protection and any policeman reading the card should give you aid and assistance. That is what it says. If you get into any kind of trouble you just show the folio to the police and they will help you. That is it."

"Very nice," said Mac. Culler whistled softly.

"Now, I am sure you are anxious to get on your way and I must get back to my office. Come, follow me, I will take you to your car."

Santos and MacMurphy followed Sunthonwet down through the entrance of the villa, where they retrieved their luggage, and out to the garage. The Range Rover looked brand new. It was black with black interior and had dark tinted windows.

Mac said, "This is perfect, Colonel, you have been of great assistance and you are a valued friend."

They threw their bags in the back and before they climbed into the Range Rover Mac embraced Colonel Sunthonwet and they exchanged deep bows and *weis*. Mac slipped the Colonel an envelope containing eight thousand dollars which the colonel slid quickly onto his pocket without counting it.

And then they were on their way . . .

CHAPTER
ONE HUNDRED-NINE

They arrived back in Chiang Mai in the early evening and ate dinner at the Chokchai Steakhouse on Singharat Road, about a mile from the safehouse. MacMurphy would have preferred a lighter meal of traditional Thai food, but Santos claimed his body needed red meat, and plenty of it, in order to continue.

After dinner and a bottle of California cabernet, they completed their journey to the safehouse. There they found the key taped over the door jam, and their gear and weapons safely stashed in one of the bedroom closets. They took a couple more melatonin to chase away the jet lag, and collapsed into bed.

Early the next morning they dressed comfortably in boots, jeans and polo shirts, loaded their gear and weapons into the back of the Land Rover, and took off for Ban Hin Taek.

Santos drove. Before they got too far out of Chiang Mai where cell phone reception was spotty, MacMurphy called Maggie for an update.

It was early evening in Ft. Lauderdale and Maggie was at home preparing dinner when the call came through.

"Mac, I'm glad you called. You arrived okay?" If she was still mad at him for returning to Thailand, it was not evident in her voice.

"Hi Maggie. Everything went fine. We had a good night's rest and now we're on our way up north. Have you heard anything from the big man?"

"Yep, he called yesterday. He confirmed that she's still there at the villa with the other fellow. He's got the place under twenty-four hour observation satellite and he's diverted the Base's Porter to full time observation and photography over the villa. He's also listening to their telephone communications."

"Great. Glad he's on top of it. What about . . ."

"He'll let me know if anything changes. He is still working with liaison to get them out, but nothing has changed . . ."

"Okay, tell him we're on our way up there. We'll be in position tonight. I'll try to call you when we're set up, but the reception is spotty up there. Just keep the phone close."

"I always do. Please be careful, and keep your phone on as well."

"Okay, Maggie. Let's keep this short. I'll call back later. Bye."

"Okay, be careful. Say hi to Culler. Bye."

Santos listened intently to Mac's side of the conversation. When Mac hung up he asked, "So what's the deal? Sounds like no change."

"Yep, no change. Rothmann confirmed they're still in the villa. He's pulled out all the stops as far as surveillance is concerned. Twenty-four hour satellite, phone intercepts and the Porter. Soon he'll have us as well . . ."

"What's the Porter? Is that a plane?"

"Yes. It's assigned to the Chiang Mai base to do aerial reconnaissance of the poppy fields. It's like a low and slow flying U-2. It takes very high resolution photos. They're also listening to every word Khun Ut and his men are saying. At least as far as telephone and cell communications. Whatever the DDO can do, he's doing. But it doesn't look like he's made any progress with the Thai government. They're still dragging their feet despite all of his efforts through our liaison contacts in Bangkok."

"Yeah, you can bet Khun Ut has them all on the take all the way up to the Prime Minister's office. Have you given any more thought about how we're going to get them out of there?"

"Haven't stopped thinking about it. We're just going to have to get up there and take a look. Maybe create a diversion. I don't know. I haven't got a clue what to do without outside help. Not a clue . . ."

CHAPTER
ONE HUNDRED-TEN

Khun Ut leaned back in his chair, his polished black Wellington boots crossed on his desk. As usual he was dressed impeccably in a light grey leisure suit, smoking a cheroot. Ung Chea sat across the desk, dressed in boots, bloused camouflage pants and a black security tee shirt.

"You're being too kind to her, Ung Chea. I've never known you to be so soft in an interrogation. You've had her for almost a week now, and still nothing?"

"But you told me not to get too physical with her, boss. If you let me get a little tough, slap her around a bit, maybe we would get better results. She has been trained to resist interrogation. Sleep deprivation, bright lights, noise, endless interrogations and all that usual stuff is not working on her. They teach that in the CIA. She is a professional . . ."

"But still, she is a woman. There are special fears a woman has. You need to play on those special fears."

"Special fears, sir?"

Khun Ut swung his good leg off of the desk, lifted his bum leg down and stood up. He limped over to the window, looked out over the town below and took a long drag from his cheroot. He turned to face the Cambodian and exhaled smoke as he spoke.

"Yes, special fears. She is a beautiful woman. The fear of disfigurement would be very strong incentive for a woman like her, like having her nipples sliced off, or cutting off her nose or ears, or even rape, or being fucked in the ass . . . being humiliated . . ."

Ung Chea's eyes widened and he leaned forward on the edge of his chair, scooting it around to face Khun Ut directly. The scar running from his ear nub to his mouth reddened. "You want me to fuck her in the ass and cut her nipples off?"

"No, damn it! I do not want you to do that. It would give you too much pleasure." He chuckled, and then got serious. "I want you to threaten her with these things. And I want you to make her believe you will do these things if she does not cooperate. You did a good job with the Hmong, now get me something out of her."

Khun Ut leaned closer to Ung Chea and gestured with his cheroot, taking on a professorial air.

"You see, Ung Chea, the Americans are stupid. They advertise to the world that they will no longer harm anyone during their interrogation sessions. They advertise to the world exactly what they can and cannot do during interrogation sessions, as noted in their famous Army Field Manual. That means no prisoner is afraid of them any longer. They would never reveal information to them. Why should they? Prisoners know they can hold out because they know they will not be physically harmed. So they remain silent, or just give bullshit answers."

He returned to his desk and sat down. "But we are not forced to operate under these foolish constraints. We are smarter than they are. We can do anything we please to our prisoners. And if our prisoners believe we will do these horrible things, really believe and fear us, they will sing like sopranos."

Ung Chea said, "But these threats did not work on the old Hmong guy, and we smacked him around pretty good, boss."

"He is a different case. Anyway, we already got what we want from him. He is not important now. You did very good work by tricking him into telling you that the two *farangs* killed his partner while they were doing something to our heroin shipment. Maybe he really does not know what the *farangs* were doing there, but the fact is they were there. That tells me the *farangs* did do something to our shipment. And that is part of the answer we were looking for. Somehow they poisoned the shipment and that is the reason for our troubles now."

Khun Ut was reflective. "Those two *farangs* are responsible, and the only question now is who is behind them. That is the information you need to get out of the woman. The Hmong would not know this information."

"I think it is the CIA, Khun Ut. It has to be them . . ."

"Maybe yes, maybe no. I agree it appears to be a CIA operation, even though it would be unusual for the CIA to do something like this. Very unusual. Not their modus operandi. Not their MO . . . But what if the *farangs* were hired by one of our competitors to make it look like a CIA operation? Or what if someone within our own ranks was behind it? Someone who wants to take over our territory. What then?"

The high-pitched whine of a single turboprop aircraft engine screamed overhead. Khun Ut flinched and then hurried across the room to look up at the sky through the balcony window.

"That fucking CIA Porter again. The sonofabitch is flying so low it's going to knock the chimney off the roof."

The Cambodian joined him at the window. "They are getting very brazen, boss. They must be looking for the CIA woman. They are coming very close. That plane is usually only used to photograph the poppy fields around here from a couple thousand feet up. Now they have it circling your house. They have the house under constant surveillance. They must know we have the CIA woman here."

"How would they possibly know that?" Khun Ut limped slowly back to his desk. He appeared tired and confused. "No, you are right. They could know. We left two men dead back at the woman's villa. Maybe they were not dead. Maybe one of them talked."

Ung Chea joined Khun Ut back at the desk. Softly he said, "There are many ways they could find out, boss. Many ways."

"How could they find out? No one followed us here when we brought the woman. We know that for a fact."

Ung Chea understood the frustration of his boss and spoke in soft, gentle tones. "The same way we found out about the return of the two *farangs*, Khun Ut, through informants."

"Yes, maybe, but we are still not sure about that. We are not certain these are the same two *farangs*."

Ung Chea dropped his head. He did not like to give his boss bad news, but he would never lie to him, and he would always give him his unvarnished opinion. "Boss," he said softly, "they are the same guys."

Khun Ut shook his head slowly from side to side, but Ung Chea continued. "We know that two *farangs* matching the description of Humphrey and Callahan left Thailand over the Nong Khai bridge in late August, right after, well, after we were chasing them. And then, the following day, two identical looking *farangs* named Santos and MacMurphy flew out of Vientiane."

Khun Ut nodded. "Yes, I know, Colonel Chatchai Sonthonwet helped them. The ungrateful bastard, after all we have done for him and all we have paid him, he helped those two sons of bitches."

"Yes, he helped them, and I think he may have helped them again the day before yesterday."

Khun Ut looked surprised and frightened. He drew heavily on his cheroot. "What do you mean, Ung Chea? What happened? You said nothing to me about this."

"That is what I came here to tell you." The Cambodian dropped his eyes and spoke softly. "I wanted to check things out first, boss. I did not want to alarm you until I checked all of my facts."

"Yes, go on," said Khun Ut anxiously.

The Cambodian took a deep breath and collected his thoughts. "Sunthonwet brought two *farangs* across the bridge from Vientiane into Nong Khai. One of our people saw them in Sonthonwet's police cruiser and reported it to Paiboon. Paiboon thought it was suspicious and checked the flights coming into Vientiane over the previous couple of days and, guess what?"

"Yes . . . what?"

"MacMurphy and Santos . . ."

"And who are they?" asked Khun Ut, suspecting the worst.

"I do not know about Santos, but MacMurphy is well known to us. We have a dossier on him. He was stationed at the CIA base in Udorn a few years ago—in the late nineties. Colonel Sunthonwet was one of his principle liaison contacts back then. They know each other very well from those days."

Khun Ut looked tired. His usual swagger and confidence was gone. But he remained as defiant as ever. "So it is the CIA."

"It sure looks like it, boss. He was a CIA officer back then, so I think it is safe to assume he still is a CIA officer."

Deep in thought, Khun Ut watched the smoke rise from the end of his cheroot. Finally he said, "I think we must have a talk with Colonel Sunthonwet. Get over there right away."

The Porter returned and buzzed low over the villa once again. They ducked and looked up at the ceiling and waited until it had passed. Khun Ut's eyes blazed with hatred.

"And take out that CIA Porter, Ung Chea. Use one of the Stingers. Take the fucking thing out . . ."

CHAPTER
ONE HUNDRED-ELEVEN

The bright sun was low in the western sky when they passed through the town of Ban Doi heading west on route 1098. They were just a few kilometers from the north/south route 110 that would take them on the final leg of their journey up through Mae Sai to Ban Hin Taek on the northern border.

They hurried to get there before dark so MacMurphy could do a final reconnaissance of the town and Khun Ut's mountainside villa before heading into the jungle on foot.

MacMurphy tilted the sun visor down and a red, four inch by eight inch card fell out and landed on his lap. He glanced at it and laughed. "Look what we have here, a free parking card compliments of the police."

"Cool," said Santos. "We can save money at the parking meters, but I don't think there will be many parking meters where we're going."

Mac laughed. "Yeah, we can park anywhere we want and never get a ticket. But seriously, this might come in handy along with our 'get out of jail free' pass from the colonel. At the very least it will keep anyone from monkeying around with our car while we are up in the hills."

"Good point. I wonder if this Land Rover also has any neat police gadgets on it like Sawat's car did, like lights and siren."

"I didn't notice anything, but then I didn't check behind the grill for lights." He checked the dashboard for a light or button of some kind. "Here they are." He flipped a toggle switch below the dash and the siren wailed. He hit the one next to it and a signal indicated the blue and red grill lights were flashing. "Whoops! I guess it does," he exclaimed. "We'll have to keep that in mind."

By the time they pulled into Ban Hin Taek it was almost dusk. The road dipped sharply down from the mountains into a long narrow finger valley lined with small homes, elegant villas and tin roofed commercial buildings. The massive Doi Tung Mountain loomed up to their right and smaller hills and mountains bordered the road to their left.

They passed a large cracked boulder lying in the Mae Kham River which flowed through the middle of town beside the road.

"Well I'll be damned! See that big rock over there?" MacMurphy pointed at the huge rock. "That's how the town got its name. Hin Taek means cracked rock in Thai."

"How do you know that? Your Thai isn't that good."

"I know the words for rock and cracked, that's enough."

"I'm surprised at how modern the town looks and some of those villas look very expensive."

"Yeah, it looks different on the ground than from the air. It really is pretty nice, actually. They get a lot of tourists here these days. Not like when Khun Sa ruled the place. Those villas were probably occupied by his lieutenants."

They drove slowly through the center of the town along the river. The surrounding hills, which under Khun Sa cultivated massive volumes of opium poppy, were now planted with tea and coffee—poppy was now grown in fields further from the towns and off the more beaten touristy paths.

Near the far edge of the town, about mid-way up on a high hill on the left side of the road, they saw Khun Ut's mountain villa. It was barely visible from the road, and the narrow drive leading up to it was blocked at the entrance with a gate manned by four sentries armed with AK-47 assault rifles.

MacMurphy drove slowly past the entrance until he was out of sight of the guards. He then turned the Range Rover around and drove past one more time, studying the mountain directly across the valley from it.

"See that tall mountain up there on the other side of the valley? That's Doi Tung Mountain, one of the tallest in the area—almost four-teen hundred meters high. Near the top on the other side, you can't see it from here, is the Doi Tung Royal Villa."

"My, you are a font of information. You must have done your homework."

"How did you guess? Never go into a situation without thoroughly researching it first, Mr. Santos."

MacMurphy pulled off the side of the road near the entrance of the Ting Ting Restaurant. It was a modern looking Thai restaurant with fresh varnish and paint and a rock garden with a gurgling carp filled stream in front of the entrance. The number of cars parked out front indicated it was a popular place to eat.

"Are we going to eat here?" asked Santos.

"Always thinking of something to eat when there's work to be done. No, we're going to stretch our legs a bit and take a longer look at this side of Doi Tung Mountain. The only thing you are going to get to eat tonight will be our usual granola bars and water."

"Great . . ."

They stopped the car and got out. Culler joined Mac on the side of the car and they looked up at Doi Tung.

Mac pointed at the top of the mountain. "See that big flag on the top? That's how the mountain got its name. Doi Tung means flag mountain."

"My, my, two more Thai words you know."

"Yep. The Doi Tung Royal Villa, which once belonged to the now-deceased mother of King Bhumibol Adulyadej, is also located high up on the other side.

"There's a narrow road leading up there. We can drive up at least that far. That's the good news. There is also a temple, the Wat Phra That Doi Tung, on the top of the mountain near the flag. You can't see it from here because it looks out over Burma in the other direction. There must be at least a foot path going up from the Royal Villa to the temple."

"Okay, so what are we doing on this side of the mountain then?"

"I'm trying to find a good place for us to set up with a good line of sight to Khun Ut's villa. We're going to have to go up the mountain on the other side and then drop down to this side. But we need to find a good place to set up the Lapua. It should be a little higher than the villa so we are shooting down, but not too much, and we also need good cover because we may be spending a few days there."

Mac pointed to a spot about two-thirds up on the side of the mountain. "I'm looking at that rocky ledge over there. See it?"

"Yeah, I see it. About where the jungle ends and the forest begins. The whole top of the mountain is covered in evergreen trees. It must be cold up that high."

"Yep, it gets pretty chilly in the evenings up that high. We won't be doing much sweating once we get into position up there. That's why they built the Princess Mother's villa up so high, to escape the heat in the days before air conditioning."

Santos looked back and forth between the rocky ledge on Doi Tung Mountain across the valley to Khun Ut's villa. "That's going to be a very long shot, Mac. It looks to be about a mile across."

"That's what I guess it to be. Maybe a little less. But the Lapua ought to handle it . . ."

CHAPTER
ONE HUNDRED-TWELVE

The two men drove back out of Ban Hin Taek the way they had come. When they reached the base of Doi Tung they circled around the southern end of the mountain and turned back north toward Mae Sai on the eastern side of the mountain.

It was dark when they pulled into the little town of Mae Sai. The main street was lined with touristy souvenir shops and small restaurants. Santos's stomach started to rumble at the thought of food.

"Mac, my stomach thinks my throat's cut. Would it be too much to ask if we pulled over to one of those noodle shops to get one last decent meal before we embark on our next jungle adventure?"

Mac laughed. "I suppose people are used to seeing *farang* tourists in this town, and I could use a little real sustenance myself. A beer would be great. I guess we can risk a short stop."

He pulled off the side of the road in front of the Sorn Daeng Noodles Restaurant and they went inside. Red plastic covered banquets lined the sides of the narrow little restaurant and, after making eye contact with the young waitress dressed in a red and gold native sarong and nodding toward an empty banquet near the door, they slid into the seats.

The little restaurant was half full with an assortment of working class Thai men and women. They were the only *farangs* in the place, but no one seemed to notice. Everyone seemed to be deeply engaged in noisily slurping noodles from the bowls in front of them. The sound of wailing Thai music played softly in the background.

When the waitress arrived they ordered the house special noodles with shrimp and crab and two bottles of Amarit Beer.

Santos ate like it was his last meal, loudly slurping his noodles like a native. MacMurphy pushed his noodles around the bowl absentmindedly and sipped on his beer.

"I don't know, Culler. I still have no idea how we're going to get Charly and Vanquish out of there."

"Relax," said Culler. "Maybe we can and maybe we can't." He sucked in a long string of noodles and wiped his chin. "The fact is maybe there is nothing we can do for them. We're going to be a mile away with a sniper rifle. That's not exactly a prescription for breaking anyone out of jail. Hell, maybe the DDO will come up with some bright idea, or maybe Khun Ut will move them out of there."

MacMurphy took a long drink from his Amarit bottle and stopped, the bottle still at his lips. Then he looked directly at Santos and slowly sat the bottle down in front of him. "That's it!"

"What's it?"

"Maybe Khun Ut will move them out of there. You said it. If they move them out of the villa, maybe that will give us an opportunity. Actually, maybe we could cause a disturbance of some kind that will give them an opportunity to break free."

"How are you going to do that? Call up Khun Ut and suggest it? Hey, Khun Ut, would you do me a favor? Come on . . ."

"General Sawat."

"What about General Sawat? We can't use him any more. They already know about our connection with Sawat."

"That's just the point, Culler. They know we're in touch with him. Listen . . ." Mac leaned forward and lowered his voice to a whisper. "What if we called Sawat and told him we were back in town and needed his help to drop us and a few other guys off on the hill behind Khun Ut's villa. We could say we would need his helicopter for that—maybe to make two or three trips."

"Okay, I get it, and Sawat would naturally report those plans right back to Khun Ut, just like he did with Khun Sa many years ago, but—devil's advocate—Khun Ut already knows that we know that Sawat talked to him about us. So why would he think that we would trust Sawat to help us again?"

"That's a good point. You're right of course. We never would trust Sawat again. Not unless we absolutely had to, that is. Like, if we had no other choice. If we were backed into a corner, desperate, and had no one else to turn to, we would have to trust him, right?"

Culler finished his bowl of noodles and pushed it aside. Then he noticed Mac's practically untouched bowl and asked, "If you're not going to eat that, do you mind . . . ?"

"Order another bowl for yourself. And get us another round of beers. I just got my appetite back." Mac attacked his dinner.

CHAPTER
ONE HUNDRED-
THIRTEEN

Bellies full, and with renewed enthusiasm, Santos and MacMurphy climbed back into the Range Rover and headed further into the town of Mae Sai. They took a left at the first major intersection where a large sign in English and Thai indicated the road to the Doi Tung Royal Villa, the Mae Fah Luang Gardens and the Wat Phra That Doi Tung.

It was quite dark, and aside from an occasional car coming down off the mountain, there was very little traffic on the paved, two-lane road that wound up the side of Doi Tung.

They passed the lights of several small Shan, Akha and Lahu tribal villages sprinkled on the mountain slopes on both sides of the road. About mid-way up they drove past the darkened Mae Fah Luang Gardens. The lights of the Land Rover illuminated the flowers and plants growing among rock formations in the gardens.

At about one thousand meters up the air began to turn noticeably cooler and the jungle and mostly deciduous forest gave way to evergreens. Further on they passed the darkened entrance to the Doi Tung Royal

Villa. It consisted of several large wooden structures built in the classic Thai way with sweeping ornately curved roofs. The buildings were surrounded by tall eucalyptus and evergreen trees and gardens.

They were pleasantly surprised to find that the road continued beyond the villa, although it narrowed to little more than one lane and the macadam ran out. Mac dropped the Range Rover down into four-wheel drive and they continued to climb upward, more steeply now.

They grinded up the side of the mountain until they passed a varied collection of statues and carvings in a dark, damp sheltered glade on their left. A few minutes later they were startled when their lights illuminated a massive stone stairway directly in front of them.

Mac hit the brakes and they gazed up at the stone stairway rising up the side of the mountain in front of them. The stairs were guarded on each side by stone half-human, half-serpent Naga warriors, eerily illuminated in the moonlight and in the headlights.

At the stairway the road turned sharply to the right and ended in the temple's deserted courtyard. Mac pulled the Range Rover into the courtyard, tires crunching on the gravel, and pulled to the far end where they parked near a grove of fir trees.

Mac slipped the red police parking pass out from behind of the sun visor and tossed it face up on the dashboard. He glanced over at Santos. "What the hell," he said with a shrug, "it's worth a try."

They cut the lights and walked to the back of the Range Rover. The weather was fresh and cool. They were alone near the top of Doi Tung Mountain. Santos opened the back of the car, pulled the two duffel bags toward him, and began sorting out their gear. They were already wearing jeans and hiking boots but they changed into long sleeved camouflage military shirts and pulled on their Ghillie-suits over the top.

"Damn," said Santos with a snort, "This thing smells rank. We should have thought to wash them after our last little outing."

"Whew, you're right. I guess we'll just have to get used to it."

Culler grimaced. "We'll have to double up on the animal repellant or we'll attract every snake and fox in the woods."

He pulled out the two .45 caliber pistols and leg holsters and screwed on the suppressors. He handed one to Mac and strapped the other to his leg.

Mac pulled out the two assault rifles and passed one to Culler. Each drum was loaded with one hundred rounds of 5.56mm ammunition. He left the spare drums in the duffel bag due to the added weight. Next they strapped on their Spetz knives, slipped on their Camelbaks, floppy camouflage hats and night vision headgear. Last, they pulled on their backpacks loaded with extra ammunition, granola and power bars, animal and bug repellant, sleeping bags, nylon shelter sheets, spotter scope and other assorted gear.

Finally, Mac pulled the .338 Lapua out of its case and grabbed two, ten round magazines fully loaded with Sierra Match 250 grain bullets. He slipped one of the magazines into his pocket and put an extra box of ammo in his backpack. He slapped the other magazine into the gun and chambered a round. He checked the safety and slung the rifle over his shoulder. "I guess we're ready," he said, passing the laser rangefinder and spotter scope to Santos. "You can carry these."

"As ready as we'll ever be," said Santos. He slammed the back door shut and pointed the remote key lock at the Range Rover and pressed the button.

Mac hesitated. "Wait a minute. On second thought, maybe we shouldn't leave our remaining gear and ammo in the back. I mean, what if we return and find the Range Rover surrounded by Khun Ut's men like before? Maybe we should cache the remaining gear in the woods someplace."

"Not a bad idea, makes sense," said Culler. He hit the remote to unlock the car. "Let's wipe it down for fingerprints as well. Wouldn't hurt, right?"

"You're right, wouldn't hurt. No sense making things easy for them." They pulled the two duffel bags out of the back and went about wiping down door handles, steering wheel and other parts of the Land Rover they may have touched. When they were done, Santos hit the remote again and locked the vehicle.

"Now, do you want to take the tourist route over the top, or shall we go around?" said Mac.

"I definitely don't want to climb any higher than we have to."

Mac studied his GPS. "Let's head in a south-easterly direction back around the stairs until we get to the other side and then we'll drop down to that rocky outcropping we saw from the other side. It shouldn't take us more than a few hours—it's all downhill."

They flipped down their night vision gear and headed off, MacMurphy leading the way.

"Downhill is good," said Santos, hitching up his backpack.

CHAPTER ONE HUNDRED- FOURTEEN

The Cambodian arrived in Nong Khai late in the evening and checked into the upscale Royal Mekong Nong Khai Hotel for a few hours of rest after his long drive. The next morning he was up early, ate a light breakfast in the hotel, and headed for the home of Police Colonel Chatchai Sonthonwet. He wanted to get there before the colonel left for work.

Like most villas in Thailand, Colonel Sonthonwet's compound was enclosed by an eight foot tall masonry wall topped with broken glass. The entrance to the compound was through a solid metal gate that was opened and closed from within by a security guard.

At six-thirty in the morning, Ung Chea drove his black Nissan Sentra up to the gate, stopped, honked his horn and got out of the car. He was dressed casually in chino slacks, a light, long sleeved, Thai silk dress shirt which concealed the .357 magnum revolver on his belt, and sunglasses.

When the guard did not respond immediately he pounded on the gate with the side of his fist. He heard the guard scrambling on the other side.

The guard slid open the peep door and asked who it was and what his business was. Ung Chea stated his name, announced that he was from Chiang Rai, and said he wanted to see Colonel Sunthonwet on personal business.

The guard slid the peep door shut and ran back to the house. A few minutes later he returned with Colonel Sunthonwet, dressed in a khaki police uniform, and opened the gate.

If Colonel Sunthonwet were surprised or nervous about Ung Chea's unannounced visit, he did not show it. He bowed deeply and the two exchanged *weis*, and then Sunthonwet extended his hand, smiling.

"It is good to see you Ung Chea. What brings you to Nong Khai so early in the morning?"

Ung Chea did not return the smile. "I have an urgent matter to discuss with you Chatchai, may I come in for a moment?"

"Certainly, certainly, come in and join me for a cup of tea and some fruit. I was just eating breakfast."

"That is very kind of you, Chatchai. I will not keep you long."

Sunthonwet led Ung Chea to the house and through to the veranda overlooking the Mekong River. Breakfast for one was set on the table beside the morning newspaper. He shouted a command to the cook, who brought another cup, plate and utensils, poured tea and then quickly retreated back into the kitchen.

Ung Chea took a sip of his tea and regarded Sunthonwet severely over the rim of the cup.

"I will come directly to the point, Chatchai. We are concerned about your association with the two murdering *farangs*, Santos and MacMurphy."

Sunthonwet started to speak, but the Cambodian held up his hand. "Hear me out, colonel," said Ung Chea sternly. He removed his sunglasses and glared at the colonel across the table. "We know you helped them leave Thailand a few months ago and we know you helped them return a few days ago. What we don't know is why you are helping them, particularly since you must know what they have done to our operation, and that there are police warrants out for their arrest."

Sunthonwet struggled to maintain his composure. He started to pick up his teacup, but then thought better of it—he did not want to display any nervousness, and a rattling teacup would not be good. So he clasped his hands in front of him, leaned back and took a deep breath before speaking.

"First of all, let me make one thing perfectly clear. I do not like the intimidating tone in your voice. You can drop it right now or I will end this conversation and send you packing back to your boss. Is that understood?"

The Cambodian stared back at him, unblinking and expressionless. Only the flare of the hideous scar on the side of his face gave him away. He did not respond.

"Good, I will take that to mean you would like to continue this conversation in a civil, gentlemanly manner."

The Cambodian remained expressionless, but Sunthonwet took even that as a positive sign.

"If you had done your homework properly you would know that Mr. MacMurphy and I had a liaison relationship when he was assigned to Udorn a few years back. Did you know that, Ung Chea?"

"Yes, we know all about that. That was then, we want to know about now. Why are you helping him now?"

"Because he is my friend. It is as simple as that."

"No," said Ung Chea, "it is not as simple as that. He is a CIA officer and he and his CIA cohort have inflicted a lot of damage on our operation. Did you know that, Chatchai? Did you know that they murdered several of our men and are wanted by the police in this country? You are aiding and abetting wanted criminals, did you know that? Do you know you could lose your position for that? Your very lucrative position here in Nong Khai is now in extreme jeopardy because of what you have done."

Sunthonwet knew what could happen to him and his family if Khun Ut decided to target him. The loss of his position in the police would be the least of his worries. He decided the best course of action was to stonewall.

"I have no idea what you are talking about. My friend asked for help to get across the border and I assisted him. That is it. Nothing more."

The Cambodian smiled his crooked grin, causing the scar to contract and redden, screwing up the side of his face. "You are many things, Chatchai, but stupid is not one of them. Do not insult my own intelligence with your stupid plea of ignorance."

Sunthonwet struggled to keep his emotions and nervousness in check. When he began to speak his voice cracked, giving him away. "I . . . I will tell you what I know and then I must leave. I am late for an appointment at the station."

He paused and cleared his throat. "MacMurphy showed up at my house with another fellow. I never saw the other guy before. He stayed in the background, letting MacMurphy do all of the talking."

"Did you not notice that they matched the descriptions of the two *farangs*, Humphrey and Callaway?"

"Not at the time. I was happy to see Mac again. He wanted me to drive them to Vientiane, so I did."

"What about their car?"

"I left it parked near the train station. It was eventually picked up as an abandoned vehicle and I assume returned to its owner."

The Cambodian stared at Sunthonwet for a long time, showing skepticism. "Okay, now tell me about their return."

"Nothing to tell, really, I got a phone call from Mac. He was in Vientiane staying at the Settha Palace Hotel. He asked if I would pick them up and bring them to Nong Khai. So I did. That is all." Sunthonwet pushed his chair back and started to get up. "Now I must leave you and get to my appointment. That is all I know."

"Sit down," commanded the Cambodian with a wave of his hand, "I am not finished. Call your office and tell them you will be late, but stay where you are."

Sunthonwet slumped back into his chair, resignation and trepidation showed on his face. "Okay, go on, but please hurry."

"By the time they returned you must have known that your two friends were the same two *farangs* that were wanted by the police for murder, correct?"

"I suspected as much, yes."

"But you continued to help them, right?"

Sunthonwet lowered his eyes. "Yes, that is correct."

"How much did they pay you?"

"Not much, a few hundred dollars. I really did not do very much for them. Just drove them across the border."

"They were not chopped into Thailand, were they? You helped them avoid going through customs. That was a pretty big favor, I would think. Certainly worth more than a few hundred dollars, especially from someone like you, a corrupt cop who will do anything for money. Is that all?"

"Yes, that is all. Now I really must be going."

The Cambodian allowed Sunthonwet to stand but made no effort to get up himself. He remained sitting in his chair. "What are they driving now?"

Sunthonwet considered lying to the Cambodian, but he was afraid they already knew about the vehicle. After a long pause he dropped his head and replied: "I loaned them my wife's Range Rover."

The Cambodian nodded knowingly, his eyes piercing into Sunthonwet's. "You filthy maggot. What else?"

"That is all of it."

"What did they tell you they were going to do here?"

"Nothing. They told me nothing."

"How long did they say they were going to keep your car?"

"They said they had some loose ends to take care of and that they would return in a week or two."

The Cambodian stood up. "I do not have to tell you that when Khun Ut hears about this he will not be happy. Nevertheless, you can redeem yourself by cooperating with us from now on. Do you understand?"

Sunthonwet nodded.

"Okay, here is my card with my cell phone number. Call me the moment you know or hear anything. Anything at all. Do not screw this up, Chatchai. Understand?"

"Yes, Ung Chea, I understand . . ."

CHAPTER ONE HUNDRED-FIFTEEN

Santos and MacMurphy circled around the base of the mountain peek and began their descent on the other side. The lights of Ban Hin Taek were clearly visible in the valley below and it was a fairly bright, moonlit night; however, they still preferred to use their night vision goggles to help them maneuver rapidly through the pine forest.

They came upon an exceptionally large evergreen tree near a bunch of large rocks and decided it was a good place to cache their duffel bags. Mac marked the spot on his GPS and they continued their descent down the side of the mountain.

"It's nice up here," said Santos. The two men moved rapidly down and across the Mountain through the trees.

"It'll get worse as we get further down, thicker and hotter."

"Yeah, I know that. Too bad. This is almost like deer country back home in Massachusetts."

After walking for about an hour they paused while Mac checked his GPS and used his binoculars to sight in on Khun Ut's mountain villa.

"We need to continue heading south for about another mile or so, and then we can start dropping down the side to that outcropping of rocks we saw."

"Better to hike through these trees than through the jungle below," said Santos.

They moved rapidly through the woods until Mac was satisfied they were directly above the rock formation and then they began their descent. The slope varied between thirty and thirty-five degrees at this point which caused them to slip and slide on the leaves and pine needles. When the woods began to thicken they were forced to slow their descent.

Soon the forest morphed into a mixture of forest and jungle. It got warmer and harder to move. At about midway down the mountainside they spotted the rock outcropping below them. The slope increased considerably. They had to slide down on their butts and dig their heels in to slow their momentum.

They were happy it was the cool, dry season and they didn't have to deal with the mud as they did when they assaulted the warehouse in Ban Mae Chan.

When they reached the rocky outcropping, they stood on the edge and looked out around them.

"We need to get lower," said Mac. "We're too high at this point. Still a little bit too far north as well."

Santos nodded. "How about down there?" He pointed to a grove of trees that jutted out of the mountainside about a quarter mile down and to their left.

"Yeah, looks good. Let's give it a try," said Mac, already heading off in that direction.

They reached the grove and found a good, flat spot on the edge and dropped into the prone position. Mac used his binoculars to survey the villa on the other side of the valley. He also searched below and around him for an alternate location to set up.

They spoke in hushed tones.

Mac said, "This is about as good as we can get. It's a good camping spot as well—decent cover, flat and a lot more comfortable than those rocks above us. What do you guess the range is from here to the villa?"

"Shit, it looks like a good mile away to me. I don't know. That's a long shot. Do you really think you can hit anything that far away?"

"I've used the 50 cal at this distance, and it was pretty effective, but this Lapua is far superior to the 50 cal. I think we're about fifteen hundred meters out. That's just under a mile. And if that's correct this rifle and I should be able to handle it. The current record for a confirmed kill by a sniper is 2,430 meters. That's about one and a half miles!"

"Then this ought to be a piece of cake, right?" joked Culler. "Well, let's just check and see what the actual distance is."

Santos dug into his backpack and pulled out the laser rangefinder. Lying in the prone position, he aimed it at the front door of the villa. The seven-power magnification brought the villa into clear focus.

"I'm putting it right on the front entrance under that portico. Let's see . . . I've got thirteen hundred and seventy-four meters. How accurate is this thing?"

"To within a meter. That's a good shot. Manageable. I wish we could get a little closer, but it is what it is."

Mac found a good spot to set up the Lapua. He extended the Parker-Hale bipod and the rear monopod, stabilized them in the dirt, and got into a comfortable prone position behind the rifle. He had attached the eleven inch Sierra suppressor to the end of the muzzle and ten rounds of 250 grain bullets were loaded in the magazine.

He settled in behind the rifle, inserted the light intensifying low-light eyepiece, and sighted through the 8x32 variable power day/night scope.

The front of the mountain villa jumped out at him, clear and large. It was a two-story, dark wood building with a curving, Thai-style ornate roof line. Darkened floor to ceiling windows ran the entire length of the top floor with another smaller, higher window under the peek of the roof. The first floor had an ornate, arched portico over the double-door main entrance with two darkened windows on either side.

A paved driveway arched around the front of the villa in a horseshoe which ran under the portico of the main entrance. The entire perimeter of the villa was illuminated by security lights, enhancing Mac's view of the building through the night scope.

Mac adjusted the mil-dot recticle in the scope at thirteen hundred and seventy-four meters and scanned the area in front of the villa. He saw two guards patrolling the front of the building and one dozing in a chair at the front door. He set the recticle crosshairs on the chest of the guard at the front door, and slid back away from the gun.

"We're in good shape," he announced.

Santos had set up a small campsite in a wooded area behind them. It had a covered sleeping area with the two sleeping bags laid out neatly on each side. That done, he went to work setting up the tactical spotting scope next to Mac.

"This thing's a dream," he said, looking through the scope. "I can count the nose hairs on that sleepy dude at the front door."

"Yep, Barker really came through for us. And to think I almost didn't bring the sniper gear on this trip."

"I'm hungry," said Santos.

"What else is new? And I'm tired. How about you take the first shift and eat your fill of our gourmet granola bars, and I'll relieve you at daybreak." He checked his watch. "It's almost three-thirty now. The sun will be coming up in another couple of hours."

"Okay, I'll wake you if Khun Ut comes out and wiggles his ass at us."

"Yeah, that reminds me." Mac dug into his backpack and pulled out a notebook and pencil and handed them to Culler.

"We need to keep a detailed account of what goes on at the villa from this point on. Everything. Light patterns—when lights come on and go off in each room—movements of the guards, people coming and going, visitors, everything that happens should be noted in this book. I have a feeling we may be here for a few days and we'll need to get a good grip on the routine of the place. Tomorrow we'll find a target someplace at the same range and do a little target practice. Nothing beats actually seeing where the bullets land."

CHAPTER
ONE HUNDRED-SIXTEEN

Santos let Mac sleep until he awakened by himself at almost seven-thirty.

"Why didn't you wake me?" asked Mac, rubbing his eyes.

"You were sleeping like a teenager. Par for the course. I didn't have the heart to wake such a sleeping beauty."

"Yeah, yeah, yeah. Anything happening?"

Santos glanced down at his log book. "A car arrived at six-twenty and pulled around back. There's probably a parking area back there. The light went on in the top left window at six-thirty. The guards changed shifts at seven. All the first floor lights went on just a few moments ago. That's it so far."

Mac walked to the far end of the campsite to relieve himself. When he returned, Culler said, "Don't forget to sprinkle some of Barker's animal repellent on your pee. We don't want anything sniffing around here and we definitely don't want to attract any hound dogs . . ."

Mac nodded and did what he was told. "You're right," he said softly, "we can't be too careful up here."

Mac ate a granola bar and sucked water out of his Camelbak. "Why don't you go get some rest and I'll take over here. When you wake up we'll zero in the Lapua."

"I'm okay for now. Let's get it over with so we know the thing is going to hit what you're aiming at. I'd hate to miss an opportunity if one presented itself."

"You got it. I've got it set at 1374 meters. So all we need to do is find a decent target at the same range in the same direction. There's a pretty constant breeze coming down the valley from north to south. We'll have to fine-tune the sights for windage as well as distance."

Mac got down behind the Lapua while Culler climbed in behind the spotter scope next to him.

Culler reduced the power on the Leupold scope from forty to twenty and surveyed the area around the villa. Mac did the same with his rifle scope.

They spoke softly, in hushed tones.

See that grassy field just to the left of the house?" said Culler. "There are a couple of good rocks sticking out of the ground that you could use as practice targets. They're at about the same range."

"Yeah, I see what you mean. That could work . . . But what if we got a whining ricochet off one of the rocks? That could alert someone."

"What kind of a wallop does that Lapua pack? It's not like a 50 cal, is it?"

"Actually, it's pretty close. The .338 round is fairly new to the sniper community. It's the first and only caliber that was designed specifically for sniping. The bullet will arrive at one thousand meters with enough energy left to penetrate five layers of military body armor and still make the kill. It was designed that way. Its effective range is about a mile, or 1600 meters, and we're just about three hundred meters shy of that."

Culler shook his head. "Wow! So that means at 1374 meters it will still penetrate maybe . . . three or four layers of body armor!"

"You got it. It's a real killer. For extreme long-range anti-personnel purposes, the .338 Lapua is the king."

"Okay, I got it. No rocks. Let's see, what's that a few meters back from the edge of the driveway there? Looks like a piece of trash." He increased the magnification of the spotter scope back to forty power. "Yep, it's a box. A cardboard box. Will that do?"

"I see it. It's a little close to the side of the house, but I think it'll work. Sight the rangefinder on it to make sure."

Culler sighted on the box, adjusting the dials. "1376 meters. Close enough?"

"Close enough for government work. Now, what do you estimate the breeze to be down there?"

"I don't know, five, maybe ten knots. Something like that."

"Let's enter ten knots. The wind kind of sweeps down through the valley. Probably stronger down there than it is up here. Okay let's try one. Got the target in your scope?"

"Got it, Mac. Take your shot."

Mac squeezed off a round and the rifle bucked, but the only sound coming out of the suppressor was a muffled pssst.

"You kicked up dirt about four feet high and three feet left of the target."

"Okay, we need to bring it down and right." Mac adjusted the elevation and traverse turrets on the top of the scope. "Let's see, one mil-dot right will bring it over one meter, and, well, let's bring it down a mil-dot as well."

Mac settled back in behind the gun again and adjusted himself. "Ready?"

"I'm ready."

Mac sighted, exhaled half a breath, and squeezed off another round. After what seemed like seconds, the box flipped.

"You clipped the top of the box. Almost in the center at about twelve, maybe one o'clock. I'd leave it right there. It sure takes awhile for the bullet to get there."

Mac thought out loud, speaking to no one in particular. "Windage is okay. We'll have to adjust when we feel more or less wind up here. But the wind will always come from the same direction during this season, and we can't anticipate gusts. Range is good too, but I could bring it down one click, one-tenth of a mil-dot, to make it better. Then all we have to worry about is windage. Okay, down one click. Let's try one more."

The last round hit the box just a few inches to the left of center.

"We may have gotten a little gust that time, but the elevation is dead on. I think we're good to go."

Santos scooted back away from the spotter scope and stretched. "Man, that's good shooting, Mac. I've really got to hand it to you. I never saw anything like that before."

"With the right equipment, you can accomplish anything. This rifle is a dream."

"How far does that bullet drop at this range?"

"Well, at fifteen hundred meters the bullet will drop about seven or eight meters. So you're actually shooting in a big arch. That's why the ammo is so important. It has to be perfect in every way to get the proper consistency. The trajectory of the bullet depends upon so many factors— distance, wind, humidity, weight of the bullet, muzzle velocity, all those things. Even the rotation of the earth."

"No shit! The rotation of the earth?"

"Absolutely. That's why I always try to sight my rifle in at the spot where I'm going to be shooting. It doesn't matter much over short distances, but when you're talking a mile or so away, it definitely affects the trajectory of the bullet. It's called the Coriolis effect. The earth rotates from west to east, so at this range firing almost due east like we are, the target drops away from you slightly by the time the bullet arrives. That means you have to aim six inches lower; six inches higher if you're firing due west. Get it?"

Culler shook his head and laughed. "And I'm supposed to be the engineer . . ."

CHAPTER
ONE HUNDRED-
SEVENTEEN

The Cambodian reported back to Khun Ut on his meeting with Colonel Sunthonwet. Khun Ut was not pleased. The two *farangs* were back in his neighborhood, and this made him very uneasy. He felt the same mixture of fear and anxiety he felt when Thai government forces attacked his father's headquarters in Ban Hin Taek more than twenty years ago.

That raid brought down Khun Sa's narcotics empire, almost totally destroyed his village mansion, and resulted in the death of his only legitimate son. The wounds Khun Ut suffered in the battle kept him from fleeing with his father, and left him with a permanent limp as a constant reminder of the betrayal.

Khun Sa was forced into permanent exile in Burma where he and the remnants of his two thousand man strong Shan United Army had to keep constantly on the move to avoid the relentless pursuit of Burmese army. Finally, after ten years of living in the jungle, with attrition and desertions of his men, he surrendered to Burmese forces and spent the rest of his life in a Rangoon prison.

While Khun Sa was in exile, the twenty-one-year-old Khun Ut, by then a seasoned veteran of the opium trade, remained in Ban Hin Taek where he nursed his wounds and quietly began to rebuild Khun Sa's empire from his father's mountain retreat overlooking the village.

His greatest fear was to suffer the same fate as his father. Indeed, he did everything in his power to assure that a repeat of that raid would never happen. The money he spent on bribes to the Thai military and government officials far exceeded what were paid by his father.

The influence he wielded within the pinnacles of Thai government in Bangkok virtually assured there would be no large scale attacks planned against him or his operations, and his control over local law enforcement, military and government leaders permitted him to operate in and around the Golden Triangle without interference.

But now the American CIA had entered into the equation. He knew the CIA was behind the downfall of his father—they had forced the Thai Prime Minister, Prem Tinsulanonda, and the commander of the Thai army, General Chavalit Yongchaiyut, to launch the Top Secret, large-scale assault that had driven his father out of Ban Hin Taek and into the jungle.

Something like that would never again happen. Not under his watch. Since Khun Ut took control he had made sure of that. But now it appeared that the CIA was taking matters into its own hands—was working against him without the consent and cooperation of the Thai government.

Could that be possible? Khun Ut didn't think so at first. But now . . . now he couldn't be certain. Certainly his prisoner, Charly Blackburn, the CIA base chief in Chiang Mai, would know the answer to that question, and many more as well. Ung Chea would extract the information he required.

Those two *farangs* had caused a lot of mischief. They had attacked his warehouse, killing several of his men in the action, and had poisoned at least one of his heroin shipments.

Now his heroin distribution network was in shambles, buyers were shunning his product, the chemists in Hong Kong didn't want to refine his heroin for fear it would taint other shipments, and worst of all, his competitors were salivating at the thought of his demise, hovering over him like a flock of vultures waiting to pick his bones.

But if his father had taught him one thing, it was that offense was the best defense. Retreat was not an option for Khun Ut. He was always more ruthless than his enemies—that had kept him at the top of the heap—and now they would feel his wrath like never before. He would start with the CIA—those two *farangs* and their all-seeing, intrusive Porter spy plane.

And perhaps, if necessary, he could use the CIA woman and the Hmong as bargaining chips. He just had to figure out how to use them in the most effective way.

CHAPTER
ONE HUNDRED-
EIGHTEEN

U ng Chea and Paiboon discussed their game plan for the enhanced
interrogation of Charly Blackburn. In the end, they were convinced
that Khun Ut was right. Humiliation and fear would work on
this woman.

They knew she had probably been through the CIA's resistance to
interrogation course, but real life was a lot different than a training
course down at The Farm. No training can duplicate the real thing.

In training, the students know that they will not actually be harmed
by the instructors—threats and harassment can only go so far. But there
would be no such certainties in this situation, and that is precisely what
they were counting on.

The mountain lodge was built into the side of the hill, so the entire
rear basement side of the lodge was below ground level. This dark, damp,
windowless space was used for storage—except for the two rooms on
each end. They had been converted long ago by Khun Sa into cells for
"special guests," just like these two.

Each cement block cell was approximately ten feet square. Aside from an olive green military style canvas cot against one wall, there was no other furniture in the room. There was no bedding on the cot, no sink, no toilet—nothing.

A single bright light bulb in a grated steel fixture in the ceiling illuminated the room. The light was never switched off. A steel plate door with a four inch by two inch viewing slot with a sliding cover was set in the middle of the interior wall.

Vanquish occupied the cell at the north end, and Charly Blackburn occupied the cell at the south end of the basement.

The interrogation room, located in the front side of the building directly under the main entrance, was actually the building manager's office. Although it too was windowless, it was a comfortable room with paneled walls, equipped with air conditioning and heat. It was furnished with a large gray metal desk facing two padded folding metal chairs and an upolstered couch along one wall. Grey metal filing cabinets lined the opposite wall, and the floor was glossy gray, painted concrete.

It had been almost a week since Charly Blackburn had been kidnapped from her home, and almost twice as long for Vanquish.

Paiboon, who had no previous experience with interrogation, was placed in charge of the care and feeding of the two prisoners. He was, of course, under the close supervision of Ung Chea, who had considerable experience with the most brutal forms of interrogation.

The Cambodian had learned these skills from his father, Ta Mok, and other ruthless Khmer Rouge leaders.

After days of sleep deprivation, constant beatings, living in his own filth, barrages of non-stop questioning, starvation and time distortion, Ung Chea was convinced that the old Hmong was holding nothing back.

He knew very little anyway. Khun Ut would make the ultimate decision as to what to do with the bloodied, broken old Hmong. That was not Ung Chea's problem. He would gladly take the Hmong out behind the lodge and put a bullet in his brain, if that was what Khun Ut wanted. He was a traitor, pure and simple, and death was the punishment for traitors.

Charly Blackburn was another story. She was a CIA officer, and a tough one at that. She had endured five days of similar treatment, absent the beatings per Khun Ut's orders, and had not given them a word of anything useful. She was totally defiant and seemingly immune to the treatment she endured in silence.

Of course, the Cambodian was unable to lay a hand on her—thus far, that is. But Khun Ut clearly was coming around to the realization that they would have to get tougher with her if they were to extract anything of value from her. Ung Chea was confident he could break her, particularly if Khun Ut would permit him to inflict a little pain on her body.

At least Khun Ut would now permit more intimidation and threats during the interrogation. That was a positive sign. At least a step in the right direction. The next step would be to follow through on the threats. The arrogant bitch deserved to be smacked around a bit, and Ung Chea looked forward to the time he would see fear and pain replace the defiance in her eyes.

This interrogation would be different than the others and he would personally conduct it. Paiboon was much too easy on her—too polite. He played the "good cop" role far too well. He actually liked playing that role.

Now Ung Chea would begin this interrogation armed with the names of the two *farangs*—that alone should shock her into revealing precious information about what the CIA's plans and intentions were— and he now had the authorization to get tougher with her. He would break her today . . .

CHAPTER ONE HUNDRED-NINETEEN

The Cambodian and Paiboon kicked the building manager out of his basement office and were discussing the previous interrogations of Charly Blackburn. Ung Chea sat behind the grey metal desk with his feet up while Paiboon sat across from him in one of the two chairs.

"Once she knows we have the names of her two CIA cohorts she will break," said Ung Chea. "She will know the game is up. If she thinks we already know everything, then it will be easier for her to confirm what she thinks we already know."

Ung Chea was proud of himself for figuring this out. Actually, he read about the technique in various manuals on interrogation, but putting it into use in this case, well, that was his idea entirely.

He also planned to use a few well-placed smacks to the head and body. Nothing that would leave any marks, but enough to shock her into submission. "Now that we can smack her around a bit, we will scare the crap out of her. That ought to do it. Go get her now. Bring her here . . ."

"Yes, sir." Paiboon rose to leave.

He returned several minutes later with Charly. The sight of her shocked Ung Chea. Her condition had deteriorated considerably over the past couple of days while he was in Nong Khai.

Her hands were handcuffed in front of her and her once shiny shoulder length black hair was now dull, matted and as filthy as a Rastafarian's. She was wearing the same clothes she had put on after her capture, a white short sleeved blouse, blue jeans and running shoes.

But the blouse was now torn, stained and covered in soot. Her jeans were filthy and she had obviously soiled herself—a large dark, wet stain circled her crotch area. Her eyes were black rimmed and dull and her face and exposed arms were black with soot and dirt. She stank of body odor and urine.

"Do not sit on that chair," commanded Ung Chea as Paiboon was about to seat her. "You stink like a donkey and you have soiled yourself. I do not want you on my furniture you smelly bitch. You can stand right where you are." Paiboon left her side and stood by the side of the desk.

Ung Chea got up from behind the desk, walked around it and stood in front of her, leaning back on the desk. She appeared to wobble on her feet and refused to look him in the eyes.

"You are quite a mess, Charly Blackburn. Do you want to tell me now about your two friends? Or would you prefer to go back to your filthy hovel."

She did not respond. She concentrated on the floor in front of her and stood on unsteady feet. The slap came as a surprise and almost knocked her off of her feet. Paiboon reached out to help her and when she was standing again Ung Chea slapped her hard on the other side of the face, knocking her down to her knees this time.

Paiboon got her to her feet and noticed both cheeks reddening from the blows.

She remained silent, staring at the floor in front of her, and began to weep. Soon her whole body was wracked with deep, uncontrollable sobs. Her tears left long streaks down her dirty cheeks. She appeared drugged, but her condition was due to the lack of sleep and disorientation she had experienced since her captivity, and this physical and verbal abuse was becoming intolerable.

"Paiboon," said Ung Chea, "put her in a chair and remove her handcuffs. I will try to reason with her now."

Paiboon removed her cuffs and sat her in one of the chairs.

She uttered, "thank you," and massaged her wrists.

"Would you like something to eat? When was the last time you ate?" The Cambodian walked back around behind the desk and sat down, putting more distance between them.

She did not respond.

"Would you like to get cleaned up a bit? Would you like a shower?"

She did not respond.

"I know you can talk. Answer my questions."

She did not respond. Her body wracked with another uncontrollable sob.

"From now on your interrogations will take a turn. They will change. They will become harsher. I am tired of playing games with you, and I am running out of time. So listen closely."

He looked up at Paiboon. "Paiboon, hold her head up so she can see me when I talk to her."

Paiboon put his hand under her chin and gently raised her head to face him. He kept her head raised. Tears continued to flow down her cheeks, washing away the grime in streaks.

"Good, now you can see me. I want you to look into my eyes so you can see that what I say to you is the truth."

Her eyes were blank and unseeing.

Ung Chea paused before speaking. Calmly he said, "I want you to know what will happen to you if you continue to sit there and not talk. You are a beautiful woman—at least you used to be a beautiful woman. Right now you are disgusting. But with some food and a shower and clean clothes, you could be beautiful again." He paused, "Unless you choose to remain silent."

Another sob wracked her body and she tried to lower her head, but Paiboon gently raised it again.

"If you continue to remain silent, I will make you permanently ugly. Do you see this scar on my face? Every day I am reminded of the piece of shrapnel that took off my ear and sliced open my face. It was not a happy day. But at least it happened quickly, in battle. For you it will happen here, in your cell, slowly, very slowly. You will feel unbelievable pain, and when I am finished you will be permanently ugly, unattractive to any man, and repulsive to children. Do you have any idea what I will do to you?"

She continued to stare blankly in his direction with Paiboon's hand cradling her chin.

He removed a hunting knife from a desk drawer and unsheathed it. He held it out in front of him and ran his thumb across the blade to test its sharpness.

"I will remove your ears—first one, and then the other—and then I will remove the tip of your nose, and then I will heat the end of the knife and cauterize the wounds. Maybe I will cut your cheeks as well. From the corners of your mouth outward. And then I will cut off your nipples. I will do all of this, I promise, if you remain silent. Do you understand?"

Her eyes widened in fear and she shook her head and muttered, "Yes."

"Good. You can speak." He continued. "But before I turn you into an ugly witch, my men and I will take turns with you. We will fuck you in your stinking cunt and we will fuck you in your ass and it will be the last time anyone will ever want to fuck you again. Do you understand what I am saying, Charly Blackburn, CIA bitch?"

She nodded and sobbed and continued to stare at him blankly.

"I see the fear in your eyes, Blackburn, you can not hide it from me."

She spoke, "Yes, I am frightened. You are a frightening, beast of a man. I believe you could . . . would, do all of those things, and more, and enjoy every moment of it. I believe you."

"So you can talk after all. That is a good start. Let us begin from where we left off the last time I saw you. Tell me about your two *farang* friends. Your two CIA friends. You know who they are, MacMurphy and Santos."

Her head jerked up in surprise. The vagueness in her eyes disappeared. She became alert and on guard. Her body language gave lie to any denials she might make. Ung Chea read the signs and smiled in victory.

"Yes, we know who they are and we know you have been in contact with them. They are CIA officers like you and they are leading a CIA attack on our operations here in the Golden Triangle. You can not deny those facts."

She laughed and shook her head in disbelief.

"Why are you laughing? Are you denying the truth?"

She cleared her throat and looked at him with an amused smile. Then she spoke softly.

"No, Ung Chea, they are not CIA officers. Your sources are wrong. Yes, they used to be CIA officers, but they were fired. They are no longer employed by the CIA, and the CIA will have nothing to do with them. They committed a serious crime and were kicked out of the Agency by the director. They were fired. That is the truth . . ."

The Cambodian stared at her, speechless and incredulous. He sensed she was telling the truth. He looked over at Paiboon, who was equally mystified.

"What about that meeting you had with them in the Wangcome Hotel in Chiang Rai last summer?" he said. "What about that? You were liaising with them, right?"

She shook her head and smiled. "In a manner of speaking, yes, I was liaising with Mac MacMurphy, but not on behalf of the CIA. You see, Mac and I have been lovers for many years. We met that one time, shortly after he arrived in Thailand, and only that one time. He told me it would be too dangerous for me to see him again. Now I understand why. Now I understand."

The Cambodian could not believe what he was hearing. It was impossible, he thought, *this can not be. It has to be the CIA.* And then he recalled Khun Ut's suspicions. *Maybe it was a competitor who hired them, or someone within their ranks.*

"You say they were fired. When were they fired and why?"

"Over a year ago. The summer before last. They were involved in an operation in Paris. They stole several million Euros during the operation and the CIA director found out about it and fired them both. After that they moved to South Florida and started a company called GSR research or reporting or something like that. They are mercenaries now. They will work for anyone who will pay them. But the CIA would never touch them. Not any longer. That would be impossible . . ."

"And who would that be? Who are they working for now, if not for the CIA?"

"I'm sorry, but I haven't a clue about that. We did not discuss that when we met in Chiang Rai, and Mac would never tell me if I did ask him."

Ung Chea was clearly taken aback by her revelations. He needed to report back to Khun Ut immediately, before he shot down that CIA plane and caused more problems for them. And they needed to get rid of these two prisoners. He did not want to compound their problems by bringing the wrath of the CIA down on their heads unnecessarily.

Ung Chea turned to Paiboon. "We will check out her information. If she is telling the truth, well, her treatment will improve. If we find that she is lying . . . Anyway, take her back to her cell. Let her take a shower and give her something to eat. And get her clothes washed."

He turned to Charly. "I hope you are not lying to me. That would not be good. Things will get very bad for you if you are."

What a mess this is turning out to be, he thought.

CHAPTER
ONE HUNDRED-TWENTY

A t that precise moment, Santos and MacMurphy were sitting cross-legged on the edge of the ledge. The spotter scope and Lapua were set up, aimed and ready, a few feet behind them. Mac was observing the lodge through binoculars.

Santos briefed Mac on the observations he had made earlier. "The whole front part of the second floor appears to be offices. The biggest office appears to be the one on the far right because all the lights came on at the same time there at about eight-thirty. It looks like it runs from the corner almost to the center of the building probably about thirty feet. The bedrooms are probably in the rear. I didn't see any evidence of bed-rooms in the front. All the lights were out by about six and they didn't come on again until this morning. I'd keep my eye on the office on the far right. I'll bet money that one belongs to Khun Ut himself."

"Here comes the Porter again," said Mac. "It'll pass right over the roof of the lodge in a few moments. That's got to piss off Khun Ut big time."

"I see it. Those guys won't let up, will they? Back and forth, back and forth over the lodge. Must be driving the sonofabitch crazy."

"That's part of the plan, you can be sure of that . . ."

Now the plane was close enough that Mac could make out the two pilots in the cockpit. It whined its way over Ban Hin Taek and began a long, slow turn to the south.

"It's following the same flight pattern over and over," said Mac, "not a very good idea in my opinion."

The words were hardly out of his mouth when something streaked up into the sky from the woods below the mountain lodge and struck the Porter amidships. The little single engine plane exploded in the air and broke in half, falling straight down to the earth like two rocks. Another explosion lit up the mountainside when the main section of the plane hit the ground on the side of the mountain below them.

"Holy shit! Did you see that?" said Mac.

"Son . . . of . . . a . . . bitch," said Culler. "That was a stinger."

"Sure looked like it. Those guys are nuts. Now there's definitely going to be hell to pay . . ."

"We've got to report this back to Headquarters right away," said Santos. "Have you got any bars on that phone of yours?"

Mac pulled his cell phone from his pocket and turned it on. "One bar. Doesn't look good. Let me try." He hit the speed dial for Maggie and listened while the call was routed to the other side of the earth. Finally a wobbly ring could be heard and then the sound of someone picking up. "Hello. Maggie. Can you hear me?"

He could make out her voice at the other end but the transmission was breaking up badly. He shouted into the phone, "Maggie, I'll call you later. Stay close to your phone."

He could hear Maggie trying to respond on the other end, but the transmission was too garbled to make anything out, so he hung up.

"Shit," he said, "I'm going to have to get higher on the mountain to get any decent reception. Hold the fort, Culler, I'll be back as soon as I can."

Mac stripped down to his tee-shirt and jeans, and looked up the side of the mountain and said, "Well, here goes," He took off at a fast pace, climbing directly up the side of the mountain.

Santos watched until he was out of sight and then turned his attention back to the burning Porter in the jungle below him. He focused through the binoculars and tried to find some sign of life, but he knew there would be none. No one could survive that fiery crash.

Mac returned almost two hours later. He was breathing heavily and drenched in sweat. He drank heavily from his Camelbak and tried to control his breathing before speaking.

"I got her," he said between gasps. "She'll pass the message on to Ed Rothmann. We'll call her again after dark when the reception is better. I hope I won't have to climb up that damn mountain again."

He fought to control his breathing. "I was thinking. Maybe this'll do it. Maybe the DDO will get approval to pull out all the stops now. They're going to have to investigate the crash, right? That means there'll be Americans on the side of the mountain looking at the crash site. It's an American aircraft that has been shot down. What will that mean for us? For this operation?"

Culler picked up the binoculars and watched several firemen climb up the side of the mountain toward the wreckage. A Thai police helicopter had arrived and was hovering over the crash site.

"With all this attention we're going to have to take extra precautions to make sure we're not spotted. I don't want us to be blamed for this."

Mac looked up in surprise as the realization hit him. "You're right. This changes everything. There's gonna be all kinds of investigations going on down there. And they're going to include Khun Ut and his mountain villa. They'll have to. Surely others saw the direction that missile came from. He's going to deny any involvement, sure, and he'll probably never be implicated due to his influence and power, but there's still gonna be investigations going on."

"So? So what do you mean?"

"I mean he won't want cops poking around his house and asking all sorts of questions while he's holding an American CIA officer there. That's what I mean. This is an opportunity for us. This is manna from heaven . . ."

CHAPTER ONE HUNDRED-TWENTY-ONE

Khun Ut sat behind his desk, head in his hands. His cheroot burned in the ashtray beside him. Things were unraveling rapidly. Ung Chea was convinced the CIA woman was telling the truth . . . and he agreed. Santos and MacMurphy were ex-CIA mercenaries. He had thought from the start that this did not smell like a CIA operation, and he was right.

But who were they working for? If not the CIA, then surely it had to be one of his competitors. But he couldn't imagine it could be anyone local. He simply didn't have any local competitors. He controlled the region and had excellent intelligence on who was doing what to whom. There were no indications that anyone here was trying to wrest control of his operation from him. Sure, there were guys would would like to step into his shoes, but they couldn't pull off anything like this without him knowing about it.

So it had to be one of his foreign competitors. The Arabs who controlled the opium and heroin trade in Afghanistan maybe, or perhaps the drug cartels in Colombia—someone wanting a bigger slice of the action. These were the most likely candidates.

And now he realized that shooting down the CIA's Porter had been a huge mistake. He had acted rashly. If only that CIA bitch had talked sooner, it could have been prevented. Now he actually would have the CIA on his case—the CIA and the two *farang* mèrcenaries.

His men had found Colonel Sunthonwet's black Range Rover parked high on the other side of Doi Tung Mountain near the temple, so they had to be close by. What were they up to this time?

He had made a calculated risk when he attacked the consulate in Chiang Mai. He had believed the combined efforts of the CIA, DEA and State Department would be pushed back by his aggressive action. He thought they would back off in their attempts to restrict the cultivation of poppy in the region around the Golden Triangle. And by all appearances his gamble had worked—efforts by the U.S. State Department and the DEA to purchase and destroy poppy fields had come to a screeching halt, and the farmers who had cooperated in these efforts were once again returning to his camp.

But now this . . .

He pushed back from his desk, grabbed his cheroot and limped slowly across the room to the window. He stood and looked out across Ban Hin Taek to Doi Tung Mountain and the smoldering wreckage of the Porter at its base.

The power of the massive mountain gave him strength. He would survive. This was just a minor setback. He had experienced other setbacks during his path to the top and had always emerged stronger than before. He had learned from each mistake and from each attempt to wrest control of his empire away from him.

Right now he had to think about damage control. His mind spun with ideas . . .

CHAPTER

ONE HUNDRED-
TWENTY-TWO

M ac, look at this. Check out the far right window on the second floor near the end of the building." Culler had the spotter scope turned up to forty-power and the window filled his vision.

Mac adjusted the scope on the Lapua. "Son of a bitch. I think that's him."

"I think we just decided on a plan, Culler." Mac clicked off the safety. "Whatever happens now, taking that bastard out is not going to make it worse." His heart pumped and his hands shook.

Buck fever, he thought, *don't do this to me now. Settle down.* He could see the man clearly, just standing there looking out of the window, smoking. This had to be Khun Ut. He set the crosshairs on the middle of his chest, let out half a breath and squeezed the trigger.

The target's arm came up as he brought the cigar to his mouth and the Lapua recoiled into Mac's shoulder. The Sierra Match 250 grain .338 bullet left the muzzle at 2,900 feet per second with barely a sound.

After what seemed like an eternity, the bullet hit the double pane thermal glass, deflected downward slightly and slammed into Khun Ut's lower left rib. The rib shattered and the .338 bullet contined to plough at a downward angle through muscle and stomach and intestines until it exited his back just under the left lung.

The force of the impact spun Khun Ut around and threw him back into the office. He hit the floor with a thud in the middle of the room, oozing blood and life onto the polished teakwood floor.

"Holy shit," said Culler. "That thing sure packs a wallop."

"Where'd I hit him?" asked Mac, still sighting through the scope of the Lapua.

"I think you were a little low and right but you hit him square enough to spin him around and knock him back into the room. It was a solid hit."

"But not a kill shot," Mac replied, matter of factly. "Damn . . ."

"Maybe, maybe not, depends . . . you got him good, though. Nice shot."

They remained in position, Santos observing the villa through the spotter scope and MacMurphy through the rifle scope. Moments later the room filled with people. One of them walked up to the window, inspected the bullet hole in the glass and looked out toward them . . .

CHAPTER ONE HUNDRED-TWENTY-THREE

Khun Ut could feel the life draining from his body. He rolled up into the fetal position and grabbed his side where the bullet had entered his body, trying to stem the flow of blood.

He called out for help. He felt like he had been kicked in the side by a mule, but he could feel no pain. Only a dull ache. He knew he had been shot, but how? From where? He was confused and panicky. He fought the feeling. He couldn't panic. But he could feel the rush of blood going to his head. His vision was blurred. He realized he was going into shock. He called out again and again and then everything went black.

Was he dreaming? He sensed people around him, moving him, lifting him up off of the floor. He was still in no pain but he was slipping in and out of consiousness. His eyes would not focus and dark spots danced in front of them. He could hear voices in the distance. He struggled to stay awake, fearing that if he drifted off and succumbed to the urge to sleep, he would never awaken.

He could feel himself being moved. People were shouting and hurrying around him. He was being carried on a stretcher, jostled around, down the stairs, out the door. People surrounded him. Someone was trying to talk to him. The face was very close. He recognized the face as Ung Chea's. Ung Chea's lips were moving but all he could hear was the blood rushing in his ears and faint voices far away.

He struggled to concentrate and finally, with great effort, he reached for Ung Chea's shirt and pulled him close. He whispered, "Who did this?"

"You were shot, Khun Ut, from somewhere outside. You will be alright. An ambulance is on its way. We will get you to the hospital right away. Do not try to speak. You will be okay. Save your strength."

Khun Ut struggled to speak. His words came out in whispery gasps. "The *farangs*. They did this. Get the woman and the Hmong out of here. Quickly. Take them into the jungle across the border, far away from here. And find those two. Kill them."

CHAPTER ONE HUNDRED-TWENTY-FOUR

antos and MacMurphy observed the commotion from their positions on the side of Doi Tung Mountain, more than three-quarters of a mile away. Santos lay behind the spotter scope and MacMurphy alternated between the Lapua scope and binoculars.

It was late in the afternoon and the shadows were growing long. A number of rescue workers and investigators had joined the original group at the smoldering site of the crashed Porter a quarter mile down the mountain below them. An ambulance wailed up the side of the hill beneath Khun Ut's villa and came to a stop under the portico at the front entrance.

"Here's Khun Ut's ride," said Santos.

MacMurphy settled in behind the Lapua. "Maybe we can finish the job right here."

They watched as three paramedics piled out of the ambulance, pulled a collapsible gurney from the rear and rushed it in through the open double doors of the front entrance. Moments later they returned with

439

the gurney. One of the paramedics held a transfusion bag of blood high over the body of the man lying on the stretcher. A gaggle of a half a dozen men and women accompanied the gurney out of the building. They milled around watching while the paramedics prepared to slide the gurney into the back of the ambulance.

"I wouldn't risk it, Mac. Too many people hanging around him."

Mac concentrated on his shot, finger poised on the trigger. Then he relaxed. "Yeah, too much commotion, can't get a clear shot. Sure hope the first one did it."

"He doesn't look too good, Mac. I can see his face. It's as white as a sheet. Hey, is that the Cambodian hovering over him? I think it is. The ugly guy in the black shirt. I think it's the Cambodian. Can you get a shot at him?"

"I think you're right. You're right. Hang on . . . Son of a bitch . . . No good . . ."

Two paramedics pushed the gurney into the back of the ambulance; the other held the transfusion bag high over the injured man and stayed at his side. The door was slammed shut and the other two jumped back into the cab, hit the siren and lights, and sped off down the hillside.

Mac slid back from the Lapua and turned to Santos. "That's it for Khun Ut. Nothing more we can do about him. If he croaks, fine, if not, well, we'll have to go to plan 'B.'"

"What's plan 'B'?"

"Haven't got the foggiest."

"What do we do now?"

"We wait."

"Wait for what?"

"For something to happen . . ."

CHAPTER
ONE HUNDRED-
TWENTY-FIVE

The Cambodian watched the ambulance speed away from the villa, sirien wailing. Darkness was fast approaching. Not the best time to launch a manhunt, but he could not let those two *farangs* get away, and he figured they were probably already on the run.

They were out there someplace, either in the town or on the hillside on the other side of the town. He was certain the shot that hit Khun Ut came from a rifle fired by one of the *farangs*, probably from a rooftop of one of the taller buildings in the town. This is where he would begin the search. He had to find them. He could not let them escape.

He entered Khun Ut's office and stood by the side of the window, looking out over the town of Ban Hin Taek in the direction of the shot. Could they see him now if he stood in front of the window? Were they still out there? Would they take a shot at him? Perhaps he could use a decoy to try to smoke them out. No, that would be too risky. He pulled the blinds shut.

Khun Ut had the town wired with informants and supporters. The two big *farangs* would stand out among the natives and be easily spotted. Someone would see them and report back. He had ordered the exits from the town blocked—there were only two, one to the north and one to the south. No one would escape via the only road in and out of the town.

But what about the mountain? They had found Sunthonwet's Range Rover parked at the *Wat* high on the other side of the mountain. He had ordered the automobile to be staked out by his men. If they returned to the vehicle they would be intercepted and killed. But what if they had another car stashed nearby, or maybe another accomplice to help them escape—someone else like a Colonel Sunthonwet or a General Sawat?

So many options, so many possibly scenarios. He felt frustrated, confused and more than a little intimidated by his new leadership role. What would his father do in this situation? He had never been in total command before. And Khun Ut was depending upon him.

All he could do was to pull out all the stops and cover every possible escape route. He would set things in motion and enlist the help of the police. After all, a man had been shot by a known, or at least strongly suspected, assailant. They should be leading the manhunt. It's their job and Khun Ut certainly pays them enough for their cooperation.

Paiboon entered the office and stood silently by the door. Ung Chea shook off his malaise and turned to him.

"Okay, it is up to us now. We need to make sure the town is sealed tight and find those two bastards. They are either in Ban Hin Taek or close by, maybe on the other side in the foothills of the mountain. They can't be too far away. Make sure the police are alerted and get every one of our men on the chase."

Almost as an afterthought he said, "And get the prisoners out of here right away. Take them across the border into the hills. I don't want any police hanging around the villa while they are in there, understand?"

Paiboon said, "yes sir," and turned to leave.

"One more thing, get the two Hueys in the air. Have them search the rooftops and the outskirts of the town, particularly on the eastern side. The shot came from that direction. Make sure you load them with enough armed troops to give chase on land if we find them."

He paused for a moment, thinking, and then continued. "No, actually, you stay here on the ground and coordinate the ground search. I'll go along with the Hueys. They may actually be our best bet to find those bastards."

CHAPTER ONE HUNDRED-TWENTY-SIX

antos and MacMurphy watched from their concealed vantage point high on the side of the mountain. The sun had dipped below the mountain behind Khun Ut's villa, casting long dark shadows across the valley. They switched to their night vision equipment.

"Things are going to get a little exciting here in a few moments," said Mac. He topped off the magazine to replace the round that had been fired and set the spare ten-round magazine next to the Lapua in front of him. "Search parties will be all over the town and patrolling this side of the mountain very shortly."

Culler checked his POF-416, making sure it was set on night vision firing, and set it down close beside him. The ammunition drum was full of one hundred rounds of 5.56 caliber cartridges. He tipped the spotter scope down and to the left and focused on the spot where the Porter had gone down.

"There's quite a crowd assembling down there by the Porter. Looks like they'll be working through the night."

"Forget about that," said Mac. "Keep your eyes on the villa. Another opportunity may present itself. They may try to move Charly and Vanquish out of there. My Spidey-sense tells me they won't want them around with the place teeming with cops and FAA investigators."

They watched two Huey helicopters lift off from behind the villa and began criss-crossing the town below, using powerful searchlights to illuminate rooftops and roads.

"I think we're safe up here for the time being," said Mac. "They believe the shot came from much closer in."

"Yeah, none of those jokers would ever believe we could be almost a mile away and still pick the sonofabitch off like you just did. They're checking rooftops and escape routes from the town."

"Which will soon lead them up the side of the mountain," said Mac. "When they don't find us down there in the village they will widen the search."

"Do you think they found our car?"

"Good point, let's find out. Keep your eyes on the villa while I give Sunthonwet a call."

Mac turned on his cellphone and checked the bars for reception. "Reception's better in the evening. I've got three bars. Not too bad. Should be enough."

Sunthonwet answered on the third ring.

"*Han lo*, Sunthonwet . . ."

"Colonel, it's me, Mac."

Long hesitation. "Hello, um, Mac, are you okay?"

"That's what I'm calling about. Am I okay?"

Another long hesitation. "They, they know you were here. They know . . . know I helped you. Please do not contact me again. Sorry Mac . . ." He hung up.

Mac brought the cellphone down from his ear, held it out in front of him like it had suddenly begun to stink, and switched it off.

"Doesn't sound too good," said Culler.

"No, not good. They know he helped us. That means they know about the Range Rover and they also know we're close by. We're going to have to figure out another way to get off this mountain, and out of the country." Mac turned his attention back to the villa. "But let's not worry about that now. We'll figure something out. Right now . . . look, see that white van going up the drive toward the villa? That's one of Khun Ut's security vans. Keep an eye on it."

"I see it," said Culler.

The van circled up the side of the hill and stopped under the portico. Two men dressed in security garb with black tee-shirts got out and slid open the doors on each side of the van. One of them turned toward the building and briefly spoke into a walkie-talkie. Then they lit cigarettes and stood talking near the rear of the van.

Culler had the spotter scope turned up to forty-power. The van nearly filled his circle of vision. "Looks like they're waiting for someone to come out. Maybe more than one person because they opened both side doors."

Mac moved the night vision scope of the Lapua back and forth between the two security men and the front entrance of the villa, and waited, finger poised on the trigger. Moments later the double doors of the villa swung open and four men surrounding Charly Blackburn and Vanquish walked out onto the porch. Two men guarded Charly and two guarded Vanquish—one on either side.

"Holy shit," whispered Culler, "there they are . . ."

"I see 'em, hands tied in front—no, they're zip-tie handcuffs. Time to rock and roll . . ."

Mac was all business, not a touch of buck fever this time. He sighted on the black shirt to Charly's right and squeezed the trigger. The rifle bucked and he brought the sights down on the man to her left and he fired again. The rifle bucked again and he sighted on the man directly behind, to Vanquish's left, and cranked off another round.

By now the bullets had reached their targets, creating chaos on the ground. Mac continued his rapid fire from the semi-automatic sniper rifle, snapping off round after round at the six black shirts around the van and on the porch.

The guard on Charly's right went down first. The bullet hit him high in the right shoulder, spinning him away from her and sending him down hard. The guard on her left was next. He flew straight back from the impact of the 250-grain bullet which caught him high in the chest. He was dead before he hit the ground.

His third shot missed one of the two men holding Vanquish and ricocheted loudly off the concrete porch behind him.

The guards dropped the Hmong's arms and drew their sidearms, looking around frantically trying to figure out where the shots were coming from. Vanquish stood there, head bowed and without his signature cowboy hat, looking dirty and beaten.

But he came alive quickly when he realized what was happening. He charged the guard nearest to him and knocked him to the ground and fought to rip the pistol out of his hands.

Mac continued to aim and fire, aim and fire, methodically, but his human targets were harder to hit because they were moving and the bullets coming from more than three-quarters of a mile away took time to reach them.

CHAPTER
ONE HUNDRED-
TWENTY-SEVEN

Charly knew exactly what was happening. Free now, she dove at the first guard to be hit. He was lying on the ground moaning. He did not resist when she yanked his .357 magnum revolver from its holster. She dropped to one knee and turned the gun on the remaining guards and started firing. She hit the one closest to her in the chest and sent him flying backward.

Next she turned the revolver on the guard who was struggling with Vanquish. She aimed carefully to avoid hitting the Hmong and shot the guard in the groin.

Bullets from the mountainside continued to rain down on the remaining guards and on the entrance doors and windows of the villa—an effort to discourage any heroes from joining the gunfight.

The Hmong looked up at Charly with a mixture of surprise and gratitude. He grabbed the wounded guard's gun and turned it on a guard near the van who was trying to run away down the hill. He shot him in the back and the guard tumbled forward into the underbrush.

The remaining guard fired at Vanquish at the same moment that Charly fired at him, and both Vanquish and the guard went down hard.

Charly ran over to the Hmong. He was holding his stomach with his two tied hands, trying to stem the flow of blood.

"I am hit bad, Charly. Gut shot. Burns like hell. You better get out of here. Leave me. Just go."

"Don't move," she said, "I'll get you out of here." She crawled over to the nearest dead guard and removed his knife from the sheath on his belt. She used it to cut through her zip-tie cuffs and then cut Vanquish free.

An alarm sounded from inside the villa and she could hear the continuing impact of rounds hitting around her and on the doors and windows of the villa behind her. The six guards were sprawled around her, dead or dying.

Still on her kness, she looked up in the direction of Doi Tung Mountain and said, "Thank you Mac, thank you . . ."

CHAPTER
ONE HUNDRED-
TWENTY-EIGHT

Culler's eye was glued to the spotter scope. "Holy shit, she just said 'thank you Mac,' she knows we're up here, she said it. I could read her lips. No shit . . ."

Between shots Mac said, "Now she better get her pretty little ass out of there *toute de suite* or . . . fuck, I'm out of ammo." He pushed back from the gun, grabbed his backpack, pulled out a box of shells and began quickly reloading his two magazines.

"She's moving now," said Culler. "She's trying to get the Hmong up on his feet . . . okay, he's up. They're getting into the van . . . okay, they're moving . . . okay . . . damn she is out of there. Sonofabitch . . . she floored it, spitting dirt and gravel all over the place, side doors still open . . . Uh-oh, they're coming out the doors. Hurry up Mac . . ."

"I've got it. I've got it." Mac slapped a full magazine into the Lapua and settled in behind it once again. Four men had taken advantage of the lull in shooting and had ventured out onto the porch. They stood there looking stunned, surveying the carnage, and watched the van speed away down the hill. One of them spoke into his walkie-talkie and pointed in the direction of Doi Tung Mountain.

Mac fired off three rounds in quick succession. Two of the men went down and the other two scattered. One dove back into the villa and the other took off around the side of the house. Mac put another round through the front doors to keep the rest of them at bay.

"Good shooting, Mac." Culler scanned the area through his scope. "Uh-oh, I think they're on to us. Those two Hueys are gaining altitude and coming our way."

Mac reared back on his haunches and grabbed his night vision binoculars. "Yeah, I think they figured it out. Let's move back to better cover."

They grabbed their gear and the spotter scope and the Lapua, and retreated further back into the pines, taking refuge in the large evergreen trees.

Culler grabbed his assault rifle and switched on the infrared laser targeting sight. He pulled his night vision gear from his backpack, strapped it over his head and adjusted the lens over his eye.

The green line of death shot out from the barrel of the rifle in front of him. He was comforted to know that whatever that green line touched when he pulled the trigger, the bullets would hit. And he knew the green line was only visible to him.

The two Vietnam vintage Huey helicopters flew back and forth on overlapping routes below them, their searchlights probing the mountainside. The side doors were open and the Huey's 7.62x51mm Minigun and door gunner were visible to Santos and MacMurphy.

Culler shook his head. "Those babies may be old but they pack a lot of firepower in those Miniguns. I'm not comfortable being on the wrong end of one of those gunships. Seems weird . . ."

Mac followed them with his night vision binoculars. "I know what you mean. Let's not get hosed down by one of those Miniguns. The Huey is heavy and slow and the belly is wide open. Let's just stay back here under cover and let'em get close and maybe we can take 'em out."

"I don't know. Maybe we should just bug the hell out of here? We've accomplished what we came here to do."

"Where the fuck are we going to go at this point? Up or down? You decide . . ."

"Yeah, I see what you mean . . . okay, you're right, offense is the best defense . . ."

The Hueys continued to scour the mountainside below them, gradually moving back and forth up the mountain. The searchlight flashed over their position and one of the Hueys pulled up level with them. The light penetrated the darkness and they shielded their eyes to maintain their night vision.

"They're checking out this position," said Mac. "They're not stupid. They recognize this as a good vantage point for the same reasons we did."

The Huey hovered in front of their location with its searchlight probing the darkness around them. They were standing motionless behind two large trees, guns at the ready, hoping it would move on.

The minigun wailed and bullets sprayed their location, knocking down branches and kicking up dirt around them.

"Fuck this," said Culler over the noise, "they saw something, they know we're here." He waited for the stream of bullets to move away from him and then moved around the tree and put the green line on the open door and pulled the trigger, spraying the interior of the Huey.

The gunner was hit first. He sprawled back onto the floor of the gunship and the minigun went silent. Bullets sprayed the interior of the Huey hitting two of the other occupants and causing panic inside.

The gunship pulled up and turned away from the mountain in a tight arc. Culler continued to fire on the exposed belly of the helicopter, bullets pinged and ricocheted off the hull as the ship peeled away and sped back toward the villa.

"Well, if they had any doubts before . . ." said Mac.

"You want to go up or down?" asked Culler. "I vote down."

"Let's wait and see what they do first."

They didn't have to wait long.

The other Huey circled in a wide arc around them, staying out of range. Finally it stopped and hovered close to the ground about five hundred meters above and behind them. Six black shirted security guards armed with AK-47 assault rifles bailed out of the Huey, spread out and headed slowly down the side of the mountain toward their position.

"I guess that answers my question. We go down, right?"

"Wait a minute, hang on. Let's think a minute. We still have the advantage. We've got night vision, silenced weapons . . . Shit, let's leave the Lapua and the rest of our gear here and go hunting."

Culler grinned widely. "Hmmm, not a bad idea, I like that. If we could get around behind them we could pick them off one by one like Sergeant York."

"Sounds like a plan. Let's do it . . . Let's get this gear wrapped up and under that tree over there. Then you circle around them to the right and I'll go left. Just don't shoot me, okay? Don't get trigger happy with that POF. Hang on while I grab the commo gear out of my backpack. We'll need that. Meet you back here when the game's over. Good hunting."

They tested their commo gear and then took off at a quiet trot in opposite directions. The combination of the darkness and their Ghillie-suits made them practically invisible. They ran parallel to the side of the mountain in opposite directions for about two hundred meters and then stopped, dropped into concealed prone positions and waited quietly in ambush, listening.

Santos heard the sounds of people coming through the woods before he saw them. He whispered in his lapel mic and scanned the woods in front of him. "They're almost on us. I can hear 'em coming."

He heard a crash of noise directly in front of him and a barely audible curse. *The sonofabitch must have slipped*, he thought. He lay still, aiming up the side of the mountain and waited, barely breathing. Soon he saw the man coming around a huge evergreen. The man was holding his AK-47 assault rifle in front of him with one hand and swiping the dirt from his trousers with his other.

Santos flicked on the green line, laid it on the unsuspecting man's chest and squeezed the trigger. Three silent rounds squirted out of the muzzle and sent the man straight back and down. Culler waited for sounds, and when there were none, he got up and moved quickly but silently higher up the hill, around and behind the dead man. He whispered into his lapel mic, "One down."

"Hang on," said Mac. Moments later he said, "I got one, too. Coming around."

Mac stealthily circled around behind the body, like stalking a deer. He moved around and up behind the line of intruders. He stopped and listened, senses acute. He thought he was behind the remaining four security guards and was surprised they were not using flashlights. He heard twigs snap and leaves rustle. *Yes,* he thought, *without flashlights or night vision gear you are blind, so you will stumble and fall and will die.*

He moved purposefully toward the sounds. He was almost upon the man when he saw him, moving through the shadows no more than twenty feet in front and to the right of him. He flicked on the green line and, holding the gun waist high, brought the line up and placed it on the man's side under his right arm and touched the trigger. Two silent rounds struck the man in the rib cage and knocked him sideways, his AK-47 flying out of his hands. He landed in a crash and a yelp, alerting the other guards.

Santos and MacMurphy had the same thought: *shit, we're blown!*

Confusion reigned among the remaining three security guards. The man nearest to MacMurphy took off running down the side of the mountain, crashing through the underbrush. Mac sprayed shots in the direction of the noise and heard a cry. The other two guards began firing at shadows, giving their positions away.

When the firing stopped, Santos moved toward the sounds in a crouch, being careful to stay low and behind cover. He stopped behind a large evergreen tree, hunkered down, and spoke into his lapel mic. "Where are you?"

"Behind them. One took off down the mountain and I think I winged him. There are two left. They're frightened. Let's take them out, but be careful . . ."

"Roger that."

They moved through the woods like hunters, stalking their prey, holding their assault rifles waist high at the ready, green lines of death dancing out in front of them touching trees and shrubbery.

One of the AKs opened fire in the direction of Santos. He hit the dirt, bullets peppering the trees above his head.

"I see him," said Mac, "hang on . . . hang on . . ." He saw the man lying in the prone position, touching off two and three round bursts from his AK in the direction of Santos. Mac moved slightly to his right to get a better line of sight, put the green line on the prone man's side and pressed the trigger. Several bullets struck the unsuspecting man and kicked up dirt under him and above him. "Got him."

"Thanks," said Culler, "one left . . ."

They heard the sound of thrashing and knew the last guard was running down the hill away from the action. "He's on the move," said Mac, "do you have a shot?"

"No . . . let him go. He's out of here . . ." The sounds of the man running and sliding downhill toward the village could be heard clearly by both of them.

"Okay, meet you back at the site," said Mac.

They rendezvoused at their original position, out of breath and experiencing an adrenaline rush from the action. They congratulated each other on the action and drank heavily from their Camelbacs.

"Let's collect our gear and bail out of here," said Mac. "They're not done with us and this is a hot spot."

"Up or down?"

"I think up. We can collect the rest of our gear up at the top and then go down the other side. Maybe we can commandeer a vehicle somewhere down in Ban Mae Sai. It's too hot around Ban Hin Taek."

"Sounds like a plan," said Culler. "I could use a little rest, too. I don't think they'll be screwing with us anymore tonight . . ."

CHAPTER ONE HUNDRED TWENTY-NINE

As soon as Charly Blackburn got Vanquish into the van she hit the gas. He was turning white from loss of blood. He had to get medical attention soon or he would die. But first she had to get away.

The nearest hospital was in Chiang Rai, *would he make it that far?* She glanced over at him and told him to buckle up. He was holding his stomach. His shirt was soaked in blood. He looked over at her and smiled. She smiled back. *Not good*, she thought, *he won't make it that far.*

Her mind spun and she remembered a small clinic in the center of Ban Hin Taek. If she could get him that far they could at least give him first aid to stop the bleeding, and maybe give him some blood.

She careened down the driveway from Khun Ut's villa toward the main road. The side doors of the van were wide open and the wind rushed through like a hurricane. She was glad she made Vanquish buckle himself in because he rocked around like a ragdoll when she hit the curves on the narrow road.

The two guards at the gate looked up as she approached the guard shack at the intersection of the main road. They recognized the speeding security van and one of them started to raise the gate. Then the other one realized that something was not quite right and ordered the van to stop. The gate came back down with a thud.

Charly slowed momentarily, downshifted and then hit the gas when she approached the gate. She crashed through the gate and the two guards dove for safety.

She spun out onto the highway and made a hard right turn heading toward the center of town. She almost passed the large red and white cross sign on the left hand side of the road. She hit the brakes hard and spun the wheel sharply left into the gravel parking area in front of the clinic.

The van ground to a halt at the front entrance and she switched her attention to Vanquish. He appeared to have drifted off to sleep. His chin was resting on his chest and his head rolled back and forth like his neck was broken.

She jumped out of the van, stuffing the .357 magnum pistol into the back pocket of her jeans, and rushed around to the other side. She ripped the door open and unbuckled the Hmong, who fell limply out of the door and into her arms.

She cried out for help, but when no one came she eased Vanquish to the ground and ran into the clinic. She returned a few moments later with two men, a female nurse and a stretcher. She quickly explained that Vanquish had been shot and asked them to care for him. While he was being carried inside, she slammed the side doors shut, jumped back into the van and headed south, out of town.

Near the edge of town she saw the roadblock in the distance and knew she could not bully her way through it. She pulled off to the side of the road to think. Her mind raced. Where could she go? She was certain the other end of the road would be blocked as well.

And then she remembered . . . the Porter. The plane had been shot down and crashed on the mountainside across from Khun Ut's villa. She had heard the staff talking about it and saw the smoke still coming from the site when she made her escape. Mac and Culler Santos were on the mountainside as well. Maybe . . .

She turned the van around on the highway and headed back toward the center of town, all the while scanning the mountainside up to her right for signs of the wreckage. Two Huey helicopters circled around in the distance on the side of the mountain. Surely they were looking for Culler and Mac.

It was almost dark and the looming black mountain made it difficult to see the smoke that would be still emanating from the wreckage.

She saw a small dirt road off to her right. An emergency vehicle and several other cars and trucks were parked at the base of the road near the highway. Her mind raced. Rescue workers, paramedics, firemen, maybe even American embassy or aviation officials might be up there at the site of the wreck. The Porter was an American owned plane . . .

She pulled off the road and parked next to the emergency vehicle. She opened the door and stood on the running board of the van, looking up the side of the mountain for signs of smoke or the wreckage. Nothing. Then she noticed what looked like a wisp of smoke about a mile from where she was standing. *That's got to be it.*

She made a mental note of the location, sat back behind the wheel of the van and headed up the dirt road. She bounced and skidded up the rutted road, wanting to get as close to the location as possible. One of the Hueys passed overhead, causing her to duck instinctively.

The road ended about four hundred meters up at an old barn. Several cars, probably belonging to rescue workers and investigators working at the crash site, were parked in front. She pulled the van in and parked beside the other cars. She looked up at the mountain, got her bearings, and headed off on foot into the jungle in the direction of the wrecked Porter.

As she came close to the people, some in uniform, mostly civilian Lao and Thai, a Marine at the edge of the crowd happened to turn around. His face lit up when he saw her.

He stepped toward Charly and reached for her hand. But Charly stumbled and fell forward into his arms.

"Ma'am, I'm sure glad to see you." He was flustered and embarrassed at holding a senior embassy officer in his arms. "Are you alright, Ma'am," he said, trying to hold her at arms length.

Charly straightened up and smiled. "I'm fine, Corporal. I didn't mean to attack you." She brushed her hair back out of her eyes, which were welling up. The relief at feeling safe at last begin to hit her.

"Ma'am, you kind of look like shit." He was immediately contrite. "I mean, I wasn't, I mean . . ."

Charly laughed and grabbed the young embassy guard by the elbow. "I'm sure we both know exactly what you mean, Corporal. Let's head down and get me back to the nearest safe phone."

The Marine called over his shoulder, "Swanson, come with me and Miss Blackburn. Henricks, you and White stay here with the counsel. Don't let 'em out of your sight. And get 'em out of this fucking jungle before dark." He winced and pulled slightly away. "I apologize, ma'am."

Charly pulled him back to her side, as the other Marine joined them. "Get me out of this fucking jungle too, Corporal."

CHAPTER ONE HUNDRED-THIRTY

I t was well after midnight when Culler and Mac arrived back near the top of the mountain where they had cached their excess gear. By all appearances, the search, at least on the mountainside, had been called off. The Hueys had returned to the villa and no other search parties had been deployed on the mountain—none that they could detect, anyway.

They were bone tired, dehydrated, and needed rest, food and drink. Mac spread out a green shelter sheet on the ground and the two men plopped down on it. They lay there, using their packs as pillows, looking up at the star filled sky.

Culler drank heavily from his Camelbac and munched on a power bar. "So what's the plan now, general? Steal another car?"

"I don't know. I can't think any more. It's a big mountain. I think we're pretty safe as long as we stay under cover and away from the populated areas. I'm not worried about getting us out of here and back across the border into Laos. Colonel Sunthonwet is not the only friend I have in Northeast Thailand. We'll get out okay."

"Well, truth be told, I'm looking forward to getting back to Ft. Lauderdale and the routine work at GSR. I've had enough excitement for awhile. This is a comfortable spot. It's cool, no bugs, nice breeze, I suggest we spend a relaxing evening right here, camping out under the moon and stars."

Mac yawned, "You're right. This is as good a place as any to rest up. I don't think I could stand up anyway."

"Me too. Do you think Charly and Vanquish made it out okay?"

"My guess is as good as yours. Vanquish didn't look too good. I don't know, maybe . . ."

Culler pulled more power bars from his backpack and tossed one over to Mac. "Well, there's nothing more we can do for them. I'll never forget the look on her face when she looked up at us and mouthed 'thank you Mac.' She knew we were here and she knew we could see her. That was truly amazing."

"Yeah, gives me goosebumps. I hope they're okay. Charly's a ballsy woman. If anyone can make it out of there safely, she can. And if she makes it out okay, I guess you could say we accomplished everything we came here to do."

"Yeah, that's right. Even if Khun Ut recovers from his wound, I think he and his operation are finished. That mission has definitely been accomplished. Getting Charly and Vanquish out of harm's way would be a real plus. I hope they make it, I really do . . ."

They lay there quietly, looking up at the stars, and slowly drifted off into deep, dreamless sleep.

CHAPTER
ONE HUNDRED-
THIRTY-ONE

POSTSCRIPT

K hun Ut survived his gunshot wound, but the publicity over the shooting down of the CIA Porter, and the deaths that resulted from people
using his heroin, ended his reign in the Golden Triangle.

On direct orders from the Thai Prime Minister, he was arrested at
the hospital and brought to Bangkok where he was tried and convicted
of heroin trafficking and multiple murders. He was sentenced to life in
prison without the possibility of parole and was incarcerated in the
infamous Bang Kwang maximum security prison on the banks of the
Chao Phraya River north of Bankok.

Bang Kwang is called the "Big Tiger" by the Thais. It got the name
because it ate all the people who entered it.

Ung Chea moved into Khun Ut's mountain villa in Ban Hin Taek where he attempted to pick up the pieces of Khun Ut's much diminished heroin business. With the distribution networks in shambles, he concentrated on the opium growing part of the business, selling the raw opium to other distributers.

Vanquish died quietly at the clinic in Ban Hin Taek moments after he was dropped off by Charly Blackburn. Months after his death a young American man appeared at the home of his widow and, without explanation, delivered an envelope containing $50,000 in cash. On the same day, another courier delivered a package containing $100,000 to Linda Peoples at her home.

Edwin Rothmann, the DDO, personally traveled to Chiang Mai to award Charly Blackburn the Distinguished Intelligence Cross, the CIA's highest honor for extraordinary heroism.

Culler Santos and Harry MacMurphy walked out of the jungle two days later in Ban Mae Sai. They waited for the cover of darkness at the edge of the town and stole an old Toyota pickup truck parked behind a seedy apartment complex. Culler finally got to use his technical skills to hotwire the truck.

Early the next morning they ditched the pickup in a busy parking lot in Nong Khai, and Mac called an old contact of his who was engaged in smuggling all sorts of people and things back and forth between Laos and Thailand.

The smuggler took them across the Mekong River in a small fishing boat and then delivered them personally to the familiar Settha Palace Hotel where they relaxed for two days before flying back to Ft. Lauderdale.

They both looked forward to resuming a life of routine in the GSR offices, and hoped that Edwin Rothmann would not call again too soon.

Exactly one month after the shooting of Khun Ut, the seemingly unrelated murders of Police Colonel Chatchai Sunthonwet and former Police General Sawat Ruchupan were reported in the Thai press.

Sunthonwet had been shot once in the side of the head at close range while sitting alone in his police cruiser in downtown Nong Khai; Sawat was found floating face down in his swimming pool in Chiang Mai. His throat had been slashed.

There were no suspects in either killing.

******

ABOUT THE AUTHOR

F.W. Rustmann, Jr. is a twenty-four-year veteran of the CIA's Clandestine Service. He retired as a member of the elite Senior Intelligence Service (SIS), with the equivalent rank of major general. One of his assignments was as an instructor at the CIA's legendary covert training facility, "the Farm." After retiring from the CIA, he founded CTC International Group, Inc., a pioneer in the field of business intelligence and a recognized leader in the industry. His numerous articles on intelligence and counterintelligence have appeared in the Baltimore Sun, Miami Herald, Palm Beach Post, Newsmax and elsewhere. He has been frequently quoted and interviewed in many national and international publications including Time Magazine, USA Today, New York Times, New York Daily News, Far East Economic Review, CNN, FNN, Reuters, Newsmax and the Associated Press, among others. He is the author of the best-selling non-fiction book *CIA, Inc.: Espionage and the Craft of Business Intelligence,* and the novel, *The Case Officer.* He lives in Palm Beach, Florida.

FALSE FLAG

BY

F.W. RUSTMANN, JR.

CHAPTER 1

The drive from Belmopan to the central prison of Belize in Hattieville, affectionately known as the "Hattieville Ramada," took almost two hours, mostly on narrow, dusty jungle roads. The seventeen prisoners, each one handcuffed to his seat, bounced along in an old, gray school bus with dead shocks and springs.

Culler Santos was in a foul mood. The prisoner sitting across the aisle from him, a heavily tattooed young man of mixed race named Aduan, would not stop glaring at him. Santos had heard about Aduan in the Belmopan jail. He had a reputation for being a psychopath, the worst of the worst.

Although he was only a few months past his nineteenth birthday, Aduan had admitted to killing six people, including one of his uncles. The latter murder, the killing of a close relative, had elevated him in the ranks of the Crips. Each of the murders, with the exception of the last one, which landed him in prison, was recorded on his chest in a row of tattooed, half-inch circles.

The Crips and their archrival gang, the Bloods, were strong in Belize, having immigrated there from Los Angeles in the mid-eighties. And nowhere were they stronger, or more heavily represented, than in the Belizean prison system.

Santos decided it was best to ignore the kid, so he concentrated on looking out the window at the passing jungle scenery. But each time he looked over, he caught the kid staring at him.

He didn't need this. On top of everything else, he was still wearing the jeans, tennis shoes, and sweat-stained, white polo shirt he had been wearing when he was taken into custody. He had not had a proper shower or shaved in the four days since his arrest. He knew he reeked because the stench of the other prisoners reminded him of a horse barn.

The kid was dressed in rags like most of the other prisoners. He wore stained, khaki cutoffs, a pair of worn out flip-flops and an Army camouflage tee shirt. The sleeves of the tee shirt were cut off to better display his powerful, tattoo-covered arms. He sported a head full of long, filthy dreadlocks, a stringy Fu Manchu mustache, and a braided goatee.

They reached Hattieville at the two-mile marker of Burrell Boom Road. A guard walked down the aisle unlocking handcuffs. The prisoners were led out the door in single file, through the main gate of the prison and into the prison yard. It was surrounded by stained, two-story, white-cement-block buildings, which housed the cells. A chain-link fence topped with hoops of concertina razor wire surrounded the entire 225-acre plot of land. Guards armed with AK-47 automatic weapons patrolled along the roofs of the buildings and stood in towers in each corner. The entire facility stank like a barnyard.

After a short "welcome" speech from the warden, who laid out the usual warnings about the consequences of escape attempts, the group was split into smaller groups and led to their cells in the "Remand Section" of the prison. There they waited for trial. Some of them had been there for more than five years. The judicial system in Belize was in no hurry.

Santos was led to a cell on the ground floor along with four other prisoners from the bus, but not before each one surrendered his belt. All other pocket litter had been confiscated at the Belmopan jail. He assumed the belts would be added to those other belongings. After the surrender, some of the men had to walk with one hand holding up their drooping pants. Santos reflected on the "low pants" tradition that was common among young blacks in American ghettos. This is where it all began—in prisons. Why those kids wanted to emulate prison inmates was totally beyond him.

One of the prisoners in his group was Aduan. Santos cussed his luck and immediately began to think about how he would neutralize this obvious threat. Aduan was hugged and high-fived by several other inmates when he entered the cell. This macho display added to Santos's dismay.

The filthy, twenty-by-twenty-foot cell was already filled with more than a dozen inmates. Santos counted the double bunks that lined two of the walls—there were four. That meant eight beds for about sixteen smelly men. *This is going to be cozy*, Santos thought.

All of the bunks were occupied, so he looked for a place on the concrete floor where he could stake out a space. Grabbing one of the bunks was out of the question. It would have meant an immediate confrontation, and he was not ready for that. Not yet.

In one corner of the room, he noticed a plastic milk carton cut in half and realized it was being used as a toilet. *Better stay as far away from that as possible*, he thought. He found a spot near the corner on the other side of the room, plopped himself down between two other inmates and put his head on his knees.

Hurry up, Mac. Get me out of here. Please hurry...

The crowded cell was a cacophony of smells and noises. A few of the prisoners, like Santos, sat quietly with their eyes closed and arms folded around their knees, trying to block out their surroundings, submerging themselves in their thoughts.

It did not take Aduan long to saunter over to Santos's side of the cell and stop in front of him. He stood there, swaying back and forth, glaring

down at the American. The cell suddenly became quiet. Three other
heavily tattooed prisoners, all with long dreadlocks, moved across the
room and converged alongside of Aduan.

Santos sensed the arrival of Aduan and his fellow Crips and watched
them from the corners of his eyes. He sat there quietly for a few moments
and then looked up and locked onto Aduan's threatening stare. He knew
now that confrontation was unavoidable, but he was not afraid.

His thoughts centered on how best to neutralize the four thugs. With
one attacker, it would be simple: take him to the ground and dislocate
his arm with an arm bar. That was the quickest and easiest way to neutralize an opponent. But in this case, there were too many of them. He
needed to remain on his feet while sending them all to the ground. Tac-
tics spun through his mind. He knew he could beat them. It was just a
matter of how.

His head rose slowly and he quietly asked, "Do you want my spot?"
Aduan threw his head back and laughed heartily. He looked around at
his friends and then began to reply.

As soon as Aduan's mouth opened, Santos unleashed a sweeping
kick with his right leg that knocked Aduan's legs out from under him
and dropped him hard on his tailbone. There was an audible thud as he
hit the concrete floor, forcing the air from his lungs in a gasp.

Santos spun to his feet in one motion and caught the tall Crip to
Aduan's left with a roundhouse, backhand punch to the side of the head,
dropping the thug like a stone.

He turned to his right and confronted the wide-eyed, fat Crip who
was swinging a lame roundhouse at his head. Santos blocked the punch
with his left forearm, stepped in close, looped his right arm under his
attacker's right arm and, with two hands grasping the wrist, snapped the
arm down. An audible pop and a scream told him the elbow was dislocated. He followed up with a sharp right elbow to the temple and the
Crip went down in a heap, unconscious and with his arm jutting out at
an awkward angle.

Aduan jumped to his feet and attacked. Santos stepped back with
his left leg to dodge a right hook, crossed his right leg over his left and

launched it screaming toward Aduan's head. Santos's foot connected at the ear with a sickening thud. Aduan careened across the room, into the wall and down in a heap.

In a blur Santos spun around and delivered a side kick directly to the knee of the forth thug. The force of the kick snapped the Crip's knee backwards, dislocating it and sending the thug to the ground screaming in pain. He was no longer a threat.

Santos dodged a kick to the head from the only standing Crip and delivered two sharp blows to the solar plexus, knocking the wind from the thug's lungs and sending him to his knees. He went down into a fetal position.

Santos stood, panting. He surveyed the carnage. Two of the Crips were permanently out of commission with dislocated limbs. Aduan was unconscious and the other Crip was moaning and gasping for breath in a heap.

He stepped over to Aduan who was lying face down on the floor. He stood over him, brought his leg up high and stomped down on Aduan's right shoulder with the heel of his shoe. He heard the shoulder crunch, rendering the arm useless.

He turned to the remaining Crip, moaning and lying on his side. He brought his leg up again and brought it down hard on the femur, snapping the bone and eliciting a scream from the thug.

Satisfied, Santos surveyed the carnage he had inflicted. Now all four of the Crips would be taken to the hospital with broken or dislocated limbs, which was Santos's plan in the first place. They would be removed from the cell and no longer a threat.

Santos walked to the center of the cell, looked around at the inmates surrounding him and addressed the motionless, gawking group. "I had nothing to do with this, get it? These guys got into a fight and beat the crap out of each other. Understand? That's your story when the guards get here." He glared around the room, locking eyes with each one of them in turn.

The shocked inmates nodded in agreement, some muttering in approval and awe of what had just occurred. Santos then walked over to the nearest lower bunk, pushed aside two inmates standing in front of it, and plopped himself down.

Lying on the bunk with his legs crossed and his hands behind his head, he said, "And this is where I will spend the rest of my time here, right on this bunk. Does anyone have any objections to that?"

There were none.